Saga OF the
—Nine—
ORIGINS

||||★||||

KAWIKA MILES

This is a work of fiction. Names, characters, places, and incidents either are the product of the author's imagination or are used fictitiously. Any resemblance to actual persons, living or dead, events, or locales is entirely coincidental.

Copyright © 2022 by Kawika Miles Black

All rights reserved. No part of this book may be reproduced or used in any manner without written permission of the copyright owner except for the use of quotations in a book review. For more information, address: kawika@damnitiloveamerica.com

First hardcover edition October 2022

Book editing by: Lorie Humpherys Lorie@BookBossEditing.com
Book design by: Kawika Miles Black

ISBN 978-0-578-28565-8 (hardcover)
ISBN 978-0-578-28566-5 (ebook)
www.damnitiloveamerica.com

To my God, Family, and Country

"The positive sides of propaganda must be made as effective as the negative."

— Aldous Huxley

PROLOGUE

Origins

Denver International Airport
1993

They got leaked…

"Sullivan!"

How? How the f—? It had to be someone with a security clearance. That's the only way this could've gotten to the press. At this thought, he lets out a soft chuckled sigh of relief. *Let's be serious though,* Sullivan thinks to himself, *if that's the press, then I'm the damn president.*

"Sullivan," the pestering continues. "Sullivan, what do we do?"

"Nothing," he mumbles, a smirk growing.

"What? Did you say—?"

"We do nothing. Tell them what they want to hear. Tell the Illuminati whatever project, or whomever is running these conspiracy campaigns, what they want to hear."

Unable to fathom what he's just heard, the nervous wreck's head nearly explodes. "Wait—are we doing nothing or am I telling them—telling them the truth?"

Shaking his head, Sullivan walks away. With the gravel of the construction site crunching beneath his leather designers, he begins to mull over the marketing campaign in full. Murals—for the zealots that *love* reading between the lines. Leak a faux set of blueprints to confuse and disorient the internet masses, and maybe bring in some "investigators" to catch wind of "a super army." People love that shit.

"Sullivan, are we doing nothing or are we—?"

"They want a conspiracy, so give them a conspiracy. Give them everything that adds, takes away and creates chaos. Post the headline: *Denver International Airport Conspiracy* and then let them do the rest."

Precariously dodging a pallet of rebar, the assistant just can't help it. "That doesn't sound like nothing—it sounds like a whole lot of work!"

And this is why Sullivan can't stand working with this generation. Soft, uneducated, and ignorant of truth. If he thought it'd help, he'd not only quote, but he'd throw the entire library of Miyamoto Musashi, Sun Tzu, and Lieutenant Colonel Grossman at him. If the wiry millennial had anything to benefit from it, tossing him in a class of jiu-jitsu, Krav Maga, or traditional kung fu would teach the kid that doing nothing can be more productive than senseless work.

"Where are they?" Sullivan asks.

"Where are who?"

The nervous quiver in his voice is sand on metal, so, in as clear and precise a tone as he can muster, Sullivan stops, turns, and grabs his assistant by his off-brand collar, tearing it from the seams. "Find the reporters and set up a meeting."

"For—for what time?"

Letting go, his grip imprinted on the collar, Sullivan pivots away. "Set it up!"

Dumbfounded to say the least, the assistant pulls out his Blackberry and begins looking for divine guidance to move his thumbs over the proper keys, not realizing in the slightest that he's performing the last task his employer will give him.

I

THE GATHERING

ONE

Area Thirty-Eight

Winter's arrived, in the same bitter cold manner as it does every year. If certain precautions are taken it's not unbearable. If your physical activity slacks though, the dry, dull air causes knuckles to crack and fingertips to bleed. Huffing and breathing warmth inside his hands, the man's attempt is feeble in preventing this inevitable outcome, and as the warm mist seeps from the slits of his clenching fists, last month's encounter floats up to the back of his mind. Officially, the statement was "an assault on seven of the PPA's best and most decorated." Unofficial gossip coined the event "The Brawl."

Like it did then, anger gets the best of him as he clenches his fists, reopening the freshly scabbed breaks on his frozen skin. It was an ambush, not a brawl. A brawl implies that the fight was unbiased—a two-to-one ratio even. This was *definitely* not that. The head of the little PPA gang had held a gun to the man's temple, slipping off and stealing his refined leather gloves, and then to show how fair and unbiased the officer was about the situation, punched him in the face. Because he attempted to fight back, the entire encounter left him with a broken nose, old, dirt-saturated snow to reduce the swelling, and a week in detention.

"Protectors of the People's Freedom," the man scoffs out. They are to receive no disrespectful acts, for they uphold The Government. The People-Protection Agency? *Hogwash*, he thinks. Memorized, recited propaganda. More like Petty. Prick... Assholes. It is what it is though. Which is worse? A broken nose, or an execution? Better to keep your head down and wait. Pain, discomfort. It can't last forever.

Thrusting his cracked hands into the frosty pockets, the man turns his head east, catching a perfect angle of the rising sun creeping from behind the wintery horizon. Spotting the sky with hues of orange, red, and hints of purple grey, sunrays stroke the bottom of the winter clouds. For some it's just the signal of another workday in Area Thirty-Eight. For him? For him it prods at something more.

Hope. At least he'd like to think it's hope, but really, what does a word like that mean today? In all honesty, he's not even familiar with the sentiment, but as the morning light glitters and bounces off the dust and snow-scattered streets, he looks from the potholes to the rusting lampposts and forgets what hope might've felt like. From the leaning buildings to the unfortunate citizens that call those outside walls their home, it's a perfectly sad sight. Every twenty feet a barrel of fire warms these makeshift families, and while kids find comfort in snuggling up to the warmest grownup, the women persevere and gather whatever will help them make it one more day. And as usual, the passed-out drunks clench their version of hope nestled underneath their chins, no doubt dreaming of their utopia.

"Take it in your own way," his Grandma Lisa's voice sounds, echoing in the back of his mind.

He swears it was "make your own way," but the trivial debate is next to null as it's not like she's around to correct him anymore.

"The task is at hand," she then states in his mind.

Finding white-knuckled motivation, the aroma of gasoline, burning wood, and charred gruel hovers in the air as he approaches his home away from home—the Mill. Meager wages practically make it slave labor, but two meals a day? Where else can you get a deal like that? The only thing that prevents this situation from moving to the next level are the overpaid Petty Prick Asshats as the overwatch.

Fatigued and drowsy, the man steps in with the masses to be herded inside. A tap on his left shoulder greets him, but knowing exactly who, he instead looks right.

"Mornin', Jax!"

Kip. Kip Wright. Wright on the right, exactly where Jax knew he would be. With a goofy fur hat and a peppered bearded smile to match, Kip looks up to his tall friend from underneath the bushes he calls eyebrows, which if you ask Jax, have always seemed to have been placed lower on his face than the average human being. It's always given Kip a jolly Neanderthal visage.

"I thought I had ya that time—when I tapped yer shoulder and all," Kip bellows, drawing dozens of lethargic gazes their way before turning back to their stale lives. The same life they all share—all except Kip.

Chuckling, Kip slams his fists into Jax's shoulders. He may be short, but he's a mini locomotive that could run just as fast as one if you put him up for the challenge.

"Not this time, Kip," Jax says, tapping the side of his head. As annoying as one might find Kip's childlike sense of humor, the guy's company and jolly attitude are like having a tiered outdoor pool with a hot tub in the middle of a wintery, dumpy motel.

Kip tosses his arms in the air. "Man, Granny Lisa would be disappointed in me." Kip knew her long before Jax was ever around, and they always seemed to share the same sense of humor, which Jax never has gotten. "I miss her, Jax."

Jax has never been able to ascertain how or where Kip found Granny Lisa, though he's asked numerous times. Her unique skin tone made it very clear that she was not biologically related to either of them, and it makes Jax wonder why there's no one else that looks like her. After her passing though, it didn't matter because thirteen years old is an awfully young age for anyone to learn how to take care of themselves. Between the two of them, Kip and Jax have been able to make it.

"I do too," Jax slowly says. "You good?"

"I'm cold and a little tired and annoyed but did ya see that sunrise on the way over?! I mean, look at it!" Enthusiastically, Kip points to the same hopeful sunrise that warmed Jax's walk over. The guy's a simpleton, but he's right. It's beautiful.

"What's holding up the line?" Jax then mumbles, tired of being in the cold. Usually, the line feels like a slow pull on the fingernails, but today the herd is at a complete stop!

Never having been one for rhetorical questions, Kip answers the loose-ended query in Kip-like fashion.

"Looks like there's a new cutie!"

It's shallow, but Jax can't help but be intrigued. No one can, as each person in line strains their necks for a better look at who Kip is referring to.

"Who is she?" Jax casually asks.

"Some new PPA chick," Kip says, shrugging with a smirk. "I saw her before I came over. She has no clue what she's doing, but she's a looker!"

Finally, as the line steps forward, Jax is able to snag a peek where he coolly tries to see if Kip knows what he's talking about. There have been countless instances where Kip's called out a "cutie" when the *she* looked more like a *he*. However, there are the rare finds where Jax has no choice but to agree with Kip. This—this is one of those extraordinary occasions, and with three other men casually glancing up ahead they, along with Jax, all raise their eyebrows.

"Wow," Jax mumbles. Even with the boring standardized PPA brown, this woman manages to captivate every single man that lays his eyes on her.

"Told ya so!"

With the line continuing to move towards the rusted, creaking mill, the duo continue to get a better sight of the Looker. Ten people away. Nine. And now eight. By the sudden change of pace, it seems like she has gotten used to the registration process. Three people. Two, and finally, after all his giddy anticipation, it's Kip's turn for processing.

"Name, Area number and residency identification," she says without looking away from the screen and with the kind of tone that states she's not above a swift throat punch.

Despite this, she's beautiful. The golden waves of hair radiate a glow, but at the same time consume all light into shaded curls. She no doubt is in lean, athletic, killing shape—her frame yielding a slight taper from her shoulders to hips, and the hips don't lie. Some guys are rather "beautiful" here in Area Thirty-Eight, but you can always tell by the hips whether they're a female or pretending to be one, and she—she is a woman. Lastly, her supple, tan skin only adds to her mystery. The singular flaw the woman seems to have comes from the uniform she wears.

"Kip Wright. Area Thirty-Eight. Residency ID two-two-one."

"Thank you. Next."

But of course, Kip can't leave it there. "So," he begins. "Did you know that you're a looker? THE Looker from what I can tell."

With the line at a standstill, Jax shakes his head. Did he just give her the name the Looker? He's slightly embarrassed for Kip, but mostly, scared for the guy's life. Apparently, he didn't pick up on the throat-punching tone.

"Please move forward, sir. Next!"

"*Sir?* Nobody's ever called me sir before, little beauty."

Two guards step forward, but casually, she waves away her male counterparts before slowly standing. Moving from behind the computer screen and taking each step with precision, she brings herself within two inches of Kip.

"Sir," she says, her tone more deliberate. "Move, or I will move your ass myself."

Just like Kip, she isn't very tall, but rather, holds her sporting build with stoicism—treating her body as the weapon she's trained it to be, capable of removing Kip from existence. As they stand eye to eye, Kip enjoys every moment of it, and sensing the pleasure emanating from him, she steps back half an inch. If Kip dares to move forward, closing the minute chasm, she'll be ready to hit him right where Kip's brain seems to be at the moment. Sure enough, Kip moves forward as the "Looker" pulls her knife out, aiming it between his legs. Looking down to the blade and then back at her, Kip makes it clear that he's not going anywhere.

"Ya think that little thing's gonna stop me? Hate to break it to ya, but—"

He hates to love him, but Jax plows his shoulder into Kip, knocking him out of the way before she turns the guy into a eunuch. Jax, not Kip, is now the one standing within an inch of the Looker, making his groin her knife's new target. Being a head taller, she lifts her light, gold-brown gorgeous eyes to Jax, revealing a series of tiny scars at the base of her neck. They are perfect cuts—tally marks almost.

After what seems like an eternity, the Looker lowers her weapon, where it rests at her side as she continues to bore her gaze into his.

"Jax M. Rouge. Area Thirty-Eight. Residency ID two-two-zero."

On account of Kip shaking off the snow and mud, he doesn't fully realize it yet, but his friend just saved his ass. The Looker, sheathing her knife, turns back to the computer, inputting the newly obtained information.

"Next!"

As Jax moves forward, he straightens up a muddy Kip before smacking the back of his thick skull.

"Ouch!"

"Just shut up," Jax whispers, continuing their rush out of her vicinity. Glancing back though, Jax can't help but to hope that she's watching them leave.

"Y'er strong for being so scrawny," Kip complains, rubbing feeling back into his ribs. "That or a sack of bones," he then offhandedly mumbles.

"And you're an idiot!" Jax says, ignoring the lack of gratitude.

Plopping down next to Kip at their usual table, Jax violently slides Kip's tray across the table's surface before slamming his own tray of slop down.

"What'd I do?" Kip demands with a mouthful of gruel, a drip making its descent down and off his bearded chin.

"Don't be stupid, Kip. You know."

"Know what?" Kip sputters out.

"The damn law, you fool."

"Ah." Kip's eyebrows rise. "The law. That wee law. *Their* law."

"There's them and then there's us. There's no 'we' in any of this."

"There is though."

Jax looks perplexed as he forces a bite down. "What are you talking about?"

"There is a 'we,'" Kip smirks. "If you go down a hill in a cart, hold your hands up in the air, and yell…" And he actually yells it, "WEEEEE!"

"You're a child!" Jax can't help but laugh as everyone else within the range of the echoing screech falls somewhere on the startlement and annoyance spectrum.

"In all honesty though," Kip begins, bringing it back down to a normal level. "Did ya see her?"

More closely than you know, Jax thinks. Skin, body, eyes, and all.

"I don't care what uniform she had on, I just had to talk to her!" Throwing his hands behind his head, Kip replays the magical moment back inside his one-track mind.

"It was still stupid."

"Whatever. Ya should thank me. I got ya closer to her than ya ever would've been, ya chicken shit coward," Kip says, playfully loading a spoon full of mush before launching it at Jax's face where it smacks him in the cheek. Wiping away the cardboard porridge, he smirks at Kip's reasoning.

It was nice to catch her attention…

"Ya know, that's why I'm here." Picking up his tray and standing, Kip slugs Jax in the arm where it instantly goes numb, and not leaving it at that, a swift right hook to Jax's diaphragm knocks the wind out of him. "That's for shoving me to the ground. See ya after work?"

All Jax can manage is a thumbs up as he feebly attempts to catch his breath from Kip's sledgehammer blow. After a moment of not knowing whether he'll die, Jax is able to stand up and dump his own tray before moving over to the gaggle in front of the assignment board. With a prayer in his heart, Jax steps up to find his chore for the day. His cracked, scabby hands can't handle another day working outside without his gloves, and with his eyes scrolling down the list, he grins.

Processing!

There is a higher power looking out for him after all. In a skip-jog combo, Jax moves towards building four, and as he steps inside, an instant aroma of oak, pine, and redwood fills his nostrils, warming the depths of his soul. No outside today! He'll take the ear-splitting machinery and the suffocating ventilation if that means his hands stay away from the winter bite.

"Gather around!" a rather jolly, round-faced PPA officer commands. In quick succession, assignments are divvied out and inventory quotas are assigned per Area needs. "Twenty-Five and Thirty-

Three are both in need of forty tons of redwood. Areas One, Two, Five and Ten need whatever oak and cedar the Mill has to offer, in both raw and processed forms, and all of last week's drivers will be reassigned to Area Forty-Eight tonight." Upon hearing this, Jax can't help but feel tinged with jealousy. One of the warmest Areas all year round…

Offhandedly, as Jax makes his way over to his station, he notices the surplus of guards both on the ground and on the overhead walkways. A number of new recruits it seems. Explains the Looker—sort of.

For starters, she didn't have any guards around her like a new private would. They acted more like security detail, and in fact, she waved them away at one point. She must be an officer at the very least, even at the lower level. However, if Jax was to bet, she's probably higher up on their food chain. She had three gold triangles on her shoulder, each one encompassing a silver star in the middle. Jax heard one time that one triangle is a private, a second means they're a specialist, and a third is some rank of officer. Every solider he's seen inside the Mill only has one of those three options. No stars. The Looker does, so, what the hell do the stars mean?

Lastly, the only reason there would be this many officers and soldiers would be due to some sort of incident earlier in the week. Safety protocols or whatever, but the last accident Jax remembers was over two months ago. Kip saw the whole thing. A man was working on one of the bigger saws and got into an argument with a single-triangle PPA private. Kip couldn't remember what they were talking about, but the private was enjoying the confrontation like some sick game. The worker was older, and like all older guys, patience was wearing thin. After telling the private to shut up so he could get back to work, the young arrogant Petty Prick punched the worker in the stomach before swinging his fist and smacking the old guy under the jaw. The man then fell backwards where the middle of his right hand got sucked into the spinning blade. The PPA private was sent home for the day while the old man was put into detainment with a couple of bandages and some kind of disinfectant. If the roles were reversed, the private would've been given a fancy prosthetic hand in less than twenty-four hours, and the old worker would've been shot on sight for illegal provocation. Yes, illegal provocation, giving the PPA "legal provocation rights." But again, that was two months ago, plenty of time for things to settle down and get back to normal.

Jax shrugs it off. Something is going on here, but no way is he about to start asking what. Not here anyway. Kip won't know, and Jax has his conspiratorial ideas, but that's nothing new. There are other ways of getting information though. Jax will just have to exercise some patience.

―⸳⸳٭★٭⸳⸳―

Lunch is disgusting. It's free but barely tolerable. Breakfast doesn't pretend to be anything but the buttery gruel it is, making this "dessert" just a backhanded compliment. Is it possible the sweet cocoa is a genuine accident? Sure, but the more conceivable explanation is the PPA is mocking everyone with the sugary soil. Donning a fun aura in practically every situation, even Kip feels as if the state sponsored meal is an insult, coining the meal as "chocolate dirt." Even better was that Kip not only pointed this fact out to the guards on shift one day, but his critique landed him in lockup for two days. Not long after that, Kip was moved to a different shift, and without him, lunch is as unbearable as the chocolate dirt.

Alone at their adopted table, Jax sits as he shovels a spoonful in before gagging. It's a concentrated batch today, and he should've just been patient. It's better to let the warm, sandy texture cool down—

"Look what we have here. What's for lunch today, boys? Gravel mush?"

They're late, but inevitably the lunch guards grace the cafeteria with their domineering presence. Mealtime guards became irrelevant long ago, because seriously, what can anyone do with a plastic spoon? Prison shank someone, maybe, but why would any of the workers attack each other? They all know who to thank for their miserable lives. Now, that doesn't stop the occasional scuffle, but that's just venting some frustration that's easily self-policed, which is the major reason the PPA got rid of the breakfast shift altogether. The lunch shift though… Can't blame the Mill's management, but rather, the only rational explanation Jax can muster a reason for is the authoritarian sadism of The Government. It's not like anyone is starting a revolution with spoons when in every corner are armed PPA.

"Looks delicious," one guard says before picking up a bowl and pouring it on top of the worker's head where it drips into his lap. "Smells appetizing too." He pretends to gag, and like an animal dying, makes an awful throaty gurgle.

Again, everyone knows who the real enemy is.

It's clockwork as they make their way from table to table doing the *hilarious* routine of throw-up sounds and poking fatter people's stomachs while slapping around the more skeletal framed individuals. Bacteria even has ingrained patterns, and like Kip with his shoulder-tapping joke, the PPA's lunch routines are never funny, but still, they laugh as if they are state sponsored comedians. The difference is that Kip doesn't laugh at the expense of others.

Muscling down his chocolate dirt before the lunch guards get to his table, Jax quickly cleans up before standing to leave, but of course, he's stopped. With an extraordinary amount of weight on his shoulders, two massive hands force Jax back down to his seat. He ate fast, but not fast enough, and as he looks over to the door holding his salvation, Jax sees that it's dammed off by another guard. He isn't going anywhere—not until everybody has had their turn.

Like a seductive secret, the guard whispers in Jax's ear, his breath smelling of onions and some unknown rot.

"Going somewhere?" he asks before rounding the table, standing directly in front of Jax. His shoulders are easily twice as broad, he is a head taller, and as his intimidating glare bears down on Jax, annoyance easily replaces the intended fear.

"I was hungry, what can I say?" Jax shrugs. They hate it when people play along with their maniacal games. He knows he'll regret participating in a moment, but right now Jax could care less. Hell, what's wrong with occasional fun?

Not used to blunt and sarcastic responses, the beastly man searches his pea-sized brain for a clever retort, but the best the guard comes up with is, "I bet."

Rolling his eyes, Jax begins to stand, but again is forced back down by the beast's pals.

"What now?" Jax whines, turning the fun meter up a notch. Kip's careless demeanor is really beginning to rub off on him. "You want to pour food on my head or something?"

"No," the guard on his left says.

"We want you to get on your knees and beg," the guard to his right states.

Weighing his options, Jax determines that if he tries standing again, he'll get punched in the face. He's had worse… He could just awkwardly slide off the bench, which would be hilarious, but as an unprecedented maneuver, it stands to reason that their reaction is equally as unpredictable. Fighting is always a riot of a time, but the risk versus reward isn't worth it today. At a loss, Jax decides to stay seated.

"Beg for what? Mercy? More food?" Jax sighs out.

"Yeah, both of those sound good. Since you love the sandy shit so much, you don't mind eating more, do you?"

From their quick response, Jax realizes that they were going to say yes to whatever he said. Why the hell didn't he ask to see if they'd let him kick them in the nuts? Cursing at the wasted opportunity, Jax knows exactly how this will play out. He'll ask, then they'll just refuse to give it. Rinse and repeat this process a couple of times, until finally they just dump it on his head.

"Can I have some more food?"

The monster man looks at him and smiles. "You can."

This—this is unexpected. It doesn't make much sense until Jax follows the trajectory of the beastly guard's arm one table down where he motions for the other worker wearing the chocolate dirt to come over.

"Eat it from off his face."

Sitting down next to Jax, the worker with the chocolate mask refuses to move or acknowledge the situation.

"This is bullshit," Jax mumbles. Standing up for a third time, he doesn't get hit in the face like initially predicted, but he does get punched. He receives a solid blow in the middle of his chest from across the table that instantly knocks the wind out of him. Tumbling backwards, the back of Jax's head smacks the bench behind him before he thuds to the floor. Dazed and trying to refocus, Jax feels warm blood trickle down the back of his neck as he rolls forward. Before he gets too far though, searing, crunching pain in his wrist stops Jax from moving any further, and as he follows the crushing boot all the way up to the same intimidating glare he saw before, the beastly guard's fist hits Jax in the side of the head.

"Did I tell you to stand up?!" The playful banter in his voice is long gone at this point, and as the guard aims four vicious kicks into Jax's stomach, he's lifted off the ground each time.

"No!" And with that final word, the beast tops off the beating by batting Jax's head to the ground a third and final time. Wiping his bloody fist off on Jax's coat, the beast and his gang tromp out of the cafeteria.

Breathing is painful but it's doable, and as Jax slowly gets first to his knees, after a little exertion, he's able to stand. Out of fear, everyone turns away, and not a single helping hand is offered to Jax.

Everyone knows who the enemy is, but not one of them has the sack to do anything about it.

Two

Boston
March 19, 2036

One, two, three, four, one, two, three, one, two, one.

The cadence—the rhythm repeats.

One, two, three, four, one, two, three, one, two, one.

The game has changed—the arena evolved. Technique has improved, equipment modified, and fighters enhanced. From bare knuckles to canvas gloves to leather fists—all of which simply circles back to skin and bone. Boxing is a dead sport. It was dying in the 2000s, had a resurgence in the 2010s with McGregor V. Mayweather and the celebrity fights following, but turned downward exponentially shortly after as it permanently fused with the world of mixed martial arts. However, the original technique is here to stay.

Without loading your hips, a hook is a slap no matter how dressed up, and when properly aligning the ulna with your grounded feet, it's not hard to crack a rib or split an eye. The only difference the antiquated sport has with the new and improved game is there are more ways to hurt the other guy—or gal—if they step in the ring. Instead of sheer blunt force trauma being the sole strategy, holds, locks, and chokes are thrown into the mix, both upright and on the mat.

That there is an equation for entertainment.

All of this wouldn't be complete, though, without bureaucratic evolutions. Technique and equipment have improved in this arena as well. From the open market to the black, if the people want a fight, they'll get it and not a single government entity or regulation can stop that, even with their for-the-good-of-the-people bullshit.

My ass.

With the "violent" sport of football the next to be regulated into oblivion, it's anyone's guess the true motives politicians will have for the people and the markets that surround them. One would think that the "people's elected" would have learned from the Prohibition. Taboo activities will only pique public interest, especially when the money moves from Washington oligarchs and into the pockets of everyday Joe and Jane.

The only reason he fights is that it's the most powerful middle finger he or anyone has towards the bureaucracy.

The rhythmed cadence starts as a whisper before growing progressively louder as the speed of the rope increases. The slapping of the rope skipping and keeping time, his feet glide back and forth as every second adds to the agonizing sear within his thighs. With a sharp beep of the timer, in his final minute he looks into the mirror, willing himself through the fiery finale. He concentrates on his brown eye for the first thirty seconds, and then his blue eye for the final stretch, the bell echoing for him to stop. The time is done, but he's not as branded memories ignite something inside of this man, and not only is it exhilarating, but it's outright terrifying. As the rope continues to clap in rhythm, each gunshot in his mind, every cry for a medic, and all of the final breaths he's seen cauterizes his soul until finally, his body gives in, dampening the flame. Never can the fire be extinguished, though. Never will he let it.

Mica Rouge: "The American Devil." With two years inside the Underground, he hopes there will be many more to come. His newfound therapy has turned into a passionate affair, one that no other woman has been able to compete against. Maybe that's why he and his ex had to just be friends. From study buddy to banging partner to nemesis, they ultimately agreed that the best route would be to just remain friends. Fighting has always been his way of coping with darkness. It's why he enlisted—to bring some meaning to the less than savory upbringing his parents provided. All of it metastasized into post-traumatic stress, a now tainted term and one he's actively avoided. That's always been his real problem. Mica never went through "acceptance."

Gag.

And that's exactly what he told his ex. That and many other choice words each time she brought up his "baggage." They were absolute poison for each other. He couldn't see it then, but Mica was bound by her sexy, sadistic nature that exacerbated the fundamental differences the two of them had. There was actually a profound sense of gratitude that came from her cheating on him. His eyes were opened to his own fallacies while he could simultaneously ignore hers. In fact, he realized that she only comprehended minor facets of his life because not only did he wall her off, the two were so wrapped up in the carnal nature of their relationship and the appearances it yielded that they were unable to have a healthy conversation about anything productive in nature. But alas, not only was their relationship like terminal cancer, her roommate seemed to be a form of chemo, allowing him to purge his system of his ex once and for all. He's not proud of that bit, but the two of them have managed to stay on good terms once that intimate connection was surgically removed.

Stepping into the locker room, the musky aroma of sweat and bleach fill his nose, and tossing his rope onto his back, Mica moves to turn on the shower, followed by his portable streaming radio.

"Now's not the time for him to veto the bill! It makes absolutely no sense for him to make such an arrogant decision."

That tone. Man does he love the resonance of her smooth, burning voice. Nothing better than an empty gym, followed by an empty locker room meant for him and her kindled rage. It's more than just serene. It's intoxicating the way she lights her victims on fire with the cerebral weapons she wields.

"You're telling me you'd rather sign and pass something that not only would put us in another war, but put the military budget above ten percent?"

That's who she's debating? This is what she's been stressing about? The guy sounds like a weasel rapist! His voice alone should put her at ease because the only people who sound like that are stupid-smart people and people who have forceful intercourse with rodents. Although the former are dangerous for society and the latter extremely disgusting, people that fall within this spectrum shouldn't be anything for Kim to worry about.

"Yes, because none of what you said is true. Moving the embassy and signing a budget relief plan for our military have nothing in common. You're conflating two separate arguments!"

Mica can't wait for it. He knows exactly where this guy is going with his argument. He glanced at her notes once or twice and knows that the weasel rapist is in his final year at Harvard, naturally giving him the divine knowledge of everything. He is *the* prime example of the Dunning-Kruger Effect, and as he sits on the peak of Mount Stupid, Kim's just licking her chops with a match in hand. The kindling has been set, she's just waiting to ignite and then push.

"*I did a case study last semester—*"

"*You did or you read?*"

And that's why he fell in love with her. Cuts right through the bullshit.

"*Does it matter?*"

"*Yes, but let me stop you right there. This is why you're wrong. Our military is ranked seventh in the world, behind China, Russia, and even France. The Relief for the Military Budget is a bill that will give our military a much-needed boost in the R and D department—actually pulling us out of the wars we are currently in—by reallocating funds for those wars back to our energy independence, which is why we're back in the Middle East in the first place.*"

And now that he's on fire…

"*That's not—*" he begins.

"*And! And, when we do end up moving the embassy, it'll take us out of a region that's been a fallen state since 2013. We spend billions of tax dollars each year to uphold a third world government when we can't get our own shit together at home.*"

…there he goes down the mountainside.

Point, set, match. Mica has nothing more to hear as he hops in the shower. At this point, it'll just be sad listening to the guy tumbling down in a heap of flames, trying to slow the fall, while simultaneously attempting to smother the embers of his glorious combustion. The only question now is will Kim be able to chillax, allowing for them to have a normal evening? Or will she notch off the kill only to set her sights on new prey? Maybe she'll finally notice all the work *he's* put in at the gym. There's no doubt Kim would appreciate his newly cut-for-weight physique, if she only took the time to pull her head from the books and eyes off the screen.

Turning off the shower, the meditative dripping of the water is immediately replaced by disrupting stressors that chemically disturb Mica's peace of mind.

"*You can't possibly tell me you believe that?!*" Kim blares out.

"Shit," he mumbles. In a handful of minutes, the weasel rapist not only slowed his tumble, but is at a complete stop and has managed to put the flames out before climbing back up the mountainside.

Kim continues. *"You have to admit that there is at least some correlation to the missing individuals and the rumored 'Children of the Ordean Reich.' With their involvement in the North American Union, there is too much evidence to deny—"*

Kim is the one cut off this time, and Mica can see it now. Her cheeks bulging, glowing a dark red while her luscious green eyes twirl into a deep black. Accidentally learning that early on was a blessing in disguise: let her finish her train of thought.

"A conspiracy theory is all the 'Ordeans' are. Even if your premise is correct, the North American Union is a great thing for the world! The ability to unite continents began with the EU and has shown to be quite effective," the rapist says.

Sidebar for a minute. It's not an exaggeration to call this guy a rapist. Yes, he probably isn't literally going out, violating women and men left and right. Based on the sound of his voice, Mica's willing to bet he weighs a buck fifteen and couldn't even attempt such a feat, and in fact, if anyone is getting physically raped, it'd be this guy. That aside! He is taking advantage of language, cherry picking data, and bastardizing ideals all in the name of "social justice" or whatever the hell they want to brand it as these days. Ideas have consequences, and this weasel rapist is no different than the slew of people out there pushing the same copy-and-pasted agenda. They call themselves "warriors of democracy" but don't realize they are simply cheap marketers that know how to utilize mob rule and propaganda. Holy hell, it's like he's talking to his ex all over again!

"What about the police report of the missing man downtown?" Kim continues. *"One day he's frantically calling for a police investigation on his neighbor for 'secretive gang activity' he was quoted as saying in the police report, and the next day he is nowhere to be found."*

"Quote 'secretive gang activity' does not suggest an Ordean Reich is trying to overthrow the U.S. government. That's called treason for crying out loud! Which, if found and convicted, is the death penalty."

He's done it now! Kim rule number two: don't ever, under any circumstance, never, ever, ever quote or state the obvious hoping that it will win the argument. Not only will it *not* shut her up, she'll blast you with fact after verified source so far up your butt that your nose will bleed and ooze truth.

"I know what it is! But just because something like treason is, quote 'illegal,' that doesn't mean people don't still do it! And to think that people cheat in card games but draw the line when it comes to political systems and power is not only naïve, but fatal to the American way of life."

Looks like a nice evening will not be happening anytime soon. Sighing, Mica turns off the stream and can't help but feel a little sorry for the rapist. Everyone will be reading it in tomorrow's news: "Man-boy Murdered on Live Stream by Sexy Genius Woman."

Listing and counting as many romantic, cheesy, flowery gestures as he can muster to subdue Kim's fury, Mica finishes packing his things. Usually, she's not one for that "lovey-dovey crap" as she calls it, but at this point he's willing to bet the odds that it won't matter. Perspective. That's how he'll have to sell it. They're in love. They both have amazing social circles, and their careers are on the rise. She has something with this Ordean Reich theory, and just because one guy doesn't believe her doesn't mean she's alone. There's sound evidence out there; she's just got to keep finding it and sharing. True journalism—truth no matter how ugly.

Stepping onto the first floor of the library, Mica finds a table in a remote corner and waits for Kim to come out of the studio. It isn't long before he watches her gleefully bound out of the elevator—not the Charlie Brown walk of shame he was expecting.

"Good mood?" Mica asks with a gentle kiss, wrapping his arms around her.

One thing that has and continues to attract Kim to Mica is that even though he's the stereotypical man's man—rough around the edges and a gym rat—he's got a compassionate side that's always putting her first. In more vulgar terms: he's a beast in the sheets and a gentleman on the streets.

As they part from their kiss, she gazes into his bicolor eyes before leaning back in for a second taste of her man.

"What do you mean?" she asks, and then, in a split second of mulling over his question, she puts the pieces together. "Did you not listen?!"

"I did!" Mica quickly states, realizing that he apparently turned off the interview too soon.

"You turned it off early, didn't you?" That stern look of hers. It's the same rigid expression Mica receives every time he's not perfectly awesome at being her boyfriend.

"Yes..." Mica slowly admits. "Only because you seemed really upset!" he then quickly interjects.

"Whatever." She lets go of him. It really irks her when he doesn't listen to her entire broadcasts, and let's be honest, it wouldn't bother her so much if that was the only thing that he doesn't finish! He doesn't finish meals all the way, he *never* finishes books, falls asleep in movies and shows all the time, projects around the apartment are always incomplete, and he never finishes their arguments. He just lets them float in the air, hoping they float away and disappear into the atmosphere. She knows it's an emanation of his commitment issue, and *he* knows it, which makes it even harder. Veteran or not, Mica needs to figure his shit out before she pops smoke and leaves.

"Your loss. You missed the best part," Kim simply states, letting out a vengeful smirk.

"I was still right though, wasn't I?"

"About what? That whole Ordean Reich thing?"

"Yeah," he says, holding out his hand, asking for what she owes him. After that little charade, that lovey-dovey crap is out the window. He wants what she owes.

"Oh, come on! You know he was just being stubborn. There is too much evidence to deny the fact that someone organized is behind these kidnappings!"

"Kim," he patiently says, continuing to smile. For the most part it's frightening, but there are moments her wrath is cute.

"Even if it's not some political group looking to assassinate the President, there is a mastermind—"

"Kim?"

"The systematic silencing of news sites, Congressmen and women suddenly changing long-held positions on practically every policy—"

"Babe?"

"What?!" she shouts, causing students and faculty to drop books and spill coffee from her resonance.

"I never bet that I wouldn't believe you. I only bet that *he* wouldn't. And..." He can't help but smile when saying this because it hardly ever happens. He might as well enjoy this glorious victory as he waits for her to finish his words, and awaiting his prize, Mica continues holding out his hand.

The stubborn woman she is, Kim ignores the obvious gesture and simply grabs his hand, calming down and smiling the moment she does.

"No," Mica shakes his hand away from hers. "That's not how this works. You gotta say it! Say it, then pay it!"

"You can never take me seriously can you, Mica Rouge?!" she bellows out, causing a few shushes to spurt out from among the dedicated students and staff. Reaching into her bag, she rips out the bag of M&M's, hurling them at him, but not surprised when his reflexes save his face from getting pelted by the candy. "You were right!" she hisses out before turning a one eighty, nearly bowling over a poor freshman.

Chasing after her, he apologizes to the young, confused victim caught in their crossfire, before catching up and grabbing her hand.

"I'm not joking about the Ordeans..."

He's done it now. She was in a good mood, and he just screwed it all up. It's a loop he just can't seem to get out of.

"I never said you were, Kim."

She tries to pull herself away, but he continues to grasp her hand, bringing her in closer. While people entering and exiting the library must inconveniently maneuver their way around the two as they have this moment right in front of the entryway, Mica gently pulls on her chin, bringing her gaze back to his.

"I'm sorry I didn't finish your interview."

Kissing him, she places her head on his chest. "It's fine. I'm just mad you won the bet."

"I know, it's hard sometimes being wrong," he says, smiling as he brushes his hands through her hair, knowing full well his words and gesture will piss her off.

"Excuse me," a man says as she yanks herself away, backing into the guy entering the library.

"You, sir, are on thin ice!" she states before pivoting yet again into a brisk walk away.

Hustling alongside her, Mica finds himself letting a long awkward silence ferment, figuring he's out of cute cards to play. But amidst it, Kim grabs Mica's hand and gently squeezes it. In a moment just long enough for her fury to subside, he asks, "You coming tonight?"

"To what? Your fight?"

Mica nods as they continue to walk down campus.

"Are you going to get hurt?" she sarcastically asks.

All jokes aside, she really does hate going. Every fight she worries. She's seen him break his nose, fracture his shin bone, and get a concussion. That was all before they were seriously dating—when there was cute infatuation and lust. He's definitely gotten better, but those memories still linger in the back of her mind. She won't outright complain about his fighting, though, because the training keeps him fit. She knows he thinks she hasn't noticed, but he's gotten a lot yummier. Muscles are firmer and sharper than ever before.

That being said, the two have moved from lust to love. Unlike any ex she's known about, Kim's the only one that understands how fighting is his therapy. She'll never fully understand, but Mica needs someone who is patient as he works through these things. With a major distrust of "experts," professional therapy is out of the question, and on the days he misses the gym, she notices. He may not, but she does, so she lets him fight.

"Well, are you?" he asks again, ignoring her sarcasm.

"Are you going to get a bloody nose? Will you need me there to kiss your boo-boos better?" She creates a pouty face and puckers her lips.

"And you say that I can't take anything seriously…"

—⋆ ⋆ ⋆ ⋆—

All the hours spent training and sacrificing have come to this. The chump in front of Mica has no idea what he's gotten himself into. *He's the one who challenged The American Devil*—and Mica, being the generous guy that he is, granted the request.

Looking over to the front row, Mica finds Kim where he gives her a wink before she sends one back his way. She does a good job at hiding it, but her anxiety, as subtle as it is, is still there. She masks it with her unenthusiasm and cynical humor, but Mica sees the angst in her hands. The twisting and wringing of an imaginary towel is all he needs to see in order to know that she's in a state of discomfort. Today, rather than putting on a show for the crowd, Mica decides to finish it as quickly as possible. Kim's been through enough today. The least he can do is put her jitters at ease. Then again, the audience has been dull to say the least, which is never good for his marketability.

It may be a finer line to walk tonight than he'd like.

The creaking gate of the ring opens, in walking the announcer and referee to take their place in the middle of the arena.

"Ladies and gentlemen, for the first time in the IFA, we had a public challenge!"

The crowd perks a little from their comas upon hearing the announcement that they are witnessing fighting history.

"Last week, Johnny 'Smash' challenged The American Devil's title!"

The crowd's enthusiasm continues to grow as the referee motions the two fighters to the center.

Smash? That is the stupidest name Mica's ever heard.

The referee looks to Johnny Johnson. "Does the challenge still stand?"

Vigorously, Johnny *Smash* Johnson nods his head, his mop-like hair flailing as he does.

"I need a verbal response," the referee states.

"Yes, damn it!" That picks the crowd up even further. Everyone loves good tension in a fight.

Turning to Mica, the ref then asks, "Do you accept the challenge? Rejecting the challenge forfeits the fight and your belt."

"I accept," Mica says, nodding his head.

"Then let there be a clean fight. Fighters, touch fists, and at the sound of the bell, start the show."

Mica reaches out his fists towards his opponent, but the man stays resolute, set on defeating the arrogant champion.

"I'm gonna smash you up!" Johnny says to Mica.

Mica's not one for trash talking, but due to the rude nature of the fella in front of him, he can't help himself. The bigger the ego, the harder the fall. "You practice that in the mirror?"

Mica no longer needs to ponder it as he decides the best course of action is to build the guy up a little before taking him down.

Sorry, Kim, but guys like this need some humble pie.

The bell sounds and Mica sees the cheap shot coming a mile away. Blocking the knee to his groin, he lets Johnny hit him with a wild right hook to his face. Mica quickly recovers, slipping a grapple before jabbing and testing the waters of his opponent. Smash quickly and arrogantly grabs the back of Mica's head, bringing Mica's face to his knee. In a swift rush, Smash then rips Mica's feet from off the mat, throwing him up in the air before Mica's face comes smacking down on the canvas.

"That was dumb," Mica mumbles into the floor.

"Finish him! Crush his skull!" someone from the crowd yells.

That, combined with the takedown, does anything but ease Kim's cool angst as she grips the invisible towel even harder.

Mica pushes himself up from off the canvas, narrowly dodging a stomping foot and an uppercut. Kicking Smash square in the thigh, it doesn't look or sound like much, but Mica notes the cringe on his opponent's face. Mica could feel it on impact—his heel striking the tender area of his inner thigh. Limping it off, Smash attempts a third volley of strikes. Not letting him get a hit in this time, Mica jumps, bringing his left knee to Johnny's jaw. A risky but show-off move that instantly dazes Smash, who staggers, unable to focus on anything. Lifting his arms in the air, Mica looks to the crowd as he starts a countdown. The once bored crowd, now hysterical and on their feet, watches as Johnny "Smash" Johnson continues to wobble, and once the countdown reaches one, Mica closes his fist, knocking his opponent out cold with an uppercut from the devil himself.

"Finally." Kim drops her invisible towel, grabs her purse, and heads to Mica's locker room as Mica tries to blow her a victorious kiss.

Damn, he should've just gone for the quick knockout. Not even taking the referee's hand as he announces the winner, Mica ignores the formal accolade and crowd approval as he hops the side of the cage and makes his way to Kim. Cautiously, Mica steps into the quiet locker room where the crowd is muffled by the closing door.

"Here," Kim quickly states, throwing a real towel at him. "When?" she then asks.

They've had this discussion a thousand times and Mica just can't seem to avoid it. Everything in him wishes he could just tell her. Next week is what he wants to say, but there is so much more to her simple, one-worded question. Another fight finished, another workout complete and she still feels like she's taking the silver medal on the podium of Mica's life.

It tears him up, but he has to say it. "I don't know…"

"It'll be a year next Friday."

"I know…" But what more can he say? "Why are you bringing this up now, Kim?" It sounds insincere. He knows full well why now. Every fight, it's brought up, but his joke won't have anything behind it if he doesn't ask, and Kim desperately needs a joke.

"Are you serious?"

"You bought me a ring, didn't you?" he asks, slapping his hands to his cheeks. There it is. Let's see if the joke holds its ground now.

It does. He sees a smirk rise to the surface as Kim's entire demeanor relaxes.

Wiping the sweat from his brow and dabbing the blood off his lip, he puts a shirt on and approaches his girlfriend. "Kimberly."

"Why not now?" she mumbles, burying her face in his musky chest. "Why can't we just move on?"

"Because," Mica begins, setting the stage for another joke, "I have a headache, I'm hungry, I'm sore, and I just want to have victory sex with my girlfriend. And then maybe cuddle and watch a movie."

"Fine…" she continues to mumble into his chest. She doesn't laugh and guffaw, but the quip landed. "I love you, Mica Rouge."

"I love you too, Kim. Now let's go get freaky."

This time she does laugh and guffaw as she pushes him away.

The couple holds hands as they exit out the back and continue down the steps before Mica brings up a more serious topic.

"You gonna write down my win in your diary, or whatever?"

"It's a journal first of all, and you should write in one. Posterity and shit. And second, no. You think you're the center of my universe, but you're not!" She says this with such comical attitude that he can't help but kiss her.

The two embrace and continue their walk home. As they round a corner, they're stopped dead in their tracks as three hooded figures stand ten feet away.

"Who are they?" Kim whispers, Mica shrugging his shoulders in response.

"You have said too much," one of the hooded figures says.

"Who are you?" Kim demands. Mica loves that she isn't afraid to speak her mind, but sometimes he wishes that she had a usable filter.

"Either join us in our cause, or keep your mouth shut," the figure states.

"Hey! Don't you—"

Mica cuts her off. "Listen. We don't want any trouble."

"Whether that's true or not, your girlfriend found trouble, Mica."

Mica hesitates for a moment in shock. "How the hell do you know my name?"

"You have a week from today to decide, Kim. We will be waiting, and we will be watching." And without anything more, the three hooded figures turn and walk away, and until they are out of sight, Mica and Kim stand and scan their surroundings.

"That was freaky…" Kim says, squeezing Mica's arm.

"Yeah, you should write that in your diary too."

Kim doesn't need to say anything. She just punches Mica in the arm.

———★★———

The Pentagon

In a finely pressed suit and a briefcase in hand, he makes his way down a hallway of one of the finest and most secretive buildings in Washington. It's not the first time, and if all goes as planned, it most certainly won't be his last. As he turns a corner, his footsteps continue their resonating echo down the desolate corridor. After recent events, it's rare for no one to be rushing through the rows of offices, trying to subdue the madness, but unconventional and unprecedented times come with such an atmosphere.

Rounding one last turn, his steps are suppressed as the tile merges to carpet, and now in a remote wing of the building, he approaches a door before knocking four times. With no response, the man looks at his watch and sits down in a chair within arm's reach of the door. Placing his briefcase on his lap, carefully and methodically he beats a nervous rhythm with his thumbs as he begins a quick rehearsal in his head. Everything is concealed safely on his lap, but once he opens his mouth, it will be fair game. The program will either succeed or fail in a matter of minutes. Before he can delve too deeply into the various ramifications, however, the door opens, and a red-haired woman steps out.

"Mr. Carter," she says, "the council will see you now."

Swiftly, he stands, grabbing his briefcase before walking into the dark room. It takes a moment for Carter's eyes to adjust, but as they do, he sees a solitary desk in front of him with a padded office chair at its side. Determined, he approaches without any apparent fear and as he sits, he takes notice of the nine decorated men and women of the board. A long silence fills the room as both Carter and the council stare each other down. Like most military types, they keep quiet until the proper moment. Figuring that they're waiting on him, Carter inhales as he opens his mouth, but upon doing so he is immediately interrupted.

"Mr. Carter, your proposal?"

Nodding, Carter takes a moment to gather his thoughts. "Council, if I may before I begin, I'd like to explain how this program hopes to—"

"Mr. Carter, your proposal is all we ask for," the council president states.

Not being one to set his opinions aside so easily, Mr. Carter argues. "But certainly, there are some doubts and concerns with the reformation of White Eagle, and I wish to—"

Again, he is interrupted, this time with more authority. "The proposal!"

Frustrated, Mr. Carter reluctantly shuts his mouth and opens his briefcase to pull out a single file labeled "The Minutemen Division."

"This country is on the brink of a second civil war, not due to slavery, but the lust of a greater power and tyrannical control, and after the recent national divorce, this all is cause for great concern. Organized crime has risen to new heights caused by the efforts of the Children of the Ordean Reich. Congress, as well as the President, believe it to be a conspiracy theory along with many other Americans, which is only exacerbated by the media. But you and I both know, from sad experience, that this popular opinion is wrong."

He opens the anemic-looking file to reveal the information of a single American citizen.

"Few are capable and willing to fight, but a few, ready citizens are all we need," he continues. "Those few who know our pains, know our desires, and know our enemies will step up if we but ask them to. In order to get our President and our country to believe the realities of these domestic threats, we must expose this enemy. However, with the progress organized crime has made, White Eagle is no longer enough, and I come to you with this reformation to address the very real and imminent threats on American soil. This program, The Minutemen Division, was created to accomplish just that."

Short and direct, just like he practiced. However, there is a void of silence before the military board discusses what's been presented, and even then, Mr. Carter's stomach is tied in knots as he listens to the whispered critiques, none of which sound promising. After they quiet down, the president of the board asks a solitary question.

"What do you propose we do next then?"

Pulling out the citizen's file, Carter responds by slapping down a photograph. "Kimberly Blackham. Independent reporter and journalist."

THREE

Area Thirty-Eight

"What happened to yer face?" Kip asks, with a rare, horrified look.

As they check out of the Mill, Jax sees dozens of similar questioning expressions. It's too easy to pick out those who saw Jax's visage used as a punching bag versus the innocent ignorant. Their gazes are either up, or down in shame.

"Had some fun with some guards at lunch," Jax tells Kip, a sense of pride beginning to grow as he reflects on it.

"Did you have a safe word?" Kip smirks and jests. They're simply trying to lighten the mood, but man, Kip wishes he'd been there—it's been his job for years to look after the kid. It also would've added some fun to his own day.

Jax shakes his head. "They were in too much of a rush." Which isn't entirely true, but he doesn't want Kip to feel worse than he already does.

"And ya was sayin' that I needed to stay outta trouble… Y'er just as big of a problem as I am!"

"It's true," Jax says, not knowing what more to say other than to add a shrug to the statement. "It's mostly by accident though."

Kip scoffs. "Bullshit. Ya love the attention."

Jax holds his tongue at the joke. Yes, he has a rebellious side to him. Name him one person his age these days who doesn't. However, not many of his peers find themselves asking what the point really is—what good does all the angst do? For Jax, it just seems to hurt more and more with less of the fulfillment he used to get when he was younger. Bruised ribs, swollen eyes, and fat bloodied lips aren't as glorious as they used to be. Jax just needs to accept what Granny Lisa taught him; governments rise and collapse all the time and like them, the Nine's reign will fall into this natural order of civilization. He's just got to stay in one piece until that time comes.

"I didn't like it today," Jax finally says.

Kip knows that tone all too well and has just the thing to add some remedial comfort. As the line advances, Kip nudges the man in front of them to the side to reveal the pick-him-up. Still at that same computer, being unknowingly seductive to every single guy in line, sits the Looker.

"She did that to ya, didn't she?" Kip jokingly asks.

"I wish," Jax chuckles out. And part of him believes that. Jax is no masochist, but any opportunity to get to know her identity is something he's willing to do. She's just different. The way she moves, talks, and even the way other PPA soldiers treat her is different. Take the single triangled private next to her for example. If it were any other female PPA, he'd be eye banging her up and down and all over town as he hands out the daily wages. But he's not. It's as if she's harnessed the power of fear.

"Y'er up," Kip suddenly says, nudging Jax forward.

"Name, Area number, and residency identification," she dully demands.

"Jax M. Rouge. Area Thirty-Eight. Residency ID two-two-zero." Crossing his fingers, Jax prays to whoever will listen that the report of his fight wasn't filed. The last thing he needs is another pay dock.

"It says here that you provoked a guard during your designated lunch hour," she says, looking up to his black and blue appearance. "Did you?"

The question is solely out of protocol—standard operating procedure. The report was apparently already filed, therefore, it's rather useless to tell his side of the story. She won't believe the truth in a million years.

"No—no I did not," Jax says with absolute resolve. But while trying to keep his demeanor, his eyes drift downward, catching sight of the tiny, tallied scars on her neck. They're too perfect—too deliberate to be accidental, and as Jax begins counting them, his eyes shoot back to hers as he realizes what it looks like he's doing.

"Sure, you didn't," she says, pulling her collar upward as if she noticed that *he* noticed. "You'll receive a docked wage of fifty percent."

"Ridiculous," he mutters.

The guard next to her hands him six credits, which Jax takes as he smothers his dissatisfied grunt, but despite how pathetically annoyed he is, Jax can't help but wonder. Does she think less of him? More? Has he left any sort of impression on her? It's doubtful, but in the end, does it even matter? She's a Legacy and he's a Labor worker. She'll forget about him before her head even hits her soft pillow tonight.

"Eh! Jax, wait up!" Jax slows just long enough for Kip to catch up before returning to his brisk, enraged pace. "Did ya get another credit cut?"

"Yeah. It is—"

"What it is," Kip says, finishing the sentence for him. "Hold out yer hand."

"Why?"

"Here." And without verbally answering the stupid question, Kip grabs Jax's hand and places six credits into his palm.

"What's this for?" Jax asks, his eyebrows rising as high as the swelling allows.

"For savin' my ass this morning; and the five other times. A credit for each time," Kip says with his same classic, goofy smile.

"I... Thanks, Kip." Jax is at a loss for words. Kip's always been the older brother, despite a myriad of reasons he might not look or act like it.

"No problem. I'll see ya at the Gathering."

"Where are you going?" Jax asks.

"I gotta get something from my place 'fore I head over." And with that, Kip jogs ahead, not giving Jax a chance to even try and give back the credits.

Stuffing the money in his pocket, Jax continues his lonely trudge towards City Hall. Already exhausted with aches and pains he knows will only worsen, there's still the hour-long ritual he must stand through. Rounding the corner, Jax steps in line with the masses, and as they all pass under each yellow streetlamp, he can't help but notice the distortions in both the lights and shadows of each sad soul by his side. Their lives are as meaningful as the grey snow beneath their feet, testifying to the hierarchy that controls each worker's life, and if that wasn't symbolic enough, there's City Hall to rub salt in their wounds.

Its illuminating lights from within the glass walls shine as a horrendous beacon for all to see. At the tip of the magnificent building rests the only non-transparent piece of the structure: a dome with the star and eight stripes engraved on its north, south, east, and west faces. The chandelier, said to have been made by the Oligarchy itself, hangs from the center of the one-roomed building where it hovers just above the heads of the gathering classes within.

PPA officers line the walls both inside and out, while the flood of attendees are individually scanned upon entering. As Jax approaches, the flickering light of the optical reader instantly disorients him.

"Make your way in quietly and orderly please," one of the guards shouts out.

"Oi! Jax!" Kip rushes forward, blocking the epileptic flashing with his hand. As he does the white turns red, alerting the PPA guards of a deviant.

"Sir! Lower your hand for the scanner."

Kip unenthusiastically puts his hand down and lets the scanner blind him. The scanners change back to white, and in a handicapped fashion, Kip eventually grasps Jax's arm after stumbling from person to person.

"Cutting it close, don't you think?" Jax tells him.

"I know, I know," Kip says with a firm blink, trying to clear the floating spots from his vision. "I seriously think I have a condition."

Methodically, the duo moves towards their usual spot in the back right corner before Jax decides to ask, "You notice that there are more assholes than usual?" There are at least four dozen guards outside and six dozen inside—easily three times the standard PPA numbers.

"Yeah, and at the Mill too."

"What do you think is going on?"

"Bet we're about to find out."

Just as Kip says this, The Government's anthem begins. With no words, the small orchestra plays a few harmonized measures of the Nine's motif. Funerals and the occasional announcement of appointed officials are the only times anyone hears the anthem in its entirety.

As the string instruments finish, a line of PPA privates push a group of individuals on stage. Normally the same few people are forced up there—workers who don't abide by The Government's law. However, there's the occasional exception. Tonight, those exceptions are a boy and girl barely the age of ten. With the "criminals" facing their audience—their peers—the Area Leader approaches the stage to unenthused clapping.

Caspian Stone, son of Sullivan and Bella Stone, the barbaric founders of the PPA. Rumors and assumptions are all anyone has of that family. It's rumored that he has three siblings, but the only member of the Stone family anybody in Area Thirty-Eight has seen is Caspian himself. From a distance you can't appreciate how pale his skin truly is, not even on the giant screens flanking the stage. Until you stand next to him it's impossible to know how close his complexion resembles that of a ghost.

"Welcome to the Gathering." Caspian's voice projects throughout the room of City Hall, extending his skeletal arms, the shiny eagle rank upon his shoulder catching the chandelier's light.

"Do you think...?" Jax begins, looking to the children on stage before trailing off as he watches Kip's head nod, answering the unfinished question.

"Tonight," Caspian continues, "I have the heartbreaking responsibility of reminding you all of the law. Normally, we have the typical drunks infringing on the law and attacking my officers," he says walking in front of two middle-aged men, pushing each with his bony finger.

Immediately, four of the triangle privates beat the two men unconscious.

"There are the workers who try seducing them—*my* PPA." Caspian now touches a young lady with the same white finger where two more privates, one of them being a woman, beat her in the same fashion.

Nothing like equality, Jax thinks, scoffing to himself.

"Those who are too frail to work," Caspian then mockingly states without even bothering to lay his finger on the crippled elderly couple before they, too, are beaten within an inch of their frail lives.

Stopping his waltz, Caspian Stone finds himself standing in front of the little boy and girl.

"And then there are the thieves of the community."

A long moment passes, forcing everyone to take in the cruelty of the next moments. Pulling out a thirteen-inch metal rod from within his coat, Caspian's long thin fingers wind around the handle as it glistens in the building's light, and with no more PPA privates lined up, it's clear that Caspian personally wants this experience.

Unable to watch, Jax shifts his focus to the dark, wooden floor, saving his eyes from the awful sight, but not willing to risk being seen covering his ears, nothing can save him from the children's screams and yelps as Jax is forced to listen to their young cries. In a matter of moments, they abruptly stop, but the sound of the rod bluntly hitting flesh and bone continues its rhythmic violence. This is wrong. Everybody in this room knows it, but what can they do? All they have is the sickening feeling within their stomachs to testify against the truly evil and barbaric acts the Nine burdens them with every day.

Finally, the fleshy beating ceases.

"What is the law?" Caspian demands, wiping his bare knuckles and rod clean with a brown and white handkerchief before dabbing specks of blood off the metallic eagle on his shoulder.

"The law states," the Gathering chants in unison, "one, no disrespectful acts towards the Nine or The Government which upholds them. Two, praise the Nine by our actions and with our words. Lastly, live, work, and if needs be die, so that the Nine and their Government may continue to prosper and bless."

"We give you food," Caspian shouts. "We give you shelter. We give you work. We give you purpose. All we ask is for you to keep the law. Let tonight be a reminder of what happens when someone breaks it. They in turn are broken. Perfection is coming! Do not disrespect us. We will not be mocked!"

"How long do ya think he practiced that?" Kip asks, giving Jax a nudge with his elbow.

"Tomorrow," Caspian announces, "you will all have the privilege of being in the presence of my family."

Gasps litter the grandiose room. The entire Stone family? The founders of the PPA in City Hall?

Holding up his arms for silence, Caspian quickly gets his wish.

"Be on time. I will not fail nor dishonor my family by having rebellious and disobedient workers."

"Is he asking us for a favor?" Kip asks Jax, the question making everyone around them uncomfortable.

"Always remember the law," Caspian concludes before finally making his exit.

The orchestra plays the same melodic anthem, and until it finishes, everyone stands in abject silence as Caspian's council looms overhead. Once permitted, Kip and Jax are the first ones to escape the asphyxiating building where neither says a word the entire walk home.

The founders of PPA—two members of the Nine—and the rest of their offspring will be here in Area Thirty-Eight. Is regulation going to change? Will there be additions to the law? Nobody would know—except one person, maybe.

"Ya have any plans for the day off?" Kip asks Jax, breaking both the silence and Jax's concentration.

"Possibly. I've got the usual errands to run."

"Well, I'll see ya sometime tomorrow, yeah?" Kip asks, punching Jax in the middle of his arm before taking off at a brisk jog towards his house.

Jax can't help but respect the tenacity Kip has brought into Jax's life. They're some of the lucky few—if you want to call it that. While ninety percent of the population lives in high density areas, Jax can't help but count his sole blessing of having a tiny, rundown state sponsored shack all to himself—his piece of heaven in hell next door to Kip. Grandma Lisa most likely had a heavy hand in making sure both he and Kip were prepared once she died, realizing that if they shared a lodging, they might just tear each other apart.

Running his fingers along the chain linked barrier, he lifts his hand slightly to skip the seven, sharp and rusting holes. His boots crunch onto the crumbling walkway as he approaches, his senses heightening with each step as he listens to the subtle shuffling and rummaging of his things coming from inside.

This home is a piece of shit, but it's *his* piece of shit—making it a common practice for those who are even less fortunate to try and acquire what little The Government has given him. Both he and Kip have had their run-ins with these vagrants and Jax will be damned if he lets them win tonight. Reaching the front steps, Jax skips the missing second stair before reaching for the door handle. Barely touching it, the door creaks.

"Here we go…" Jax whispers.

Flipping on the lights, attempting to catch the criminals off guard, Jax kicks the rest of the door open just in time to see three cats scatter from off the kitchen counters, knocking anything and everything to the ground in a shattering crash.

"Damn cats," he mutters, not seeing anyone or anything threatening.

Turning around to close the door behind the exiting felines, it slams shut on its own accord. In less than two seconds an arm shoots across the front of his neck while another grips the back of Jax's head, immediately cutting off his air supply. The enormous weight of his attacker buckles Jax at the knees where he falls to the ground face first, breaking his nose and letting blood freely flow onto the wooden floor. Jax swings his elbow at his attacker, but it's useless, and with a second attempt, Jax quickly finds himself blacking out. However, before his sight goes completely dark, his attacker whispers in his ear.

"Surprise."

Immediately, the pressure on his neck is released allowing Jax to take in a deep inhale before attempting to push himself up.

"I got you good," the bear of a man says, smirking at his small victory as he shoves Jax back to the ground, using the guy to help him stand.

"Not that good," Jax mumbles, finally able to get to his knees. "You made it pretty obvious that someone was here."

"Please," the bear growls out.

"You left the door open!" Jax states before standing, his nose continuing to drip into the tiny puddle of blood on the floor.

"I still caught you off guard," he brags to Jax.

"Connor?" Jax asks the bear.

"Yes?" Connor slowly says, not sure where Jax will take this conversation.

"Shut up!" Jax casually shoves Connor as he walks past him, sending the burly man flying into the door frame.

"Man," Connor chuckles, "if only you fought like that every time."

"It's called labor strength."

Jax has always been strong as an ox, labor force or not. Lucky for Connor, he manages to still catch Jax off guard. Built like a truck, Connor's shoulders are just as wide as a diesel's frame, and yet even with all his experience within Area Thirty-Eight's PPA, Jax's natural strength and ability is frightening. If Jax just tapped into that, he'd be deadly. All that being said, Connor has battle expertise on his side, and all the raw talent in the world can't compete with wisdom earned from blood and sweat.

"You're out of regs," Jax casually says to the guy he's been friends with for as long as he can remember, grabbing a towel and sitting on the edge of his kitchen table. Aside from the unconventional uniform he's got on, Connor's black stubble strewn about his face says it all: he's been in the field, which means there is some juicy stuff happening around the Area.

"Two things," Connor begins, rubbing his stubble. "Don't tell me to shut up. And two, you shut up! What if I was a criminal or one of my men? How would you—what happened to your face?" He's somewhat shocked when he sees Jax's discolored and swollen appearance.

"One of your men…" he tells him. "And thanks for the broken nose on top of it, by the way."

"I haven't seen you this bad since that night I first met you in overnight lockup," Connor sarcastically states.

Jax chuckles at the memory. "You were in the cell next to me."

"I was there for training. You were in there for breaking the law." Connor shrugs while he rummages around in his pockets. "So, what happened?"

"I got in a fight at lunch." Jax dabs some more blood from his nostrils with the towel, squirming at the stinging pop his broken nose makes.

"Of course. Did you start it?"

"What do you think?" Jax sighs out. "It was some new guy throwing his penis around. I wasn't listening to any of his *directives*, and this is what happened," Jax says, framing his face like a picture before moving to the sink.

"A new guy," Connor mumbles as he tries to pick his brain for who.

"The guy was huge. Bigger than you."

"Oh. I know who you're talking about. His name is Don Kraft."

"I don't care what his name is," Jax snaps. He doesn't care what the names of any of the PPA members are. Plus, he's not supposed to know them, only their rank, which he also couldn't give two shits about.

"He was recruited from Area Forty-One to help us with security tomorrow."

"And I don't care why he's here," Jax says, mumbling more to himself than to Connor this time.

"You heard about that, right? The Stones coming to Thirty-Eight?" Connor asks, walking into the kitchen to clean up the mess the cats left.

"Caspian just barely announced it at the Gathering. When were you going to tell me that they were coming?" He usually gives information freely to Jax. As soon as Connor knows, Jax knows.

"I'm not allowed to tell you *everything*. You're lucky I tell you anything." He risks his class status and life every time he talks with Jax outside official business, giving out insider information. If there's one thing he learned in that survival course, though, it's that he is no different from anyone else in the Labor class—something Jax unknowingly opened his eyes to those few weeks in confinement.

"Can I ask you something?"

"Is it about the Stones?" Connor asks.

"Yes," Jax says, realizing what Connor is going to say before he says it.

"Then no," Connor smirks.

"Dude…"

"But I'll let you anyway," Connor finishes, wishing he hadn't. If it was any other kind of information, sure, he'd tell Jax. But it's not. It's the Stones. The one group of people that has any control over him.

"How many of them are there?"

"Five."

"Only five?" Jax figured there'd be a whole herd of maniacs running around on stage, punching babies and kicking old people. "Who?"

"The parents: Sullivan and Bella and their kids: Caspian, Rhett, and their sister Renn," Connor says, counting them on his hand.

There is one more, Connor then thinks to himself, but again, he doesn't have to tell Jax everything.

"When are they coming?" Jax asks, rinsing out the blood-soaked towel.

"Tomorrow," Connor says with another clever smirk.

"I know that! When tomorrow?"

"You've got to be specific, man!" Connor laughs out, but upon seeing Jax's broken, sullen mood, decides to quit playing games. "The parents will be here at about seventeen hundred. Caspian is obviously here, but Rhett and Renn came in yesterday."

"Hold up. Rhett and Renn are already here? Who are they?"

"What happened to you not caring about who the PPA are?" Connor chuckles, sitting on the kitchen table, the surface bowing under his weight.

"C'mon, this is good stuff!"

"You'll find out tomorrow."

Jax can't help but search his brain to solve the looming mystery. Not a lot happens in Area Thirty-Eight, but when it does, Jax gets fixated—like the Looker for example. There are dozens of women in the PPA, and even more men, so it's worthless to guess, especially after the influx of security.

"It's been fun messing with you. Reminds me of the good old days," Connor says, hopping from off the table. "And sorry about your nose. I tried to keep you standing, but you just fell forward like a bitch." Reaching into one of his dozen pockets, Connor pulls out a small pouch, tossing it to Jax. "Put that on a damp towel and then put the towel on your face. Do it before you go to sleep and make sure you reset your nose before you do. You won't look so ugly in the morning."

Examining the package, Jax looks up to thank him, but Connor's gone.

One day, Jax thinks. One day he'll learn how to do more of what Connor does, but tonight—tonight is not the night. Placing the medicine pouch on the table and looking for something to satiate his hunger, like usual, Jax finds nothing.

The first cut stings as she continues across her arm, letting out a much-needed sigh of ecstasy. Blood seeps out of the fresh laceration, dripping onto the white towel draped across her lap. Pulling up the knife, Renn visually calculates another inch of skin before making the forty-seventh parallel incision on her body. Ferociously, the door to her room bursts open, but without a flinch, Renn Stone fails to waver from her conviction. Placing the cold steel to her arm, she tallies rape forty-eight.

"What is going on?" her mother screeches.

"Just documenting progress," Renn sarcastically states, taking her combat knife and wiping her blood from the steel, forever staining the white towel on her lap.

"Look your mother in the eye when you address me," Bella Stone hisses out.

"Noted... Bella."

Slamming the door behind her, Bella shakes the entire room—everything in it except Renn.

"Now, what are you doing?"

"What does it look like?" Renn thought it'd be obvious, but then again, she and her mother have never really seen eye to eye.

Bella grabs for the knife, but Renn whips it out of her reach, and before she can attempt another snatch, Renn sheathes the blade, unable to keep from smiling at her mother's juvenile nature.

"Give it to me!"

"Come and get it," Renn coldly states, her fingers wrapped around the hilt. Bella is more than a pretty face. She is well trained and more impressive than one might think, but Renn's skills supersede hers by a long shot. That being said, Bella's feats and value have never been in physical confrontation, but rather deception and manipulation.

"I am very disappointed, Brenna. In both you and Rhett."

"I honestly don't give a damn," Renn mumbles. She doesn't understand the half of what Renn's been through—what the Nine's policies have forced her daughter to endure. Bella's either turned a blind eye to it or condones every offense Renn has been forced into. Either way, their relationship is beyond repair. "Make sure to keep Caspian away from me then. Wouldn't want to taint his perfect record."

"What is going on?" Rhett Stone asks, stepping into the room and gently closing the door as he enters.

"She is your responsibility!" Bella yells, pointing an accusing finger at Renn's bleeding arm.

Seeing the fresh blood, Rhett's fiery heart drops to his stomach. His responsibility—it's one he doesn't take lightly. Time and time again, Rhett has searched for the men who have taken their turns in breaking pieces from his sister's soul, but the system is fraught with corruption as everyone tries to take their slice of the pie. All Rhett does is the next best thing a brother can. It's a process Bella will never understand.

"Mother, leave. I'll take care of this."

"Take care of it?" Bella's high-pitched screech echoes. "If you call this taking care of your sister then—"

"Then what?" Renn shouts. "You going to kill him like you kill all of the Unapproved?"

"You little bitch…"

"That is enough!" Rhett throws his hand across his mother's mouth, and before the confrontation can escalate any further, the radio on each of their shoulders clicks on.

"Is everything all right?" Caspian's voice asks.

Bella glares into her son's eyes before back to her daughter's bloody arm, and throwing Rhett's hand from her mouth, hits the radio.

"What is it, son?"

"Is everything all right? I heard shouting."

"Everything's fine. Just having a discussion."

"That's what this is called?" Renn scoffs.

Caspian is unconvinced but he would rather not get into the middle of whatever their "discussion" is about. "Well, Connor is back."

"Who?" Bella asks.

"Connor, our brother. Your son. He's back. We can eat now."

"We'll be right down," Bella says, clicking off her radio before taking one last condescending look at Renn. "Get that cleaned up. Now!"

Opening the door and slamming it behind her, Rhett locks it behind their mother before turning back to Renn.

"Renn, I thought you were doing better…"

"Yeah, well shit happens." She hates hearing the disappointment in his voice, but what other outlet does she have? Confined and constricted by Bella's chokehold, as of right now, there is no light at the end of Renn's tunnel.

———★———

Thanks to a repetitive loud bark that quickly morphs into a growling grudge match between two wild dogs, there's no better time than now for Jax to wake up and meet the shit of the day. Reluctantly, he pulls himself out from under the sheets, the medicated towel having dried up, sticking stiffly to the side of his face. Jax cringes at the abhorrent smell of the medicine, but it feels like it worked. Able to see out of his once-swollen eye, the broken feeling he felt in his face is virtually gone. The true test is seeing if what he's feeling is a reality.

The icy cold tile underneath his bare feet helps knock off the drowsiness, and as Jax tentatively peeks in the bathroom mirror, a wave of relief rushes over him at the surprising look of his face. With only a scab at the corner of his cut eye and some tender bruises that haven't fully healed, it looks as if the beating never happened. Splashing chilled water on his face to wash the rest of the lethargy away, Jax moves to scrub off the stench from the medicine. Stepping outside moments later, with credits in his pocket, Jax immediately notices the unusual warmth of the winter morning. The sun's coming up, and already too many people make their way to the market square. He hates crowds and distrusts anyone who genuinely enjoys being around people. Some masses can be avoided, but most seem to be inevitable to Jax.

In five minutes time, Jax is shoving his way through the rabble of people to make it to the only shop he trusts—Mari and Ann's. With the day just beginning for them, the two already look exhausted. Ann's moving crates that must be at least twice her weight, and as the little girl struggles to move one of the dozen boxes of potatoes, she manages just long enough to drop it in a violent, but controlled manner before kicking and cursing at it for being so heavy. As if the tent canopy felt offended for the box of potatoes, when Ann turns to move another crate, her long brown ponytail gets snagged on a hook from one of the canopy's supporting poles, yanking her head back and the little girl onto her butt.

"Damn," Jax can't help but chuckle as he rushes over to help the little girl up. Before he can get there though, Mari is by her side smiling and shaking her head.

"How many times have I told you," Mari says, untangling Ann's hair from the hook. "Put your hair in a bun."

Finishing the disentanglement, Mari stands, the woman's eyes meeting Jax's as he approaches. The brightness in her almond gaze has always brought a smile to Jax, and her rosy cheeks are an added gorgeous bonus. As he returns the smiling gesture, a rush of shocking euphoria runs through him, his eyes diverting to her thick black leather coat before moving down to her matching black tight jeans. The moment's brief, but Mari notices, and for her, nothing is more attractive than a man like him.

"Jackie!" Ann shouts, darting over and barreling a hug into Jax.

"Morning, Ann!" he says, picking her up to his eye level.

"Morning!" she shouts, her ear-piercing screech of excitement deafening Jax. "Guess what?!" she asks, giggling at his pain.

"What is it today?" She always has some piece of trivia for the guy. They're mainly animal facts, but every once in a while it's something a bit more exciting.

"It's my birthday today!" she blurts out, revealing the biggest smile a girl her size can.

"Really?! How old are you? Five?"

"No, Jackie," she says with an exasperated tone.

"Six?"

She punches him in the shoulder. "I'm eight."

"Oh, got it. Well happy birthday," he says, pretending to rub feeling back into his shoulder, a joke which never gets old with Ann. With her sense of humor, it's still a mystery to Jax as to why Kip and these two have never gotten along. In an uneasy truce, it's as if Ann sees Kip as competition for the funniest kid on the block. Mari on the other hand just prefers Jax's sexy young visage over Kip's older brother look.

As Jax glances over at Mari, she feels his eyes on her and can't help but let her smile grow a little bit wider.

"You better go on and help your sister. Looks like you guys have a lot today."

Jax isn't sure where or how those two really met. All he knows is that they aren't really sisters and that before they got here a year ago, Area Thirty-Eight was a much duller place.

"What can I do for you, Mr. Jackie?" Mari asks, putting her hands on the table and leaning forward, her feet lifting slightly off the ground as that smile Jax put on her is still plastered to her face.

Looking around as if confused, Jax relishes in any opportunity to mess with her, especially when it comes to her height. A full head shorter than he is, not only is Mari defensive about her abbreviated status, she's aggressively defensive, making it a dangerous game for Jax to play. Dropping her feet back to the ground, Mari punches Jax square in the chest.

"You see me now?" Mari growls out.

"Yep!" Jax says, a little more struggle in his breath. It's like the tides have shifted with the jokesters. When it comes to Mari, Jax is like Kip, abusing jokes to their death.

"Wise guy," she says, the sarcasm seeping from her voice. Her eyes are rolling, but it won't take much to get that girlish smile back.

"Charming too." Jax smirks. And there it is—Mari's smile returns.

"What can I get for you?" she asks, all business now.

"Seven cans of tomato soup, three pounds of turkey, a pound of cheese, three loaves of bread, five apples, five oranges, two dozen eggs, and a pound of your finest powdered juice."

"So, the usual?" she asks, bored by the request.

"What's wrong with that? It keeps me fueled."

"Nothing's wrong with it, it's just boring is all. Have you ever tried cooking? I could teach you some recipes, you know." The hesitancy in her voice does not go unnoticed by Jax. It's not the first time she's made the offer, and it won't be the last. She likes him! The ball is always in his court though… "Fifty credits," she then says, taking off her gloves and holding out her hand.

"Finally got those gloves, huh?" Jax nervously asks, her delicate skin now at the forefront of his mind.

"Yep! Fifty credits," she repeats, teasing him along as she dances her hand in front of his face.

Pulling out the money, Jax subconsciously makes sure to make contact as he places the payment in her palm. Then, taking Jax's crate of food from Ann, Mari places the order in Jax's arms.

"I like having you around, you know?" she slowly says, standing on her tiptoes to ruffle her hand through his cropped hair. And then in as forward of a move as she's done, Mari kisses his cheek before Ann's tiny body squeezes its way between them, prying the two apart.

"Get outta here!" Ann shouts out in a foreign accent. "We're workin'!"

"See you tonight?" Jax asks, still fighting Ann's little pushes.

Making sure that he knows it's up to him as to whether they do, Mari simply gives a flirtatious shrug at his question. She's got time—everyone's got time around here, so there's no reason she can't keep tossing the bait out there for him to nibble.

By the time Kip and Jax get to City Hall that night, the building is packed, and not just with the lower classes. Hundreds of Legacies and Oligarchs in their clean, crisp clothes line the walls, while three-triangled PPA guard posts are mounted on the roof and squeezed into every crevice that could possibly pose a security breach. There's no tolerance for the incompetence of privates on an evening like this.

Shoving their way through the mob to get to their spot on the floor, Jax accidentally aims an exceptionally harsh shove towards one particular individual.

"Dick!"

Recognizing the tone, Jax immediately stops to search for Mari, but he can't find her or Ann.

"Down here, wise guy."

Glancing down, Jax winces as he sees Mari flat on her back.

"Hey! Long time no see!"

"Just help me up…" she says, unenthused to say the least, and holding out her hands, Mari expects him to get the message of annoyance she's projecting.

"Where's Ann?" Jax asks, grabbing and yanking Mari to her feet.

"Right behind you."

There's a tug on his coat where Jax turns around to see a grinning Ann.

"Ninja…" he whispers, the little girl giggling at his shock and awe.

Brushing the dust from off her butt, Mari's heart begins to beat in an uncomfortable rhythm as she hears Kip's low, baritone voice.

"Hello, Mari," Kip says, his seductive tone an embarrassment to all who hear. Then, in Kip-like fashion, he begins pinching his fingers together as he motions towards Mari.

"This—this is the kind of shit I don't like!" Mari firmly states. "You want to keep those fingers?" she then asks, causing Kip to immediately put down his hand, the smile being wiped from off his face. "That's what I thought…"

A moment later, before Jax or Kip can apologize for their offenses, The Government's anthem starts to play, everybody falling silent as it does.

"Good evening," Caspian Stone blares, his voice echoing as he climbs the stage. Oddly enough, he's by himself with five red velvet armchairs, and holding out his skeletal hand, silences the remaining chatter, the room quickly coming under his complete control. "As I mentioned yesterday, tonight you will have the honor of being in the presence of my family."

"You think they're here to just visit?" Kip asks, the surrounding people tentatively looking at him as he does.

"May I introduce my mother and father: Sullivan and Bella Stone."

As commanded, the crowd claps as a man and woman mount the stage, revealing their faces for the first time in twenty-five years. Sullivan Stone's face appears on screen first, sending a shiver down everyone's spine. While one eye scans the masses, the other hides behind a matte black eye patch. No smile. Not even a frown, only a neutral, disinterested expression. Bella's face then blips on screen, pulling thoughts in a completely different direction. With a porcelain visage that is as uncanny as it is disturbing, Bella Stone's surgically lifted cheek bones scrunch her eyes into her forehead. While the weight of her glare bears down on them, the perfect, crisp movements of her body don't go unnoticed, and it's as if every movement she makes is programmed into a perfect algorithm.

As the two parents sit, they wave to their audience—their people—the lack of applause of little importance to the couple.

"Next my brother, Rhett Stone, the newly appointed Section Leader for Section One of Area Thirty-Eight," Caspian announces as a strapping mini—but slightly meatier—version of Caspian in standard PPA browns walks onto the stage, embracing his brother.

"What happened to the other Section Leader?" Jax asks Kip. Usually, the sections have a lifelong appointment. Promotion to Area Leader or death are the only ways of being released from duty. Since Caspian is still in office, the only logical explanation is the latter.

"Killed in an attack by the Raiders just outside of town," Kip says, Jax grinning at the news. "It's weird to see Caspian so…" Kip continues, searching for the word that's on the tip of his tongue.

"Humane?"

"No, that's not it."

"Benevolent?"

"Benevo-what?" Kip asks before snapping his fingers three times, the word slowly eluding him.

As he takes his seat next to his mother, Bella pats Rhett's leg, feigning pride in the man her son's becoming.

"Finally, my dear sister, who has ranked higher than any other woman within the People-Protection Agency: Renn Stone."

"Of course, the three children have to outrank all the other PPA mem—" Jax stops, his sentence dropping to his stomach along with his heart. "Kip, is that…"

"Yup. It sure is all right; his sister is that one PPA chick from yesterday."

"The Looker," Jax whispers, his eyes glued to the woman in PPA brown.

Four

Boston
March 20, 2036

"Mica! Where's your toothbrush?"

Kimberly, I know commitment... Commitment is...

Really? That's how he's going to start off?

"Mica?" she yells out again.

He lets out a sigh, knowing all too well that her hearing his expulsion of annoyance will distort the dynamics of the conversation—that is if you can call this little exchange a conversation.

"What do you need my toothbrush for?"

"To brush my teeth!"

Disgusting, he thinks. Dropping his pen, Mica storms to the back of his apartment. "No. Nope, no and no."

"Why?" Kim asks, she now being the interrogator.

"Really?" Mica asks, as if he needs to create a dissertation and rebuttal, but by the exasperated look she's giving him, yes, that's exactly what he must do. Holding up his index finger in the most Kim-like fashion he can, he begins. "One, gross."

"And...?" Kim says, rolling her hand for him to continue.

"And two, no."

"What?" Kim states, throwing her hands in the air. "What the hell kind of argument is that? None of those are reasons! How is it gross?"

"How is it not?!"

"We've kissed! You know, your mouth has touched my mouth. Your tongue, my tongue. That, and your mouth has been other places on my body that—" Kim starts, but before she can finish, Mica's rolling his eyes and moving back to the couch.

"It doesn't need to make sense!" he just ends up yelling out.

"You're going to be a great father!" she shouts back. It's supposed to be a jab, but butterflies flutter in her stomach at the thought. "If you ever propose..." she mumbles, the afterthought quickly incinerating the infatuated little insects mid-flight.

"I heard that!"

"Good," she mumbles again, placing a strip of toothpaste on her finger. As she shoves it in her mouth, she emphatically stomps her foot. "Good!" she repeats.

Meeting you, I immediately knew that we'd be spending the rest of our lives together.

Better. It's on the right track, but it's still—it's still missing something.

"You know what?" Kim begins, storming into the kitchen foaming at the mouth.

Completely unaware, Mica thought she was still fuming in the bathroom, but as she walks in, he fumbles the pen in his hand, hastily closing the notebook as if he was looking at old school magazine porn.

"What are you doing?" Kim playfully asks.

"Nothing," he says, knowing full well that this holds as much water as his toothbrush argument.

Rather than asking a second time, Kim leaps forward, landing on top of Mica before frantically and futilely reaching for the secret notebook. Mica sees it coming a mile away, and rather than trying to yank it out of reach, he just throws his body in her way, caching the notebook in the couch. They fight for a bit, but quickly the combat turns into a tickling match. Cheesy? Maybe, but when you're in love, even the corniest things have sentimental charm. In less than ten seconds, Mica has Kim pinned on the floor, exposed for a relentless volley of tickles with the only goal being a deep, roaring belly laugh.

"Stop! Stop, stop, stop it!"

"Nope!" Mica states, continuing the merciless assault.

"I'm gonna pee, stop!"

Taking this as a legitimate threat, Mica ceases, letting Kim catch her breath. It takes a few deep inhales, but on the third, she kisses him with everything her freshly brushed teeth can offer. She has an ulterior motive though. Even while seeming to be living in the passionate moment, she begins to maneuver her hand towards Mica's hidden notebook.

"Nope," he simply says before stopping her hand, returning to the kiss.

"What's the big deal?" she asks, breaking away, still fruitlessly attempting to obtain Mica's secret stashed between the cushions of the couch.

"We're not talking about this."

"Says who?" Kim coolly asks, knowing that her next move will get him to laugh, lowering his guard. "We're already living together."

Appalled, he forces a chuckle—exactly what Kim anticipated. "One night does not count as living together."

Again, even as Mica's eyes roll back, giving her the opening she aimed for, Mica is too damn fast.

Putting all his weight on her as he gets up, it's enough of a stunning effect to let him grab the notebook and throw it on top of the entertainment center where he knows for a fact she won't be able to reach it.

In utter denial at what Mica just did, Kim expresses her disappointment in the most aggressive fashion she can as she flops over onto her face. "That was rude," she mumbles, her words of malcontent spoken directly into the carpet.

"You started it," he says with a shrug, and moving towards the kitchen, opens his pantry. "You want anything to eat?"

With his eyes doing a shakedown of the pantry, Mica can't help but notice the sudden, loud silence. Fearing the worst, he jerks his focus from food to notebook, but sure enough, Kim isn't on a chair attempting to nab it, but rather, is still lying face down. Deciphering the situation, Mica notices her discomfort in the sole gesture of her wringing out that invisible towel.

"You okay?" he asks, knowing that she isn't.

Shaking her head, the imaginary towel continues to be throttled as her body jerks and as she gasps, tears making their way out from behind her closed eyes.

"Shit…" Mica whispers before rushing over, practically sliding into second as he comes next to her, scooping her head into his arms in the swiftest but gentlest of movements. "What's wrong?"

Again, she shakes her head. It won't do any good to pry further, so Mica simply wipes and pats her tears away. Who could imagine that their playful scuffle would upset her this bad? There must be something he's not seeing. What though? What could be this upsetting? Not even her lacking the fiancée status pulls out this frustration and discomfort.

As Kim continues to breathe, concentrating on each breath, the tightening wringing of her hands grows.

"Do you—do you think—?" she begins but immediately is riled right back up at the mere thought, twisting her grip before loosening it as another hail of tears floods her eyes.

"Hey…" At a loss for words, this is all Mica can manage, and without calming back down, Kim lets him know exactly what is bothering her.

"Do you think they'll come back?"

He foolishly thought that a good night's rest would ease the whole situation, but again, his naïvety has led them to this juncture. "No. It was political theater," Mica says.

"But what if they do?"

"If they are that stupid, then I won't let anything happen to you."

This calms her a little, but not much. "Do you think I should drop the story?"

"No!" Mica states without hesitation. "You'd never forgive yourself."

Finally, expelling a harsh breath, she wraps her arms around Mica. With her tears wetting the crook of his shoulder, Mica finally feels her heartbeat slow and her breath calm. Picking her up from off the ground, he moves to the couch where he places her on his lap, lightly kissing her tears away.

When Kim pulls her face from Mica's embrace, she finds comfort as she gazes into his eyes, fixating on the favorite of the two.

"Why aren't both of your eyes blue?"

"Well, you see," he chuckles. "There are these things called 'genetic anomalies,' and my eyes happen to be under that scientific definition, one of them being brown and the other blue."

"Hardy har!" Kim begrudgingly tries to pull herself away from Mica, but he won't let her. Pulling the love of his life even closer, he makes sure his kiss is soft and comforting, and as Kim's body relaxes, she returns the intimate gesture.

"I'm not kidding," he mumbles, his lips still tangled with hers. "I will kick their asses if they show up again."

"Mmm hmm," Kim says, going back in for another kiss. "How about you start by slapping mine around a little?"

"I'm serious," Mica says mid-kiss.

"I know," she mumbles, her passion growing. "So am I."

"How big is this party supposed to be next week, by the way?" Mica then asks, not entirely picking up on her hints.

Pulling away and grabbing his cheeks to emphasize the situation, Kim just looks Mica in his bicolor eyes. "Will you just shut up so we can— you know…"

"Right," Mica says. "My bad…"

——— ★ ———

New York
March 27, 2036

With each stride, his knees hit a little bit harder, forcing him to suck it up, cranking the speed for the final stretch. The treadmill belt whoops at a consistent rate of nine miles per hour, a pace that in his prime Carter could easily hold for the full twenty-six point two miles. But, years later, his career and dedication to his country have both taken their toll.

His last marathon, April 15, 2013, not only made history, but revealed his calling in life, forcing him to give up the sport for good. It taught him that there are more honorable things bodily pain and anguish can be used towards than personal accolade. The vivid smells of sweat and ash will forever brand his memories, and since that dreadful day in Boston, Carter has dedicated his life to his nation—no matter the price. As a young college graduate of political science, that moment in history shifted Carter into an early career change, and once in the CIA, the bigger picture became clear.

With three beeps, the treadmill hums to a slow, cool-down pace. Matching the relaxing speed, calming his breathing, Carter glances down at his phone. Once his heart rate reaches a hundred-forty beats per minute, he takes one last heavy inhale before making the call. Stepping down and closing the door to his office, each ring heightens his level of anxiety—anxiety that he has not felt since his first mission. He will be damned if he fails *this* assignment. He can't. For years, Washington has been a biased group of politicians and bureaucrats with predetermined and established agendas. With political term limits now nonexistent, the only accountability one has in office are the pockets of their benefactors.

Checks, policies, and favors. Crony capitalism at its finest.

Of course, Carter didn't discover any of these conspiracies until after months in the Central Intelligence Agency, but exposing fraud wasn't enough. Even his own agency was corrupted. It's pathetic. Call him a saint if you want, but Carter has never been interested in the finite nature of political power. For the American people's sake, he's found it pointless to attack the corruption head on. Instead, he and a small group began compiling a new tactic.

The Minutemen Division is going to turn everything around. From the legal gaps in the system, to targeted collusions and political scams, the Division will achieve what Carter was originally trying to accomplish with his service in the CIA. The rules of war have changed, and Carter must change with them, even if that means going against orthodoxy and governmental doctrine.

With one final ring, Carter gets the voicemail.

Irritated, he punches end on the screen, tossing his phone on the desk where its protective case bursts open. Pacing back and forth in his office, he begins going through every planned contingency. To avoid any leaks in the process, his contact was supposed to tell him the when and where, but now it seems that it's not going to happen that way. Out of all the assignments to have problems, it's the one with the most important potential asset.

The target's in Boston, but where?

Before Carter hyperventilates and makes an irrational decision, his phone buzzes and he quickly answers.

"Yes?"

But nobody responds.

Confused, Carter looks at his phone only to see a small notification. Clicking on it, Carter reads:

Arnold Arboretum Boston. 2230. Three agents.

Not needing any more information, Carter quickly changes, grabs his gun, holsters it, and leaves to retrieve the Division's most valuable agent.

Boston

It doesn't matter if you're a college dropout, or a prestigious law student on scholarship. Much like the illegal underground fights, parties are an outlet. Not from the finals or anal professors, but from the never-ending economic depression, censored media and political propaganda and misinformation being rammed down everyone's throats. Anybody and everybody attends these events regardless of group, party, or clique. They're a time for those in the present to live independently from the shady past and hopeless future. Partying is the only common ground people have these days.

Ever since the last presidential election, people stopped caring. Persistent fraud tends to do that. Protect them from this. Create equity for that. All of it turned from a good idea into a not so good one, but by the time the realization of lost personal freedoms and democratic components was made by the collective, the very republic was out from under everyone's feet. Some can argue—and still do—that good came out of it, but that's only because no one can truly admit that they were manipulated into being a useful idiot. Being equally shat on is technically still equity.

"Are you ready yet?" Kim asks for the fourth time.

"I wasn't ready thirty seconds ago, and I'm not ready now."

"If we don't hurry, we're going to miss everything!" Kim dramatically says.

If Mica just got his ass out here, he would see why Kim is being so adamant! In contrast, if she had a little patience herself, then Mica could finish up the final touches for the perfect evening. Not only does he know she's been looking forward to this little masquerade shindig, but it's their one-year anniversary.

Kimberly, you are everything I need that I didn't know I wanted, and you're everything I want but didn't know I needed.

Stuffing the ring into his left vest pocket, one year ago this day, Mica spilled Sprite all down her shirt. There really is no better time than tonight.

Casually he smooths out his pinstripe suit, fits his mask to his face, and pats the ring in his vest one last time for luck before stepping out to see his fiancée to be.

"How do I—?" he begins but is immediately stunned by her beauty. Her dress is perfect. Mica begged her to let him see it, but she refused, and he's glad she did. Hugging her every curve, Mica wants to throw the whole night out and take the gown right off her.

"You sure you want to go to this party?" he asks. "We could just skip to the end of the night…"

"You look devilishly handsome yourself and I want you. I really do," Kim says, his offer becoming awfully tempting. "But delayed gratification…"

"Fine. Shall we get going?" he asks, and as Kim places her masquerade mask on, she reaches for his arm and hands him the pièce de résistance.

"Your cane, sir," she says, donning an English accent.

Taking it in hand, Mica can't help but admire the fine custom work Kim had done on the antique. The new stain and polish have brought life back into every detail of the engraved redwood, and as he wraps his fingers around the hilt, despite the age of the item, it's like it was made for Mica Rouge.

"It's beautiful…"

"Thank you! And you're welcome," Kim states as the infatuated couple steps out into the cool spring night.

"So, where is this party?"

"Just on the other side of the park," she smiles, skipping forward.

"Hold up," Mica says, reining in her enthusiasm. "Can we go around?"

"Why? It's just right there," Kim says, pointing to a house a quarter mile away on the other side of the darkened park. The music can be heard, and the flashing lights seen, so what's the big deal?

Having an uneasy feeling is a difficult argument to win when you're a *tough* guy. "I just don't want to walk through the park."

Kim lets out a guttural laugh. "C'mon! You scared or something? I thought you could kick anyone's ass!"

Kim's confidence in Mica flatters him, and yes, he has comical self-confidence, but he is also hyper-aware of his inferiorities. Briskly, Kim is the deciding vote, and as the couple make their way through the park arm in arm, Kim casually dreams of the night's events while Mica cautiously analyzes every dark corner. However, a portion of the park goes unnoticed by Mica, and from the shade of one of the moonlit trees a voice interrupts the couple's stride.

"Your time is up."

"They're back?" Kim whispers, her panic stopping the couple abruptly.

"Have you made your decision?" one hooded figure asks, stepping from the shadows of their flank.

"Does it matter?" Mica asks.

"It does," the figure immediately states. "Times have changed, and a new united government will reign."

"I was right. The Children of the Ordean Reich are real," Kim whispers.

"Yes, Kim, we are," the hooded figure on their right says. "However, our fate will be determined by us, not your deceit."

"What is your decision?" the hooded figure directly in front then asks.

"She'll keep her mouth shut," Mica quickly states. She won't—he won't let her—but lies to get out of the situation. It's clear that these guys aren't messing around, and now is not the time to negotiate.

"So she shall."

The middle figure is the first to advance. Swiftly, the other two follow and all three pull out thick, long knives.

"Run!" Mica yells, pushing Kim and swinging his cane at the closest attacker, cracking him in the jaw. Kicking the one on his left square in the chest, Mica knocks him back and tries to reposition himself to face all three. Swinging at the nearest foe as he pivots, Mica narrowly misses as the hooded figure ducks under and bolts towards Kim.

"I said run!" Mica repeats before being taken to the ground.

Petrified by fear, Kim attempts to flee but is stopped short as she's tackled to the ground, her elbows and knees scraping the asphalt upon impact. Her scream of pain goes unheard by those at the party and only fuels the hooded figure's desire to silence her voice forever. He lunges a stab at her, but it falls short due to a wild, direct hit in the throat from Kim. Dropping the knife, he is then immediately kneed between the legs before Kim kicks off her heels to run for a second time.

Mica, doing everything he can to get to her, is constantly thwarted by the two other hooded figures. Using his cane as best he can to defend himself against their blades, Mica is slashed once across the chest, his tie cut in two, and as the bottom half of his tie falls, Mica is then sliced across his thigh. One of them eagerly goes for the kill, but as he moves closer, it's a fatal mistake. Close is where Mica is the most comfortable. Easily, Mica dodges the stab, and grabbing the arm of his attacker, breaks it with ease.

Kim begins running, but she is dropped instantly back onto the pavement as a knife cuts into her heel. She cries out, but Mica is the only concerned audience to her agony as the party on the fringe of the park doesn't skip a beat.

"Kim!" Mica calls out, smashing his cane into the throat of one of the hooded figures. There's an audible pop as the assailant permanently drops to the ground. Mica lunges towards Kim but is hurled backwards and away from his girlfriend.

Grabbing her bleeding heel, Kim painfully discovers that she can no longer stand. Doing the next best thing, she crawls towards the party on the edge of the park, but getting to his feet, her attacker stops Kim with a stab in the back of her leg. Kim opens her mouth to let out another deafening scream, but it too is cut short as the killer squeezes her airway shut. Slowly, he pulls the knife from her leg, twisting as he does, and upon seeing tears from Kim's eyes gently rolling down from behind her mask, the hooded figure relishes in this infamous moment.

"It's a shame your boyfriend couldn't save you," he says, his blade rising in the air.

Mica breaks his final opponent's leg, then cracks his cane across the guy's temporal lobe before turning too late to Kim's aid. The murderer's knife is deep in her stomach, angled up towards her heart, and Kim, gasping for air, feels the blade violently pulled from her body.

"No!" Mica sprints forward, smashing his cane right into the back of his enemy's skull, killing him instantly. Dropping his cane, he falls next to Kim, frantic and afraid. "No, no, no…Kim…"

Pulling his masquerade mask off, Mica's eyes are drawn towards Kim's hands grasping her invisible towel. As she grips the air for a sense of relief, Mica knows that this time there is nothing he can do to alleviate her pain.

With his hands on hers, rain begins wetting the back of his hand. "Mica, it hurts so bad," she says, her tears mixing with the sky's showers.

"Please, no," Mica prays.

"Mica…" Kim then says, quieter than before. "Make it stop—it hurts."

As she continues to wring her hands together, Mica removes the invisible towel, placing his hand into Kim's, and taking off her mask, Mica drops it into the puddle of blood and water.

"Help! Somebody help!" he shouts, but no one hears his plea. The party is raging, and less than a hundred feet away, someone's life is ending.

Turning his attention back to his love, he begs her to stay. "Don't close your eyes... Kim. Kim?"

Her grasp on his hands becomes weaker every moment, and just as suddenly as the pain came, it goes, giving Kim a sense of peace in her final moments.

"Happy one year, Mica..." she says with a delicate smile.

Seeing the fading light in her eyes, Mica stifles a cry. "I-I—here."

Frantically, Mica searches his pocket for the ring. Pulling it from his vest pocket, he shows her the band, the same one she picked months ago in a casual shopping trip one weekend. "I didn't forget..."

"I love you, Mica..." Kim again smiles. Her hidden pain just beneath the surface quickly turns to sorrow as the life she envisioned quickly begins to fade.

"I love you too, Kim... stay—stay with me, love..." The rain falls faster and becomes heavier by the second, but as Mica feels the slack in her grip, he slides the ring on her finger.

"Bye, Mica..." are Kim's final words to her love before her eyes close one last time.

Mica tries to say the word goodbye, but he can only mouth it as he drops Kim's hand from his fingertips into the puddle of blood. With his world being forever changed, Mica gasps for air.

"Somebody help!" he shouts, his gaze catching sight of one lone figure staring back at him from the edge of the park. Standing, Mica's foot hits something that clinks and tumbles across the wet pavement, and glancing down at the object, he finds a small metal skeleton key.

Looking back up to the park's boundary, Mica finds the lone man has vanished. Falling back to his knees, Mica picks up and pockets the key before taking Kim's hand back in his. Sliding the engagement ring off, he holds Kim in his arms, stroking her cheek with his thumb, and with ease, he stands, picking up her lifeless body in his arms.

Exiting the park, a lady sees Mica and Kim, convincing the young man to let her drive the two of them to the hospital. Pulling up to the emergency room, Mica knows there is nothing any doctor can do for her, but where else is he supposed to go? The staff's penetrating and brutally honest questions blend in with the sounds of the hospital chaos, and blatantly, Mica ignores them. Insulted, confused, heartbroken, he walks off and sits to the side, the clean tile underneath him puddling with blood, mud, and water dripping from off his pinstripe suit.

Awaiting the police, Mica twirls the skeleton key in his hand where it helps him pass the time and fuel a newborn rage—one that all his years in the service couldn't create. This loss was not in a foreign country fighting some politician's war. Rather, it was in his own backyard and in a fight Kim chose. He killed them, yes, but they were just insurgents—mere peons. Kim knew something that their general didn't want exposed, and because of that, she's dead. So many things could be brought to the hypothetical table, but Mica doesn't focus on any of it. He's heard his mother bring situations to that very table many, many times after his dad left and it did nothing. Her queries didn't bring his dad back home, and sitting down where his mother once sat won't bring Kim back either. The only thing he can do is ignore the table. Ignore it or flip it over.

"Mr. Rouge?" A detective steps into the room and over the puddles of red rainwater. "My name is Detective York. I was wondering if I could have a few minutes of your time?"

"Do I have a choice?" Mica says, standing to meet the detective's eyes.

"This way please," York says. Guiding Mica to a chair in an empty hospital room, the detective takes the seat across from him. "I know you don't want to discuss what happened, but we need to."

"You mean relive the nightmare I just went through?" Mica asks, grabbing his face and holding back the tears. "While it's still fresh?"

"Arnold Arboretum, is that the park you were cutting through?" York asks.

"Yeah," Mica nods.

"And the lady that picked you and Kim up, what—" York begins to ask, but his question is cut short by another police officer walking into the room.

"Detective, a moment?"

"You want some coffee or something, Mr. Rouge?" York asks as he stands.

Mica doesn't say anything, giving the detective a silent answer before he leaves. He isn't alone for long before another man silently walks into the room, locking the door behind himself. Wearing a grey suit, soaked from head to toe, this is no cop, but makes himself at home anyway as he sits down in front of Mica. About to give him the same respect he did the detective, when Mica looks into this man's eyes, there's a familiar darkness; they're eyes that have experienced the evils of battle. This is not a beat cop sitting in front of Mica, but an old soldier and one that still has some fight left inside

Holding out his hand for Mica to shake, Mica does.

"Hello, Mica Rouge, my name is Mr. Carter."

Five

Area Thirty-Eight

"What was that?" Bella shrieks, throwing her finger into Renn's shoulder before turning to Rhett and doing the same. "When asked for a speech, you give a speech!"

"Bella," Sullivan calmly states, the consistency of his tone matching the brown liquor he's pouring into the pair of glasses.

"Don't *Bella* me!" she snarls, glaring at him in his one good eye. "We are on the verge of one of the greatest genealogical breakthroughs and the twins go and pull a stunt like that? Their image is our image, and if they're going to behave like that at the Gathering—"

Sullivan approaches his wife, placing her drink into her hands. "Here…"

Ripping the cup from her husband's outstretched hand, Bella sloshes her drink onto the tile below. Snapping at a nearby servant, she points to the spill before taking in a deep breath and sipping the liquid.

"Your mother is right."

Renn looks to Rhett, gritting her teeth. Giving a slight shake of his head is all he has time to do, but her ire still outweighs his admonition.

"How the hell is *she* right?" Renn blurts out.

Coughing on her second sip, Bella screeches as her tonic dribbles down the corners of her mouth. "You know very well, you ungrateful bitch!"

"Bella!" Sullivan's rumbling voice echoes out, his agitation bringing his wife down to a simmering mutter. Then, as if he never lost his temper in the first place, he continues in the same breath. "Let me handle this."

"She's no better than all those experiments we bring in," Bella scoffs, draining the rest of her drink, then, approaching her daughter, she haughtily lifts up Renn's bandaged arm. "By the way, she's been doing it again."

Yanking down and away, Renn slaps her arm back to her side.

Whipping the heavy wooden door open, Bella pauses for one last prod. "And Rhett's letting her."

With that, the mood, although quiet, is far from relaxing as the door thuds behind Bella's exit. Sullivan stays resolute as he looks to Renn's arm and then up to Rhett, downing his drink in one gulp before moving for a refill.

"Do you know why we are here?" he slowly asks. "In Area Thirty-Eight?"

Rhett shakes his head at his father but Renn, she keeps her eyes burrowed into the closed wooden door, seething at the maternal lineage that she comes from.

"It's where it all started."

Again, in a single swig Sullivan drinks the bourbon and placing the empty glass upside down, moves over to the flickering fireplace, his eye matching the intensity of the embers.

"And this—this is where we feel it should all end."

"What do you mean by 'it'?" Rhett asks.

"Stand tall when you speak to me, son," Sullivan states, his gaze not moving from the warmth of the fire.

Doing as his father asks, Rhett lifts his shoulders and puts his gaze forward. "Can you clarify what you mean by 'it'?"

Taking a long blink, Sullivan rolls his focus towards his son. "It: the genealogical work your mother and I have been working towards for the past nineteen years."

"And what does that have to do with us?" Renn asks. Knowing her father's next statement, like Rhett, she stands up straight and puffs her chest out, deliberate in her mocking contempt. "Sir!"

"Because you're family."

"You mistake my question, sir!" Renn shouts, continuing the jeering show. "What does it have to do with us, and more specifically me, being in the PPA, sir?!"

Sullivan silently scoffs at her attitude. Approaching his daughter, he gently tilts her chin to bring her thousand-yard stare to his. "You'll learn soon enough." And then pausing, ensuring she feels the gravity of her insubordination, he stares a moment longer. "When you behave in such a manner, as you have with me just now, it is almost certain that you will be adding more tallies. Rhett?" Sullivan asks, dropping his daughter's chin.

"Sir?"

"Keep a better eye on your sister," he says, strolling towards the room's exit, his coat over his shoulder. "Things tend to happen after encounters like this."

Stoic in her demeanor, Renn continues to stand in her mocking form of attention, but as their father closes the door behind his exit, the burden she endured to uphold finally collapses her to her knees. As she crumbles, her face falls into the recess of her hands that quickly pools with tears.

Dropping beside her, Rhett holds his sister, letting her weight completely fall into his arms where she continues to sob.

"It's not true," Rhett calmly says.

"But it is…" she whispers. Conveniently, Rhett is on assignment each time their father orders her to "learn" a lesson. "They're evil."

Rhett has been with Renn since before they were born—they have a bond that goes beyond just a blood line. Through thick and thin he's strived to be by her side, and so when she says that their father and mother are evil, Renn isn't just making a cynical observation, but rather is eluding towards something more.

"What are you thinking?"

Renn's breathing slows as she figures out how to best say it. It's been on her mind for weeks and having specialized in operations like the one she's considering, now might just be the time to set some things in motion.

"What do you know about the Raiders?"

Rhett shrugs. "They're rebels. Rebels with genetic defects in the Unapproved class."

"Do you believe that?"

"I don't think it really matters what I believe. I have orders and so do you."

"I know," she says, nestling her head into his chest, contemplating the risks and rewards. This is no fleeting thought, and if she's willing to collude and conspire, then it must be done right. There is no room for half-measures.

Quickly, her train of thought is shattered as the door to the room bursts open, only this time with a welcome sight.

Looking around the room, Connor rushes forward, encompassing the two in his thick arms.

"Came as soon as I could."

"'Bout time," Renn states, her sarcastic remark muffled within the embrace of her two brothers. Half measures will not only get her killed, but the lives of the only men she cares about will be on the line.

"Connor?" she then asks, pulling herself up and out of his hug.

"What's up?"

Again, Renn looks to Rhett for silent advice. The commander in him tells him to shake his head, but the brother side of him forces him to nod. No matter what their parents say—no matter how they treat and exile him from the family, Connor is more of a brother than Caspian ever will be to Rhett and Renn. They can trust him.

"What do *you* know about the Raiders?"

"Whatcha thinkin' about?" Kip asks, his question breaking the silence of the winter night.

"Nothing really," Jax replies halfheartedly.

"Ya thinking about Renn Stone?" Kip asks, jabbing him with his elbow.

"Why would I be thinking about someone in the PPA?"

"Dude," Kip scoffs. "Really? Not only does she have a rockin' bod, she's Renn Stone…"

"Exactly my point," Jax mumbles, tossing a pebble to the side. "Look who she's related to."

Caspian's tolerance for human suffering is pretty damn high, but that's not really the question or the point Jax is getting at. Articles have been written and stories told about Sullivan and Bella Stone. Mass public killings over all the Areas. Some were for alleged infractions of the law. Most, however, were under the guise of protecting the Labor class. Caspian learned it from somewhere, so, how is Renn any different?

"She's still cute! I'd become a Legacy if that meant I had a shot with her."

Jax can't help but chuckle at Kip's one-track mind.

"And didn't it seem like there was something different about her?" Kip asks.

"Like what?"

Shrugging his shoulders, Kip lays out his simple case. "She didn't wave to us like the rest of her family. And her smile was fake—like she was embarrassed to be up there. Not to mention, when asked to say something she just turned and walked off stage," Kip says.

"You sure you don't have a thing for dark, twisted women?"

"Believe me, I sure as hell love me some kinky women, but I'm telling ya, she's different. Renn Stone isn't like her family."

"Whatever you say…"

As the two continue to meander their way home, Kip looks to Jax before glancing back to City Hall, and after three more times of this, Jax lashes out at Kip's fidgeting behavior.

"What are you doing? Did you forget something back at the Gathering?"

Shaking his head, Kip states the most obvious piece of information.

"Mari's kinda cute."

"Don't!" It comes out of Jax's mouth quicker and more hostile than anything he's said to Kip before. Jax doesn't know what it is, but a fire is lit inside—one that he's never experienced before.

"What?" Kip asks with a truly innocent look, trying to hide his knowing smirk. "You got the hots for her too?"

"I don't have the hots for Renn…"

"Hey man," Kip states, throwing his hands in the air. "I'm not one to judge. I'll take whoever you don't, but ya gotta pick. Mari or Renn."

"You're hilarious," Jax sarcastically states, slugging Kip right in the ribs.

"Son of a bitch…" Kip mumbles, grabbing his side.

"My bad," Jax responds, immediately regretting his actions. A wild swing to the floating rib is a dick move on any front, not to mention Jax's natural left hook.

"Ya got a thing for Mari, I get it," Kip retorts, shrugging the cheap shot off before things get out of control.

"I don't!" Jax denies, never having thought through the ramifications of what a relationship with Mari would look like. "After Granny Lisa died, you, she and Ann are the closest people I have to a family. You know?" Jax states, making sure to keep Connor's unknown status out of the lineup.

"I miss Granny Lisa," Kip says solemnly, his expression saddening as he shuffles a rock in the snow. However, Kip can't help but smile and chuckle at a newfound thought.

"What now?" Jax asks.

"Since ya don't have a thing for Mari," he slowly says, trying not to laugh. "Do ya think I could have a go at her?"

"Get out of here!"

———✦✦✦———

They're looking for something. Ever since Sullivan and Bella stepped their sadistic feet on Area Thirty-Eight soil, they've been systematically parading around town, ransacking every residence, making it that much more obvious that they're not on a routine visit.

"You alright?"

Not to mention Renn Stone's face. Like Jezebel, she looms over him, taunting and haunting his emotions every time he registers in and out of the Mill. She's beautiful and yet she's a Stone.

"Jax!" Mari yells, her forceful tone shaking the images of Renn from his mind.

"Sorry," he says. "Was thinking…"

She flirtatiously flicks a well-placed pebble at his forehead. Wishing she had more time with the guy is putting it lightly…

"About me?" she asks. It's forward, but before she sees her coy question play out, angst jumps in, tossing the potentiality of sheer embarrassment at her face like her pebble at Jax. "What can we get you today? The usual?"

"Yeah," he chuckles. "The usual." And then with a reassuring smile, he adds, "I've been thinking about those cooking lessons you offered."

"Yeah?" she casually states, feigning an unenthused response. Turning to Ann to have her fetch Jax's supplies, Mari decides to dive into Jax's intentions a little deeper. "So, what were you thinking of cooking?"

"You tell me!" he jokingly blurts out. "I have no idea where to start."

Holding out her hand for payment, Jax places his credits in her palm, her spine shivering as their hands touch. It's childish, yes, but it's Jax. There aren't many guys like this, and that's no exaggeration.

"What are you saying, Jax?" She tries to play it cool, muffling her impending excitement, but the overwhelming sentiment forces its way out, crinkling her dark eyes behind her lifted cheeks. "You want me to come over or not?" Mari then asks, folding her arms over her chest, intentionally perking up her breasts, only it's not as effective as she would like due to her heavy leather jacket.

"Yeah! I'm trying to ask if you wanna come over and teach me some cooking things?"

"Some cooking things?" she snorts out, unable to keep the laughter at bay.

Handing him his bag of supplies, Ann decides to jump into the conversation.

"Where am I supposed to go?" the little girl asks.

"I've got some toys and what not," Jax reassures.

"Oh, cool!" And then, in her trademark girlish grin, Ann swings a punch at Jax's leg that he easily slips, picking her up in a relentless tickle.

"Will you stop hitting me?" he playfully growls. It's only when she begs him to stop that Jax lets up on the tickle assault. "How does tonight after the Gathering and before curfew sound?"

"Can we, Mari?" Ann asks, looking hopefully to her older sister. "Please, please, please, please!"

And Mari thought she was excited. "If it gets you to shut up! Holy hell, get back to work," she states, ruffling Ann's hair. "And put that thing into a bun while you're at it."

"So, I'll see you at the Gathering?" Jax asks.

"Fine!" Mari answers, making sure he knows that it is more than okay.

Giving her a beaming smile of his own, Jax sends her a wink that throws butterflies and all sorts of giddy emotions whirling throughout her body. Once his back is to her, it's like she's slapped across the face with reality.

"I am such a girl," she mumbles to herself.

"What about being a girl?" Ann asks, not sure if she heard her sister correctly.

"Shut up, Ann!"

Not knowing what to do with that bit of information, Ann just rolls her eyes and moves to get the supplies for the next customer.

On his way back from the market, Jax finds Kip sitting on the icy dirt in front of the gate, asleep. Resisting the urge to show Kip how to truly scare someone, Jax nudges him awake instead.

"Enjoying your nap?"

"Twenty minutes," Kip says with a yawn.

"What?"

"I've been waiting for twenty minutes."

"For?" Jax then asks, his one-word question doing a piss-poor job at solving the mystery.

"Hanging out. Shooting the shit."

This time, Jax has nothing but a perplexed look.

"It's our day off, man!" Kip says, really wondering if he's the slow one.

"Right," Jax apologetically says. "C'mon in!"

Ushering in Kip, Jax closes the door, moving over to the kitchen to put his things away. "By the way, Mari and Ann are coming over after the Gathering so—"

Before Jax can finish the phrase, he is tackled and thrown into the far wall.

"Ya serious?" Kip exclaims, picking up the kid, tossing him first onto the couch and then back at the far wall where Jax's butt leaves a permanent indentation.

"What the hell…"

"That's awesome!" Kip says with a beaming smile.

"I appreciate the enthusiasm, but that hurt, man." Whatever excitement of his own that Jax had, it fades fast as he examines the concave shape his backside made in the wall.

"It's about time!" Kip continues, throwing pillows, rags, whatever else he can towards Jax.

"Will you stop it?" Jax shouts, picking up a pillow of his own to chuck at Kip.

Kip dodges the incoming projectile before finding a nearby can of soup.

"Don't even—" Jax begins, but before the warning registers with Kip, he hocks it in Jax's direction where it narrowly misses and clunks into the wall, bringing the roughhousing to a sudden halt. Upon hearing the odd metal sound, Jax holds up his hands for a cease fire.

"What was that?" Kip asks, but instead of responding, Jax pulls the can from the drywall, and rather than a gaping void from damaged sheetrock, a rusty red metal backing is found. As Jax continues to burrow into the wall, the more he unveils. Except for the marks left by the can of soup, what was once probably a bright, shiny crimson, is now a weathered and faded red—from years, decades maybe of being concealed in the wall. After a few more chunks of drywall are removed, Jax is able to pull out a metallic box.

An object like this is bound to catch some unwanted attention, and as Jax thinks about it a level deeper, the fears of the recent house searches come to mind.

That's it, Kip thinks to himself, immediately recognizing the artifact in Jax's hands. It's exactly like Dan's described, and in surprisingly good condition. The only question now is what's in it? Kip's been briefed, but everything he knows has hinged on speculation. Nobody except the legend himself knows what's hidden inside.

"Open it!" Kip states, no longer able to contain his excitement.

Not knowing if he should, Jax takes the box in his hands and rotates it around in search of a way to do so. On what Jax is assuming is the front facing end, he sees a single word—a name neatly engraved in the metal surface.

"Kim?" Jax whispers.

Kip cocks his head as he hears the name. Nowhere in the briefings did he hear about a Kim, only adding to the doubt of whether this is in fact the box he's been sent for. It's possible there could be more than one still out there. As Jax reaches for the rusted hinges, ready to answer the stacking questions, a loud explosion shakes the house's foundation.

"Uh oh..." Kip prays that's not what he thinks it is. Two more explosions quickly quake, each significantly closer to the house than the first.

"Get down!" Jax screams just before a fourth explosion wobbles the frame of his home, shattering the front windows. "Hide it in the fireplace!" Jax then yells, handing the box to Kip before immediately making his way to the door to make sense of the growing madness.

Hundreds of feet from the house, gunshots flash as the two sides of the battle shape and evolve. As armored PPA vehicles rush from the direction of City Hall, gravel and bullets spit down the street and on towards the invading enemy which has already begun their infestation of the district.

"What are the Raiders doing here?!" Kip yells out over the peppered gunfire.

"I don't know," Jax says, doubting that this is in any way a coincidence.

Bullets begin traveling their way, kicking up dirt in his front yard before reaching the house where the metal projectiles begin splintering the wooden deck. Both Jax and Kip dive inside and behind any solid object they can as the gunfire takes out the remaining glass within the shattered windows. After the short volley, the two stand and move back onto the porch.

"You think it's because of the Stones?" Kip asks.

"Maybe—" but before Jax can finish his thought, he and Kip are catapulted forward and off the porch from an earth-shattering explosion. Instantly the battle goes silent as a high-pitched ringing fills Jax's ears. Allowing his eyes to refocus, Jax sees nothing but grey smoke and brown dirt littering what remaining snow there is. Carefully, he pushes himself up, feeling around for Kip. But suddenly, before Jax can orient himself, he feels his body lifted onto its feet and pushed forward through the smoke until again, he is slammed back down to the ground.

"Are—okay?" a female voice shouts.

"What?!" What the hell is going on? Shaking his head, finally getting some semblance of his surroundings, Jax focuses on the woman that apparently picked him up like a backpack, moving him to the bunkered crater that an obliterated armored vehicle now inhabits.

"Are you okay?!" Renn Stone repeats, the sporadic gunfire making a resurgence.

"Yeah," he responds, peering from around the corner of the destroyed PPA vehicle to begin looking for Kip.

"I couldn't find him!" Renn says, answering his concern.

Sitting upright, Jax makes a move to bolt for his house before being jerked back down by his collar.

"You idiot!"

"I gotta find Kip!"

"Stay down!" she adds, quickly looking around and finding a small group of PPA soldiers just up ahead. Before saying another word, she darts in their direction, firing three-round bursts periodically until taking cover next to them.

Ignoring her admonition, Jax gets to his knees and again begins searching for Kip. Amidst the chaotic scene, Jax finds himself rather calm—calm, focused, and determined. It's not the first time he's seen a Raider assault, but it is his first time being involved in one.

"Kip!" he shouts, pausing to listen for a response. He yells Kip's name two more times before finding it futile. Taking matters into his own hands, Jax sprints back to the house, which is now in more than two dozen pieces. Praying that Kip's not underneath the mess that was once his domicile, Jax begins moving pieces of rubble around.

"Over here!"

From behind, Jax turns to see his friend taking cover behind a fallen tree, and immediately, Jax runs towards his friend before remembering the treasure they just found. Skidding to a stop and turning back to his demolished home, Jax slides next to what is left of the fireplace. Frantically, he searches, but it's in vain as it is nowhere to be found. Not even the destroyed remnants are amongst the concrete rubble. Before he can mourn the object he didn't even know existed until minutes ago, bullets begin ricocheting and shattering the bricks of the once-fireplace, and turning on the balls of his feet, Jax weaves his way over to Kip with rounds continuing to chase him around the battlefield.

"I thought you were dead, you moron!" Jax accuses.

"Would a moron find this?"

That big old brute managed to find the box! If they weren't in the middle of a firefight, Jax would kiss the hell out of Kip.

"Let's get out of here."

"Yeah," Kip happily agrees.

With the gunfire moving away from them, the two rush over next door to Kip's house, which is miraculously mostly intact. Before they are completely out of harm's way however, curiosity gets the best of Jax. Looking back, he notices the downed vehicle Renn took cover at moments ago. With two other PPA soldiers huddled next to her, Renn fights for all three of their lives as her calm, serene composure dwarfs her panicky comrades. Hunched at the right, back end of the vehicle, Renn occasionally leans and takes a quick three-shot burst towards the team of oncoming Raiders. Each shot is timed and aimed perfectly, slowly diminishing the advancing group of Raiders. But the group is too big, and as they continue to press forward, the private in the middle finally decides to muster some courage and fight back. Standing up to take a shot over the hood of the armored vehicle, he is unsuccessful as a handful of shots fatally find him, the last one hitting him square in the head.

It's in this moment that Jax realizes something devastating. It doesn't scare him, only pisses him off because it's the last thing that he wants to do. If those two die, there is nothing standing between the Raiders and him and Kip.

"What are ya doin'?!" Kip shouts over the gunfire, but not a fan of either of his options, Jax makes up his mind.

"Stay—" Again he's cut off, only this time it's by a bullet hitting the tree next to his head. Looking up and to the left, Jax sees two Raiders on the outskirts that have spotted the duo.

Kip thinks of waving a surrender, but in this circumstance he's more likely to get his hand shot off. Either that or even the dumbest officer can connect some dots.

"Get to the house!" Jax orders.

Before Kip can argue, Jax reluctantly weaves and maneuvers himself towards Renn, figuring that he can wait and be shot, or he can try to stay alive with a weapon in hand. Bullets whistle by his head, only adding to the motivating speed he's taking, and as one shot grazes his neck, he slides next to the dead private. Picking up the rifle, Jax looks to Renn.

"There are two more on the left!" he shouts.

"Shoot them then!" Too preoccupied to glance over, she has no idea who is beside her in this fight.

Even though it's illegal for him to know anything about a firearm, Jax knows quite a bit thanks to Connor. Relatively speaking that is. Placing the butt of the gun to his shoulder, Jax takes aim and pulls the trigger once the red dot is on the Raider's chest. Nothing happens. Just a click.

Panicking, Jax ducks as a bullet narrowly misses his skull and he turns to the scared soldier.

"It's jammed!"

The two-triangled specialist doesn't respond quickly, but timidly he takes the gun in his shaking hands, slaps the bottom of the magazine and loads a round by flipping a switch. The dead private didn't even have a round in the chamber...

Huddling next to the left side of the vehicle, Jax searches for his target but is quickly blinded by an explosion of dirt right in front of him. A little startled that he almost got his head blown off, he peers over at Renn. She pokes her head out for a brief scan, brings it back, and then leans to take a three-shot burst. Easy enough. Miming her, Jax takes a quick glance to see the two Raiders advancing on their left. Then, leaning out just like it was demonstrated, he lines up the shot and pulls the trigger. With a burst, he narrowly misses, but the shot forces the two of them to hunch down behind a thick log, one that is too small for both to hide safely behind. Seeing one of their arms poking out, Jax takes aim for a second time and shoots his target's elbow. The other Raider pops up from behind his cover to return fire, but Jax leans back behind the truck just as the bullets hit metal near his knee.

Jax takes another quick glance. The Raider still stands and takes a shot that barely misses. He'll have to make this next shot fast. Jax does, and the three bullets hit the Raider square in the chest.

Letting out a chuckle, Jax turns to the terrified specialist. "It's not as hard as I thought it'd be!" But all the soldier can do is give a shaky thumbs-up.

"How many left?!" Jax shouts to Renn.

"Two!"

Slightly moving away from the truck, Jax crouches down next to the dead private. He risks another look by standing up and crouching back down, marking both Raiders in that one swift look. One is next to a broken-down vehicle, and the other is running up on Renn's location. Knowing there is no other option, Jax stands up and takes a shot at the one running. One bullet hits him in his stomach, another in his chest, and the final one in his jaw. Without crouching back down, Jax aims to take the final shot at the remaining Raider, but the Raider's gun is already aimed, ready to kill.

"All clear on the west side," Renn says into her headset as her shot sounds, just as Jax's life flashes before his eyes.

With the last target lying dead, Jax stands baffled that he's not in the dirt too. Looking over to his savior, he notices that although her hair is a tangled mess, she is downright attractive at the same time.

Turning to face who she thought was another PPA soldier, Renn's head whips from Jax to the dead private.

"What did you do?!" she demands, all beauty fleeting from her as she does.

"Nothing! He got shot so I took his weapon," Jax stammers out. "It looked like you could use some help."

Turning her wrath, Renn glares at the scared specialist before looking to Jax.

"Where'd you learn to shoot?" she asks, slinging her gun over her shoulder and storming towards him.

"That guy," Jax lies, pointing to the two-triangled soldier. "He told me to just point and shoot."

An inch away from him, she looks up into his eyes just like that first time they met. *My ass*, she thinks. There is only one person she knows that would teach someone from the Labor class to shoot, but that isn't the immediate problem. Snatching the gun out of Jax's hands, Renn turns towards the specialist and asks the question she already knows the answer to.

"Did you?"

All the soldier does is nod, despite both he and Jax knowing it's a lie.

"Stand up when you acknowledge an officer!" Renn shouts, the soldier quickly following the order.

"And why did he have to save me exactly?"

It was logical self-preservation. Jax wasn't saving her. He was just saving his and Kip's ass. Then again, maybe he does care about Renn.

"I was too scared," the soldier mumbles.

"What was that?" she calmly asks.

"I was too scared," he repeats louder, the trembling in his voice increasing.

"When were you promoted?" she asks, looking to his two triangles before glancing down at the singular one of the dead private.

"Last week…"

"When people get scared, people die, specialist," she says, her voice calm and quiet but with apparent authority. "That private's life is on your head, not mine."

"Roger!"

"Go get some help. Now!" she then commands. He salutes, glances at his dead comrade, and then leaves. "You," she says as she turns to Jax. "Get out of here before I hand you over to Caspian for using a firearm."

Not needing to be told twice, Jax is gone and off to find Kip before she changes her mind. The most perplexing thing about that entire encounter is not that he survived, but that Renn let both him and that other soldier live. Maybe Kip was right. Maybe there is something different about Renn Stone.

SIX

Boston
August 5, 2036

In a minute cloud of dust, Mica's bag slams onto the desk, and carelessly tossing his phone into Kim's old, poorly made mug, Mica walks past the unsanitary counter and straight to the fridge. With the door loose on the hinges, he pours himself a glass of lukewarm milk before making his way to the couch, downing the beverage, the mustache of his spotty beard leaving a white chalky dew.

Mica had been out of his depth with her. The only thing he knew for certain was that he loved Kim from the moment he laid eyes on that handmade mug of hers. She absolutely sucked at anything crafty, and the mug reflected exactly that. With a lopsided heart on one side and a concaved smiley face a toddler could have drawn, Kim was unabashedly proud of every inch of this creation. Her self-confidence was what made her glow. After that first date, Mica knew his life would be different and each kiss, each touch, each conversation they'd had was a reminder of that. Now, every time he sets eyes on that mug, he's reminded that "different" can take many forms.

Her absence has left both him and the apartment in shambles. With an overwhelming pile of clothes and bagged garbage in one corner, and the growing mound of dishes in another, what was once a manageable and organized disarray of living space, has become one of the many scars Mica carries. Since the dark day of their anniversary, the lipstick she kissed and the note she wrote on his bathroom mirror remains Kim's sacred territory. Still painted with her dried blood, her masquerade mask painfully rests next to his off to the side, but the deepest scar of all is one that Mica takes everywhere he goes. As it dangles from a chain, Kim's engagement ring hangs next to the skeleton key he found from her killers, both touching his chest, just over his heart as mementos of love and hate.

The rhythmic clattering vibration of Kim's mug brings Mica back from his trance, and out of sheer annoyance, Mica stands to answer his phone.

"What?!"

"It's time to get back to normal, Mica," Carter says on the other end.

"No thanks."

"This is not life advice. It's an order."

Irritated, Mica asks, "From who?"

"The country that you work for, Mica. The people."

Kim's death was tragic yes, but not near as tragic as it is for millions of Americans that have not only been made outlaws and radicals overnight with simple changes to laws and policy; people are literally dying due to the whims of mob justice and rule, all of which has been funded and defended by the Ordean Reich. Mica has no choice but to get his act together. It's what Carter trained him to do.

"What do I need to do exactly?" Mica asks with a slow exhale.

"You've been enrolled back at Harvard. Classes start Wednesday. You'll also be an intern helping Governor Reuben G. White with his campaign." Carter takes a momentary pause, allowing Mica to process the information. Nothing is harder than moving on after a loved one's violent removal from your life—a concept that will never be lost on Carter.

"Is that all?" Mica asks.

"No. I have an assignment I need you for tonight."

"Roger. I'll be ready."

That all-too-familiar tone resonates with Carter.

Jim... Carter thinks to himself.

"Mica, clean some dishes, talk with your friends. Get out. For what it's worth, I know—"

Mica ends the call.

Gripping the phone, the more forcefully he does, the smoother the tears dripping down his cheeks become, and resisting the urge to shatter the phone against the wall, Mica gently, almost reverently, places it back in Kim's mug.

——⋆★⋆——

"Another one?" the sales rep sighs out as a scruffy biker walks in.

Honestly, what other demographic would he expect at Harley Davidson? A biker chick is the only pleasing variance, but even then, they too are frightening. Fresh out of high school and with his only experience being tinkering in the garage, naturally the kid's experience didn't allot many options. That and his dad forced him into the family business of sales. If he had his way, he'd be designing the bikes, not selling them.

Unkempt beard and all, in a rather odd and bored-like fashion, the biker passes by the high-end and elite bikes most men would whore their girlfriends out to have. The LiveWire 2037. The Road King Special V.3. Not one of them captures his attention for more than a couple seconds. That is until he approaches an "old school" design—the Harley Forty-Eight 2013 edition. Built to rumble through the urban streets, this piece of beautiful machinery spews attitude from the exhaust and can reach face-ripping speeds in 1.9 seconds flat.

Set on making this sale stick, the salesman approaches. "An interesting piece of hardware. Quite rare in fact."

"What makes it rare?" the biker asks, his skepticism of the kid's history bleeding into the conversation.

"Well for one, the year. It's over twenty years old. It's completely off the grid, no wireless internet connection—all updates must be done manually. More importantly though, an exact replica, this particular bike has been modified to have a test part installed straight into the engine—"

"Is it fast?" he interrupts, the details and the monologue of little interest to him.

"Yeah!" the young rep replies. If the biker would've just calmed down, he was in the process of sharing that piece of information. "It's the fastest street bike we have available to the public."

"And what about the ones not sold to the public?" the biker asks, slowly raising his eyebrows.

"I'm sorry, but they aren't for sale."

"Money's not an issue," the biker bluntly adds.

The salesman is taken aback by this tidbit of irrelevant information. "I can't just sell—"

"What if I wanted to look at one?"

"You'd have to talk with a manager. I don't have access to the warehouse out back. I've only been here a month."

Obviously, the biker thinks with a smirk, holding out his hand in thanks.

"Well thank you, Mister…"

"Childs. Charlie Childs." The kid grasps the man's rugged hand, regretting the decision the second he does.

"What time do you close, Charlie?"

"Nine," he states, squirming under the grip before managing to finally pry his hand free from biker's vice.

"Perfect." And before the salesman delays him any further, Mica turns and exits the dealership.

— ★ —

Mica never was one for breaking and entering, but these past months have shed light on the advantages it yields. Kim's death was just the beginning—a nudge. That's all Carter needed. However, despite all the training and the prospect of revenge hanging over Mica's head as motivation, he can't find a way into the warehouse.

Speak of the devil, Mica thinks, his earpiece giving a subtle vibrate. "Yes?"

"What are you doing?" Carter casually demands.

"What you asked."

"Didn't I specifically say to utilize legal means?"

"Within reason. Which is what I did. I tried being *reasonable*, but it wasn't working," Mica states as he continues to study the vertical obstacle in front of him.

His stubbornness and outside-of-the-box thinking are the traits that made Mica a viable candidate for the Division. It's also what makes working with him extremely frustrating.

"I gave you a handsome budget. This organization cannot and will not—"

"Yeah, got to go." He's heard this lecture before, and as he spots his target over the fence line, Mica taps his ear, ending the call. Dashing towards the adjacent building, Mica kicks off the wall. The leverage propels him over the perimeter where he silently lands on the fractured concrete on the other side.

Again, his earpiece vibrates.

"Mica," Carter immediately begins. "There's a time and place, and the Minutemen can't be founded solely on illicit activity."

"Isn't the Division illegal in the first place?" Mica refutes. "They're no National Guard or government sanctioned militia, that is for sure."

"I used my words intentionally. There are arbitrary aspects to the law that must be taken into consideration."

"My point exactly," Mica retorts, hanging up a second time.

Prowling around the enormous warehouse, Mica eases his way around a corner, conniving a way into the actual building.

"They really need to tighten security around here, don't they?" Carter says, emerging from the shadows of supply crates and slowing Mica to a halt. "Just because you can break into the facility doesn't mean you should."

"Your training."

"Tools in a box, Mica. They are to be used with prudence. You were recruited and serve as a soldier. It is not your place to make judgement calls for the Minutemen."

Scoffing, Mica ignores the admonishing piece of advice. "The bikes in there are faster and better than the ones they have on the show floor."

"And all this puts you above the law? Your ability to obtain and the mere desire of having a better bike?"

"Arbitrary aspects…" Mica mumbles.

"We have all the money and equipment you'll need to accomplish any assignment, including the simple one of getting an effective mode of transportation."

Mica rolls his eyes before stepping past Carter where, in a rather impressive manner, he begins scaling a shaky rain gutter.

"In order for the greater good to succeed," Mica grunts, gripping a portion of the wall with his fingertips, "the greater good must live outside the law."

Having noted the unstable apparatus Mica is using to scale the building, Carter marks the open window at the top, which Mica is no doubt climbing to.

"I hate to break it to you, but you are no Prince of Thieves," Carter says.

Loving how well this conversation is going, Mica finds a precarious foothold as he approaches the window, allowing him to shift his weight from his feet to his hands. "What about Batman—the Dark Knight legend himself?"

Clearly not getting through to him, Carter picks up a splintered fragment of two-by-four that will help facilitate one of his crash course specialties. It's the heart and ingenuity that makes a soldier, not gadgets or toys. Timing the moment where Mica will make his transition from the wobbly rain gutter to the open window, Carter tosses the disheveled piece of wood up and at the solitary rod propping open the skylight. Instead of a comfortable lip to latch onto, Mica's fingers jam into the suddenly closed window, and with his footing shaky to begin with, Carter takes a step back as Mica makes an epic plunge, first slamming into a stack of supply crates before his abrupt stop at Carter's feet.

With Mica writhing around, Carter makes sure he eventually locks eyes with him, beaming a simple grin at his student.

"Hi," Carter says, letting that be his one-word lesson for the humbled and humiliated agent.

The following morning, the young salesman smiles brightly as he sees his biker friend walk back in. "Rough night?" the kid asks noticing the bruises and cuts on Mica's face. "Did you have some trouble with your friends in high places?"

"I'll take the Harley Forty-Eight."

"Perfect!" With another commission in the bag, the kid walks Mica over to his desk to work out the paperwork.

Harvard University
August 9, 2036

Bored, tired, and fed up, Mica's posture says it all. In an exaggerated slouch, he awaits the inevitable torturous and monotone lecture. One down, three to go. And if that wasn't bad enough, out of all the classes Carter enrolled him in, he had to pick governmental theory. Kim had been the political nut, not Mica. He's no *useful idiot* and understands the world of bureaucrats just fine; it's his lack of patience for the entire system that makes him sick. He barfs in his mouth because of how well he understands political agendas. Even worse is his internship for the "Republic's Golden Child." Mica lets out an audible sigh of disgust at the thought. He's a proud American, but that sentiment is for an America that no longer exists and is in a time he's long since served in.

"Mica?" a woman abruptly shouts, catching his attention. "Is that you?!"

He's impressed that anyone can recognize him under his scraggly beard, hooded head, and face twisted in complete and utter disgust for life and the encompassing surroundings.

"Of course, it is! I'd recognize those blue and brown eyes anywhere!"

"Aila?" Mica slowly says, her face slowly coming back to remembrance. Lazily he begins to stand, but the process is immediately hastened as she grabs the collar of his jacket, pulling him in her embrace.

"How are you?" Aila asks, refusing to let him go. "I've missed you!"

"I've missed you too?" he awkwardly responds, unintentionally projecting his discomfort in the hug. His words are both sincere and reflective. He truly has missed friendly faces, but it's been so long, that he can't properly articulate or express any human emotion, and out of all the people to see, it's one of Kim's old roommates. "Are you in this class?" he asks as she finally releases her clinch on him.

"Yep!" She grins, revealing her perfect teeth and two distinct dimples. "I thought you dropped out?"

"I thought so too," he mumbles, scratching his beard.

"Well neat! Is it okay if I sit next to you?"

"Sure?" he states in yet another awkward question. She smiles, knowing and fully understanding that he's not put off by her sudden appearance. Apparently, he just doesn't know how to be around people yet. It took her some time herself after learning about—about Kim's murder.

"I like the beard by the way!" she quickly adds as the professor walks in.

"No, you don't," Mica chuckles.

"Yeah, it's hideous."

"Everybody, take your seat please!" the professor declares, striding up to the front of the class.

Immediately labeling herself as an enigma with her expressionless face, she slaps her briefcase onto the table. Her cup of coffee in one hand, she plugs in and sets up her digital presentation with the other where a moment later a classic picture of the White House is displayed.

"Good morning, everybody, I am Professor Lisa Rodgers, and this is Governmental Theory 3410."

"Have you ever had her before?" Mica quietly asks Aila.

"Nope, but I heard she is really good. She's not very popular among the faculty, being more of a Constitutionalist and all, but that's why I signed up for this class! Makes me question, when everyone else is just in a giant echo chamber. Plus, she's my aunt."

"Me too," Mica lies. "Wait, what? Professor Rodgers is your aunt?"

"Surrogate aunt, I guess you could say. Long story."

"I'm assuming every one of you in here belong. If not, please leave quietly."

No one budges.

"Let's get started then. Does anyone know when the two-term policy for a President of the United States was officially discontinued?" As she expects, nobody raises their hand. "It was in 2022. There is some debate as to the exact year, simply because the dialogue and implementation started nearly a decade prior, but no matter—the general consensus is 2022. Okay then. Let's see if you know this piece of historical information: the electoral college, who's heard of it?"

She knows that more people know the answer to this, but again, with debate as to its "radical nature," the topic has been shadow-banned from university studies.

"That was not a rhetorical question," Professor Rodgers coolly states.

Aila shoots her hand into the air.

"Yes." Still no expression, despite Aila's enthusiasm and her alleged relation to the professor.

"It was how we elected the President in the late 20th century."

"Correct, and it even lasted a few years into this century. Do you know how it worked, by any chance?"

Aila, impressed with her own acumen, nudges Mica, proudly nodding her head and puffing out her chest.

"Miss?"

"Aila," Mica whispers, nudging her back as he points over to the professor.

"Oh. Sorry." Aila begins to blush. "I didn't hear the question…"

Despite the scattered chuckles, Rodgers masks the embarrassment for her niece and repeats the question. "How did the electoral college work?"

Stumped, Aila shrugs her shoulders. "I actually don't know that one, Professor."

"That's okay. I doubt anyone does nowadays. But I'm willing to be wrong. Is there anyone in here who knows the answer? Last chance."

Mica is the only one who is confident enough to raise his hand but does so reluctantly.

"So, there is someone! Yes, go ahead Mister…"

"Rouge."

"Mr. Rouge. French?"

"The name is. I'm not," he responds, ashamed of the association he has with the country.

"Continue," Professor Rodgers says.

"Well, it's kind of complicated," he begins, "but in a nutshell, it came down to the political philosophy of a representative constitutional republic. Every state had a certain number of votes that went towards electing a president."

"And how many votes did each state get?" Professor Rodgers asks.

"It depended."

"On what? What determined the number of votes a state got?" she asks, again trying to get to the root of it all.

"The number of electorates, or votes, depended on the sum total of senators and members of the House of Representatives from each state, and since the House number for each state was dependent on the populace, that's where the number of electoral votes varied state to state."

He really wishes he wasn't the only one that knew this. Looking to Aila for some sort of support, all she gives is a shrug. She's careful, but as soon as Mica turns back to Professor Rodgers, Aila smiles, her charm for the man being resurrected.

"And how did a presidential nominee win the electoral votes of a state?" Rodgers asks, knowing that with just a few more questions, she'll get to her point.

"Wasn't it by a popular vote of the people in that state?" Mica asks, picking his brain for the rarely used information. "All the registered voters voted, and whichever candidate got the most votes won all of the state electorates? It was a winner take all system, was it not?"

"Yes, that is exactly how it worked. Well, kind of. It was a winner-take-all system in forty-eight of the fifty states or was supposed to be, anyway. Electorates still had the option to vote against the popular vote of the people in their state, but those were extremely rare instances. The only two states that didn't have this winner-take-all system were Maine and Nebraska."

A student raises their hand.

"Yes?" Professor Rodgers asks.

"Why is that? Is it a regional thing? Are they close to each other?"

Rodgers calms her annoyance with a slow inhale. This is no beginner class, and the fact that they don't know this basic information—the university system is killing the future. Not to mention there is the damn internet... Indirectly answering the question, the professor redirects the conversation back to her original aim.

"Write me a paper about it. I'll expect it Monday," she says, aiming a stern glare at the student. "Now, not counting Maine and Nebraska, the entire system we had in place was a winner takes all. Why? Why have a system like this and not the system we currently have?" She asks Mica but opens the question to the room. "Doesn't our system of Congress being who elects a President work better?"

Mica doesn't wait for someone to take the answer; he knows it and he knows exactly where the professor is going.

"It's more efficient yes, but less democratic."

Professor Rodgers is slightly impressed with this young man. Maybe Carter was right about him after all.

"How so?" she asks. "We elect our senators and representatives. The idea of the republic is to use democratic means in electing officials who we think will push our ideas forward, enacting laws and policies to do so, is it not?"

"Yes, but it comes down to checks and balances," Mica argues, finally getting to the point Professor Rodgers was aiming for. "If Congress elects the President, they can skew the results, creating a lot more room for corruption in the system. Unlike the electorates, they are held less accountable by us, the people."

Mumbles and silent gasps fill the room.

"He has a point," the professor says, patiently waiting for the class to calm down. "But, just to clarify: we have primary elections and censuring processes; aren't these checks against our representatives?"

"They are," Mica begins. "But with Congress having full authority to elect the executive branch, it creates a closed-loop system. We might not appoint judges, but when we vote for a President, we vote for one that we think will appoint federal judges that we as the people would appoint, or at least that is taken into account. When Congress cuts the people out of the process of electing a President, they are also cutting us out of the process of selecting judges as well. In short, it's a slippery slope, because where does the elimination of democratic processes stop that modernity has pioneered?"

Exactly, Rodgers thinks.

"Senators are now in office until they die or resign, which wasn't always the case," she teaches to the class. "The amendment that changed the way we elect a President also changed the way we elect members of Congress. Before we implemented our current election system, there were people trying to create a different constitutional amendment where when we the people voted, the person with the most votes won, period, in what is called a 'popular election.' They wanted the voice of the people to be heard from the people themselves, not Congress and not from electorates."

"Wasn't that how it worked though?" a student shouts out. "Logically, whoever has the most electoral votes has the most citizen votes."

"You'd think, but no. In 1824, 1876, 1888, and 2000 all those who lost the election won the popular vote. Seems unjust, huh? The Electoral College was essentially a hybrid of a popular vote and a congressional vote, but instead of being a democratic process, it evolved into more of a game, some would argue. A game to win the states and not the people. But that's politics for you—imperfect people creating imperfect systems. Back to what Mr. Rouge was saying about checks and balances, though. How does a lack of checks and balances create corruption? As we've pointed out, the idea behind checks and balances is inefficient. It slows down progression."

Mica knows exactly who these people are. Kim used to talk about them—about their ideas—and for that, she is where she is.

"Too many people's opinions in the political ring"—Rodgers folds her hands—"can cause the system to lock up."

"And that's a problem because?" a student asks.

"It's not, but Liberal officials thought it was, because the government could shut down, and it had numerous times. But that was the beauty of it. Progress for equity's sake is naïve and doesn't properly work out the logistics of policy and long-term effect. So," Professor Rodgers continues, "these same officials tried to simplify the election process in hopes of simplifying the checks and balances, but they went about it in a way that most didn't expect. Instead of having a pure popular vote from the people, which I don't advocate for either, the voting changed to Congress, giving more power to the government and less to the people."

"Sounds like a problem to me…" Aila mumbles to herself.

"Exactly," Professor Rodgers says, overhearing Aila's whispered comment.

Mica shrugs his shoulders at the professor, his mental political library sparce in this area. That same shrug completely catches Aila off guard. She's absolutely captivated at this point by Mica Rouge. She knows what she wants but can't think of how to go about it. Turning to Mica, Aila opens her mouth but stops as she hears nothing but utter silence from the class. If she speaks, *everyone* will hear her. Cursing her luck, Aila glances around to see if someone will open their damn mouth and save her opportunity, but no one does.

With more than a hint of frustration, Aila blurts out, "Why is our current election system such a problem?" A few in the class awkwardly chuckle at the abrasive question.

Succinctly, Professor Rodgers answers. "Because, slowly, we the people are becoming less of a check to create balance within the political system."

"I'm sorry, but that's bullshit!" a male student shouts out.

And just like that, her chance is back.

"Hey, Mica," Aila tentatively whispers, "what are you doing Friday?"

"Is it?" Rodgers belts back at the student.

"I'm not sure," Mica says, peeling his eyes away from the impending debate. "Why?" he asks, oblivious to the nervous shake in her voice.

"Gun control laws are constricting are they not? And what about freedom of religion, speech, and the press?" Rodgers firmly asks.

"What about it?" the male student belts out, again clearly stating the biases in his tone. "There have always been restrictions on rights."

Aila continues, hoping no one is focused on her. "The company I work for is having this fancy dinner at Hotel Elegancy, and I was wondering if you would like to be my plus one, or whatever?" There. It's out there in the ether.

"What books are you allowed to read? How many guns can you own?" Rodgers asks. Students search to find any answer that doesn't make it sound like they have fallen victim to the government's repressive propaganda.

"Based on all the shootings over the last few decades, I think it's safe to say guns may be best left out of the hands of everyone. They don't save lives, they take them," the boisterous student states, refusing to back down.

Mica hesitates to answer Aila, knowing he should have seen this coming. Tentatively he says, "I don't know, Aila. I might have to pass."

"Yeah, it's all good," she says, brushing off the heartbreak as if it's nothing.

"You really think that?" Rodgers holds her own ground. "What about the bombing last week? What was it the man used?" she asks, stopping as if actually pondering on it.

"A car and propane!" another student shouts out.

"Transportation and barbeque materials," Rodgers clarifies. "And where can you get propane?"

"Walmart!" the same student shouts out.

"And anywhere else that sells barbeque supplies. And how about a Corolla? And stabbings, how much have those increased?"

The cocky male student opens his mouth to argue, but Rodgers cuts him off.

"If people want to kill, they will kill, and who's to say that people don't have the right to protect themselves? You? Yes, guns are designed to destroy, but a gun in the hands of a trained, responsible citizen is safer than a mentally unstable individual or a criminal looking only to harm. How about instead of making another law restricting what we own, indirectly harming the innocent, we reform the way we teach the rising generation?"

Oblivious to the ongoing heated debate, Aila hangs her head down in a mini-pity party. It's just too soon for him. She should know this! That doesn't help stop the emotions that started coming back up the second she saw him, though. It was bittersweet when she heard that Kim died, especially the violent manner in which she did, but at the same time Aila couldn't help but wonder if it was an act of God that her roommate was killed. It's selfish and borderline evil to think about it like that, but being the staunch Christian that she is, if there is one thing that she knows it's that God's work is a mystery.

"I appreciate the invite though," he says, seeing the disappointment—not for the first time—in his friend's eyes.

With a smile, Aila sits up with the determination to ignore the stinging twinge in her heart.

───── ✦ ★ ✦ ─────

"How's he doing?" Carter asks, her last student having just bumped into him on her way out.

"Nice to see you too, Carter," Rodgers sarcastically proclaims. They've been friends for years and still the guy is business first!

"I'm sorry, Lisa. I'm stressed to say the least."

"I know, but it wouldn't be a proper hello if I didn't bust your balls," she retorts with a smirk, only to look back at her computer. "And he's doing fine. Very intelligent. He's a good find."

"And Aila?" Carter asks, this particular question a little more difficult to utter. He knew his niece was taking Lisa's class, making him hesitant to enroll his most recent operative in the same course due to the history she shares with Mica, but with every other one of Lisa's classes full, this was the only option if they wanted to maintain Lisa's federal anonymity with the university. Nothing would put the Division under greater threat than having sophists hating Rodgers more than they already do.

"She's a flirt," Lisa chuckles. She debated on whether to give Carter this bit of information, but on account of him inevitably finding out, she figured it'd be entertaining to watch him squirm.

"I don't know what to do about that girl," Carter responds in a surprisingly calm manner. He's not entirely shocked by this; Aila has always had an inconvenient choice in boys, and Mica, he has been on this girl's radar for quite some time…

"Yes, you do. You always have," Rodgers states. Since their early days in the CIA, Lisa has helped Carter raise his niece, and at times she's had to whip him into shape along the way. She's longed for a relationship with the man; however, each has their allotment in life and Lisa has accepted her marriage to her country.

"You're probably right," Carter states. She usually is. If the country wasn't in such a disaster, Carter and Lisa would be married, there's no doubt in his mind, but as frustrating as it is, they may never be able to explore a life together. "You up for lunch?" he then asks.

"I have a class in ten minutes, but after that!" His mysterious ways have always had a flattering appeal to Lisa, and not because of their clandestine nature, but simply because she is the only one that can see through his bullshit.

With a smile he turns to exit, but before Carter leaves he's reminded of something that pivots him back to face Lisa.

"By the way, you haven't heard anything about that key, have you?" he asks, the matter having made him abnormally anxious these past months.

Annoyed by his constant fretting, she answers like she always does, "If I hear anything I will let you know, John. Until then, follow protocol."

Recognizing that tone of hers, he reluctantly gives up the argument without another word. He's beginning to doubt that the Ordeans even have the Keeper's key. If they did, their operations would already be sabotaged by now. That said, he's been wrong before.

"I have a few calls to make. I'll see you in a bit."

After an affectionate embrace, Carter is out the door and back to business, pulling out his phone.

"I have another assignment. I'll be at your place in twenty."

"And if I'm not there?" Mica asks on the other end.

"You better be with how fast that motorcycle is," and before Mica can argue back, Carter hangs up.

Out of all the guys in the *world*, Aila had to pick this one.

"I have to go," Mica says.

Although he may not be ready for a relationship, he's discovered that he's ready for a friend.

"Oh. Okay. Well, see you around?"

"Yeah! Friday?" Mica quickly answers, and then inserts, "in class," upon seeing her expression, remembering the date offer she made earlier.

"Yes, in class," Aila giggles. He is more charming by the minute, and he doesn't even know it.

If goodbyes could lack grace, Mica manages to accomplish this as he waves a stiff hand up and down and side to side, before turning away and looking any more stupid than he already does.

Within a matter of minutes, he is home. He must admit, even though this slick machine wasn't in his top five, it's growing on him. The ride is smooth, handles like nothing he's ever touched before and turns on a dime. The torque though, that's what captured his attention. The moment he first hit the throttle, the roar from the engine awakened the lion in Mica's heart as he sped down the empty street that first day.

"It is about time," Mr. Carter says in an irritated tone. Gazing out the window never has had much appeal. It usually starts out as an opportunity to ponder, but it always ends with Carter finding new regrets.

"Traffic," Mica lies, unsurprised to find Carter in his apartment. With a bike like his? Not in a million years. "So, what's the assignment?"

"We want you to take out a gang," Carter casually says, his brooding still directed out the window.

Mica on the other hand, doesn't acknowledge a word he says. Moving to put his phone in Kim's mug, Mica's heart stops at its absence. Instead, a fancy knife that Mica's never seen before rests in its place.

"Where's the cup?!" he demands, picking up the blade and stabbing it where the mug should be.

"What cup?" Carter asks, turning around. That's when Mica sees it. The lopsided heart. The toddler's smiley face. Kim's mug in Carter's hand.

"For future reference," Mica spits as he storms towards Carter. "Don't ever use this cup!" Jerking the mug from Carter, Mica spills coffee over both their hands.

"Noted." Carter nods, gently snatching his coffee back from Mica and taking a sip nonchalantly. "As I was saying, the gang."

"You want them dead?" Mica asks, his agitation burrowing into Carter's soul.

"I did not say that. I said that we want you to take them out."

"Okay," Mica says with an annoyed shrug. *What's the difference?* he thinks.

"Recently," Carter begins, taking another sip, "this gang has been found funding the Children of the Ordean Reich. Tonight, they'll be making a major transaction, one that will cripple us as an effective enemy of the Reich if it goes through."

"When and where?"

"Two a.m. behind the news station." Another sip. "Stop the transaction from taking place." It is not hyperbolic in the least bit to say that this deal could be one of the last things the Division sees transpire in this war.

"What are the rules of engagement?"

"Kill only in self-defense. That is the only time you should ever take a life while working with us."

"That's debatable," Mica mumbles.

Carter's impressed with the progress Mica's made, but he has a lot to learn.

"Let the police arrest the gang, just make sure the transaction tonight does not happen," he adds, taking one final sip and carefully giving Mica back the mug. "And don't get caught."

"I never do."

"One more thing," Carter says, pointing over to a metal trunk off in the corner of the room. "We gave you some tools to work with—some are more familiar than others."

Silently, Carter then leaves Mica alone with his thoughts and preparations.

Placing Kim's cup in the sink, his eyes fixate on the chest the entire time. Drying his hands, Mica moves over, snapping the clasps up and lifting the heavy lid, revealing an array of weapons and pieces of body armor. Immediately, he moves to pick up one of his favorites: the whip. Next, his attention shifts to the blades, and like the ones he uses in training, they are simple, black-edged weapons. His bread and butter—two knives and a single hatchet. Less interesting items like the armor and the clubs don't get as much attention from the agent, but one item pierces Mica's heart more than any other edged weapon could.

Running his fingers along the outline, Mica picks up the mask. An exact replica of the one he was wearing that night with one slight modification—two devil horns. At first, he hates it, but he then loves the guise as the fear-evoking symbol Carter intended. If there is no God that their enemies fear, there sure as hell is a Devil.

Just adjacent to the masquerade mask lays the most familiar weapon of all—his redwood cane. Not a replica, but the exact one he used to kill Kim's attackers, and together, the poetic coupling of the demon's mask and his cane kindles his rage. At times, he's doubtful that any of this will make the impact Carter and the Division aim for, but that's not why he's agreed to Carter's terms. These items are tools of retribution—they are weapons of revenge, redemption, and freedom from his anguish.

Getting in position, Mica cuts the engine to his bike, coasting to a parking spot a block and a half away.

"I feel so stupid," Mica mumbles.

In theory it's cool to have everything you'll need strapped to your body, and maybe with some tweaking and adjustments it'll feel more natural, but his weapons dangle loosely off his body in an overwhelming number of buckles, straps, and holsters while his pockets bulge at the seams with everything else. This, however, is not what makes him feel like a soup sandwich. The euphoria from seeing the horned mask vanished the second he placed it on his unkempt, frizzy face. Nothing like the vigilante he pictured; he looks more like a crazy hobo high on crack.

Having approached from the north, downwind from the rear entrance of the warehouse, he waits and watches the area from the shadows. It isn't long before a small army of black Cadillac SUVs approaches, slowing to a halt before more than a dozen brawny and hardened men exit the vehicles.

"Seventeen…" Mica counts. "Seventeen?!"

He knows what he's doing, but Mica's never handled this many at one time. Carter knows this, so what the hell is he thinking? But, before Mica can radio in his complaint, three more vehicles approach, dumping out another massive group.

"Twenty-eight? Are you shitting me?!"

Putting his hand to his ear, Mica radios Carter.

"You done?" Carter asks.

"No, I'm not done," Mica states, making sure to keep his voice down. "Twenty-eight targets? You never—"

"Did they make the transaction?"

"No, but I don't see how I'm going to stop all *twenty-eight of them*!"

Before Mica can complain any further, he notices discourse among the two groups before a handful of men move to one of the vehicles. In the still night air, Mica overhears whimpering and muffled yells as five people are pulled outside, all of them with a canvas bag over their head.

"Stand by," Mica says.

After another quick study, Mica makes a horrifying observation. Two of the five are full-grown adults, which is disturbing on its own, but not as gut wrenching as seeing the other three.

"Kids?"

"Sales have gone up three-fold for traffickers since Congress elected President Westwood. Both they and he opened our border, making Cartel-Ordean activity like this easier than ever. It's also made for a rather convenient means to eliminate political rivals. What you're seeing is Governor White's Chief of Staff and his family…"

"What's the local response time?" Mica asks.

"Five minutes," Carter says without skipping a beat.

"Call them in four," Mica states before cutting the transmission.

Standing up from the shadows, Mica walks forward, calculating and planning each step and breath he takes. His mind slows down his surroundings and the movements of the targets ahead as he taps into his training. Every sight, sound, and smell is interpreted and studied as he accepts the weight of his leather armor and its Kevlar lining pressing against his body. Clutching his weapons in hand, this is not a matter of ability any longer. It's a matter of principle. Damn politics. This fight is about defending human life and childhood innocence.

"Hey!" a thug snarls, noticing Mica's advance, completely unintimidated. "Yo! Stop right there!" he yells, pulling out a Glock from his pants.

Forty-five caliber. Mica is very familiar with it, Glock being the choice amongst most of his instructors. Mica stops, and so does the activity of every criminal present as they watch, waiting for what happens to the vagrant that's walked in on their affairs.

Sliding his right hand on top of the whip, Mica unclips it.

"What are you doing here?" Mica demands. He knows how stupid it may sound, but he must stall. There are some details he still wants to finalize.

"Doesn't matter," one of the apparent leaders states, naïve as to what is about to transpire. "You best leave, though!"

Mica doesn't move as the thug pointing his Glock takes three steps forward, chambering a round.

"You best listen, old man—"

Three steps are all Mica needs. In a flash, the whip is out, slicing the back of the thug's hand wide open. Yelping, he drops the firearm while gun shots rain in from the twenty-seven others, riddling the back of the unarmed criminal and the SUV that Mica is behind before a single trigger is pulled.

"Who is that?! He with you?" one of them shouts.

"Ain't no way! He's with you!"

This is exactly what Mica was aiming for. Nothing is weaker than a confused, disorganized enemy.

"Protect the product!" one of the leaders shouts as seven criminals huddle around the small family.

"Shut up!" he yells, smacking one of the kids who's started to cry.

"Hey!" Mica shouts, standing up from his hiding spot and throwing a knife which lands with a thud, finding its mark in the meat of the thug's thigh. A retaliating barrage is shot in Mica's direction, but again he's unseen and unharmed.

"Let's get outta here!" a cowering suggestion echoes out amongst the silence.

"It's one douche—" one of them begins, but before he can finish the petty logic, he's bashed in the back of the head by Mica's cane. Mica is able to easily take out two others with the same speed and precision before they are left again to shoot at his shadow.

An eerie silence falls over the moans and groans from the injured, and with the wind strewing leaves across the asphalt, nobody moves for seconds at a time. Suddenly, a startling hiss cracks the dull air. Groaning under the lack of support from its flat tire, one of the criminal SUVs drops to the ground.

"What the hell…"

"Shut up," the leader whispers, listening to nothing except whimpers and scattering foliage.

Without warning, the worker vans parked at the warehouse begin to beep as their alarms go off. First one, then two, until all of them blare in the early morning hours, disorienting every gang member. Out of nowhere, the middle criminal is whipped in the throat, dropping him to his knees—and still not a single shot is fired as Mica breaks the various limbs and tracheas of thugs trying to stop him from running off again. In a matter of seconds, only a select few stand between him and the kidnapped family.

Cautiously, the gang approaches Mica, with the horrifying realization that this is no hobo. Unexpectedly, Mica throws his cane, cracking one skull on the far left, as the remaining fearfully advance. Pulling his two mini-clubs from off his back, Mica goes to work on their hands, knees, jaws and any part of their body that gets in the way or tries to cause him harm. Mica is only hit once by a bat with a wild swing to his ribs but slamming the mini-club into the thug's collar bone and then the base of the skull, Mica neutralizes the last threat.

With the car alarms still sounding in the background, Mica knows he must hurry as the distant sirens of the police can be heard. Scrounging for his weapons, Mica hastily approaches the family. Doing their best to move in front of and protect their cowering children, the parents face their unknown approaching savior.

"It's okay," Mica says, slowly lifting the canvas bags from each of their heads. "Is anyone hurt?"

Timidly, all shake their heads.

"You'll be fine," he then says, kneeling and looking into the eyes of a little girl. With her eyes red and cheeks flushed, Mica wipes away one of her tears. As he opens his mouth to say one final thing, he is stopped by a flash of white light from behind.

Whipping around, Mica sees a photographer sprinting in the opposite direction. Snatching up his cane and other weapons, with ease, Mica catches up, tackling her to the ground just outside the warehouse's perimeter.

"Get off of me!" She fights, swinging her fists and flailing her legs, managing to hit Mica more than the combined twenty-eight criminals did.

"Shut up," he growls, picking her up from off the ground. "I'm not going to hurt you, stupid. I just need—" Mica begins but freezes upon seeing her face. "Aila?"

Seven

Area Thirty-Eight

"Open it!"

The suspense is murder. How many years has it been since he last saw one? Kip was just a young thing, and if it wasn't for this assignment, he guarantees he never would have seen one again.

The rusty metal box is as enchanting as it is frightening, the taunting mystery captivating both as Jax carefully picks the lock and tentatively flips up the latches.

"Why the wall?" Jax mumbles.

"What?" Kip snaps, confused at the comment.

"Why was it was hidden in the wall?"

"Because it's worth killing for," Kip solemnly states, the Raider attack fresh on his mind. *It's also a rather clever move on Granny Lisa's part,* he then thinks. This box has been Kip's mission for years and it's what he and Granny Lisa would talk about at night after Jax would be asleep. She apparently knew it was in this house the whole time, and it's what she trained Kip to be ready for when the "time was right." Never thought a can of soup lodged in the wall would be it…

"You think it's got illegal stuff in it?" Jax asks, not sure if he's looking for reassurance on the matter.

"I do…" Kip calmly says, and it's only things like that that have any chance of sparking hope in anyone.

Who determines the illegality of books—of anything for that matter? Who says information and history is prohibited? The Government, and why? All documents are conspiring documents in their eyes. Audio disturbs the peace. Pictures disturb the minds and hearts of their people. Compound those subjective terms with words like "propaganda" and "conspiracy" and you have an organization like the Nine and their Oligarchy whose sole purpose and drive in life is the accumulation of power and control.

"Should we?" Jax asks, slowly finding his courage as he rests his hands on either side of the lid.

Despite all his drive and emotion, Kip has to take a moment to ask himself the same question. His whole life has been to find out what's in this box, thinking—believing—that its contents could change their world, and now that it's here he's apprehensive. What if he's been wrong this entire time? What if Lisa died for nothing more than trinkets and memories? What if the entirety of Kip's life has been without purpose?

"Yes," is Kip's slow, yet confident response. "Open it…"

Finding resolve in Kip's stoic answer, Jax pries the rusty box open, diminishing all doubts with it.

"A book…" Kip whispers, memories and hope flooding back. Yanking it out, he flips dust in every direction as he turns through the delicate paper pages.

Frozen in place, Jax counts that book and every artifact carefully, methodically creating a mental inventory. A black fat book, three identical dark blue books, an audio device of sorts, a series of discs, and a chain necklace. Once the surreal weight lifts, Jax reaches for the only object that *might* not get him killed.

Placing the tiny, delicate metal links of the necklace around his neck, the silky metal texture slips between his fingers as he releases the jewelry. With the relic dangling from the elegant chain, the ancient key swings left and right in a mesmerizing pattern until the corner of Jax's jacket stops the swaying momentum.

Finding a surge of determination, Jax quickly reaches for the audio device.

"Holy Bible? Odd word, bible," Kip blurts out, completely comfortable with the illicit nature of their situation. "Wonder why it's holy," he then chuckles before slamming the black book down in another wave of dust. Frantically, Kip then reaches for one of the metallic-looking discs.

"What's an iPod?" Jax mumbles to himself, reading the shiny lettering on the back of the audio device. Flipping it over, Jax notices a small red button, and upon pressing it, the square screen illuminates, revealing a petite white apple before a bright menu takes its place.

"It still works?" Kip proclaims.

Connor's told him about these power sources that are essentially infinite. Nuclear is the word that comes to his mind, but he isn't quite sure if that's the right term. It was a technology that was being developed before The Government was founded and could be retrofitted for just about any electronic device, old or new. However, it was all lost as soon as the Areas came into existence.

"What do you make of these?" Kip then asks, handing him a small stack of shiny discs. Pulling one out of its plastic case labeled *John Mayer*, Kip is quick to discover the bright glare when aiming its surface at just the right angle towards the light. Right away, Kip sees the humorous potential in this discovery as he begins blinding Jax.

"These things are awesome!" Kip giggles.

Scrolling through the various menus of the iPod, words like artists, playlists, and albums are all nouns with no meaning or context for Jax. Yes, he's aware of the basic concepts of the English language—nouns, verbs, adjectives. It's rare, but with Grandma Lisa in your life, there's a certain privilege that comes from being associated with someone as educated as she was. Even Kip can read and process complex ideas simply from being around her instruction and upbringing. It's not until stumbling on a completely different series of terms that Jax must stop and reflect on her past conversations and lessons.

"American Backstory, The USA: a Founding?" He's heard some of these concepts before, but damn if he can remember any of the details.

"Who do you think Kim is?" Kip asks, picking up the box and seeing the name written on the front of its surface. If this is the box they've been looking for, this was a name Kip was not briefed on. *There it is,* he then thinks, picking up just the evidence to prove that yes, this is in fact what he's been looking for all these years.

"This one has yer name on it, Jax."

"What?" Jax asks, perplexed at what Kip has just said.

The Rouge Family
DIA BBQ Minutemen HQ
Oct 14, 2037

Shivers run up and down Jax's spine as he reads those words on the shiny disc, then, upon picking up an aged, tan envelope found inside one of the blue journal books, his heart stops as he makes one more discovery. With the small paper package in hand, Jax compresses the contents, feeling several folds of paper before spinning it around and revealing an uncanny piece of information.

To Jax
From Mom and Dad

These words he knows. Reverently he reads them, a momentary pause being created in his mind as he begins comprehending their simple meaning. His parents were here in Area Thirty-Eight.

"Kip," he says, urgency building inside him. "Put everything away."

"Why?"

"Now!"

"Not without an explanation."

"Books are illegal, not to mention, we don't even know who this is from."

"Yeah, we do!" Kip retorts as he points to the *Rouge Family BBQ* disc.

There's no denying the reality staring right at him, but...*tact*. That's a word Connor uses all the time, and until now the term was elusive.

"I want to talk to somebody first," Jax ends up saying, hoping that the rationale will get Kip to comply.

"Who?!" Kip demands. No matter who was training him, the lesson of patience was something Kip always struggled with, and now, in a real-world situation he is being asked to exercise some.

"A friend." The one person Jax knows he can trust with information like this.

"*I'm* your friend!" Kip says to a Jax who suddenly seems blind to this fact. "This is dangerous stuff, Jax. Who is it?"

For obvious reasons, Jax hesitates, but seeing reason in Kip's apprehension and noticing that Kip seems to know more than he's letting on, Jax finds no good excuse to keep Connor a secret any longer. "He's... Connor."

"He's Connor?" Another name that never showed up in any of his briefs.

"He's in the PPA," Jax sighs, releasing this last bit of information.

"He's what?!"

Kip's worst nightmare. Everyone's worst nightmare. The only thing that might be remotely close would be if Jax said he was going to set a match to it all, which the PPA might very well do, but not before murdering them for conspiracy, sedition, and treason. "Y'er going trust one of them? Over me?"

"I am..." is Jax's brief answer.

"Ungrateful bastard. Ya have no idea what sacrifices Lisa and I have made for you!"

Jax doesn't. How does a child comprehend the reasoning of a parent, and how can Jax comprehend those early years with Kip and Grandma Lisa as his only defense and hope for survival?

"Kip, I—"

"Save it for the PPA. Hope ya know what y'er doing. If not, we're all dead."

"What choice do I have, Kip? Connor is—"

"What choice do you have?" Kip retorts. "I don't give a damn who this Connor is. You bring in the PPA and any choice ya thought ya had will be gone, and one, if not both of us, will be dead." Kip scoffs. "Do whatever ya have to. I sure as hell will be."

"What's that supposed to mean?"

Kip bites his tongue. *Patience*, he thinks. "It's time for the Gathering. Let's just go do our civic duty, and we'll worry about it tomorrow," he says, having a very different idea of when the box should be opened next.

"I thought you were going to be a no-show and ditch us there for a second," Mari whispers, her lips closer to Jax's ear than she initially intended.

"No-show? Never. Ditch you, maybe," Jax says with a wink.

"Shut up," she chuckles, shoving him as she does.

Maybe it was a subconscious desire that her lips were practically brushing up against his ear; regardless, when Mari and Jax are together, the world seems to be in its proper order.

Adjacent to the love birds, Kip gives Ann an innocent wave that the little girl blatantly ignores. She's not being rude, it's simply because it's Kip. He's never really shown them much attention, let alone a friendly wave, so what's the girl to do? Rather than waving back, Ann just sticks out her tongue.

To her surprise, the guy isn't fazed in the least bit as he mimics the juvenile gesture in a playful manner. With an immediate cold shoulder, it's clear that Ann didn't take Kip's joke the way he intended. Surrendering to his apparent frustration, Kip throws up his arms and rolls his eyes towards the stage.

As the anthem fades in, reaching the crescendo, Caspian and Rhett take their places, and with the music finishing its final note, Caspian turns on his microphone as he begins to pace.

"This week has been a disappointing one for us in the PPA," he solemnly states in a feign of sorrow. "My parents continually encountered disturbing intel on each one of their citizenry tours."

Nodding to the foot of the stairs, on cue, two PPA privates drag a bruised and bloody man, tossing him sluggishly in front of Rhett. His gapping cuts, deep bruises and profound amount of blood testify that he's not some casual offender of the law.

"This was found in his house," Caspian says, pulling from his pocket a gorgeous pearl white novel with a blue, silver embossed spine. "*Brave New World*," he then slowly announces, displaying the book's cover page as he paces in front of the damaged criminal.

Wrenching the broken man to his feet, Caspian's eyes meet the green of his brother's, and with his back to his audience, the darkness in Caspian's eyes shift and burrow into the soul of this deviant before him.

"Does anyone know what brave new world this book is referring to?" Caspian asks, turning towards the crowd, pausing as if waiting for an audible answer.

Without a word, Jax looks to Kip. While he expects to see fear within his elder brother's eyes, Jax sees only anger. Kip knows that the Raiders may not have been specifically after their collection of illegal items, but they're after something. The two of them are on the cusp of a renaissance—a new fringed enlightenment—and it's only a matter of time before they either succeed in starting the revolution or die and fail.

"It doesn't exist!" Caspian chuckles out. "This *Brave New World* is a myth—a myth that will only poison your minds!" Turning to the man, Caspian slaps the book across the criminal's face, its resonating impact echoing throughout the chamber. "What has The Government stated about books in our society?!"

This question is not for the audience, but for the lone man Rhett continues to effortlessly hold upright.

"We gave you the chance. We gave you all the chance to have personal copies, and what did you do? You abused. That. RIGHT!" He turns around, his boney jaw clenched with rage. "What is the law?!"

In unison, everyone sounds: "One, no disrespectful acts towards the Nine or The Government which upholds them. Two, praise the Nine by our actions and with our words. Lastly, live, work, and if needs be die, so that the Nine and their Government may continue to prosper and bless."

"Why is that so hard to understand?!" Caspian asks, nodding to Rhett who releases the man to thud to his knees. As Caspian methodically switches places with his brother, the skeletal sadist pulls a small, metallic lighter out from the inside of his coat and ignites the book's pages before deliberately tossing it in front of the prisoner.

"Close your eyes, Ann," Mari whispers sharply. Ann immediately obeys, and snapping her eyelids shut, desperately reaches out for the nearest grownup. He doesn't care that she thought less of him a few minutes ago, Kip grabs the little girl's shaking palm and pulls her into his embrace.

Grabbing Ann's other panicked hand, Mari in turn grabs Jax and looks to him as if pleading for him to stop the nightmare. He can't. All he can do is stare back into her dark, tear-filled eyes and hope that it's all forgotten by morning.

That's impossible though. This is just one book. Jax and Kip have four.

"He," Caspian shouts, pointing to the criminal, "claims that he hasn't even opened it. Say that we believe him, does it matter?"

Behind the kneeling man, Caspian draws his weapon from his hip, and pointing it at the man's head, pulls the trigger without a flinch of remorse. The earsplitting sound reverberates off the glass walls of City Hall as the man falls forward, his head landing directly on the burning book. What flames are left from the sudden whooshing impact begin to singe the hair of the lifeless man's head.

"No, it does not, for we will not be mocked." And as Caspian exits stage left, the anthem begins to play.

"Can we go?" Ann asks, peeking up from Kip's grasp on her.

"Of course," Kip says, picking her up and carrying her out of City Hall.

As the group trudges back home, they let the silence of the winter air do the talking—the moon and stars their only light source guiding them home. Rounding corner after corner, all their thoughts take them to different places. Mari's to Jax's warm home. Ann's to a fresh meal filling her cramped belly. But as for Jax and Kip, each of them think of their own ways to handle the possibility of being prosecuted as transgressors of the law. Jax thinks only of Mari and how she would cope if it was him up on that stage, let alone Ann being able to process the visceral image of his death. Would Mari protect Ann's eyes like she did tonight, or would she let her watch, knowing that it would be Ann's last chance to see him, her brother and father figure? Would his death have meaning? Did that man's death have meaning? Jax would like to think it did—he would like to think his would, but what value is there in a life if no one takes to heart the actions of your existence?

"Ya doing alright?" Kip asks Ann before placing her down and kissing her little forehead.

"Yeah, thanks Kip," she says, wrapping her arms around him one last time before he runs the rest of the way home, not taking a second look back.

"You've known him for a long time, huh?" Mari asks with a smirk.

"Yeah… He looks meaner than he is. His heart is practically jelly. After our Grandma Lisa died, I had nobody—nobody except Kip raising me before I could begin pulling my own weight."

"Do you know what he did before all this?" Mari asks, bewildered by someone that she's never really thought twice about.

"I don't. I've heard him talk about things that happened before The Government, but he keeps a lot of that to himself and I only catch bits here and there."

"Really?" Mari says in awe, keeping quiet for a long moment. Never has she met anyone who knew a time when the Nine didn't exist. Not even in her previous life when she was privy to delicate information did she hear of a time before all this. Anyone who should be old enough to remember are the dead, nonexistent elderly individuals. She's thought about it obviously, just like everyone, but when formulating unapproved ideas, it's best to internalize those kinds of musings than discuss them.

"Have you ever wondered what it'd be like?" Mari tentatively asks.

"Wondered what *what* would be like?"

"Wondered what it'd be like without them—the PPA. The officers, the Stones, the Nine. The Government…"

"Mari," Jax slowly begins.

"It's just a question."

"After what we just saw, it's a question you shouldn't ask…"

"That's exactly why I'm asking. They hate us," Mari says, whispering the thought. "They don't take care of us. We take care of *them*. They don't deserve our obedience or loyalty, Jax."

"But they do take care of us," Jax slowly says, not even believing his own words.

"Do they?" Mari retorts. "Do you really think you're taken care of by the *merciful* Nine?"

"What are you suggesting? That we fight them or something?"

He's fed, he subsists on the credits he gets for his honest work, and as long as he stays in line, what reason is there to revolt? It's basic survival instincts, and yet the devil advocating inside of him *knows* every bit of what he just said and thought is absolute bullshit. Just the other day he passively resisted basic orders and got beat to a bloody pulp because of it, so he can't even kid himself that he hasn't teased the idea of starting something bigger—that he hasn't loathed the fact that no, The Government does absolutely nothing for him or anyone else under their wing. It's that exact dilemma that makes finding the box so difficult to comprehend. He's leaning towards just wiping his hands clean of the whole situation and handing it over to Connor. He's the soldier. He's the tactician. Jax—Jax is just a Mill worker. He's just someone who buys food from Mari's market.

"What happened?!" Ann shouts, jabbing her finger towards the bullet graze on Jax's neck.

"I had an accident at the Mill," he lies, hoping this wouldn't come up. Now he's really got no other choice because Mari sees right through his crap. She heard about the attack—everyone listened to the explosions and gunfire, bunkering down as they waited, and some, like Mari, were praying for a Raider victory.

"Bull!" she calls out, pushing Jax completely off balance.

"Hey!"

"You were at the Raider attack, weren't you?" she accuses.

"Yeah, I was, alright? My place got blown up," he states, quickly clearing up the lie before more of her terror rains down on him.

"Your place *what*?" A fright-filled gasp emits from Mari, and charging up her attack, she begins whaling on Jax with both her fists, pounding his feet, legs, and whatever appendage will result in the most pain. Ann, not caring about the severity of the situation Jax put himself in, just laughs at the comical ass kicking.

Just kiss her already! Ann thinks. Every day she wishes that Jax would get his head in the game—that he and Mari would just get together. All she's ever wanted is for a happy home and as far as her little eyes can see, Jax makes Mari very happy.

"Why didn't you tell me?!" Mari blares, her next jab striking his sternum.

"I never had the chance!" he blurts out before blocking a final wild kick aimed for his groin.

"Are you okay?" she asks.

"I don't know, am I?" Jax scoffs, finding her question rather ironic.

Ignoring his sarcasm, she asks, "Do you have a place to stay?"

Ann's ears perk up at this question and she immediately crosses her fingers as she rattles around with excitement. "Say no, say no, say no," she whispers.

"Yeah," Jax says, instantly cutting the power to Ann's enthusiasm. "Kip's place is still intact."

"Good. Let's go, Ann," Mari orders, grabbing her sister's hand before the two begin storming off.

"You can stay with us if you want!" Ann shouts over her shoulder, making one last desperate attempt. "We'd love to have you!"

Mari stops, waiting for his reply, secretly hoping Ann's petition comes true.

Boy, does he want to. There is no denying the rising sentiments between the two, but as he slowly warms up to the idea and starts to accept the offer, he silently and abruptly shuts his mouth.

"The box..." he whispers. He can't leave Kip alone with something that dangerous. Not only is he unsure of Kip's intentions, but after what happened tonight the two of them are far safer together.

"Thanks," Jax shouts back. "I want to make sure Kip's okay, though. I'll see you two tomorrow?"

Mari, clearly disappointed, ignores his question in a storming rage.

"You handled that well," Rhett sarcastically states.

Hearing the cynicism in his brother's voice, Caspian ignores it as he steps in front of the door, sliding the delicate key into its slot. With a quick twist of his wrist the airlock seal is broken as the door hisses open.

"You coming?" Caspian asks, turning for a response.

He doesn't want to but what choice does he have? "After you," Rhett says with a universal up-yours gesture.

Despite his love for his brother, there are times where Caspian imagines concaving Rhett's face to an unrecognizable mush. Not to mention the slew of ways he'd publicly display the body after the fact, showing that not even his own blood is safe from insubordination. It's one of those days when the only thing saving Rhett is the restraint Caspian exercises. Fraternal contention can't ruin the Stone family vision.

Stepping into the secluded room, the far wall is lined with numerous shelves encumbered by ornate artifacts and hundreds of books in an organized beauty.

"Why do we have these?" Rhett asks, picking up a rusted metal box that he can tell was once red.

With a heavy sigh, Caspian pulls a second metal box from the far end, and with some exertion, pries the lid open, tossing the charred book back inside where it came from earlier that day.

Truth is subjective, is it not? Caspian ponders. *Sometimes all it needs is a little nudge.*

"With time, you will understand," Caspian says pressing the lid back on before lobbing the box towards his brother.

Catching it, feeling the weight of the artifact, Rhett asks himself if that man really had to die under the lie his brother propagated.

"That is how they get you," Caspian scowls, seeing the fallacy of thought Rhett is spiraling down. "Do not become attached. They're nothing more than workers."

"It wasn't his book though," Rhett states, his eyes glued on the closed container in his hands.

"Doesn't matter." Caspian steps forward, taking the box and shoving it back on the shelf. "It's what needed to be done. A small sacrifice of freedom and life for the bigger task at hand."

Freedom and life? Shoving his way past his brother, Rhett attempts to exit the chamber and create as much distance between the two of them as possible.

"This line of thought cannot continue, brother," Caspian says, hitting a button and closing off Rhett's escape. As the door seals the two inside, the floor abruptly moves, the entire room beginning its scraping descent down a concrete shaft.

"It's time for you to see for yourself how close we truly are," Caspian spits.

As the room continues deeper into the unknown, sounds of an elegant melody begin filling Rhett's ears.

"Also, you better shape up that attitude," Caspian drawls, clenching his jaw in an attempt to calm his nerves. "Sounds like Mother and Father are here."

Rhett's not intimidated by these repetitive scare tactics of Caspian's. However, without having any idea what the hell is going on, he finds it best to keep his mouth shut and analyze rather than feed his elder brother's insatiable ego.

Once the room hits ground level, the doors open, and rather than the elegant room they entered through, a desolate concrete tunnel awaits. With just enough light lining the walls in the blackened abyss to lead the way, an overwhelming stench wafting through the underground structure, and with the echoing symphony, Rhett can't help but have a sense of terrifying awe.

"This way," Caspian gestures forward and to a door off to the side. Opening it, light and melodic sound spill into the underground chamber, and stepping inside, Rhett again is overwhelmed by the hundreds of shelves, ledges, displays, and mantles. From books to schematics and antiques of every kind and design. Building blueprints. Scientific processes and formulas. Artistic renditions. Caspian doesn't give anything a second thought—he's been here countless times. Rhett on the other hand, is in sensory overload as he tries taking in as much information as possible. This room and the one they just came from serve as a stark reminder that no one person, family, or organization should have this much power and influence over information.

"You made it!" Sullivan declares, reaching towards Caspian, and while in their embrace, Sullivan notices the other one. "You really think you're ready for this?"

"Let's try and be grateful he's here!" Bella callously says as she wraps her plastic arms around Rhett more out of decorum than genuine affection.

Rhett's always been disturbed by his mother's artificial appearance. Combat is but a fractional reason for all her surgeries. The deeper motivation to Rhett is the fact that Bella is literally trying to symbolize her pursuit of immortality as she embodies the marriage of scientific engineering with the beauty nature intended.

Everyone dies, Bella. Everyone dies...

"Please. Sit," she says, a slight banshee giggle present in the back of her throat. "We have some things we need to discuss."

Taking their seats, Rhett immediately notes the missing family members.

"Where are Renn and Connor?"

"Renn..." Bella scoffs, turning and waltzing in the other direction.

"They're on another assignment," Sullivan says flatly.

Rhett's heard enough lies come out of his father's mouth to know when one is spoken, but like his brother's ego, this is something better left unfed.

"How do you perfect a nation?" Sullivan asks, looking to Rhett with his one good eye.

Rather than play his games, Rhett just shakes his head. "I don't know…"

"A brave new world, like that book you killed the man over. How would you create one?"

"It's why we're here, isn't it? It's why we have the experiments—to create the perfect society," Rhett says. He's never been explicitly briefed on what's going on in Area Thirty-Eight, but that doesn't mean he hasn't had access to the historical archives. Limited access and speculation are all he's ever had at his disposal.

"Correct," Sullivan intones, smiling at his son's intuition. "Harris Crowe, the founder of this great nation, he had the idea—the vision—but not the means." And then gesturing to both his wife and himself says, "That's where the Stone family comes in."

As his father reveals this little piece of information, Rhett realizes that his mother's fabricated appearance may be more than a skin-deep pursuit—it might be more than a self-indulged attempt to outlast the clock of mortality.

"We, as in, our family?" Rhett asks.

"That's the whole point of the Continental Union, the North American Union just being a facet of it." Sullivan nods in agreement. "It's why we have the guardians in the PPA. Ideology. If you control that, you control a nation. However, there is more to it than ideas, narrative, and political organization."

"And Mother's been at the forefront of your experiments," Rhett concludes.

"No, I am the result of the successful ones. As are you and Caspian. We have become literal perfections of the human body," she interjects, sitting a little taller. "Perfect the body and the mind will follow."

"Only *some* of our experiments."

"It's not that simple then," Rhett quietly states. It never is with his family.

"No, it is not. Some reject philosophy as if it was a virus in the bloodstream, which has made the attempts we've performed on your mother rather finite."

"And?" Rhett asks, now looking over to Caspian.

"It's not so much about perfecting one individual, but rather it must begin with a thorough cleansing of the human race. Only then will the individual person follow in both mind and body."

"Reconstruction then?" Rhett asks.

"Literal, collective perfection all the way down to the molecular level. That is why we are here in Area Thirty-Eight."

———⟫ ٠★٠ ⟪———

The Mill

"Rough night?"

Far from having the desire to make small, senseless talk, Jax lets out a grunt, rubbing the dark circles under his eyes.

Careful as to not draw attention from everyone at the Mill, Kip tentatively looks for any potential looming ears before whispering his next question.

"Ya thinking about—about the thing?"

Standing by his no-talking policy, Jax just nods his head.

"And?"

Jax shrugs.

"Yer friend…" Kip clarifies. "It's still happening then."

Kip's feelings about the whole situation remain unchanged. However, the more he thought last night, the more he realized that Jax has earned a level of trust from Kip. But the PPA? This is the one factor that Kip can't get over, and in all honesty, why should he? What makes this PPA friend of Jax's—who was kept from Kip's knowledge until twenty-four hours ago—such a reliable source? What kind of friend keeps a secret like that? This PPA *confidante* will more likely get them killed than help the two out.

"As far as I know," Jax finally says, breaking his vow of silence. "I really have no way of contacting him though. He just shows up when he has the time."

"Oh," Kip mumbles. So not only does this secret friend have murderous privileges, but he also has complete control of the communication situation. After a night's rest, one normally finds solutions to a problematic circumstance, and as Kip listens to Jax, other courses of action begin formulating in his mind.

"He knows where to find ya now that yer house is—?" Kip asks, miming the explosion and mayhem part.

"He should. He knows who you are," Jax says with another casual shrug.

"Say again—?" Kip begins, his frustration beyond comprehension. He knows nothing about this mystery PPA friend, but the mystery PPA friend knows him?

Uncomfortable with the amount of eyes Kip's reactions are getting, Jax tries shifting focus a little.

"Mari and Ann might be coming over tonight."

"Ya changing the subject?"

"Yeah, I am," Jax replies, exasperated that he even has to mention it, and before Kip gets any more riled up, Jax grabs him by the shoulder and pulls him to the side of the registration line. "Listen, you've got to trust me on this."

Kip defiantly bumps Jax's grip from off his coat.

"Please, Kip. It's not like I want either of us to be on that stage. If anyone will know what to do, it'll be him."

There is nothing ideal about any of this. Kip was briefed that none of this would be easy before being stationed in the district. It was a long time ago, but it's as vivid as it was the day it occurred. When one's life mission is laid out at that young of an age, how could it not be? Lisa ensured he'd be successful too. She was aware that she wasn't going to make it through to the end, so she prepared Kip accordingly. But, now that it's here, he has no idea what to do. Trust Jax and they could die. Don't do anything and they *will*.

"Fair 'nough," is all that Kip can manage, moving back into the shuffling line awaiting his turn to check in.

"Next," Renn Stone barks, slowly moving the line forward. "Name, Area number, and residency identification."

"Rouge, Area Thirty-Eight, residency ID two-two-zero," Jax quickly says before turning to leave her beautiful evil.

"Mr. Rouge," Renn says, stopping him in his tracks.

Kip can't help but chuckle at the ironic sight. Jax can place his trust in the PPA while still detesting the person whose family upholds their sadistic policies.

"Your record states that you've had a number of incidences where you've provoked guards, particularly during lunch this past week."

"It won't happen today, ma'am," he tells her.

"I hope not because if it does, you'll be in overnight lockup."

I'm lucky that I haven't been already, Jax thinks.

"Also, you've been transferred to the lumber transportation unit. Hopefully it mitigates your apparent *problem*."

That means he'll be with Kip. "Can I go now?"

"No," she replies, bringing Jax's frustration to a boiling point.

Battle of the control freaks! Kip is having the time of his life as he watches the sexual tension and drama unfold before his very eyes.

"Mr. Rouge, your pay will also be deducted for insubordination. You leave when I say you can."

Staring at her, gritting his teeth and exercising all the patience his frame can muster, Jax nods and acknowledges the plight.

"Next!" she yells out, giving the indirect command that now he may get out of her face.

"So, y'er with me," Kip chuckles, nudging Jax in the ribs. "Guess all that trouble ya've been causin' has paid off."

"They really know how to incentivize people around here, huh?"

"Since it's yer first day, I'll drive," Kip says as he jumps into one of the massive lumber trucks. "C'mon! Chop chop!"

Jax rolls his eyes because he knows that Kip is loving how he had his ass handed to him by Renn Stone. A little pedestal to stand on after Jax just rammed the Connor situation in his face.

"You know that I'm a better driver than you," Jax drawls as he makes his assent into the cabin.

"Yeah, but I'm already here making the checks. So, ya can secure the perimeter, yeah?"

"Damn it," Jax quietly curses before hopping back down.

Some hundred feet away, unknowing to the duo, stands Connor. As he watches Jax, he can't help but contemplate the coincidence of the events over the past hours. All this time, right under his nose. Growing up as an adopted Stone, he is still aware and educated on the early resistance and their attempt to undermine the Nine. The tactics used in the clandestine battles were iconic—not because of the sophistication of their methods but rather the simplicity. The Resistance almost won the conflict.

It was a war of pride and humility. While The Government was using advanced satellite technology to communicate and coordinate, their adversary had paper and pen. The Nine had thousands of troops, drones, and electronic weaponry at their disposal, but all the Resistance needed was an improvised EMP explosive to control the entire battlefield. To this day the absence of the Resistance's complexity is baffling. Jammed signals and a nonfunctional arsenal essentially crippled the PPA, because pen, paper, and mechanical engineering was all the defiant rebels needed. Inked ideas helped the Resistance remember that which they were writing in blood for the rising generations.

With this realization, the Nine tightened the leash overnight. In a sweeping decree, any form of written communication and technology not authorized by The Government was prohibited. Book burnings took place in the streets. Technology and possessions were confiscated with finesse and efficiency, and for the uncompliant, they too were burned and eliminated with that same aggressive elegance. In less than a month the decade-long war ended. History was not only the Resistance's link to the old world; it was also their lifeline to a new one. It was a glorious victory for the Nine, but as always, the enemy's spirit was not put down without a fight. In a single last effort, the Resistance utilized a series of protective metal boxes, hiding what surviving documents there were. They knew it wasn't going to help their generation win, but future posterities would hopefully benefit.

That was what Connor was taught anyway, and he speculates that details were shuffled around and omitted. That's how the Nine operate—limited and propagated information, compartmentalized so that one has just enough to accomplish a mission but not too much as to let the soldier think for themself. He's been raised under the constant reminder that although he is not a Stone by birth, he is a Stone at heart, making it his duty to put a stop to opposition. The Stones are the security for the future. Area Thirty-Eight is ground zero for the Resistance, and since being assigned here his entire mission has been this—his mission are these boxes. It's why he's gone for weeks on end. It's why he's never at the capital, and with a recent resurgence of these containers, he knows he is failing.

"You okay?" Renn asks, approaching from his flank.

"Just thinking. Don't you have somewhere to be?"

Renn chuckles. "I just finished checking everyone in. Where else do I *have* to be, huh?"

"You think that the Raiders came for the box?" he asks.

"You know they did," she says, glancing over to Jax in the distance and folding her arms in slight skepticism. "They didn't have an exact location, but why else would they come and attack a residential area?"

"Something just seems off about the whole thing," he muses, turning from watching to Jax to face his sister.

"How so?"

"Out of all the people to have a box it's him."

When she found out, Renn was enraged by Connor's decision to befriend a citizen. Then again, he's never really fit into the family—and not just because he's not blood. Renn senses that the reason goes deeper. Connor remembers more about his childhood than he discloses. Renn's done the math. Unlike Caspian and Connor, she and Rhett were born after the Founding, and although her elder brothers were young, they were old enough to have memories. Of what, she does not know. Caspian doesn't talk about it either out of shame or pride, she can't tell which. Connor though, if Renn had to guess, doesn't talk because he was happier then—because he hates life now.

"I've always kept your friendship with him a secret," she says. "But this—this is out of my control."

"Do you think they found out and framed him?"

"Mom and Dad? That's absurd." She says this but knows that it's not—that it's in fact a very real possibility. Renn's seen the room filled with those boxes. It'd be easy to take one and plant it in someone's residence and let the consequences unfold.

Giving a weak smile, Connor drapes an arm around his sister. "Something's not right—it's all out of place. Sullivan and Bella here, the Raiders, the box. All of it happening at the same time…"

"Talk with Jax tonight, and we'll go from there. Maybe this is a test to see if you'll do your duty."

Renn prays that he won't. She wouldn't.

"Maybe," Connor coldly states.

"By the way," Renn says before turning to attend to other duties, "he's staying at Kip's place. The attack the other day destroyed his house."

"Thanks," Connor says, again, in a cold, expressionless manner.

Renn wishes she could say more—wishes she could do more for her brother, but in the end, she leaves knowing that solitary contemplation is his only place of serenity. It's the only time she thinks he can remember happier days.

"That was kind of fun," Ann states as the group walks home from the Gathering.

"How the hell can ya say that?" Kip declares, shocking both Jax and Mari with his brash tone towards a kid.

Ann, however, is unfazed.

"No one died!" Ann says, sticking out her tongue, playfully punching his leg.

"Fair—that's fair!" Jax chimes, joining in, slugging the big oaf.

"She's allowed to hit me," Kip says, clearly irritated, and just to make sure his point is taken, tackles Jax to the cold ground, wrestling the kid into submission.

"How embarrassing!" Ann giggles and taunts.

Mari on the other hand just rolls her eyes. "Alright, tough guys. Get up!"

In this moment, Kip is struck with sudden brilliance. Yanking Jax to his feet, he makes eye contact with him, putting both on the same page. Normally Jax wouldn't go along with something so bold, but figures, what the hell. In a swift, coordinated effort, Jax leaps for Mari and Kip for Ann, where together the duo takes down the girls, assaulting them with a barrage of tickles. While Ann laughs and squirms, Mari fights like hell as if life and death are in the balance.

"Stop it!"

Jax ignores the warning and plea, foolishly continuing the onslaught on what he thinks is a defenseless woman.

"Stop!" she demands, her second warning shot giving him plenty of time to retreat, but when he doesn't, a swift kick to his groin is all that's needed to immediately end the fight.

"Geez, Mari," Jax says in a falsetto voice.

"Shit... I meant to hit your stomach." Rushing over to him curled on the ground, Mari unsuccessfully masks her laughter.

"She just killed him," Kip states.

"You think that's bad? You should've seen her last boyfriend when he didn't listen," Ann says, horrifying Kip the instant she does.

After a few agonizing moments writhing in pain, Jax gains enough composure to stand up.

"Lesson learned," he moans out.

"You caught me off guard..." Mari smiles apologetically, her laugh hiding any genuine remorse.

Mari then takes his face in her hands, squeezing his cheeks and giving her best puppy dog face. She does all this mockingly but quickly something more occurs as infatuation sets in. Without another word Mari's lips crash onto his, kissing Jax in a passionate embrace. Ann gasps almost as loud as Kip, and not knowing what else to do, Kip quickly covers the little girl's eyes, pushing her away from the romantic scene.

"It's about time!" Ann shouts, fighting against Kip's efforts to create privacy.

For a moment, the two simply brush their lips against each other's, but as time wins out, they begin to intertwine and dance their mouths together.

"How sweet," a creepy voice in the distance proclaims, cutting the passionate moment short, parting the two love birds.

Looking to the left, Jax sees four drunken PPA privates approach: one bald, one ugly, one short, and the last a lanky twig.

"You got her all warmed up for us!" the lanky one says, drool practically oozing from the corners of his mouth.

"In your dreams!" Mari says, her disgust apparent.

"He's not talking to you, bitch," the ugly one snarls, moving to slap her, but Jax instinctively shoots his arm out, blocking the blow.

"Whoa!" Kip shouts, rushing over and separating Mari from the four PPA creeps. "You guys better move yer asses outta here."

As if solving nuclear physics, the bald one cleverly says, "No."

The other three snicker, but all the retarded comment really accomplishes is signaling to Kip and Jax that Baldy is the leader.

"Now," Baldy begins, "while we're still being nice, get out of here and we'll forget any of this happened. When we're done, we'll walk her home for you, how about that?" He grimaces, placing his face an inch away from Jax's.

"No thanks," Jax replies, pushing Baldy back as he waves away the alcoholic stench from the soldier's breath.

"Your funeral," Baldy casually responds, taking a swing and hitting Jax in the side of his head.

On impulse, Kip shoves Mari back before ramming his forehead into the bridge of Ugly's nose, blood spurting down his face on impact. Jax, barely fazed by Baldy's wild punch, kicks him back and pulls Lanky to the ground, giving the skeleton a swift kick to the head. With Ugly on the ground grabbing his broken nose, Kip turns to Shorty, and grabbing him by the throat, effortlessly lifts him off his feet.

"I said, get outta of here."

"You're in so much trouble," Shorty defiantly rasps, grossly misjudging his current standing.

In response, Kip drops him to his knee before pummeling him into the frozen ground with half a dozen punches.

"Go, Kip!" Ann cheers, her mouth instantaneously covered by an embarrassed and scared Mari.

Upon seeing his three comrades on the ground, Baldy cowers backwards.

"You two are in so much trouble."

"See," Kip belly laughs, pointing to Shorty's unconscious heap. "That's exactly what yer friend said."

Attempting to scramble and run, Baldy is tripped up by his own panic, and Jax and Kip both casually drag him back to his fallen comrades.

In order to paint the proper picture, Jax picks up a brick from the gutter.

"If you breathe a word of this to your superiors, I'll bury this brick in your head. Am I clear?"

"Yeah!" Ann declares, stepping up to the scared PPA private before kicking him—well, in his privates.

"Hey!" Kip snatches Ann off her feet and throws the girl over his shoulder. "We need to get goin'."

"I know." Without warning, Jax smashes the rubble over the side of Baldy's head, before grabbing Mari's hand and disappearing into the night.

"How'd you two survive before you met Kip and me?" Jax asks, once at Mari and Ann's house.

Playfully insulted by the misogynistic question, she holds up her hand to halt any sort of other thought fallacy he might have.

"Hold up!" she begins. "One, I can handle myself just fine. I am rape free in Area Thirty-Eight all on my own, thank you very much. Second, the creeps didn't start bothering us until after we met you."

"I'm serious," Jax says, irritated. "Now's not the time to flirt."

"And so am I!" *If only he knew...*

Her former life's experience has gotten her and Ann this far, and how frustrating is it the second she finds a good guy—a great guy—the universe turns itself against her as if she hasn't properly atoned.

Recognizing and completely disliking the awkwardness, Kip lightens the mood. "Have the creeps always looked that funny?"

With a chuckle, Mari smiles first looking to Kip, and then Jax.

"I haven't been your biggest fan, Kip," Ann bluntly says, shocking everyone by the comment. "But you're cool." And as Kip tries to discern whether she gave him a compliment, character critique, or both, Ann throws her arms around him in a squeezing embrace.

"Hey," Kip says, picking her up. "Let's give them some privacy, yeah?"

Knowing that if any sort of vulnerability is going to come out, it'll be when Ann is out of sight, Jax turns to Mari and asks, "Are you okay?"

"I'm fine…"

She's not, but that's okay. Jax picks up on the tone, and rather than saying anything more, pulls her in, hooking her chin underneath his fingers so that they can finish the kiss the two were sharing moments ago.

―――ᾳ ᐧ★ᐧ ᾳ―――

"Where is he?" Renn asks. "It's been over an hour."

At a loss for words, Connor shrugs. Ironic; the one day it's imperative they talk is the one day Jax breaks curfew.

"He knows the penalties, right?"

"Yes, Renn," Connor sighs. "I'm just as anxious, but we have no choice but to wait. He'll be here…"

"Is that what anxious looks like to you?" she asks doubtfully, his stoic demeanor telling her a different story.

It's the nature of what Connor does. The killing of the Unapproved. The taking of their records—their history. All of it allows him to be numb to the angst Renn is discovering and being forced to meet in this moment. While she sees it as a privilege, it is Connor's curse to be able to stand here, his attention focused on apprehending another box.

In a violent moment that takes both Renn and Connor from their internal reflections, the front door bursts open, Jax charging in armed with a stick and Kip with a rock.

"Connor!" Jax sighs in relief, dropping the branch he was wielding. "You scared the shit out of—"

"Where is it?"

Startled by Connor's abrupt tone, Jax's thoughts begin fumbling. "Where's what—what are you talking about?"

Connor ignores all of this and simply repeats his question. "Where is it, Jax?"

"Connor, I have—" Jax begins, but stopping the second he sees Renn staring back at him.

"Shit..." Kip whispers. If this is the friend, then they're in serious trouble.

With Kip frozen in place, Jax easily pieces everything together. Connor knows what they found. He knows and he sold them out to the Stones.

Tired of asking, Connor moves and grabs Jax by the collar. "Where is it?!" he shouts, his grip cutting into Jax's shoulders.

"Back off!" Kip steps forward and is instantly forced back as Connor punches him in the sternum.

"This is the last time I'll ask. Where is it?!" He's irate and conflicted, but far from captivated by tunnel vision, his focus trained on the entire room. Pinning Jax against a wall with one hand and drawing his weapon with the other, Connor aims it right at Kip. "Drop 'em!"

Clearly outmatched, Kip reluctantly lets the rock and newly acquired knife fall from his grip.

"Connor..." Jax says in disbelief.

Kip was right. What fight is there when he's betrayed at this magnitude? Lost and stumbling for a fighting position, Jax looks over to Kip's fireplace.

"Finally," Renn sighs. Moving over to mantle, she scans briefly before moving the grate covering the bed of coals so she can peer up the chimney and retrieve the box. "Have you opened it?"

"Hell yes, we did!" Kip blares out.

Tossing Jax aside before moving over to Renn, Connor takes the box in his hands. The second he touches it, both the soldier and the human within him are at odds. Jax, a true friend and someone he cares deeply for, has come across something that is worthy of death under penalty of the Nine's law. Collecting these boxes—these pieces of war history from the Raiders—has been his mission for years. What is he without the mission? Where is his faith placed? The Nine? Their Government?

Flipping the clasps up, the rusty metal grinds as Connor lifts the lid. He's confiscated a lot of boxes, but never has he opened one. Why? Blind duty. These have been hidden; people keeping these from the Nine and their Government have died by his hands trying to protect them. One hundred and nineteen boxes—three hundred and sixty-three guardians—and after every single one he's collected, not once did the Stones allow him to see the fruits of his labors.

"Connor…" Renn slowly says. She sees the conflict within him. She trusts his judgment and would follow him onto any battlefield, but never has she been able to gauge where he stands with Sullivan, Bethany, and the agenda of the Nine. On the surface—even after everything he's done—Connor appears loyal to their orders, but Renn knows better than anyone that a piece of his soul dies each time he obeys them. The question is, does Connor still have any of his soul left?

"Connor?" Jax asks.

"Books?" Confused by this, Connor turns to Jax. "Did I kill for *books?*"

Desperately, he turns to his sister. "Renn?"

How does she let her brother know that every life he's taken has been over novels, writings, pamphlets, atlases, magazines, and digital recordings? She's seen, read, listened, watched, and archived every piece of material that Connor has blindly collected. It's why she hopes Connor will make the right call this time.

"Yes," is Renn's short answer.

"Why—why would they give an order like that?"

"Seriously?" Kip interjects. "You and all yer fancy schooling and ya can't even fathom an answer? Were ya not at the Gathering the other night?"

Connor stares blankly back at Kip.

"He's not authorized," Renn states.

"Why am I not surprised?" Kip blurts out. "Ya missed quite a show. Her brother," Kip sneers, jabbing a finger into Renn's shoulder, "killed a fella right on stage fer having a book. *One* book!" And moving over to Connor, Kip picks up each of their four. "So, ya gonna kill us or not?"

"He's my brother too," Connor sheepishly says.

"What?" Jax asks, getting lost further as details continue to pile.

"Sullivan's yer—that's fantastic!" Kip chuckles out. "So, yer the secret sibling who's been killing *my* brothers and sisters—*my* family while collecting *their* history."

Did Kip just admit—? Jax thinks. "You're a Raider?" he asks.

Kip ignores the naïve question, his gaze still burning into Connor's. "This is yer friend, Jax? The savior ya swore would know what to do? Look at him!"

Jax is, and all he sees is a confused, broken individual. Someone who went from a savage dog to a beaten pup in the blink of an eye—a foreign entity whom Jax has never met before.

Not surprised by Jax's lack of response and the soldier's thousand-yard stare, Kip slams each book back into their box before boldly returning to his former question. "Ya gonna kill us, or not?"

"No," Connor quietly says in a somber realization—the frivolity and trivial nature of his life following orders, having been used as a useful idiot.

Without even asking, Kip then snatches the box from Connor before handing it to Jax.

"Connor," Renn begins. "We don't have to kill them, but we need that box."

"There's nothing to talk about," he says.

Again, she'll follow him onto any battlefield. If this is the one he has chosen then they need to figure out a plan—they need to strategize. These workers have no large-scale combat or strategic experience.

"Seriously, Connor. We can't get ahead of ourselves..."

"Listen," Kip chimes in. "If yer not going to kill us, then get the hell out. Ya sure ain't doing any favors to anyone by staying here."

Shaking her head, Renn takes matters into her own hands. Connor will thank her later.

"Have you read any of the books?" she asks Jax.

"Haven't had time," Jax says, opening the box back up.

"Is that all you have?" she then asks.

"What the hell do ya want, Miss Stone?" Kip asks. "You two were supposed to be *the answer* to our problem here. And now one of you is in shock while the other one is complaining about a plan. The two of us should be dead, and since we're not, it's best for all our sakes if ya just walk yer pretty ass out that door—"

Unsheathing her knife, Renn charges Kip, backing him against the far wall, her knife shaving the stubble from underneath his chin.

"I am helping, you idiot," she growls. "If you couldn't tell, the two of us are on your side now, so shut up and let me get up to speed with what's happening before we *all* get killed."

"Ask away then," Kip chuckles, his ass having just been handed to him by Renn Stone yet again.

"What else is in the box?" she asks, sheathing her blade and turning to Jax.

"A bunch of these CD things, an audio device of some sort, a chain necklace and a letter," Jax says as he rummages inside the box.

"I think I can get ahold of some tech to read whatever is on those discs and play that mp3."

"M P what?" Kip asks.

"Don't worry about it." She waves his question away. "What's the letter say?"

Jax shrugs his shoulders. "I don't know. Haven't read it. All I know is that it's from my parents."

Connor's ears perk up at this. "Your parents are dead," he says.

"He speaks!" Kip cheers. "And no shit, genius."

Connor ignores Kip and stands, making his way over to the box. "What's your last name?"

Now Renn is the one in shock as she realizes the connection he's making. She's a fool for not seeing it earlier! Jax has checked in and out of her station at the Mill how many times, and only now is she realizing who he might be? It's buried deep in the history files—mentioned only once, but it's there, and she has read it.

"Connor," she says, "we really need to talk about this."

"I know…" he says, noticing her change in tone. "Can I read the letter?" he asks, turning to Jax.

"I guess," Jax slowly says. He never thought of the contents of the box as sacred or something that he owned. He just found it. But this letter—this is *his*. His name is on it and although he's wanted to read what it contains, apprehension has also held sway on him opening it.

"I've got to know," Connor desperately says, holding out his hand.

Looking into the soldier's eyes, Jax sees his friend, so he hands it over to Connor, who carefully opens it before hastily reading.

Shaking his head in disbelief, he shows the letter to Renn, and as she reads, she has the same reaction.

"It's him…" Renn whispers.

They know him. Jax thinks. *They know my dad.*

"Is there anything else besides the books and the letter?" Connor asks.

"Like what?"

"Anything. Have you flipped through the pages of the books? There could be more letters, documents, or even pictures stuffed inside."

"Really?" Kip asks in disbelief. Immediately turning to one of the books, he begins turning page after page in search of another mystery. To his and everyone else's surprise, out of the first book a folded document tumbles out and onto the floor. Dropping the book, Kip picks up the new discovery and begins the laborious process of unfolding it, and as he does, the paper doubles in size.

Rushing over, Jax scatters the contents of Kip's kitchen table, making room for the giant piece of paper. Once laid out, upon quick study they discover it to be an old map with only part of the North American Union depicted.

"What's Colorado?" Jax asks.

"Where'd you read that?" Renn asks.

"Right here, where Area Thirty-Eight should be." Jax points and sure enough, instead of Area Thirty-Eight, it says "Colorado," instead of Area Forty-Five, the word "Utah", and instead of the North American Union the map reads, "United States of America."

"Is this real?" Jax asks.

"Well," Renn begins, "it very well could be. I have read something about the United States, which this map clearly says it is, but I always thought they were somewhere overseas…"

"It is real," Connor finally says, the memories coming back to him.

"So, what do we do?" Kip asks.

"Nothing," Connor says. "We do nothing, because we can do nothing."

"Bullshit!" Kip shouts out. "There's always something we can do!"

"Not right now," Renn says, taking Connor's side. "We have to—"

"Are ya outta yer minds?" Kip yells, his voice continuing to rise. "We'll be dead in less than a week if we just sit around."

"That's not true," Connor refutes.

"Yeah? Tell that to the Raiders. Tell that to yer friends!"

"You're with the Raiders," Renn says. "Contact them!"

Kip shakes his head. "Ya guys are as dumb as those shit-colored uniforms y'all wear. The only reason the Raiders haven't taken over the Area yet is because they're a bunch of factions."

"A bunch of what?" Jax asks.

"Factions. Clans. Groups. It's not how it was supposed to work out, but the Raiders are fragmented and can't get their heads on straight. I come from *one* faction just to the West. One of dozens. Maybe even hundreds now. And I haven't been in contact with my own people for years. Half of them I'm willing to bet think I'm dead."

"Then what do we do?" Renn asks, her tone matching Kip's anxiety.

"We leave. Tonight!" Kip states.

"We can't just leave…" Jax says, his thoughts turning to Mari and Ann.

"We take Mari and Ann and leave. Head for the woods. Head for my faction."

Connor and Renn roll their eyes.

"Hey," Kip abruptly says. "If what ya read in that letter is as important as ya think it is, y'all know we can't stay."

"We have to," Renn says. "Connor and I can't just get up and leave either."

"I don't give two shits about y'all. I didn't trust ya before tonight, and I have no reason to start now. I promise, we'll be dead by week's end if we don't leave now!"

"Seventy-two hours," Connor says. "Give us seventy-two hours to prepare. That'll give you time—"

Kip doesn't listen to the rest. What need is there? Snarling at everyone's incompetence and apathy, Kip moves to the door and slams it behind him as he walks out into the night.

"He's going to be a problem," Renn whispers to Connor.

"I know…" *But what choice do we have?* he thinks.

───※★※───

The Mill

Kip never came back. Jax waited up for hours, praying the entire time that the guy didn't do something stupid, but after waking up in the same chair he was waiting in, Jax feared the worst for his friend and brother as the house was just as silent and empty this morning. Feeling as if there was no other choice and their hand was forced by Connor and

Renn, Jax made the decision to begin waiting out the next three days. With the Gathering as anyone's only source of news and information, Jax was also left with no choice of his own but to go about the day as if a world-shaping event wasn't on the horizon.

Not in the entry line nor at his shift or lunch, the entire day came and went without Kip. If he did end up doing something stupid, everyone would know. They'd know because they'd be forced to watch Kip participate in the Gathering. On the other hand, no news may be good news. If Kip ended up acting out last night and covered his tracks, Jax would be the only one to know that the guy pulled *something* off. In all reality, Kip probably did do something. So, it's not a matter of "if," but "what?"

"So, what we gonna do?" Kip's whispered question sounds.

Startled and deeply annoyed, Jax turns around.

"You son of a bitch…"

The guy Kip cut in front of ends up doing what Jax wants to and grabs Kip's collar to give him a piece of his mind. Not having the patience for decorum though, Kip yanks down and in on the guy's wrist, forcing him to his knees, and just before the guy can let out a yelp of pain, Kip slams a rock-hard closed fist into the man's jaw, turning him into a limp, unconscious noodle. Then, looking up, his visage asks if any of the other sheeple in line have complaints of their own. Nobody does and glance around as if not having seen a thing.

"Where the hell have you been?" Jax demands.

"What are we gonna do?" Kip repeats, still not having time for bullshit.

"She's right there," Jax says, pointing to Renn at the exiting desk.

"Where are the books?" Kip then asks as if no one is eavesdropping or noticing the pair's agitation.

"Shut up!" With a swift elbow to the stomach, Jax knocks the wind out of his dimwitted friend. A moment ago, he was worried sick. Now, he kind of wishes he were dead…

"Name, Area number, residency identification," Renn asks.

Jax pushes Kip forward.

"Next." Renn moves Kip along and Jax steps up.

"Rouge, Area Thirty-Eight, ID two-two-zero."

Having noticed the minor confrontation the two were having in line, with a single look Renn says: *Clean this up, or I will.* The last thing they need is to lose the edge they currently have.

"Next!"

"You're an idiot!" Jax kicks his friend in the butt and shoves him forward as they exit the Mill.

"You really think I care right now?" Kip defiantly states. "You have no idea how serious things have gotten."

"Like hell I don't! I'm the one who found the box—"

"And that's all you've done!" Kip shouts, the final word echoing throughout the alleyways of town. "You found a box, Jax! I've been in this fight for years—since before ya were even born."

"What do you mean before I was born?"

"I met yer dad, Jax… I know exactly who wrote that letter to ya."

"Wait, you what? Why haven't you said anything before?"

"I couldn't, but he was a big deal. He was my hero…" Kip somberly says. "I was fourteen, Jax. Fourteen when they recruited me, and fifteen when they assigned me to Lisa and you. I made a promise to her before she died that if Rouge's box was found, I'd do anything to get that back to the clan. So again, I don't give two shits what your box-finding ass has to say or think…"

What can he say to that? Jax thinks as his gaze shifts down to the frozen ground, feeling his finite perspective.

"So," Jax slowly begins, bringing his eyes up to meet Kip's, "what do we do?"

"We leave. Tonight."

"What about Mari and Ann?"

"We bring them with us," Kip says, shrugging his shoulders as if that's the dumbest question he's heard. "Let's go over, get them ready, and while you three go to the Gathering, I'll get things finalized at my place."

"The PPA will know you didn't scan into City Hall."

"So," another stoic shrug. "I haven't been doing what I should be all day, and we'll be long gone before they can go over the records and see the no-shows."

Connor and Renn never gave him a choice—they didn't even ask for his input. Their expertise far outweighs either of Jax or Kip's, but what good does all that knowledge do if you have blind spots and ignore the source of the intel? Jax thought that that's what Kip was doing after he left last night. It seemed as if everyone was taking matters into their own hands, and yes, Kip made it very apparent that Jax is relatively new to this whole combatant thing. It's been maybe twenty-four hours since Jax has thought of a life and purpose outside of The Government's purview, but upon finding that box, he's been pulled into the fight whether he wanted it or not. So, yes. His choice has value because his skin is in the game now.

"Alright," Jax says. "Let's go get Mari and Ann."

Surprised, but not showing it, Kip gives a wide, toothy grin.

It's going to be quite the mental shift for Mari, and especially Ann, which worries Jax. He's had time to process and feel a morsel of the situation's gravity. He's fought Raiders who were after what he possessed. He saw a man murdered for *holding* one book while he himself had four locked away. He's met with Renn Stone—he's seen that woman's resolve, and Kip—he's had Kip to lean on this whole time. But Mari, this is all being thrown at her and she's going to be expected to accept it and act on it in a matter of hours.

"Mari!" Jax yells, running up to the front door. "Mari!" he shouts, rapping on the door.

"Holy moly..." she says, whipping the door open with a glare. "What?"

"Can we come in?"

Recognizing the urgency in his tone, she invites the duo in without hesitation.

"Ya might want to sit down," Kip states as he watches her offer the two of them a seat.

"Where's Ann?" Jax asks.

"In the bathroom!" the little girl shouts out.

"Can ya hurry up?" Kip bellows out. There's a momentary pause before a whooshing flush breaks the heavy silence.

"Excuse me?" Ann asks, whipping the bathroom door open in a Mary-like fashion.

"Please," Kip says in an apologetic tone. "It's important..."

Like a flip of a light switch, Ann's attitude beams into a blissful demeanor as she runs forward, throwing her arms first around Kip and then Jax.

"I'm glad you're here," she says.

Not knowing what to do, Kip pats her head with a stiff hand before prying her away from Jax and placing her on the couch. Mari, still confused as to what all this tense urgency is for, throws her arms up at Jax.

"What is going on?"

Carefully, Jax looks to Kip for how to proceed. The overall situation and reasoning might be better explained with Kip's knowledge on the bigger picture, but on account that Mari and Ann have only started to trust Kip, the heavy news might better be delivered by Jax.

"We have to leave," Jax says.

"But you just got here!" Ann belts out, a giggle following her clever quip.

"What do you mean 'leave'?" Mari asks, seeing the depth to Jax's statement.

"We have to leave Area Thirty-Eight..."

"Leave the Area? Why—?"

Again, Jax looks to Kip for help.

"Mari," Kip begins, gently grabbing her shoulders. "It's not safe here, not anymore."

"For who? You two?" Mari tentatively asks.

Why does she have to be so difficult?

"For all of us. For you and Ann," Jax says, and then pushing Kip aside, places his own hands on her shoulders. "We found books, Mari. Four of them."

Her eyes widen and Jax can't tell if it's due to shock, excitement, horror, or all the above.

"Books?" she whispers.

"It's why there's been so many Raider attacks lately. It's why Caspian executed that man the other night. Everyone is looking for what we have. It's not safe for Kip and me anymore, and when we leave I wouldn't be surprised if they came after the two of you."

And just like that, despite all his frustration with Connor and Renn, he is now doing the same thing to Mari and Ann. The lack of free will in this situation is a lot. Ann feels it. Standing up from her seat, she makes her way over to Kip for a hug—for a sense of comfort from the overwhelming burden and sentiment. Mari, however, seems rather comfortable with the weight, and like she always has, surprises Jax with her response.

"When?"

"Tonight. After the Gathering," Kip says, and then giving Ann a squeeze, looks at her. "I know this is scary, but I need ya and yer older sister to pack up and get it ready to go so when ya get back we can all leave. Can ya do that?"

Looking first to Mari for some clarity, upon seeing her older sister nod, Ann turns back to Kip and gives him the same assurance.

"I'm not gonna be at the Gathering. I'll be packing some things, so don't worry if ya don't see me there, okay?"

Again, the little girl gives a courageous nod as Kip gives her one more squeezing hug. Before placing her down, he motions to say something else but can't. The big oaf chokes on a single tear in his eye as he rustles his hands through Ann's hair. "Love ya…" he mumbles, and then, before he further embarrasses himself, bolts out the front door.

Ann's eyes well up with tears of her own as she sees Kip leave, and neither Jax nor Mari can bear to watch her. Together, the pair pick up the confused girl in their arms. Ann's no stranger to change, but this time there's just something different happening that she can't put her finger on.

"We'll see him tonight after the Gathering," Mari reassures. "Right now, though, we need to get packed up and ready to go."

Nodding, wiping away her tears, Ann hops out of their arms and runs upstairs to do as Kip and Mari asked.

Mari would have to agree—there is something big happening and it scares the shit out of her. Their world just got turned upside down in a matter of minutes and their home—their home is no longer going to be anything but an abandoned building.

"You okay?" Jax asks, pulling Mari into his arms.

For too long has she been keeping herself locked inside her own heart. Tragedy and trauma does that to a person, and as she sits in his embrace, she can't help but be grateful that Jax is at least willing to pick the lock. Maybe that's where her outburst and kiss came from last night. She's had to be strong and lead all her life, so it's been nice to share that burden with another person.

"Yeah, I'm good," she says, pulling away just far enough to give him a kiss; not like the passionate spasm last night, but one of endearment—of understanding that she will go wherever he does as long as they go fearlessly together.

The Gathering

"Are you sure everything's ready?" Jax asks as they walk towards City Hall.

"We better be… You helped me!" Mari says, taking his hand into her own.

"I miss Kip…" Ann quietly says.

"He'll be waiting for us after the Gathering," Jax reassuringly whispers.

As their eyes are scanned upon entering the glass doors of City Hall, Jax takes Ann's hand before moving to their corner and awaiting the ceremony. Seconds quickly turn into minutes as the trio wait and watch the masses pack themselves in for their regularly scheduled indoctrination.

With the last worker making her way in, the doors hiss shut, signaling for the anthem to begin.

"He's not here!" Ann whispers.

"Ann," Mari says. "We already told you. After, okay?"

She knows what they said, but something's not right.

The Stone family seeps onto the stage, and like always, Rhett carries the offending Laborer. Renn follows, her neutral expression heavier than usual, and as the parents take their soft velvet seats, they begin sipping drinks in anticipation of the night's event. Dropping the masked worker to his knees, Rhett and Caspian flank the demoralized individual.

"This is the first time they've ever put a bag over someone's head," Mari whispers, making sure the comment doesn't find Ann's ears.

Looking at the masked man, Jax's gaze is drawn to the tattered clothing and his bruised, exposed chest from underneath. His knees, saturated with fresh, un-clotted blood, the detail signaling that they've either been torturing him all day, not allowing for the body to heal, or this man was recently caught and therefore quickly and viciously scourged. In either case, Jax concludes that maybe a bag is simply hiding a grotesque image.

"Look at him…" Jax whispers, letting Mari notice the same gory details.

"What is the law?!" Caspian solemnly states, his voice echoing throughout the somber room.

In unison, all recite the statute.

"One, no disrespectful acts towards the Nine or The Government which upholds them. Two, praise the Nine by our actions and with our words. Lastly, live, work, and if needs be die, so that the Nine and their Government may continue to prosper and bless."

"No disrespectful acts towards the Nine or The Government," Caspian says in a rather peaceful tone before he makes his way over to the masked victim. "Not really that hard to abide by…"

"Kip!" Ann whimpers, the bag being ripped from off his head.

Horrified at the sight, Jax shifts his gaze to Renn. They've always been safer together. Jax should never have let Kip leave his sight. Did she?

Did she turn him in? He reluctantly trusted her simply because Connor did—without question he had confidence in Renn Stone.

Her eyes said it all at the Mill. *Clean this up, or I will.*

Grabbing Jax's hand, Mari squeezes, her eyes fixated on the stage, fright and panic filling her lungs, stomach, and heart.

"KIP!" Ann shouts out over the crowd.

Looking up, his gashed and swollen face searches the corner of the masses where he instantly finds her standing between Mari and Jax.

Ann, Mari, and his friend—his brother.

Mari reaches for Ann's hand and pulls the girl into her arms, but Ann fights. Tears roll down her young cheeks, washing over Mari's hand that has found its way over the girl's mouth.

"You are getting worse!" Caspian shouts out, bringing the attention back to him and from the child. "We are on the road to perfection, and yet every day, we find more evidence that tells us that you are not ready! We have the books and letters that we find, the occasional workplace riots that we keep under control, but this man has reached a new level of chaos." Holding up a tiny paper symbol, too miniscule for anyone to see, he has its image projected onto the screens flanking the stage.

"What's that?" Mari asks Jax.

He saw it only briefly, but the stars and stripes are so distinct that Jax recognizes it as a symbol from the map.

"Treason!" Caspian says, continuing his monologue. Crouching down, he then turns to Kip, glaring at him as he does. "It is time that we help you understand the seriousness behind what you've done."

Staring past him, ignoring Caspian entirely, Kip focuses on the crowd. He focuses on his family. With one good eye staring at him, it's in that moment, Jax realizes a dark truth: that he'd give anything to be kneeling beside Kip—to be someone to comfort him. To be someone to *suffer with* him.

"Who are you looking for?" Caspian tauntingly asks Kip. "Your friends hate you, and your parents are dead, remember? Nobody is here for—"

Jerking his gaze from Mari, Ann, and Jax, Kip spits a mouthful of blood onto Caspian's bony face. Without hesitation, Rhett knocks Kip over with a swift kick in the ribs. Slowly standing, Caspian chuckles before in an outburst of rage, he kicks Kip repeatedly—the stomach, his face, groin, and wherever Caspian can find a suitable place for a steel toed boot.

"Kip," Ann again whimpers, burying her face into Jax's hip. All she wanted to do was tell Kip about the cute boy she met today at the market. She didn't want to leave home. She didn't want to be a grownup and learn about all these grownup problems… Over and over, the sound of boot meeting flesh and bone matches the rhythmic falling of Ann's trickling cry, every deep thud causing Ann to squeeze Jax a little tighter until finally, the last kick is heard.

"Disrespect will not be tolerated," Caspian says out of breath, and while wiping his face clean, spits onto the back of Kip's head. Kip is surprisingly still conscious as Rhett moves him back to his knees. His head only hangs for a moment, but that is all the time he needs to find the strength to lift it back up, holding it higher than Caspian will ever be able to reach.

"Do something, Jackie," Ann begs.

What? Jax thinks. Never has he felt more hopeless than now. All he can manage is to place his hand on Ann's soft brown hair and hold her close, trying, but failing to comfort her broken heart.

"This man," Caspian announces, holding up the tiny American flag, "was found with the mark of treason this morning. And a book!"

Kip continues to hold his head high, despite the obvious lie.

"Pick him up," Caspian orders, shaking his head and pulling out a gun. "Nothing we do seems to work on you people."

Rhett, obeying without question, picks Kip up, standing him on his feet before a quick aim and shot sounds from Caspian's firearm. The sound reverberates off the glass walls and in a violent burst, Kip's right knee opens, instantly dropping him to the stage in an excruciating cry.

"Pick him up," Caspian again orders.

Rhett lifts Kip up yet again, only this time with slight reluctance. Limply standing, Kip faces Caspian before another shot is fired, opening Kip's left knee and dropping him back onto the stage.

"Pick him up," Caspian orders for a third time.

Rhett looks at Caspian, hesitating to obey his brother this time.

"Pick. Him. Up!" Caspian quietly roars.

Rhett obeys. Lifting for a third time, Kip is able to stand, but only long enough to cry out in pain before falling back to the stage.

"Pick him up."

"Caspian," Rhett whispers. "He can't stand."

"Up!" Caspian yells.

Defying the order, Rhett steps to the side.

"Do it," Caspian calmly says, pointing his gun at his brother, forcing Rhett to attempt the feat where again, Kip falls to the stage moaning in pain.

"Pick—!"

"No!" Rhett cuts him off.

Holstering his weapon, Caspian moves towards Kip, and although significantly smaller than Rhett, Caspian lifts Kip up with absolute ease.

"He can," Caspian says, kicking Kip's knees back, locking them in place with two distinct echoing pops. "Hold him!"

Rhett does as he's told, keeping Kip balanced as best he can.

"Caspian? Son?" Sullivan gives his wife his drink, stands from his chair, and walks towards his eldest. The whispering is brief, but with a simple nod, Sullivan Stone looks at the audience, and then to Kip with his single eye before turning to sit back with his wife.

Slapping the American flag to Kip's chest, Caspian slowly moves behind him. Breathing calmly, he watches the movement of the back of Kip's head, finding exactly where to shoot.

"For the Nine."

And without another sound, Caspian pulls the trigger.

Jax,

Son, we hope you are the one to find this box, but whoever does, we hope the contents will be an inspiration. It's not much, but it is all that's survived the genocide.

Life is not what it used to be. When you read this, you will not have the freedoms we once had but now have lost. Where it was once acceptable and admired to speak your mind, you'll die if you do. There was once harmony in differing ideologies, but opposing ideas are no longer approved—also punishable by death.

Death finds so many these days, and the future doesn't look any brighter. As you very well know, life is hard, and despite what you believe—who and what've you've lost—there is light out there to be seen. No matter how dark the shadows may be, they are proof of a shining light. Don't give up, son. Along with many other good virtues, there is fight in your blood.

We love you—we always will. The pride that we have for you is as great as the things you are meant for. We hope you find value in what we have left behind.

Remember to never forget.

It has been said that "we would be unworthy sons if we did not have the spirit and strength to retain in ink what they wrote in blood."

Find a legacy to follow while creating your own.

With the deepest love parents can have,
Mica and Aila Rouge

II

Amidst Violent Chaos

EIGHT

The Pentagon
September 11, 2036

"Mr. Carter, do you have an explanation?" the head councilman asks.

Since the founding of the Minutemen Division, they have been looking for fallacies and cracks within the organizational structure. They've been unreasonable in their scrutiny and have been overtly subverting every one of Carter's efforts, all because they never believed.

With the news headline beaming from his tablet, Carter gives the only response he can. "What defines bravery?" he simply questions.

"This is not the time for—" the head councilman begins.

"Heroic action despite flaw, weakness, or fear."

"Your point?" another asks on the council.

"My point is that those we have selected as a part of this program are not perfect—they're not the 'cream of the crop,'" Carter finger quotes this part. "They have their flaws, and yet they act for the good of this country."

"Mr. Carter," the head councilman begins again. "What we're talking about is merit versus outcome, and the fact of the matter is, a building collapsed because of Mr. Rouge's actions."

The headline makes Carter more than furious. The whole point is for the Division to circumvent conventional rules of engagement. However, he can't let loose his fury. Not right now anyway. For now, he'll simply push the obvious. He is far from enthusiastic about Mica's approach, but a good soldier adapts and overcomes, accomplishing the mission by any means necessary. The council has provided little to no operational support, and if Carter's hand is going to be forced like this, he sides with the results his soldiers get.

"Yes, but no one was killed, *and* the primary objective was met—the local Ordean cell was stopped. This Division was set up to expose and cut the throats of the enemies of our nation and more specifically this Fourth Reich—"

"Carter!" The fury unprofessionally hissing from the councilman's mouth. "Citizens are calling members of the Division vigilantes. That is not the business we are in, and what will happen if Mr. Rouge, or any other agent is compromised? Reputations are at stake."

Last time he checked, the court of public opinion is mob rule, and luckily for them, they're siding with the Division, but even if they weren't, who the hell cares what they think just so long as the mission is accomplished? This is what infuriates Carter with politics and the giant PR magnifying glass people like this use. They care more about image than results—political aesthetics than patriotic restoration.

"That won't happen. I can assure you," Carter says, holding his tongue with the direct approach.

"Can you? Your agents have been shedding unnecessary light on the program."

"A single agent," Carter corrects. "Mr. Rouge has acted alone in every one of these situations you are fixated on."

Eyeing Carter, the head councilman abruptly changes gears. "How is your investigation going?" he asks, flipping open a crammed manila folder.

"It's ongoing," Carter says, unsurprised. He hoped it wouldn't come to this, but he's prepared for the contingency, nonetheless.

"Division Agent Trax cannot carry out his duties properly without that key."

"I am very well aware of that, but if the Ordeans had it, we would have been compromised already."

"You don't know that, and frankly, that is not the issue."

"It sounds like it is," Carter snorts.

Through a forced, unnatural smile, the councilman states his ultimatum. "The progress you've yielded is not sufficient to what we have put into its expansion."

"What are you saying?"

"You're operating at a deficit. If there is no improvement in two months' time, we will terminate the Minutemen Division and other avenues will be pursued."

Since the day he stepped foot into Langley, Carter's seen both operatives and officials alike get cold feet. As detrimental as the past is, people are more comfortable with reverting to that than pursuing an unprecedented future. In an on-demand world, patience is in short supply, and as they say, the vision of Rome was not built in a day. Neither was this nation. Missions *never* go as planned. The moment the first bullet is fired, tactics evolve and any soldier who's had their boots on the ground knows this. Politicians, lawyers, and academics alike don't—and from Carter's experience—never will.

With nothing to lose, Carter stands to give his final statement.

"There is a constant debate as to what the real motives behind Lincoln's Emancipation Proclamation were. Some say he hated slavery all along and it was always his plan. Others argue that it was a strategic move to bring the Union back together through military force. Even if Lincoln abolished slavery solely for strategic purposes rather than a moral obligation, it is clear by the time he was re-elected, he found slavery to be an abomination. Although the Civil War *may* have begun to preserve the Union, it ended with the liberation of *all* slaves. How often do we start something knowing what the middle and end results are going to be?"

"You have made a mistake by creating a false correlation between the past and the present, Mr. Carter," the head councilman shouts, slamming the dossier down. "And you have made an even bigger mistake by presenting it here—"

"Then why don't you tell me what you truly expected the Division to accomplish, because it'd be asinine to expect results like the ones I clearly have," Carter begins, stepping forward.

"Sit down!" the head councilman yells, rapping his gavel on the table.

"No." Carter ignores the order. "Enlighten me. How has the successes of one unorthodox agent brought reason to cut funding to the most efficient and successful program this government has brought into law? Please. Explain!"

"That is enough!"

Scoffing, Carter answers his own question. "Just because you have lacked the capability of micromanaging every part of this operation, that does not mean results cannot and are not made!"

"There will be order in here!" he shouts, breaking his gavel into two.

Carter does not sit, nor is he finished. "You're all hypocrites, not patriots—"

"I said that is enough."

"American lives have been saved. Children have lived to see their families again, and parents are better able to raise their kids in security because of what my team is doing." And before he can listen to any more of their bureaucratic reprimand, Carter shakes his head and turns to walk out.

"We have not finished debriefing you!"

"Go to hell!" And with that, Carter exits and slams the door behind him.

With clear profanity being muffled behind the thick oak door, Lisa Rodgers looks up with a giant smile. There are only two things that can change Carter's cool, tempered demeanor into the hothead he is right now: bureaucrats and stupid people. Often, the two overlap.

"Went well?" she asks, handing him a fresh cup of coffee.

"Walk with me?" Carter asks, grabbing the much-needed drink.

"What'd they say?" she asks. "We in the green?"

"We're not even out of the red," Carter scoffs. That's not what needs to be the focus though. If they don't find that key, the Division's funding is the least of their worries. "Where is that key, Lisa?"

"Is that what they were giving you trouble over?"

Carter shrugs. "In part. Please tell me you have a lead…"

"We do, actually."

Carter stops dead in his tracks. "And?"

"And." She hesitates, trying to figure out the best way to put it. "And you're going to be pissed."

———✦———

Boston

"Save the USA!"

"No more cults!"

"Where is your God now?"

Never-ending protests. This isn't necessarily a bad thing, but so many opinions these days are not backed with any sort of legitimate facts; which if you think about it, yes, it is a bad thing. Emotion is the main tenet of argument and the deeper the opinion, the more flamboyant the emotional drownings of reason are. But hey, that's an unintended consequence of the First Amendment protection guarantee: stupid ideas are allowed to be heard. Validation of said moronic opinions—that is an entirely different discussion, and one few are willing to have.

Aila works her way through the atheist, scientific, and political worshippers, all of whom profess brainwashing of others without seeing the irony of the Critical Theory propaganda they fill their ears with. First off, don't these people have jobs? Even if they don't, the most effective use of their time is shouting en masse? Secondly, yeah, they have the right, but what good is cynicism? Everyone knows Congress is doing jack squat. The private sector has always been more efficient at building. Everybody also now knows about the Children of the Ordean Reich and their efforts to undermine the constitutional republic and dismantle the democratic processes that allow these idiots to be out here in the first place. A little less talk and more action from the everyday citizen would go a long way—after all, faith without works is dead. Their protest is just organized speech with no clout, making it a moot effort. No point in quoting scripture to these people though. Anybody who does just gets eaten alive like every other minority throughout history.

Finally making it through the suffocating crowd, nearly being slammed up against the giant glass window of Ned's Sandwich Spot, Aila sees him. Forgetting the claustrophobic conditions of the unhygienic sweaty protesters, her whole world stops and pinpoints this moment. With Mica's pleasing grin melting her heart, he no doubt is reading the article said to "reshape history." Although the story focuses more on debunking the mysterious vigilante known as the "American Devil"—a less than obvious rip-off of comic books—that isn't what she thought about when reading it herself through the lens of her journalism expertise.

No photo has been taken of him. No one was killed in the event, dozens were rescued, and it appears that the Ordeans have been outmatched yet again. Reading between the lines, the man's heart is strong, immense, and will only continue to grow as he acts for the citizens of this nation. In a poor attempt, Aila tries rubbing away the rose tint that her blushing cheeks have created upon thinking of the devilish American, but it only makes the blush more prominent as she steps into the restaurant.

"What are you smiling at, Mr. Rouge?" she asks, hoping he doesn't notice her schoolgirl infatuation.

"It's just good to see someone trying to make a difference," he casually says, looking up to Aila. "And"—he holds up the article to show her the headlining photo— "no one knows what he looks like. All they have is his trademarked 'USA' tagged on a wall. That and the victims swearing that a demon attacked them."

Stuffing the article into his journal and then into his backpack, Mica's grin remains plastered on his face. Where most would see narcissism, she just sees a guy who's proud of a noble achievement. Granted, it may be getting to his head a little.

"Well, I heard that a girl got a photo of him one time. She thought the horns on his mask were kind of cute..."

Mica's beaming smile is wiped off his face, and in turn, is put onto hers. Nothing like humbling her man—well, a man. One she hopes will be hers...

"I'm pretty sure that he insisted that she properly dispose of it," Mica says.

"And she did. No digital copies, only a single hard copy. Rumor has it those were her exact terms."

"Did you ever think that he was still a rookie when she got that photo?"

"Excuses are just like armpits. Everyone has them and they all stink," Aila says, her smile getting bigger as she watches him squirm. All women are sadistic to one extent or another, are they not?

Mica, mocking her with a set of annoying puppet hands, completely misses a chip Aila throws his way, the salty snack poking him in the eye.

"Real mature..." Mica laughs. Taking a bite of his sandwich, Mica nearly spits out his food with a thought he's been mulling over. "Have you thought about—?"

"Just a second," Aila cuts him off and drops her chin to her chest, bowing her head before muttering a prayer under her breath.

"Not here..." Mica mutters, checking over his shoulder with a ready excuse for anyone shooting them a weird look. However, an amusing idea comes to him, and as he chucks a chip of his own at Aila's bowed head, she manages to block the incoming projectile with a flick of her wrist. Lifting her gaze a moment later, she can't help the smug look that creeps across her face.

"Hiyah!" she whispers.

"Please! How'd you do that?" Mica rolls his eyes and picks up the chip she just swatted down, tossing it a second time. Attempting to repeat the ninja feat, she fails miserably as it falls right down her shirt.

"We walk by faith, not by sight," she mumbles, weaseling the chip out before popping it in her mouth. "Anyway, what were you saying?"

"Have you thought any more about that key?" he asks.

"Kind of," she says with a shrug and bite of her own sandwich, glancing at the chain hanging around his neck. Following the connecting links to his chest, her thoughts quickly divert from the key to his broad chest that it hangs in front of...

"I'm starting to think that it's not linked to the Ordeans," she blurts out.

He scratches his bare chin. Not having his beard is still a foreign experience, but in all honesty, shaving has been the most logical thing to do. Trends come and go, and right now beards are obsolete by today's aesthetic standards, and with him being a masked hero, the risk outweighs the discomfort of his itchy neck.

"But they had it on them that night."

"Maybe they stole it."

"From who? The Division didn't exist then."

"Says who?" Aila asks lowering her voice. "Who says you were their first recruit?"

Not buying it, Mica shuts down the conversation as people begin filling in at an exponential rate. Apparently, protestors got to have their union-sanctioned lunch break too...

"Maybe we should talk about this somewhere else."

Aila reluctantly concedes. It's not that the two of them have nothing else to talk about, but it's nice to see progress with Mica. He never explicitly says it, but he mourns Kim every time they bring up topics like this. She sees the change mostly when talking about the Minutemen Division. His motives used to be about revenge, but as time has gone on—as they've talked through the past—it's become clear that Kim's tragic death has blessed many lives. It was a spark over a puddle of gasoline.

That's the radical nature that many subscribe Christianity to these days, simply because these people of faith work to make sense of life's madness, finding God's hand in sorrow. Disregard the Muslim extremists who actually believe that a chauvinist's wet dream will be their reality if they bomb infidels to kingdom come. Ignore the irony of radical atheists as they worship powerful governments or themselves rather than a power that supersedes man's reach, giving these finite groups the ability to alter the liberty of humankind. Yes, there are radical Christian sects, but no, the moderate white Christians are specifically the problem of the century. People are so terrified of a tyrannical theocracy that they don't realize one is being created right before their eyes as they pay homage and their respective tithes to the State.

"You still up for tonight?" Mica asks her, taking the last bite of his turkey-swiss sandwich.

Before she answers, her phone vibrates, and she holds up a finger. "Uncle Carter!" she smiles and blurts out the name, freezing Mica to his core.

He's known for a while now that Aila is Carter's niece, and upon Mica learning that Carter knew that *he knew* that Carter knew he was hanging out with said niece, the anxiety from the circular logic has only grown. The slew of issues really began when he originally approached Carter about the photograph situation. He couldn't hide it—it was all caught on the security footage that the Division pulled to doctor up before putting it back in the system. That's when Carter made it very clear of the thin ice Mica is now on, putting an obvious underlying sentiment at play here. Having never mentioned his boss by name, Aila is blissfully unaware of this in-the-head drama Mica is constantly engaging in. All she knows about Mica's superior is that the guy is a power-hungry, anal-retentive prick.

There's always the possibility that parental love will override Carter's senses and he'll order Mica to leave Aila alone. She's Carter's only living relative and he, hers. The tragic death of parents or a sibling is never an easy thing. Mica knows this better than most, but for some reason Aila has always looked on death with optimism and hope. Instead of going into a destructive shell, she holds her head up. She never became weak, using her circumstance as an excuse to give up or do something stupid—unlike Carter and Mica, both of whom let emotions get the better of them.

So, one would think that this maze of clandestine information would be where Mica's anxiety was thriving, but it's not. His freakout comes from the worry that his boss will discover the secret key. He's been hesitant to tell Carter about it and he's not sure as to why. The fact that he found it the same night Carter approached him may be coincidence, but it also might not be, so, rather than deal with that conversation, Mica just follows the deep feeling in his gut and keeps quiet about it.

"Uh huh," she says with a pause, sending the most natural wink Mica's way, his heart giving a surprising flutter. "No, I'm just at lunch with Mica."

"Tell him I say hi," Mica says, forcing his enthusiasm.

Another wink with another flutter.

"Okay, I'll do that. I love you too. Oh, by the way, he says 'hi'... Okay, bye," she says, hitting the end key before looking up with a wide grin. It's been a long time since she's felt this happy. She has her good days and her bad ones, like everyone, but since her parents—since that time, she's never felt true joy until maybe today in this sandwich shop. "Of course I am still up for tonight," she exclaims. "I've been looking forward to it all week!"

Mica's been booked literally every day this past month, taunting the newspaper and saving lives, so they haven't been able to simply hang out. She constantly must tell herself that it's part of the process. Romance or not, she must take a step at a time—here a little, there a little. He likes spending time with her, and for now, that's enough.

"You're in charge of the movie. Snacks are all mine!"

"Deal," Mica says, giving her a wink of his own, and like him, her heart dances. Checking his watch, Mica's eyes nearly pop out of his head. "Crap!"

"That thing with the dude, right?"

"I'll see you tonight." Darting from the diner and onto the street, he almost gets hit by an erratic taxi making its way through the mostly peaceful protest.

"Don't go dying on me now, you devil," Aila whispers.

Glancing down at her uneaten sandwich, she sees that Mica left his backpack, unzipped with the top of his dark blue journal peeking out from inside. He's always religiously scribbling away in that thing. She asked him about it one time and all he told her was that ever since Kim's death, he's kept one. That's it. Who knows what he writes or why. Mica might not even know the reason in all honesty, but with fate tempting her to open it up and answer her questions, part of her is terrified by the potential darkness of the man she's falling in love with. Belief in God's hand in our lives yields the natural realization of the Devil's. In the end though, if she hopes to start a relationship with him, trust must be there, darkness or not.

Instead of giving in, she shoots him a quick text. *Hey, you forgot your bag. I'll bring it tonight.*

A split second later she gets a reply. *Thanks, you're the BEST!*

As she reads the words he sent her, the roar of Mica's beefy motorcycle quickly erupts, zooming past Ned's Sandwich Spot, clipping the leg of one of the more aggressive protesters.

"They had it coming," he'd say, shrugging his broad, meaty, rock-hard shoulders at the senseless quarry...

Damn, she thinks. *I am head over heels for this man.*

White's Campaign Office

If Mica's being honest with himself, there is a future with Aila. Now whether it's intimate or not he has yet to figure out, but as of right now, he absolutely loves Aila's friendship. It comes down to trust, and not from her, but from himself. He doesn't know what he's ready for in life, let alone in a relationship. Despite it being out of character, it's why he hasn't made any rash moves with her. His relationship with Kim and every relationship before her was fiery to say the least. However, when she died, so did the old Mica.

"You're late," a boyish man arrogantly announces.

Walking into the stuffy office, Mica's completely amazed the room isn't inside an American history museum. The bookshelves don't have the pseudo-wear that franchised designers give new furniture and could very well be decades old. There's a direct correlation to quality and mass, and Mica is willing to bet that if he had to move one that their authenticity would be proved by their weight. Frames line the walls wherever a book-burdened shelf isn't and are filled with torn-out pages from journals, historical original black and white photos, and signed documents from what Mica can only imagine are the nation's founding. Even the desks and chairs arranged around the room have a classic look that complements the interns, employees, and volunteers who all seem to have gotten the dress code memo—donning suspenders, dresses, and attire fitting the ambiance of the 1990s. Thank goodness though, that the only things that don't look like they were crafted in 1993 are the computers and technology that support the functions of the office.

"Did you hear me?" the boy-man asks, indirectly repeating his disapproval of Mica's lack of punctuality.

"My bad," is all Mica says as he continues standing in awe at the decor.

"Governor White does not tolerate these kinds of things."

Mica smirks as he looks at the kid trying to be a responsible adult.

"Tardiness. That's what you want to say, isn't it?" Mica says with a raised eyebrow as the man-child just scowls. Then slapping the kid on the shoulder, Mica digs into the ego a little deeper. "Chill out, this isn't student body president we're campaigning for."

"That's exactly my point," he retorts, folding his arms across his chest.

"Do you have any gold stickers by chance?" Mica asks. "Star ones are best."

This question throws the kid for a loop as he responds. "Why?"

"Don't worry about it," Mica chuckles. The joke would be beyond this kid.

"The meeting has already started," the man-child says, having nothing more to contribute to Mica's amusement as he points to an office off to his right. "Be sure to keep quiet as you enter."

"I'll tiptoe." Like he did in grade school, Mica obnoxiously creeps towards the office. The bit backfires on him as these doors are also decades old, and as Mica opens the conference room door, his entrance is announced by its loud screeching hinges. Immediately, Mica tries to quiet the noise by opening it slower, but it only heightens the pitch.

"Ah, Mr. Rouge. Nice of you to join us."

"Thank you," Mica tentatively replies, stepping inside.

Governor White, former tight end for New England Patriots turned beefy politician holds out his thick arm. "If you can find one, have a seat." The conference room is packed with a fuggy atmosphere, and rather than climbing through the huddled employees to the empty seat on the opposite wall, Mica stands where he is.

"Sorry I'm late."

"Not a problem. We were just discussing the media cycle," the governor says, his rough hand clicking the remote and bringing up the all-too-familiar headline. There is something rather entertaining about watching a man as large as Governor White stand and give a PowerPoint, Mica thinks. Like a bear in a shirt and tie.

"Who is this?" White asks. "The media is stumped by this vigilante, and so are the police! But are we? I want to pose the same question to you that this article is: Who is the American Devil?"

The room is filled with an awkward silence which pleases Mica. Despite all the attempts to unmask his identity, nobody knows who he is!

"That was not a rhetorical question," White states, folding his fingers while he continues to wait, ignoring a deep, dark shaking urge.

If there is a single drop of alcohol within smelling distance, his hands shake, the aroma being second nature to him. Many times has he considered prohibiting drinking on the job, but in today's political climate, you might as well hope for wings to sprout from your back as you jump off a building.

A timid young intern raises her hand, bringing White's mind back to reality.

"I think it's a man, and I think it's rather obvious," she claims, hushed whisperings emerging at the *sexist* comment.

"Okay…" White is happy that someone at least speculated. "Any other conclusions out there?"

A rather proper and prestigious-looking woman immediately shoots her hand into the air, clearly having an important clarification. "Why do you think it's a man?"

Mica shakes his head at the ridiculous, postmodern route she is bound to take this discussion. Semantics and minutiae are what they are about to argue over.

The timid intern makes her stand. "For starters, most interpretations of the Devil are masculine and male."

When you look at the world through a fundamentally flawed lens, you'll never have truth revealed to you—and yes, there is such a thing as objective truth. There is also the argument that all points of views are flawed as the human condition lays out. We are all susceptible to fallacy. However, the systems of modernity allow us to find truth easier than ever before, and the critical theories that seek to uproot that are viruses, not remedies to human progress.

Appalled by such a preposterously broad conclusion, the stickler woman shouts out as if her world view is common sense, "The Book of Genesis likens the Devil to a snake, which is a common symbol for *woman* due to its venomous nature."

Pretty sure she pulled that one out of her ass, Mica thinks. Even if it was true, why is she so desperately wanting the term "devil" to be associated with women?

The timid intern holds up her finger, her fortitude shocking everyone. "If you'd let me finish, bruises the size of a man's fist have been found on the criminals in question. Not to mention the reports and testimonies from said criminals."

"That's rather misogynistic…"

"Oh my!" Mica can't help it anymore. "Get off your high horse, lady!"

"Excuse me?!"

"You really think that any of these details matter?" he then asks before the quiet clamoring in the room begins to roar.

White's shaking hands begin vibrating, staying firmly clenched. The longer this contention goes on, the more irritated he becomes and the stronger the damn withdrawals grow. He can handle the Marxist-progressive perspectives all day—his tough skin makes the opinions of useful idiots like water off a rock. It's why he's hired as diverse a people as possible. If he's going to stick to the water analogy, White is also aware that all viewpoints have value—that truth coupled with patience will cut through the most embedded of false ideologies like a stream in a canyon. At the end of the day though, tolerance is extremely hard to come by for him, and as he thinks of his daughter Tiffany, the governor wills himself to block out the alcoholic aroma, the argument over political correctness, and refocus on the task at hand.

"Okay, shut up!" his shout the release of tension he needed, the room immediately obeying the command. "It was a simple question that nobody apparently knows the answer to... I am the American Devil!"

As White waits for that to sink in, one man bursts out in laughter.

"Sir, you obviously could do some damage, but frankly, a man was seen at the crime scene, not a bear!"

"You are an American Devil," White bellows out, cutting off any laughter the man's joke may have stirred.

The man abruptly clamps his mouth shut in confusion.

"We are all American Devils," White concludes. "Men and women are both responsible for this nation, viciously fighting America's enemies."

"But sir, we're talking about an individual—" the pompous woman says.

"Wrong," Governor White bluntly shouts. "This character—this vigilante, whatever you want to call *him*—he gets what I'm trying to tell you people. Put the fear of God into those seeking to destroy this country."

Mica almost raises his hand to protest the erroneous claim but resists the unwise impulse. *It was just a simple publicity stunt*, he thinks. Carter gave him the mask and he just rolled with it. Marketing 101.

"And since the United States of America is its fighting citizens," White continues, standing as he does, "that is exactly how we will approach our campaign for the presidency—we appeal to the American people."

The room explodes in another uproar of dissent and grievance.

"The people do not elect you; Congress does!"

"And the people elect them!" White roars back at the pending riot. He's never had a temper, not in the Corps and not even when he drank, but this bureaucratic bullshit just might change that. "If we appeal to them, Congress will have no choice but to listen and vote with them. If Congress is filled with the men and women that I know it is, they will vote for me out of fear of losing their seat of power."

"That's rather idealistic, sir," the timid lady states. "Members of Congress are in office until they die. *Or...*" she slowly states, given her uncertainty with even this option, "in the rare chance they give up their seat of their own free will and choice."

"The people can remove them from office," White simply states.

Raised eyebrows and uncomfortable looks scatter across the packed conference room, vaguely recalling the history lesson of a Stanley Braithsworth. For the better or worse it's what the media does best—sways the court of popular opinion. Not only do they have the uncanny ability to do so, but they are also incentivized through grants, tax write-offs, and a dozen other programs and loopholes the federal government provides them.

Taking in a deep breath, White continues, hoping to pop the faithless bubble that has been blown up around these people.

"There have been some in this country that have done a very good job at masking the most important part of the Twenty-ninth Amendment. Section two states that 'if at any time a member of Congress abuses his or her power and privileges, the citizens may petition for a removal of said official.'"

A variety of wide eyes emerge as people turn to their smart devices for instant fact-checking capability.

Not waiting for people to realize that he has his history down, White repeats himself. "Again, we will appeal to the American people."

"So," Mica raises the first concern, "the campaign is using fear to get you into the White House? Vote for me or else…"

"That's a vulgar conclusion, Mr. Rouge, and the answer is no. We will be the voice of the people. We empower them as the original founders intended. The idea and value of checks and balances has eroded due to past corrupt election cycles. The ability for leaders to hear the people's voice is gone, and it won't be long before it is written as ancient history."

White knows there will still be reluctance to this proposed strategy, but they will see soon enough. The Ordean Reich is gaining ground and has infiltrated numerous government resources to push their tyrannical, Marxist views forward. They've done it in such a brilliant fashion that the public considers them a conspiracy theory rather than the reality they are. This genius tactic is extremely difficult to combat. It usually is exposed through hubris as those implementing this art of deception begin announcing their intentions rather than misdirect the public. Politicians these days often forget to apply Saul Alinsky's rules—however, the Ordean Reich has not made this mistake.

As he begins to see the fear and doubt spread across the team, White summons a tone that he hasn't used in quite some time. "Trust me. This will take some aggressive patience, but it is our best course of action—we appeal to the American people."

It's an old school tactic, but how can anyone argue with the kind of hope, vigor, and stoicism that Governor White brings to the table, let alone Mica? Plus, he wasn't put on this detail to market campaign mottos. Mica's here to protect the governor. Carter believes this man to be the foundation that will obliterate the Children of the Ordean Reich, and although he doesn't have the whole picture, in the short time he's spent in this room Mica has seen enough to believe. This guy is so idealistic it's crazy, but a little hopeful insanity might just be what this country needs.

"Let's get to work," White finishes, and with no other invitation needed, the team begins shuffling their way out of the stuffy room.

"Mr. Rouge," White says before Mica can exit. "You have a moment?"

The governor leads Mica into his office, before taking a seat. Glancing at the desk he sits behind, Mica does a double take.

"Is that—?"

"It is," White smiles. "The original desk in the Oval Office. After the last presidency remodeled the entire White House, this was one of the first things to go."

"How did you get it?"

"How did you get this assignment?" the governor asks with a smirk hinting at their mutual associate. "I appreciate you coming on the campaign."

"Carter always seems to come through," Mica says, acknowledging the obvious character strength of his boss.

"Yes, he does. He is also very loyal," the governor says, pausing and reaching for his mini fridge to collect his thoughts, the cool brisk air reaching Mica across the room as he opens it. "Would you like something to drink?"

"Water will be fine."

The governor chuckles, reaching and tossing Mica a bottle. "Not a drinker?"

"Never have and never will be," Mica says, cracking the bottle open, taking a swig of the icy, bottled beverage.

"Don't ever go back on that," he says, eyeing Mica for a moment. White pops open his can of Coke Zero, the hiss of pressurized carbonation echoing in the room before he takes a sip of the bubbly liquid. "I used to be."

"What made you drop it?" Mica asks, taking a seat.

"My ladies."

"Your wife and…?"

White likes this kid, but he doesn't entirely trust him yet. "She was one of them! A remarkable woman. I hope you have the chance to meet her," he says, taking another sip before redirecting the conversation. "You have a wife, Mr. Rouge?"

Chuckling, Mica simply shakes his head. "No, sir."

"A girlfriend? Boyfriend?"

"Nope." Mica gives another slight laugh. This guy does not shy away from anything.

"That's a bunch of bullshit. Look at you! Why would someone like you choose to be single?"

As the governor says this, Kim's ring dangling from his neck instantly becomes heavier. Mica tries to shrug it off. The governor meant nothing by it, but for some reason, the brief flash of her memory makes a physical appearance in his discomfort.

"I haven't really had the best luck with relationships," is all Mica can manage.

"So I've heard," White solemnly says, being reminded as to why Carter recruited Mica in the first place. "I take it you understand the real reason you're here on my campaign then?"

"I do," Mica says.

"And I know that *you* know of the Ordeans?"

Again, Mica confirms, nodding his head.

"Do you know what they're after, Mr. Rouge?"

"Power, like anyone in politics."

"I won't take offense to that," the governor chuckles, leaning up to face Mica. "The Reich believes that the system we have is fundamentally flawed because of its checks and balances—that we aren't as efficient as we could and should be."

"I'm not quite following, sir."

"They think we are grid-locked beyond repair—that the Constitution is out of date. Their plan is to make our three branches of government into one in order to 'perfect and purify' our society, and are using the guise of class warfare to propagate their agenda."

"How do you know that?"

"I just do," White says, cutting off the long discussion before it even begins. The idea and realization came the second he put down the bottle and walked away from Harris, his eyes opening as this clarity became part of his vision.

Mica, however, just assumes Carter is how he came by this information, so instead asks, "How do they plan on doing it?"

"That is the real question, and one that I cannot answer right now. My guess, if it were me: eliminate the power and agency of the people first. After that, choose a branch of government that meets the agenda's needs, eliminating the other two."

"Okay," Mica begins, not entirely sold on the idea. "Which branch of government?"

"You're making me guess some more," White says, taking another sip.

In an almost apologetic fashion, Mica takes a sip of his own drink, not knowing how to proceed other than shutting up. If Carter were here, he'd about have a heart attack seeing a speechless Mica.

"The law makers," White then says, giving the kid a break. "Although the Ordeans have already infiltrated the presidency, Congress represents the people the best, and if they are to have a compliant populace, sway the officials of said populace."

"So where do I come into play?" Mica thought he knew what his assignment was, but with this new information, he's sensing there is a difference in what Carter expects and what the governor does.

"They want me dead because of what I know and have speculated. If elected, I can and will throw a massive wrench into their machine." Finishing his Coke in one gulp, White crushes the can. "Protect me and hunt them."

"Simple enough," Mica says. "Just me?"

"Mr. Carter has a lot of confidence in devils."

The governor knows, Mica thinks. He knows who Mica really is. "I hope I can live up to those expectations then."

"You and me both, my friend!" White chuckles.

Another long silence fills the room, and White knows that there is something else is on Mica's mind.

"Sir?" Mica tentatively asks, trying to find the best way to articulate his question. "Can I ask you a personal question?"

"Ask away." White is hesitant but not entirely resistant.

"Is it true? What the media is saying about you?"

It always comes to this, that's no surprise. White can't keep running away from it, but now—now is not the time and in a kind, but firm admonition, the governor cuts Mica's thought process off.

"The only answer you need right now is that no matter how dark an individual's past, inspiration always starts from somewhere."

"Fair enough." Mica humbly nods, knowing how true that statement really is.

"Before you go, Mr. Rouge, there is somebody I want you to meet," White says, standing up and walking to the door. "I want you to meet your partner."

"I thought you were confident in my abilities," Mica jabs, giving the governor a hard time.

"I said Carter was; I still have my doubts," White jabs back. "Mica Rouge, meet Officer Dan Trax."

In front of Mica, a freight train steps forward, holding out the biggest hand he's ever seen. The governor is big, but it is more because of height and status as a former football player. The man in front of him, he is another breed of massive.

"Nice to meet you," Mica states, surprised but not the least bit intimidated.

"And it's nice to meet you."

Dan already sized the man up when he saw him step into the meeting. The sarcastic attitude towards the secretary wasn't entirely impressive, but the kid at the front desk is an ass, so he gave Mica the benefit of the doubt. As for the reputation coming from Carter, Dan has yet to see it.

"Well," Governor White awkwardly says, "I'll let you two love birds get to know each other." He slaps Mica on the shoulder before leaving the room.

The meeting took longer than he expected, and as much as he'd like to chat with a train, Mica's not going to cancel his night with Aila.

"Hey, I've got to get going, but let's sync up tomorrow morning to talk security stuff, yeah?"

"Whatever," Dan scoffs.

Mica's ears perk up at the asshole tone. "Did I miss something?"

"Are you serious about this job or not?" Dan coldly asks.

"I am. And like I said, did I miss something?" This guy may be big, but Mica's taken down big guys before. They have the same weaknesses that any bro has: a hyoid bone, knees, and a pair of testicles.

"Then let's walk and talk. Wouldn't want you to miss your date."

"Who said I have a date?" Mica retorts, looking at the chip on Dan's shoulder.

"No ring on your finger, eager to leave. It's a date." His detective skills always pay off and catch people by surprise.

"Alright, Sherlock. Let's walk and talk then," Mica says, bowing, like the good gentleman that he is, letting Dan the Man take the lead.

Stepping into the darkened city, Mica starts walking without giving Dan the opportunity to see the direction, stopping in front of his bike.

Not believing what he's seeing Dan asks, "I was wondering who's that was."

Now his tone changes, Mica thinks, chuckling to himself. "Impressed?" he asks, pushing the ignition button, bringing the beast to life.

"Man," Dan moans, having missed that sound. The roaring engine, the purring idle, and most of all, the wind in his face as he grips the handlebars.

"You have a bike?"

"Had," he replies, his eyes shut tightly, picturing fond memories.

"What happened?" Mica asks, surprised that he wants to hear more.

"Ex-wife." Avoiding any further explanation he gives the short reply. "Another story for another time."

Mica picks up on the hint, bringing the conversation back to business. "So, what makes you think the two of us have what it takes to protect the governor?"

Dan shrugs his shoulders. "I don't know about you, but I've been a cop all my life. My dad was a cop, his dad was a cop, and now I'm a cop."

"Is that your resume or genealogy?" Mica asks.

"What makes you think you're qualified for the job?" Dan shrewdly asks.

Wouldn't you like to know? Since Mica can't use his real reason as to why he's qualified, he uses his cover. "I was in special forces and started my own security firm after I got out a couple of years ago."

"You look awfully young."

"And you look rather old—"

Before Mica can finish, he is tackled to the ground. Instinctively, he rolls onto his back just in time to see a knife coming straight at him. Shooting his arms up in an X, the forearm of the attacker slams into the block, and as Mica slithers his way up and out from underneath his attacker, he knocks him unconscious with a knee to the groin and an elbow to the brain stem.

"Look out!" Mica shouts, but Dan already senses the attack.

Dan dives as a shot is fired from behind, the projectile missing its mark entirely. Mica isn't as lucky though, as a second shot goes off, the bullet grazing his arm. Before he can move and shift his fighting position, Mica is grabbed from the side by two more attackers. Seeing this, Dan picks up a bottle from the gutter and tosses it to Mica. Catching it, Mica smacks one of his attackers on the top of his head with a loud hollow thud.

A third shot is fired, hitting the wall Dan's using as cover. As it ricochets, the sound tells Dan exactly what he needs to know. Fearlessly, he picks up a broken brick, and immediately finds the shooter. As one more shot rings out, Dan charges, closing the ten feet between them in half a second. This panics the man and before he can get a final shot off, his skull is crushed.

Dan turns to help Mica, but there is no need. Mica stands victorious with the glass bottle in one hand and a thumbs up in the other.

"Nice work." Mica took out three while Dan took care of the one. Granted, Dan's attacker had a gun, but it's the speed with which Mica took care of them that's impressing the former cop.

"Maybe you're not such a patsy after all," Dan says.

"You thought I was a patsy?" Mica responds incredulously.

"You ever been shot before?" Dan asks, seeing the blood on Mica's arm.

Mica shrugs. "I've been stabbed."

"Well," Dan says, "you're lucky it was a low caliber bullet. It could've been a lot worse."

"How'd you know it was low caliber?"

"The sound, and"—Dan points to the wall— "when he shot at me, it didn't do any damage to the wall when the bullet hit. Just bounced off."

"Is that why you charged him?" Mica asks, liking this guy's fighting style.

"Yep. Knew if I did get shot, chances were it wouldn't be too bad."

"What if he got you in the head?"

"He was too scared and shaky to aim that well. Pissed himself when he saw me coming."

Mica laughs in agreement. These guys were no professionals but even so, it isn't a coincidence that they attacked the two of them when and where they did.

"You think they were Ordeans?" Mica asks.

Dan lifts the sleeve of the shooter to reveal a small tattoo of a single, white star. "Yep."

"What's that?" Mica asks, staring at the tattooed star.

"It's their mark."

How has he never noticed this before? Out of all the Ordeans he's encountered, Mica has never noticed a uniform tattoo on any of them. "How'd you know about that?"

"Remember that genealogy you were making fun of me over? My history of law enforcement comes with its perks."

"Right." This guy knows more than he's telling him, but now is not the time to interrogate him. Mica's late.

"I'll take care of it," Dan says. "I know the department and it'll take less time for me than you. You can leave for your date."

"You sure?"

"Go, before I change my mind," he says, waving Mica away.

"Thanks man. I'll see you tomorrow then."

Mica ignites the engine and the bike roars to life. Hitting the throttle, Mica peels out of the alley leaving Dan alone and envious of such a beautiful machine.

———※ ★ ※———

There's a wooden rap at the front of her apartment, one that causes Aila to beam from ear to ear upon hearing it. Plugging in her popcorn maker, she skips over, twists the rickety knob, and whips open the entrance to her apartment where her Cheshire grin is immediately wiped away.

"What happened?!"

Blood-soaked, Mica glances at his sleeve, continuing to clutch at the injury. "Ran into a little bit of trouble."

Aila prods at the wound. "Sorry!" she declares as Mica lets out an annoyed wince. "I'm really sorry. It's just—never mind."

In the years she spent with her uncle overseas, she became rather accustomed to battle injuries. Most of what she saw were on the level of Mica's gunshot, but there were the occasional serious ones that brought the reality of her situation closer to home. Never did she think the fight and its effects would be at her front door, but gazing at Mica's injury, Aila is reminded of the solemn reality that yes, the country is in a Cold Civil War.

"I have some stuff I think," she says, locking the door behind Mica.

It honestly looks worse than it is, but Mica doesn't let her know this and leans into the drama. He'd never admit this out loud, but Mica is one that slightly relishes theatrics, especially when attractive women are involved.

Adding another wince upon Aila's return, Mica turns on the charm. "I still brought the movie."

Encumbered by an enormous first aid kit, Aila lets out a slight chuckle. "I'm glad, because that was the first thing I thought when I saw you bleeding all over."

Whipping out a rag, she soaks it in isopropyl alcohol and pulling out a pair of sheers, cuts Mica's shirt off before he can give any sort of protest.

"Geez," Mica says. "Buy me dinner first."

Blushing at his comment, Aila reciprocates the sarcasm by pressing the alcohol-soaked rag right onto the grazed wound. Completely taken off guard by the pain, Mica bites his tongue, holding in the slew of profanities that he is dying to release. After a moment of watching him squirm, Aila removes the cloth before gently blowing on the wound, her minty breath causing any remaining alcohol to evaporate. Yes, she brushed her teeth, swished some mouth wash, and threw in a piece of gum for good measure before he came over. She likes the hell out of Mica!

"Was it them?" she asks, the memories of Kim's death hovering in the back of both their minds.

"Yeah," Mica quietly says. Not only did the smell of her breath wafting back at him bring him to a state of sobriety, but the way her eyes shifted to his forced him to immediately reflect on her—on them and their future. He cares for her, much more than he ever thought he would. He can no longer afford to be flippant with his missions or with his life.

"I wasn't alone though," he says.

"Oh? And who am I to thank for saving your life?" Aila asks, only partly mocking him, but at the same time relieved. Who knows how much worse it could have gotten?

"I was with some retired cop."

"Is he okay?" she then asks, cleaning the rest of his arm with ease before bandaging it.

"Yeah. He's the one who took out the gunman."

"My hero," she says, knowing full well the comment will annoy Mica. "How many of them were there?"

"Four."

"How many did you take out?" she asks, her eyes widening in surprise.

"Three."

She knew what she'd signed up for the moment she let her heart fall for Mica. The life of soldiers and their spouses is a familiar one, and as dangerous and heartbreaking as a life like that can be, Aila likes hearing that Mica is not only competent, but extremely effective. That and there will always be a certain level of sex appeal to toughness for her.

After a momentary silence while Aila finalizes her first aid touches, Mica finds the courage to ask her something that has always puzzled him. After everything he knows she's seen overseas with Carter, after all the heartbreak she's been through with the death of her parents and Kim, not to mention the global catastrophes and bureaucratic pandemics, she still finds a way to believe.

"How do you do it?"

"Do what?"

"How do you do this optimism thing you always do?"

"It's belief. It's faith…" She smirks. It's vague and definitely not the answer she knows he wants, but it's the truth! She just does.

"That doesn't really answer my question," he chuckles. "Fine, let me be frank with you then. How do you believe in a god?"

"Is that why you have a devil as your *symbol?*" she jests.

"I'm serious. How do you believe in a god?"

"How do you *not* believe in a god?" she retorts. There's no jest in this comment. There is a clear difference between white knuckling life and belief, faith, and hope that a higher power has her best interests in mind.

"That's not a fair question," Mica scoffs.

"And why not? Why are you allowed to question *my* faith, but I can't question your lack of it?"

"I'm not questioning your faith—"

"But you are," Aila states, cutting Mica off. "And I don't mind if you do, but let me ask you this. Why is it wrong to believe, despite the horrors of the world?"

Isn't it obvious? Mica thinks. Isn't it obvious that a loving "God" wouldn't make room for greed, lust, murder, sloth, envy, all of which happen on a global scale? Isn't it obvious that if there was a "God," they're just watching humans destroy themselves? There are men and women who think they are gods, and it is these kinds of people that are the ones orchestrating the travesties of the world, or at best are being allowed to by the "God" Aila believes in.

"It's not," Aila then says, answering her own question. "Because it's not God who murders, rapes, who's involved with the trafficking of children, and who has allowed for corruption to infiltrate our institutions. It's mankind who does those things."

"Then why doesn't God do anything about it? Why doesn't he just make people do the right thing?"

"Are you being serious right now?" Aila laughs. *Does he not see the irony in what he just asked?*

"Of course, I'm being serious! If He's so perfect and omnipotent, then why not make us do what's right?"

"That sounds like communism and fascism, does it not?"

Mica clamps his mouth shut. "That's different..." he mumbles.

"No, it's not, and you know it!" she chuckles. "America was founded on the belief in God and the idea that we should all have personal agency and liberty. Ironically enough though, if we didn't have the ability to choose then we'd have the fiction of Utopia. But that's not the case and whether by chance or accident, like with my parents, or due to targeted nefarious purposes, like with Kim, shit happens."

"You really believe that?" Mica asks doubtfully.

"I do," she nods. And although secular walkers of life and atheists alike die a little inside every time she mentions this, she says it to Mica anyway. "If you believe in what America stands for, you believe in a god whether you like it or not."

Having leaned towards the ironic religious dogma of atheism like many of their generation, Mica chews on this for a minute. It's been messy. It's been bloody, but what other country in the world allowed for personal choice and growth on a massive scale before 1776? There was the royalty and the serfs. The elites and the slaves. It varied from generation to generation and from culture to culture, but there really wasn't any form of large-scale freedom and agency before America.

The cynic inside didn't allow for him to think like this, let alone believe any of it. After Kim's death, it was solidified in both Mica's mind and heart that if there was a Savior of mankind, the guy was giving him and everyone on this planet the good old middle finger. Now, after this brief conversation with Aila, maybe that's been a bitter and nihilistic interpretation of life and humanity.

"You thinking about Kim?" Aila asks.

"Kind of." Mica nods. "I'm thinking more about the concept of someone's faith building your own. We talked about it one time before she died."

"And?"

"And I think it might be true." Mica touches his arm and the solid bandage Aila put around it.

Yes, he handled himself around three of those thugs, and yes, he's handled himself around more, but maybe the fourth one in this instance—

maybe that one would've been the end for him. If it wasn't for Dan, maybe he wouldn't even be having this existential moment.

"Well, to an extent," Aila says, tossing her things back into the first aid kit. "There comes a point when we all will have to lean on our own faith and strength, trusting that God has our best interests in mind."

He doesn't need to say it, and Mica doesn't ask it, but Aila sees the sudden emotion within him. He wants to express everything to her, but he can't. Not right now, not like this with his shirt off… Old Mica would've, not Mica restored.

"You wouldn't happen to have anything that I could fit into, would you?" Mica asks, holding up his blood soaked and now tattered shirt.

She chuckles. "I doubt it, but I'll check." A few seconds later she comes back with a hideous sweatshirt. "This is all I have."

"Whose is it?" Mica cringes.

"No idea," she laughs. "Maybe an ex-boyfriend's?"

"Shame on you," Mica flirtatiously mocks, taking the sweatshirt and putting it on. A little snug, but it's better than being a shirtless tool.

"Popcorn?" Aila winks.

That gesture…

"Wait!" he shouts, as if popping popcorn will doom them both. Literally, it's absurd, but figuratively speaking, if he doesn't act now, it very well might be true. Everything he's felt and experienced with this woman has been leading to something more. Something that he wants to build on. Without another moment of hesitation, Mica stands, gently and yet swiftly approaching Aila.

"Wh-what are you doing, Mica?" she stammers out. She's waited for this moment for what seems like an eternity, and now that it's here, Aila freezes. Scared to death by the ramifications of the approaching kiss, she opens her mouth in protest but is silenced as Mica's lips press to hers.

Nine

Raider Encampment

Every time he whispers his sacred words, he's reminded of another life. One where he could proudly smile, looking into the eyes of his family. A life where they were safe and happy.

That was then. This is now.

From outside, the whistling wind disturbs his peace as it follows a quiet messenger into his tent.

"Yes?" the shadowy old man asks, standing to turn, his hood covering the scars tattooing his face. It's been years since he found this boy, alone and terrified within the rubble of the airport. No longer, though, is he a child, but a man.

"Kai," the old man says. "What is it, son?"

Running his hands through his beaded hair, Kai contemplates how to best present the recent intel. "It was foolish to have come," he ends up saying. "I'm sorry to have bothered you."

"You came here to tell me that you have nothing to tell me?" The man eyes his son carefully. What Kai has to say can't be good if his apprehension is this high. "Is it another box?"

The question is not asked out of disappointment, but despair—out of fearing the worst. Caspian is a pawn whether he realizes it or not. A dangerous one, but a pawn, nonetheless. The damage he has already done to their rebuilding efforts has been astronomical as he's intercepted every archived source of history they've had within reach. This is exactly how he knows Caspian is not the mastermind, but rather a loose cannon—one that has been strategically harnessed by the Stones.

"We got there, but Renn was patrolling the region," Kai says, seeing the distress in his father's eyes grow. "She knew! She was right where our intel said it would be," he adds, hoping to regain some dignity.

"Does *she* have it?" the old man asks.

"No," his son says. "One of the Insiders does."

"I thought all our people within the region were dead..." the old man states, his hope being restored.

"It was Kip," Kai states, hiding his disapproval. Not only was Kip not dead like Kai presumed, but for some reason, his father seems to value this moron. That aside, it's better that Kip have it than the alternative.

"Why the apprehension?" the shadowy man asks. "This is good news. Can we get in contact with Kip?"

"That's where it gets complicated."

"How so?"

"Kip isn't the only one involved. He found it with someone else."

"Jax…" He always felt that the boy would have a bigger part to play, especially after Lisa's passing, but as his loyalty has never been tested, he could be as much of a threat as the Stones. Having considered the matter as far as he can, the man turns to his successor. "What do you think we should do?"

"There are a lot of factors at play. It's complicated," Kai says.

"You already said that," the man says. "The real question is do you think we can still trust Kip?" he then asks, having the prompting to delve into Kai's doubt.

Kai's immediate instinct is to say no, but that would be his emotions speaking. Logic and impartiality to the situation at hand tells him that as uneducated as Kip comes off as being, he is tactical and dependable. "We can."

Just then, there's a knock on the tent frame's entrance.

"Yes?" the older man replies.

From outside, a second Raider rushes in. Completely out of breath, her eyes bloodshot and cheeks flushed, her demeanor saying it all.

"Sir,"—she inhales before wiping the tears that begin flooding her eyes— "Kip Wright was just executed…"

<hr>

"Jackie…" Ann grabs, squeezing Jax's arm, trying to smother the bloody images of Kip from her mind. Her young eyes have seen death before, but it's always a stranger—someone she's had no emotional connection to—and as the child tries to comprehend this sudden traumatic change, she holds onto Jax for some semblance of stability.

Jax on the other hand, has seen the death of someone he cared about. Before, sorrow and depression were the emotions of choice as she was taken from him—gracefully, but taken from him, nonetheless. This time—this time his sentiments match the violent nature of the thievery.

"Let's get out of here," Mari says, grabbing Ann and pulling on Jax's hand. He doesn't move. Insisting, she tugs on his arm harder, trying to move the rooted statue he's become, her eyes welling with tears. "Let's go!" Mari repeats.

"Take Ann," Jax says, his blunt command catching Mari off guard.

Never has she seen him like this. As if the world no longer exists, his cold, hardened gaze stares at those responsible. Imagining the actions that course through him as he plots, Mari fears he too will have his final moments.

"You're coming with us!" Mari begins as the anthem starts to play.

"No, I'm not." He pushes Mari away, peeling Ann off him. Jax doesn't know where the rage will end, but he knows exactly where it'll begin.

As the PPA officers scoop up Kip's corpse from off the stage, tossing it onto a stretcher, citizens begin filing out of City Hall, desensitized to the murder like every other life that has been taken on that stage.

"Renn!" Jax shouts out over the mumbled commotion of the masses.

She barely hears her name, but keeping her course she marches out the exit, ignoring the sounds of Jax's rage. But his outcry gnaws at her bones. She did this. She created the monster that is no longer afraid of the PPA—that no longer complies out of the fear of pain and death.

"Renn!" he repeats with more force.

PPA ears begin perking up at the outraged worker, which is normal after a Gathering like tonight, and upon seeing his place within the crowd, Jax is deemed a non-threat.

"Jackie!" Ann cries out, confused and in agony from the loss of one friend, fearing that she'll lose another by the end of the night.

Seeing the futility in arguing with the man she's come to love, tears pour down her cheeks as Mari picks Ann up. Now is not the time for her—the older sister—to cave to her emotion, but rather save Ann.

Unable to get to her through the crowd, Jax sees Renn leave through a set of back doors and takes a sharp left, walking outside, studying the surrounding alleys of the horrific glass building before him. That's when he sees her—alone and secluded down a stretch of corridor.

"Renn!" he shouts, his voice reverberating off the glass and brick path.

She stops but doesn't turn.

"Why?!" he yells, quickly closing the gap between the two. When within reach, he kicks her square in the back and onto the icy, snow-covered concrete.

Skidding to a stop, Jax rips Renn up from off the ground, flipping her onto her back. He wants her to look at him as he slowly crushes her windpipe, blackening the life in her eyes, but something happens that he never would have anticipated. She's staring at him, just like he wanted, but the expectant expression he riled himself up over isn't there. With her flushed cheeks, Renn's light, beautiful golden-brown eyes are watery, swollen, and outlined in a pinkish hue.

"Please..." she whispers. "I can't do this anymore..." No knife can cut into her flesh deep enough to extract the torment now welling up inside.

Growling, Jax reaches for her belt, unsheathing her knife to fulfill the request and end both her pain and his. Raising the blade over her unguarded chest, hate fills his eyes as Renn shuts hers, and whispering her last words, she wishes she could have done *everything* different.

"God, please forgive me."

But they aren't her last words. He can't do it. After all this, Jax drops the blade, and as it clatters to the ground, he follows suit, collapsing to the snow where he begins to weep. At first, it's quiet, but as he lays there crumbled with his face in the ice and back to the wall, his mourning develops into an uncontrollable sob.

Sliding her hands underneath her hips, Renn pushes herself upright, not sure as to whether she should run or stay until he calms and can finish the deed. Folding her arms, Renn curls up as she waits, and whether she lives or dies tonight, her home is no longer an option. If Jax spares her, their destinies will be forever intertwined.

Slowly, Jax gains composure, pushing himself up next to Renn. "Why? Why Kip?" he asks, his eyes in the palms of his hands. "Why not me?"

"I don't know," she tentatively says. As nondescript and illogical as it is, it's the truth. Both he and Kip defied The Government, making both guilty of treason, but only Kip was punished.

"What do you mean?" Jax asks.

"I don't know," she repeats.

"Renn?" a familiar voice echoes down the alleyway, and as Connor steps into view, seeing the scene before him, he acts, picking up Renn and then Jax.

"Go home," Connor states. "Now…" he then says, hugging Jax before pushing him out of the alley. "We can talk there."

"Jackie!" Ann shouts, seeing him shoot out from the shadows. Startled by Ann's exclamation, Mari barges toward him.

"What the hell?" Mari ferociously asks, demanding an explanation and smacking him in the shoulder. "What were you planning on doing? You selfish bastard," Mari states, hitting him a second time, this time her fist closed.

Ann, just happy to see him alive, goes in for a hug but is pushed away.

"Are you coming over?" Ann asks hopefully, needing him to say yes.

"No. I'm leaving," is his only cold reply while he walks further and further away.

"Why?" Ann's quivering voice asks.

Origins

Even though Jax's back is turned towards them, he can't unsee Ann's crying visage as she stands in pain and confusion.

"You're not the only one dealing with this!" Mari yells out, her hatred echoing into the desolate winter night. "You bastard," she then whispers, her voice tender like Ann's, unable to mask the confusion and hurt. All the aggression and resiliency from her other life cannot conceal the misery and grief, and as she tries to implement her training to gain some emotional footing, she comes to the stark realization that her past will forever haunt her.

—⋆★⋆—

With her head throbbing and her heart aching, Renn continues to ask the ever-damning question—why?

Because he didn't understand is the compartmentalized answer she gives herself.

Kip was naïve to the powers they are facing. Jax wasn't. When she made the initial call, fear drove Renn. Kip, not Jax, was moving things too fast. Rushing the decision-making process against a force like the Nine would've gotten them all killed. In the same breath though, she knew her actions to kill Kip would make her mother and father proud. It was a stroke of genius to appear steadfast while diverting her efforts to undermine them—and just like she anticipated, their suspicions came to a grinding halt and Sullivan and Bella Stone were never prouder. Renn Stone was loyal to the Oligarchy.

However, something transpired that Renn did not factor into the equation. As Kip's execution unfolded, an overwhelming sense of dread encompassed her to the point she almost cried out for it to stop. Taking a life was nothing new to her, but it always stayed on the battlefield—her enemies always knew when their lives were coming to an end and why. Kip's situation was different. He distrusted her simply because of her uniform and name; however, her mere presence in his home that night gave him hope that maybe he could trust her one day—that he could lean on Jax's trust in Connor, and by proxy her. Yes, he stormed out, infuriated that the situation wasn't completely under his control, but he came to his senses.

Kip approached her early the next morning and did so in such a way that testified of his training and true skill in tradecraft. Renn didn't even see him approach; the patience exercised to wait for the opportune moment where she was completely alone is something she and her PPA counterparts have studied but never fully understood. The interaction was brief, but he found the gap in her routine to make one simple statement.

"If we're gonna do this, let's do this right." He was no mere Laborer, but an Unapproved—Kip was a Raider.

That's all he said before leaving in the same manner he approached her, and as the day passed, those nine words continued to weigh on Renn's shoulders. There was trust, and yet at the same time there wasn't. With how quickly and silently he approached, Kip could've taken her life and no one, including her, would've seen it happen. Instead, he gave her an olive branch. That's not the part that nagged at Renn. She was afraid. That's what drove her to follow him and Jax to that woman's house, and as she listened to their conspiracy, Kip had a very different idea of what must be done, and rather than reacting, she was proactive with the terror that gripped her. She couldn't let that box leave her sight. Taking a tactic from Kip's book, she waited for the moment he was alone, and when he was, Renn made her move.

Never having seen his sister like this, Connor picks her up. For the third time she's fallen to the ground crying, saying the same mumbled words:

"His eyes…"

Connor is indifferent to what happened to Kip. It's cold, but he never met the guy until the other night, and even then, he was doubtful. Jax trusted him, and so Connor trusted Jax's judgment. That was before pulling Kip's file. Now, Connor realizes how great of a resource the guy would've been. To say that Renn's actions were foolish would be putting it lightly. It is what it is though, and as broken as both Renn and Jax are over this, Connor can't let the mission dwell on a single lost asset. The two of them have a small window before Sullivan and Bella begin finding reasons for their missing presence at the dinner table tonight. Despite Connor and Renn wanting to slow the pace of the operation, Kip's execution has made that impossible. Renn created a self-fulfilling prophecy that the longer they wait, the more they jeopardize the box falling into the wrong hands. Where speed was once their perceived enemy, it is now their greatest ally.

"Pull yourself together. Compartmentalize it and move on!" he says, taking Renn's face into his hands.

The words are harsher than most would be able to accept, but they're needed. He's right. Self-deprecating rot won't move things forward. She's a soldier and must act like one. Slowing her breath, Renn flicks her tears away as she begins to figure out how to reboot the machine Kip had in motion.

"We don't have much time," she says, standing upright.

"He'll be here. Give him a minute," Connor says, turning back to the device at the front door. He's shoddy when it comes to improvised explosives, but it'll get the job done. Finishing the final touches, Connor steps back away from the door, impressed with what he managed to rig. In that moment, the front door swings open.

"Jax..." Rushing forward, Connor encompasses his friend in his massive physique.

"We need to get moving," Jax quietly says, the weakness in his body reflected in his tone. His apathy is short-lived though as he sees Renn, the rush of adrenaline making a resurgence.

"What is she doing here?" he asks before Connor quickly puts himself between the two.

"She's with us, Jax," Connor says before moving back over to the door, shutting it and connecting the pressure plate to the staged munitions.

"You sure about that? That bitch got Kip killed!" Jax's tone rises.

"Just shut up!" Connor's abrupt, booming voice gives pause to Jax's revived rage. Now is not the time. The clearing of slates can wait. "The PPA are on their way to arrest you as we speak."

"On what charges?"

"On whatever the hell charges they want to make up..."

"I'll kill them then," Jax says nonchalantly.

This time Renn speaks, looking directly at Jax. "Don't be stupid! They *will* kill you, one way or another!"

"Do you know why that box is so important?" Connor then asks. "Why your parents left it to you?"

"Do you?" Jax spits back.

"I do!"

The short, immediate answer snaps Jax's mouth closed.

"If you want to know who your parents are, you'll shut up and come with us."

"You know my parents?"

"No," Renn chimes in. "Kip did, and we might know where to find them."

Without needing any more information, Jax runs to the loose tile under the fireplace. Pulling the rusted metal box out, Jax feels the newfound weight of its importance. One person has already died in its name, and more are sure to come.

"Here." Renn tosses him a backpack filled with equipment. Before she can elaborate any further, three pounds shake the front door.

"Jax Rouge. You are under arrest for obstruction of justice, for the murder of five PPA officers, and for possession of treasonous documents."

"We've got to move!" Connor whispers forcefully. Sneaking out the back, the three quickly create distance between themselves and Kip's house. From there, the sound of the splintering door kicked in is heard, and almost immediately following, the only tangible memories Jax will have of Kip erupt in a fiery explosion.

"Where are we going?" Jax asks. He didn't dare talk until they were outside the borders of the district, and until that time, it was awkward as hell as he sat next to Kip's murderer.

"The mountains," Connor states, his eyes fixated on the dark road.

With only one thing worth approaching out there, Jax asks, "The Raiders? Why them?"

"They're after the box too," Connor says.

"So, we just handing it over?"

"That's what Kip was trying to do," Renn calmly says.

Immediately, Jax turns to her. "And last I checked, you got him killed because of it."

Connor scoffs. "Why would she have him killed to stop him from doing exactly what we're going to do?"

Anything Jax could say would just be simple bias, and realizing this, Jax redirects his line of questioning. "How do you know that?"

"How do we know he was taking you guys to the Raiders?" Renn asks for clarification, Jax nodding as his answer. "Because he was a Raider."

He had his suspicions, but the blunt news still startles Jax. "So *that's* why you had him killed."

"No, it's not. I—" She stops, knowing what she'll say is going to sting like hell. "I was scared."

Whether it's a reality, or just wanting to make sense of her actions, Jax can see remorse in Renn's visage as she says this. Now, what Jax can do with that realization, he has no idea. He already tried killing her and couldn't follow through. Even if he could do it now, even if Connor allowed him to, what would it accomplish other than appease an emotion he's had less than four hours to process?

"It makes sense," is all Jax can manage to mumble.

"What does?" Connor asks, his eyes still fixated on the darkened path ahead.

"Kip being a Raider. The fear… The chaos of the last day. His death…" It's no coincidence that both the Raiders and PPA showed up at the exact same time, creating a battlefield with his home as the epicenter. "Is this the only one?"

Renn shakes her head. "No, but it might be one of the last."

"Where are the rest?" Jax asks, dreading that he already knows the answer.

"Where do you think?" Renn scoffs.

Jax stares at the box as he ponders this. It's something that he can't seem to piece together. What's her motive? What is Renn Stone afraid of?

"Why are you doing this? Why now?" Jax asks, turning to her. What's the worst that could happen from prying? Is there a level that surpasses loathing?

"Why are *you* doing this now?" she asks, throwing the question back at him.

"Because I hate Caspian." He shrugs. It's as simple as that. Jax is tired of the systemic abuse one class is putting onto another, and Caspian the Oligarch seems to be the reason behind all of it.

"Well, there you go," Renn says, leaving it at that.

Unlike Jax though, Renn realizes that this hatred is only the beginning and not the solution to their problems. Like the Hydra in Greek mythology, killing Caspian will not solve anything for Area Thirty-Eight. Another more vicious leader will just take his place. The Nine, they are the real problem—they are the source of her terror. It's only a matter of time before Jax realizes the true depth of what they have started.

"We're here."

Slowing the truck to a stop, Connor brings the vehicle to the edge of the mountain's tree line, and as the three step out into the chilled night air, both Renn and Connor scan the blackened horizon they just drove from.

"You think we were followed?" Connor asks, looking back, the glowing burn of the explosion long out of sight.

"Doubt it," Renn states, checking her watch. "Unless they were using a Bird, I think we're good."

"A bird?" Jax questions, unfamiliar with the military lingo.

"Don't worry about it," Renn says, throwing on her field pack. "Let's hide the truck and get going before the sun rises."

"We're fifty-seven miles past the district border, Renn, we should be fine," Connor coolly says, clipping and attaching his own gear.

"You were just the one asking if we were followed," Renn chuckles. "Plus, it's not the PPA that I'm worried about anymore."

"Here," Connor says, tossing both Jax and Renn goggles.

"There's a button on the side of the right lens," Renn says to Jax as she puts on her own pair.

After he's securely fastened them, Jax presses the tiny power button and the forest lights up as if the sun suddenly rose to midday. "Whoa!"

Connor chuckles as he watches an awestruck Jax. Pulling out a computer no bigger than the size of his palm, Connor taps in a set of commands before a transparent map appears in the goggles for both Jax and Renn.

"How'd you do that?" Jax blurts out, his excitement carrying in the wind.

"Keep your voice down. It's from a satellite."

"What's a satellite?"

They'll be there all night if they answer every one of Jax's queries.

"Just listen," Connor says. "You see the river?" he asks, highlighting it on his tablet which in turn highlights it on the goggles. "We're going to follow it upstream for about six miles."

"Then what?"

"Then they'll find us," Connor says.

This is where Kip would've been helpful. Connor's not a fan of the rudimentary nature of his plan, but that's the only way he can fathom to get an audience with his faction.

"So, they're going to capture us," Renn says, slowly coming to terms with the uncomfortable proposal. "How do you even know it'll be Kip's group?"

"I don't," Connor shrugs. "But it's the best guess we've got based on what Kip already told us."

"What if they don't know Kip?" Jax asks, thinking about the possibility. "What if we come across another group of Raiders?"

Reaching into his bag, pulling out three plastic knives and three plastic guns, Connor hands one of each to both Renn and Jax.

"Then we use these," Connor replies. "Let's go."

It's been years since Connor has been out in these parts, and the river they were supposed to be following seems to have dried up in the drought. Couple that with the low vegetation and sparse wildlife, there's nothing like the haunting silence of a night forest to relax and calm the mind. Having lived a life in solitude, Connor finds serenity in moments like these, and as a solo operator, he's had to. From Connor's experience, he'd much rather face the vices of a lone wolf strategy than to worry about the safety, security, and proficiency of someone else. No team he's ever worked with has given him a hundred percent confidence that they could save his life. That kind of trust doesn't live in the military he's been brought up in due to the simple fact that the Legacies and the entitlement they bring to their ranks kills the pride of earning one's place. As ill-equipped as Jax is for what he's signed up for, he'd take the heart of a volunteer over a Legacy soldier any day.

"We need a break," Renn says, breaking the silence of the still night forest.

"Can it wait?" Connor asks, looking at their point eight hundred yards away.

Renn shakes her head, pointing towards Jax. Twenty feet behind, huffing and sucking in air, Connor is reminded that rucking is one of the many things the Labor class are not conditioned for, and it's not just an unintended consequence of the law. As a student of cultural science, Connor knows that ideological and physiological weakness in subordinates makes them easier to control. Unarmed and mentally ill-equipped slaves are much more compliant than the armed, knowledgeable citizen.

"You tired?" Jax asks Renn, having finally caught up with the pair.

"Nope," she says, smirking as she tosses him a water bottle.

"Me neither," Jax puffs out. Taking a swig of water, he then begins to analyze her, momentarily detaching himself from the horrendous grief she's caused him. He's far from finding any reason to put his faith in her, but that minute smile is the first glimpse of joy he can recall from her. It's lofty and fleeting, but a spark of optimism flutters inside.

Wow, Jax thinks. She's beautiful...

However, before he can follow that train of thought any further, a cool metal lightly presses against the back of his head.

"You move, you die," an icy voice states.

Renn's eyes widen as both she and Connor reach for their firearms.

"I wouldn't..." the voice calmly warns, numerous clicks erupting around the three before dozens of armed Raiders step out from around the trees and rocks.

"On your knees," the voice says, pressing the metal more firmly against his head, commanding Jax to the icy dirt.

Looking over first to Connor and then to Renn, they lock eyes as she mouths for him to just comply.

"Hurry up!" the voice yells, smacking Jax on the side of his head.

Wincing from the sting in his ear, Jax watches as a man steps out from behind him.

Immediately Jax notices the black skin. The only other person he's ever seen that comes even close to resembling the man's appearance was Grandma Lisa. As Jax continues to look around at the surrounding Raiders, their appearance is the first thing observed, looking nothing like anyone in Area Thirty-Eight—Labor worker, citizen, or PPA. Some are brown and tanned, having feathers and beads ornamenting their hair, while the darker ones, like the man in front of him, have their hair done up in tiny little ropes. And not one of them is without tattoos.

"What brings you here?" the black man asks Jax.

Jax shrugs his shoulders. "What makes you think I'm in charge?" he retorts, looking to Connor for help, but as he tries looking around the black man, Jax finds that Connor is blocked by two other Raiders.

"I will not repeat myself..."

"We're here because of Kip," Jax quickly states. It's a shot in the dark, but judging by everyone's reaction, it seems to have been well-placed.

"He's lying," a Raider forcefully states. "They're on patrol."

"This far outside the wire?" Renn blurts out. This whole operation could turn south quick if they believed the three of them were hunting for more test subjects. "We got intel saying that Kip's clan would be here."

All these white PPA people are the same, thinking they are the ones in control. At the same time however, they can't be lying, Kai thinks.

Furious, Kai kicks Jax square in the chest. "Who's asking?!"

Pushing himself up from the dirt, Jax's sense of humor begins showing through as he gives the dumb answer of, "We are."

If Kai wanted to, he could cause the man unfathomable pain, but that's not the point. Crouching down, staring his captive in the eyes, Kai simply asks, "Why?"

"Because Kip was my friend. He was my brother."

Whatever commotion was happening amongst the Raiders, it goes silent as Jax says this, and Kai doesn't show it, but chills run down his spine.

It's him, he thinks. Kai can't be overzealous, though. It could cause great harm to the Clan, but after a moment, Kai determines that the three pale individuals know enough to at least be kept alive.

"Scan them!" Kai orders, and within seconds three Raiders are running scanners across the trio's bodies. "And pat them down," he adds, knowing that if these three are as smart as they look, they're prepared.

"They're clean," a Raider reports after his initial scan, but as they continue frisking, they find each equipped with a plastic knife and gun.

Just like he thought, Kai smirks.

"We also found this in the large man's bag."

Stepping forward, a Raider holds up the metal box.

"So, you are telling the truth," Kai whispers, relishing in the fact that he has what Kip could not get to them.

Throwing bags over their heads, the Raiders bind Connor, Renn, and Jax's hands before trudging them through the forest. For Jax it feels like hours, but Connor and Renn know it is forty-seven minutes and twenty-three seconds. Though the sulfuric aroma is nauseating, it is a clue for the two soldiers. Connor has patrolled near here and begins making connections as to the exact location. Upon hearing the crackling of fires and the mumbled hushes of women and children, Connor and Renn are able to picture a layout for the encampment. While Jax has no idea what is being said, having studied the Raiders, Connor and Renn comprehend almost every word and phrase.

"There's some good news and some bad news," Kai's voice intones as he shoves the three into a tent.

A deep bass voice then shakes the tent as both Connor and Renn try to identify its owner.

"Bad news first," it says.

"We caught these three trying to locate our camp."

The bass voice scoffs. "And the good news?"

"They had a box."

Connor hears Kai's gloves slide across the rusty metal surface as he pulls it out of his bag, handing it over to whom he can only imagine is the leader.

"Unmask them," the deep voice orders.

The suffocating bag's stale atmosphere dissipates as Jax inhales like an infant taking their first breath.

"He also said he knew Kip," Kai says, pushing Jax forward.

The old battle-scarred man looks to Jax, unimpressed that he knows the notorious name of their recently fallen comrade.

Lowering his hood, the old man reveals white, weathered and battle-worn skin, whereupon Connor's heart immediately stops. He knows that face. Somewhere in a distant memory… back before the Founding.

"And how did you know Kip?" the elderly leader asks, looking down at the box in his hands, reading the name *Kimberly Blackham* on the box's face. "Clever, Mica," he then mumbles to himself.

"He was my brother. We found that box together…"

"What's *your* name?"

"Jax."

"Well, I'll be damned," the old man chuckles, his eyes widening.

"Who are you?"

"Give him the box," he says, handing the box back to Kai.

Kai hesitates at his father's command.

"It's his," the old man says.

"But sir—"

"Kai, the box is his."

As Kai slowly complies, the old man looks over to the other two. The woman who is no doubt Sullivan and Bella's daughter, and the other—

The battled elder freezes as he looks at the soldier next to Renn. Studying him, all the old man can see are his wife's eyes staring back. How many years has it been that he's had to convince himself of Connor's death? Decades it's seemed, where regret has been his only solace at the loss of his son. Dan looks to the three of them before resting his eyes on Jax.

"My name is Dan Trax, and your parents were dear friends of mine, as you'll soon discover by what you'll read in that box."

Renn immediately recognizes the name, as does Connor when for the first time in years, he's looking at his actual father.

"Where is she?" he shouts, his fists cracking the table in front of him. "You said—"

"Sir," the officer interrupts. "There is nothing we could have done better."

Caspian raises his eyes to look at the bold officer in front of him. The soldier stands resolute in his conviction that they followed orders as given. Military training does an excellent job at reprogramming an individual to take a directive without question, however, the concept of an "implied task" is just as important. It allows for a soldier—especially a leader of troops—the ability to elaborate and expound on said directives and orders without oversight. This was the officer's first mistake.

One would *imply* that if Jax Rouge, Connor Trax, and Renn Stone weren't in the house when it blew up, especially since two of them have high-level security clearances, that a search would be underway, which it is not. One would *then imply* that it might not be the wisest decision to be giving such a poor update with no plan of correction in place, therefore *implying* that interrupting your commander with such asinine intel would also be unwise, which was the officer's second mistake.

"Could not have done better?" Caspian slowly and methodically asks, letting the officer feel the gravity of the misconception of his own competence. He's already sized him up, and even though there is a hundred-pound difference between the two, Caspian has always had something other men do not.

"You understand what is at stake—?"

"I stand by what I said! I lost three men in the initial explosion and will not lose any more tonight."

The officer is relying on PPA regulation, culture, and his massive frame to save him, which none of them will.

"You're so..." Caspian chuckles out, elongating the word as he searches for the right insult. "Stupid." Making a delayed lap around his office, Caspian then slows his stepping. "Your aggression is telling, Captain. First off, they're *my* men not yours, and I can do with them as I please. Secondly, you don't think I'm a proper commander—that I'm weak. Don't you?"

For theatrics, Caspian comically throws his hands up before slowly dropping them to his hips. Drawing his firearm and knife from their holsters, he carefully places them on the desk behind him, wiping his hands as he turns back around.

"You and I both know what you want," Caspian says, folding his arms, crossing his ankles, and leaning on the desk, putting himself into a non-combative stance. "So go ahead. Take it."

The officer grits his teeth and quickly plays the scenario out in his mind. With three other PPA soldiers at his disposal, the odds are in his favor. They are loyal and very effective in their craft, as is he. So, without a second thought, the officer walks up to Caspian and swings a thick fist up towards Caspian's brittle jaw.

It's like breathing for Caspian. Nonchalantly, he leans just slightly, arching his back only to feel the wind of the officer's missed uppercut. As predicted, the behemoth's hammer fist comes sweeping down. Catching it as if it was a twig in the wind, Caspian's smile shocks the officer.

Having picked their side, sealing their fate, two of the officer's men approach. With a swift punch to the windpipe of one, and a heavy open palm on the side of the skull of the other, Caspian kills one and concusses the other in a single second, all while remaining in complete control of the beastly officer's arm.

Eyeing the last standing private, Caspian simply shakes his head. "Think about it, soldier."

The burly officer takes Caspian's words as a subtle diversion, unsheathing his knife with his free hand and brining the point to Caspian's neck.

"You will yield your—"

But before he can finish the weak ultimatum, the officer's wrist is crushed to dust under Caspian's grip. Dropping the knife, it clatters to the ground, and with what strength the officer can muster, he forms a fist, striking Caspian across the side of his head. In an agonizing surprise, Caspian's head holds like a statue while the fist of the officer bends and breaks at the knuckles.

"As I was saying," Caspian states, popping his neck and then his back before breaking both knees of the officer, collapsing him in defeat. "I'm not sure you understand what is at stake. In fact, I highly doubt you understand the kind of information you let my sister leave with, and by failing to apprehend her, Rouge, or anyone else they've been involved with, you have jeopardized the entire program my family has built."

"Wh-what are you?" the beastly officer asks.

Approaching the squirming officer, Caspian crouches by his side, taking the defeated man's head into his hands before looking to the last standing soldier.

"Looks like you've been promoted."

And then slowly and joyfully, Caspian crushes the officer's skull between his bare hands.

TEN

New York
September 29, 2036

    He's made it and she would be proud. He hopes she'd be proud anyway. Holding his beautiful little girl's photo—all he has left—the governor looks down and admires her smile. Reuben's heart breaks as he remembers a time when he meant nothing to the world, but everything to her.

    Never again will he be a disappointment and a disgrace. Policies will be put into place, upholding the founding American values. Economies in every state will boom, political divides will heal, and hard work will be something to seek out rather than shirk. Meritorious behavior will be rewarded while jobs and business opportunities will always be present for those willing to take them, changing the trajectory of their destinies at any moment of their choosing. Dreams will be allowed to flourish, bringing to pass the vision of Martin Luther King Junior. That is what he will build. That will be his apology to his Tiffany.

    Change. Reform. These values still exist. The court of public opinion promotes a culture of privilege and argues against penitent individuals time and time again, presuming everyone's guilt before proven innocent. Whether that be white, black, rich, pretty, athletic, popular, smart, tall, short, two-parent, or simply having the privilege of being loved, the religious dogma feeds off guilt, projecting and using it to obtain power as they maximize the reach of their shame. Having a remorseful heart is one thing—it's necessary. Eternal self-condemnation is another entirely and is about as effective as an internet confession. True change comes by what you build, not from what you're able to destroy.

    "Governor White?" His assistant clears her throat as she pokes her head inside his office. "It's time."

    "I'll be right there," he says with a faint, placid smile.

    "But sir—"

    "Alyssa," he calmly says, "if I'm few minutes late, people aren't going to just pick up and leave."

    Mustering a smile, she nods her head, closing the door as she exits.

Folding the photo of his Tiffany, Reuben stands and faces himself in the mirror. If he could go back, he would. No amount of success and glory will be able to replace his little girl. Anybody can debate when life truly begins, but until you hold new breath in your hands—in your arms—one can't begin to fathom its complexity and its grace. But even then, deceit is a powerful tool. For him, it took holding the delicate new soul of his daughter, and then ending it because policy, law, and culture deemed it a just necessity in pursuit of achievement and *"freedom."* That naïve sacrifice blinded him to the true meaning of life. Although legally he is absolved, it will forever be his most damning use of agency.

Having finished picking his appearance of aesthetic flaws, White moves to the door and steps out. After all, they're waiting.

"Carter?" Lisa's voice crackles over the earpiece.

Why today? he thinks, practically mumbling the annoying question out loud. Of all the days to meet her *boyfriend*, Aila had to pick today. Carter tries to not let it bother him, but when a gut feeling just won't go away, well that's a huge red flag in his eyes! The fact that Mica is her boyfriend is outright baffling. Friend, that was an inevitability he saw coming. But romance? It's either bad luck or God's got a divine sense of humor.

"Carter! Check your two," Lisa repeats, erupting in his earpiece.

Seamlessly snapping back to the task at hand, Carter's eyes shoot off to the right of the stage in search of the potential risk. "It's clear. I've got nothing, Lisa."

"Brown coat!"

Another quick scan and a split second later, Carter sees the guy with his hand in his jacket pocket.

"Roger," he states, rolling his eyes at the fact that he didn't spot the obvious.

Marking the target with an infrared laser, Carter nods to the guard in the shadows. As Carter approaches in a blatantly obvious fashion, the guard covertly moves in the back.

"Sir," Carter begins, the man's gaze hardening.

In an attempt to move his hand from out of his jacket, Mica anticipates the attack. Before the man can fully draw his firearm, he is subdued and dragged off, having not drawn a single person's attention from Governor White's eloquent speech.

"Clear," Carter reports. "Good eye, Lisa. And nicely done, Mica…"

Carter makes another mental tally under the category titled "Number of Times the Boyfriend's Saved My Ass."

Mica is the best he's ever trained. That's not the problem. What it really comes down to is that Mica was trained as a soldier for the country and nothing more. The kid's arrogance has tempered over the months, but he's still young, sophomoric, and impulsive. Mica's not meant for Aila. Coming from personal experience, good soldiers aren't necessarily the most stable in a relationship.

"The governor is in his closing remarks," Lisa announces to the team. "When he finishes, Dan, take him to Rendezvous Charlie."

"How's the crowd looking?" Carter asks, his chin moving to his radio.

"Inspired," Lisa pauses. Having pieced together Carter's delayed reaction, Lisa completely understands why he overlooked the hitman. "No thanks to you," she chuckles out.

Carter shakes his head at the comment and turns to see Mica handing the unconscious would-be-assassin to the authorities.

"There will be no further questions at this time. Thank you," Dan announces to the media before escorting Governor White off the premises.

Catching Mica's eye, Carter motions towards the cars but Mica denies the order with a forceful shake.

"Can't. I told you," Mica says over the radio. "I've got to catch the flight."

"Get in the car," Carter orders more forcefully.

"You approved it earlier, and Dan's team has it under control. Plus, if I'm late you know exactly how that'll turn out for both of us."

This is supposed to be the first time the two are meeting. Not only is punctuality important to Aila, but the narrative of their first meeting hinges on the trust of that punctuality. Aila's no stranger to the unpredictable nature of her uncle's work, but he promised that things would be different once they moved back to the States. He'll have to break that promise at some point, but now—now is not the time.

"We good? I'm leaving either way, but I want to make sure before I do."

"Yeah…"

"Roger. See you in a couple hours."

Carter opens his mouth to protest something, but as a gentle hand touches his shoulder, he shuts up.

"Let it go," Lisa says.

Carter turns around. "I hate this."

"Doesn't matter," Lisa chuckles. "It'd be a lot easier if you would simply let it go, though."

Carter shakes his head. Lisa is Carter's best friend, but that doesn't mean she understands how to raise a child—a child his brother should be raising.

"Don't think I don't understand. She's as much family to you as she is to me!"

"It's not her I'm worried about," Carter argues.

"You are too!" she states, calling his bluff. "You're worried about both of them. Mica may be the bigger concern, but don't act like she's always been a saint."

"But she is a saint!" he blurts out. "She's never given me trouble until now."

"Give me a break. Italy? She was perfect in every way over there?" Lisa gives him a small shoulder check, knocking him off the curb and into a passing pedestrian.

"Sorry," Carter mumbles before grimacing back at Lisa.

"She's grown up a lot," Lisa says. "And that being said, Mica is a better boyfriend to her than you're willing to admit."

Carter hates it, but Lisa's right. It was Mica who confronted him about the dating situation and did so without her consent or knowledge, and in fact it was his idea that they meet in a controlled, staged environment, keeping both Carter's and Mica's anonymity safe. It's not an ideal situation, Mica admitted, but it's the best they got.

"It's just a defense mechanism," Lisa says.

"What is?" Carter asks, worried that she's talking about him.

"His arrogance." And then smiling, she knows full well that he'll hate her for this next part, but she has to! "He reminds me of you."

<hr />

"It's about time!" Aila flirtatiously says, opening the door for her man.

As he gives her a kiss, without pulling away from the embrace, her lips graze his with confusing but amorous words.

"Too bad..."

"What's that supposed to mean?" Mica asks, his lips still intertwined with Aila's.

"I was looking forward to some alone time before we left..."

Mica blushes at the innuendo. "Sorry, got caught up at work... You ready?" Giving her one more peck on the lips, he begins pulling her out the door.

"Hold on," she orders, grabbing the collar of his jacket, jerking him back into her apartment.

"Aila," he sighs, the door slamming behind them.

"Chill out. It's not what you think."

"I know," Mica scoffs when in reality he has no idea what the hell she's doing.

Lowering her voice to a whisper, Aila moves over to her backpack. "I found something on that key."

"Liar." He's looked at it hundreds of times and found nothing but scribbles and chipped paint.

"You doubt me?" she mockingly asks, whipping the key out and flipping it over, revealing the clout behind her claim.

"They're just scribbles and dots, babe."

"Are they?" she asks, clearly feeling even more clever by the second.

"Maybe scratches?"

"Funny," she mockingly laughs. "It's Arabic."

"Ara-what?"

"Arabic. It's a language," she says, rolling her eyes.

America's people have always perpetuated a self-centered culture, but since the closing of the war zones in the Middle East in the late 2010s and beginning of the 2020s, it only got worse. With censorship already a common practice through news sources and the unofficial corporate arms of the U.S. government, this helped turn an already narcissistic culture even more in on itself. Foreign policy was no longer a priority and with the help of certain political parties affiliated with the Chinese Communist Party—hosts of the *World Internet Conference*—it first became practice and then policy not too long after to begin censoring, filtering, and restructuring online information from other countries. This caused obvious and further distrust in the media, corporations, and the governmental information websites for Americans, and so citizens began to put even more effort in finding sources outside of the United States.

A man by the name of Stanley Braithsworth projected this as a major risk for his digital identification platform. The way he saw it, when the United States government has no trust from its citizens, it's a threat to "democracy." Creating intrusive filtering algorithms, Braithsworth found a way to essentially cut off the United States' internet from the rest of the world, creating an orphan nation that socially and even economically disincentivized its citizens—through their *Digital IDs*—from participating in "radical behaviors" the algorithms identified. Slightly increased prices for certain products and services, fewer access to said products and services, and obviously when you can shape public perception to look upon certain actions as taboo, the power of peer pressure is pushed to its full potential. Like the Patriot Act, the true intentions were without the

American people's knowledge, and for those who had accurate theories about why and what Stanley Braithsworth was doing with his tech company, it was propagandized that it was for "the security of the American people."

All of this hinged on the simple concept of out of sight, out of mind, slowly placing a bubble over the information that flowed in and out of the country, VPN or not. Braithsworth contracted with the federal government and made it easy to identify and keep the political ideologies they felt benefited the country, his company, and mutual oligarchs within the bubble, all while simultaneously forcing radical agendas such as Islamic Jihad and Chinese Communism out. To an extent, that did protect America, but briefly. Marxism still had its claws in the Liberal Left, and rather than bringing any sort of good, historical geopolitical context from other countries to refute the destructive activists, the appeal to novelty, or argumentum ad novitatem, was allowed to go unchecked. Without the distractions from foreign policy, America could go on and think about itself and its own power structures.

However, depending on who was asking, as an unintended consequence, languages and cultures quickly began to disappear from the American psyche, leaving only English and Spanish as the primary languages in the United States. Places like "China Town" and the vast communities of immigrants that flooded to the States for the free enterprise opportunity America offered, also began to disappear. Unlike native born American citizens, *they did have* the perspective and context for the dangerous ideas and policies America was implementing, saw the dangers, and abandoning what they once held onto as the "American Dream," decided to take their bets elsewhere.

Out of sight, out of mind is an indiscriminate force. The only reason Aila is aware of any of this is because of her uncle and his work abroad. With him being her legal guardian, the government couldn't stop him from bringing her overseas. She and any other child of a U.S. representative for the international community experienced life outside this digital bubble, giving them "unapproved knowledge." Most of the kids and their parents that she met within this community ended up staying outside of the country permanently after retirement.

Aila and Carter, however, did not.

"What's it say then?" Mica asks, testing her.

"They're numbers: 070476."

"Okay…" Mica slowly says, but before he can argue any further to the still questionable nature of the claim, Aila holds up her finger and continues.

"Let me finish. I thought it was a little weird too—that it seemed a little random or a mistranslation on my part, but it wasn't either of those." Rushing over to her computer, she touches a tab on one of the various web browsers and open applications. "After I checked my translation like ten times, I went with it; they're numbers after all. How complicated can six numbers be?" Once the browser loads, the site shows what looks like a locking system for a door or safe.

"What is that?" Mica asks.

"This here," Aila says with a smile, "is an antique brass mortise skeleton lockset. Or at least that's what the item description says. Anyway, the key that opens it is like the key we have here—the one that you found."

"Nobody uses keys anymore though…" Mica again slowly states, thinking that he's seeing where this is going.

Since 2025, physical locking systems and security devices have been a thing of the past. Cars, houses, safes all moved away from the lock and key model. Even the alphabet and numeric combinations began to fall out of favor. Instead, people began to invest in biometrics. The reasoning for this market shift was that *anyone* can pick a lock, and far too often do people write their passwords somewhere easy to find, or at the very least, pick a birthday or date that isn't that hard for hackers to crack. If they were complicated passwords, it was all moot as most organizations and individuals kept a digital list which was just hidden behind your basic passphrase anyway. Not everyone, though, has access to fingerprints, retinal scans, and coded heat signatures—therefore these types of biometric and memory security models were advertised as being more secure than a simple lock and key or password. In less than a single generation, the security market shifted from one form of asset protection to another.

Here's the chink in the armor. First off, not everyone had the patience to learn how to pick a lock and therefore, not everyone could pick a lock let alone crack a safe. So that marketing was just a lie. Also, people increasingly became aware of the necessity to create sophisticated passwords and combinations that were algorithmically locked, making brute force hacking methods much more difficult. Couple the deception in advertising with the speed of the booming biometric security industry, and it wasn't too long before people forgot how to even operate a simple key or input a simple dial and spindle combination lock. Like the market shift of rewind machines for VHS tapes in the '90s and early 2000s, teens and kids didn't even know how to operate these old fashion locking mechanisms.

This is the irony of it all. These teens became young adults in the work force who continued to subconsciously morph the physical security within their respective industries. They then began to learn how to hack these "un-hackable" biometrics by developing techniques to pick up fingerprints, translate photos into retinal scans, and imitate heat signatures. Customized sensory devices improved, and even the black market made it an easy task when cutting off fingers or removing eyes became more efficient and cleaner, unlocking the device and eliminating witnesses simultaneously. The good old key and combination lock stuck around, however. Thanks to antiquity collectors, these forms of security never truly died out—all they did was shift hands, becoming more secure due to their rarity and the unconventional knowledge that is needed to operate them.

"Exactly," Aila states enthusiastically. "Nobody knows about keys anymore, let alone uses them. However, I then had to ask myself, why write a numbered combination, especially on a key?"

"Who says it's a numbered combination?" Mica asks. "Maybe it's a date for when the key was made."

"I thought of that," Aila begins, "but I also thought that maybe the key was just something that held the combination rather than it being the means to open something—that it's just a clue."

"A clue to what?"

Without saying it, Aila clicks on another tab to open yet another picture: an antique 1900 Sycamore Safe from New York City—one with a spindle combination lock securing it. Just underneath the picture and product description are an address with a delivery date of December 2035, one year ago.

"How'd you get this information?"

"Had to use some of the skills my uncle showed me while living abroad," Aila says, continuing to smile at her cleverness, her acumen momentarily captivating Mica. He hasn't even seen the crux of the information. "Did you see the address?"

Moving his eyes from Aila's to the delivery location, he's in utter shock as the location is of someone who no doubt would collect antique safes.

"That there," Aila says, "is the office of the Governor of Massachusetts."

"I know," Mica says, skeptical of the coincidence and not accepting the possibility of what Aila's cleverness has presented. "I work for him."

"You of all people should know how corrupt politicians can be."

"And you know how I got this key, right?" Mica reminds her.

By implying that Governor White is involved with the Ordeans, then by default, her uncle, Uncle Carter, is also involved because he is the one that assigned Mica to protect the presidential candidate—to protect the only man that Carter believes to be able to save the Republic. That last part she doesn't know though…

"Yes," Aila softly says. "But it's nothing new for politicians to be crony capitalists. Money and power are all that matters to these kinds of people."

"Not this one… I work for him, Aila."

This shuts her up for a moment.

This isn't just Carter speaking through Mica. Mica has been working with the governor only for a couple of weeks, but for someone with a character like Reuben G. White, it doesn't take long before you see the authentic and patriotic nature individuals like that have. The way he talks about history, the sacred nature he holds for those who have died for this country, and the basic treatment he has for those on his campaign, none of this adds up as someone colluding with the Fourth Reich. If everything she is pontificating is true, it'll break Mica. After all the healing he has had to do from Kim's murder… To have the cause he believes will avenge her and everyone else whose life has been taken by the Ordeans—to have the very thing he has been fighting against be Governor White, a betrayal like that would break anyone.

 Calmly, Aila turns to Mica, putting her hands on either side of his face.

 "Hey." She gently touches her lips to his. "It might not be what you think. But we have to know for certain."

 "We're going to be late," he says, kissing her back. Standing, he takes her hand and leads her out the door. As she follows, grabbing her coat and phone, Mica slows down for a moment, just enough to grab her in his arms and say, "I love you."

 "What'd you say?" A grin, bigger than any he has ever seen before, stretches across Aila's face.

 "I said, 'I love you.'"

 "I love you too, Mica Rouge," Aila whispers back, planting a passionate kiss right on the lips of the man of her dreams.

 "Breathe," Lisa says, putting her hand on the back of Carter's.

 "They're late," he huffs, turning his hand over, grabbing her hand back with a small squeeze.

 "By three minutes," Lisa scoffs, throwing his hand away. It was cute at first, but now it's just annoying.

 Nonchalantly, he takes a sip of his coffee. "She doesn't like being late. The whole point of him leaving after the speech was to not be late!"

 Lisa shakes her head. "You're being a real asshole, you know that? Absolutely ridiculous…"

"Wow…" Carter nearly spits his drink out all over the table. He's only heard her swear on one other occasion, and they were in the middle of a gunfight then.

"You made me say it." She shrugs, not able to hide her smirk. From the corner of her eye, just outside the main window, she sees Mica and Aila walk inside hand in hand. "There they are!"

Carter looks up at the same moment the happy couple kiss.

"Get a room," he sighs out.

Her patience having boiled over, Lisa flicks him in the forehead just like her mother used to do when she was being a brat.

"Ouch." Carter rubs his head, gritting his teeth in a scowl. "Why?"

"Why do you think?"

And just like he used to do when Carter was fed up with the woes of youth, he sarcastically shrugs at Lisa, sticking his tongue out.

"What'd we miss?" Aila asks, skipping over and grinning from ear to ear.

"Nothing, dear," Lisa says with opens arms, embracing her niece. "Your uncle was just being—well, your uncle."

"Of course, he was." Aila rolls her eyes, turning to Carter for a hug.

"So," Lisa begins, beaming with excitement. "Are you going to introduce us to your boy toy?"

There's a reason Lisa's been in espionage most of her career. It's like she's meeting Mica for the first time, despite their professional relationship already established. It is a mission critical skill to become multiple people, sometimes simultaneously. Carter has seen this Lisa numerous times in the field, and yes, it's still Lisa, but this version is the only "Lisa" Aila has ever known.

"C'mon…" is all Carter can say at the awkward comment. She's being a little over the top, but nothing Aila hasn't seen before.

"Well… he's in your class, so you already know him," Aila slowly states, catching weird vibes herself.

"Not officially though," she says, holding out her hand.

Taking her hand, Mica shakes it and smiles, trying to mirror Lisa's enthusiasm as best he can.

"Professor Rodgers."

However, it comes off as him trying too hard, something Aila also notices. *Maybe it's just Mica's unnaturally stiff posture*, she thinks, filing it away for later analysis.

"Call me Lisa outside of class—unless of course you want me to call you Mr. Student?"

All right, Aila thinks. *There is definitely something weird going on!* Not only is it Aunt Lisa's pseudo-drunken behavior, but her uncle is unusually surly. Clearly there is something behind the scenes that she isn't seeing.

Chuckling, Mica turns stiffly to Carter hoping to anticipate the next socially approved behavior.

"And this is my Uncle Carter," Aila slowly says, carefully watching Mica's interaction with her uncle. "Whom you've never met…"

"Do you have a first name?" Mica chuckles out, always having wanted to solve the mystery of his first name.

"Mister or Uncle, take your pick," Carter says, firmly grasping Mica's hand just long enough to make it uncomfortable for Aila, and with Carter's eyes burrowing into Mica's as if he's attempting self-combustion, she can't handle it any longer.

"What the hell is going on?"

Aila's always been very aware of the nature of Carter and Lisa's work, but when they were transferred back to the States, she assumed that they'd have more of a paper-pushing role. All of that is thrown into question though, as she begins reading between the lines of what Mica's told her and this previously held knowledge.

"We ordered some cheeseburgers and milkshakes," Lisa announces, diverting the awkward atmosphere. "Mica, I hope you like cookies and cream!"

As the group sits down, Aila whispers in Mica's ear. "What's going on?" But rather than even attempting to address it, Mica gives a flat, toothy grin.

"So, tell me, where are you from, Mica?" Lisa begins, trying to normalize the situation with obvious small talk.

"Please," Carter mumbles.

Swiftly, Lisa kicks Carter's shin, forcing a rather hilarious yelp from the boorish old man. It doesn't go unnoticed by many, including a little girl one booth over who screeches out in a fit of laughter before sticking her tongue out at Carter. With the world against him, Carter throws his arms in the air and storms off towards the bathroom.

"What is going on, Aunt Lisa?"

"He just had a rough day at the office."

Everyone at the table knows *that* is bullshit.

"I'm going to go talk with him," Mica says.

"Don't!" Lisa and Aila simultaneously exclaim.

"He just needs a minute," Lisa then calmly says with a wink.

"I have to use the bathroom anyway," Mica says, ignoring Lisa's passive aggressive order. Squeezing Aila's hand, Mica returns Lisa's wink as he stands and makes his way in the direction of Carter. Confidently, Mica approaches the bathroom door, but as he opens it and walks in, anxiety and angst flood him from every angle.

"You okay, sir?" Mica asks, seeing Carter standing at the sink, his hands gripping the countertop as he just stares at the dripping droplets from the sink.

All Carter can muster is a nonverbal response—a glance fiercer than any Mica's seen in training.

"Okay," Mica slowly begins. "Just thought I'd check in."

Turning to exit, figuring there is nothing that can be said to alleviate whatever Carter is going through, Mica gives a small shrug, more for himself than Carter's coarse mood.

"I practically raised Aila," Carter states, stopping Mica's exit. "Lisa helped, but Aila never was her responsibility." Then, shifting his gaze from the sink to Mica, Carter stresses his last statement. "Take care of her…"

Aila's told him the story, as much as she can remember anyway. Three years old is young, but Aila has an impressive, vivid memory, and for the details she couldn't recall, Mica turned to the archives, knowing that Carter wouldn't give him the time of day.

Sincerely, and with as much feeling as he can muster, all Mica says is, "I will."

There's no need for anything more—say it once and say it right. Mica waits for acceptance, and once Carter nods and gives it, Mica quietly leaves.

━━━✦✧✦━━━

White's Campaign Office

"Now, was that so bad?" Aila whispers, knowing that the whole dinner was a complete lie. She managed to get a lot of information from her aunt after Mica left to find Uncle Carter, and although Lisa didn't spill anything specific, Aila knows when there's something being kept from her.

In all fairness, there's a lot she's not telling them either. For starters, there is a lot about Aila's past that she has yet to reveal to Mica—her promiscuity in Italy being one, which wasn't entirely her fault… Yes, she was targeted by a foreign asset, but she was unnecessarily reckless to say the least in her formative years which made her a prime mark to begin with. Now, when it comes to Carter and Lisa, Aila's never had the security clearance to know the details about anything they do, but she's not dumb. She's made some logical conclusions about the things Carter and Lisa were involved with overseas for the U.S. government. Combine all of this with what she knows about Mica, and Aila is willing to bet that their little meal earlier was not the first time Mica's met either of them. In fact, if a gun was held to her head, she's absolutely certain that it was her uncle who recruited Mica. If that's the case, she's that much more apprehensive about their current breaking-and-entering situation.

"Let's just stay focused," Mica softly says.

Heading off a conversation that he's not quite ready to have, Mica knows she's prying. She'll figure out the truth eventually if she already hasn't. Like Kim, Aila has an amazing knack for reading accurate information between the vaguest of lines. It's why she was friends with Kim to begin with…

Looking up into his bicolor eyes through his devilish disguise, Aila's heart melts, and as he stares back at Aila through Kim's old masquerade mask, countless memories and emotions flood him. He debated for a long time whether he should've pulled Kim's old mask out, but it ultimately came down to the simple fact that Aila needed a disguise—that and it was time to completely let go of the past.

As he reverently grazes her cheek with the back of his hand, Aila is reminded of the night Kim put it on her own face. The jealously she had for her friend was damn near unbearable. She wasn't envious of Mica or of Kim by any means—Mica was a friend and Kim, she was one of the best people Aila knew, but she longed for what the two of them had together at the time. The dynamics between those two were fiery to say the least, making Mica and Kim the ultimate power couple. While the fighting cage was his arena, Kim destroyed her opponents through broadcast and old school journalism. Wearing this mask is not only a memory of that, but it's a symbolic weight of the void Kim's death left in both Mica and Aila's lives.

"You still think it looks good on me?" she asks.

"Definitely…"

And with that one word, Aila's natural confidence shines.

"So, how's this all work?" she asks.

Studying the exterior of the building, Mica easily spots every camera.

"Security here has always been low, so getting in and out shouldn't be a problem."

"You're on the security detail, aren't you?" Aila jokingly asks, pointing out the irony in what Mica just said.

"I don't have a say in everything… You brought the key, right?"

Reaching for her pocket, Aila begins to fret as she frantically pats herself down. "I think I dropped it."

"You think you what?!"

Then, Aila turns off the panic as quickly as she turned it on, coolly slipping the key into his hands. "Just kidding."

"Don't do that..." he snaps, refusing to laugh.

"We could've just written down the code," she says, her wide grin still plastered to her face.

"OPSEC," is all that he says to this.

"Whatever, high speed," Aila mumbles, sarcastically throwing her hands in the air. "So, where do you think the safe is?"

"If they have a basement, my guess is it'd be there," Mica shrugs.

"What do you mean, *if they have a basement?*"

"I checked the blueprints and there is no basement in the original design of the building. Secondly, I've been in every room from the main floor up and haven't seen any safe that matches your intel."

"What are you saying? That I'm wrong about the safe?"

Mica chuckles. "No. I'm saying that this might not be the place."

"Where else would it be then, his house?"

"It's possible," Mica says, *but not probable,* he then thinks. It makes more sense to keep crucial intel—especially the type that could prove treasonous behavior—away from home and in a secret location.

Leading the way inside, Mica weaves his way through the shadows towards the back entrance as Aila closely follows, trying to resist the urge to stare at his perfectly sculpted butt. Yes, tighter, stretchy clothing is tactically more practical, but it also acts as a sexy addition for his ass…

Quickly analyzing the door, Mica pulls out his knife and snips the wires of the alarm system.

"That was easy," Aila mutters.

"So far."

Sneaking their way into the building, Mica gently closes the door, listening for the secure click as he does.

"Stay here for a second," he tells Aila.

Crouching behind a desk, Aila watches as Mica methodically moves about the first floor, clearing it of any potential threat. Three minutes later, satisfied that the area is secure, he begins searching for the room that technically doesn't exist that is housing a theoretical safe.

"Anything?" Aila whispers as she sees Mica approaching.

Mica shakes his head.

"Well, it wouldn't be obvious, would it?"

"No." Mica thinks about this for a moment. The floorplan isn't that big and where else would you be able to hide a safe?

"What about a crawl space or a closet?" Aila suggests.

Of course, Mica thinks.

Gesturing to Aila, the two rush over to a small cleaning room off to the side. Like all maintenance closets, it's not elaborate or complex, but something has always seemed off every time Mica has had to get something from it. Three of the four walls are encumbered with shelves, tools, and storage of all sorts, making the barren fourth wall a rather odd anomaly.

"Well, if you're looking for something like a hidden room it's kind of obvious…" Aila mumbles.

"But where's the door?" Mica asks himself rather than Aila. Sliding his fingers across the blank wooden wall, Mica begins searching for anything remotely resembling a handle, button, or keyhole. After three passes along the edges and its surface, he's about to call it when a sharp edge in the lower right-hand corner of the wall cuts his finger. Lifting the ridged, tiny metal flap, Mica uncovers a small opening.

"Looks like we need the key after all," Aila says, and before Mica even asks, she pulls it out and hands it over. It slides in perfectly. Slowly turning it, making sure not to snap the fragile piece of metal, Mica is barely a quarter of a turn in when he hears a distinct click and the pattering of feet at the front of the office.

"What was that?" Aila hisses.

Quietly, Mica removes the key and places it back into his pocket before rushing up to the closet entrance. Slowing his breath, Mica listens for any clue as to who it could be, praying that someone forgot something in the office. Signaling for Aila to hide against the far wall of the tiny room, Mica angles his body, allowing him to pie the corner and slowly reveal pieces of the office without exposing his location.

It's not a forgetful intern. In the middle of the office, Mica sees two hooded figures rummaging through desks and shelves as they search the entire floorplan. Cursing at himself for not being more careful, before Mica can determine any sort of plan of action, he stops upon seeing one of the hooded figures pulling out a small cardboard box from out of his cloak and placing it beneath a desk. Beneath *his* desk!

Shooting from out of the compact room, Mica catches the hooded figures completely by surprise. With one freezing in place, the other runs for immediate cover. In a swift manner, Mica takes down the self-paralyzed one with a sharp open palm to the underbelly of his jaw, dislocating the mandible and knocking him unconscious. Before he even hits the floor, Mica searches for the remaining enemy.

"Mica."

Aila's soft, echoing whisper stops him in his tracks.

Having heard the woman as well, the second hooded figure dashes in Aila's direction. Mica sprints to cut off the direct path of the hooded figure, but as he approaches, Mica's dealt a swift kick to the chest that sends him toppling over a filing cabinet. Bolting upright, Mica sees the enemy's shadow dart into the maintenance closet, and in a single second, Mica kicks open the closing door where to Mica's horror, a knife is pressed up against Aila's neck.

"Stop!" the figure commands, a slight trickle of blood tracing the blade's edge before dripping onto Aila's shirt collar.

Terrified, Aila still manages to keep her composure, it not being the first situation like this that she's been in.

"Let her go," Mica growls.

"We've already warned you, Mr. Rouge!" the hooded figure calmly states. Extending his hand, the figure reveals a small, metal switch and with his thumb compressed, time slows as the building shakes, glass shatters, and the room in which they are standing in ignites into flames.

Carter screeches to a halt in front of the smoldering building, slamming the car door shut as he exits and marches towards the ambulance.

"Uncle!" Aila states, rushing forward.

"Where is he?" Carter asks, holding on and squeezing her as tightly as he possibly can.

"He's just over there." Aila proudly smiles, pointing over to the entrance of what was once the office.

Mica reacted with such agility. There was no stopping the bomb from going off, but in a flash, Mica moved and tackled both her and the hooded figure, putting himself within immediate reach to grip the blade pressed against her neck. As the three of them fell to the ground, Mica positioned his hand just above the clavicle of the hooded figure, and upon hitting the floor, Mica put him in a simple but violent forearm choke that coupled as a shell of protection for Aila from the fiery debris. Once the immediate burst was over, and before she or the enemy knew what was happening, Mica had the hooded figure on his stomach, twisting his arm around, pinning him to the floor.

"He almost got you killed, Aila." Carter rolls his eyes, seeing her giddy smile.

"How?" she asks, appalled. "We were picking up something that he left at the office." Lying to his face, Aila insinuates that this was merely a case of being in the wrong place at the wrong time.

"Aila…" Carter's not buying it.

"He saved a man's life," she then says, trying to score some additional points for her boyfriend.

"Yeah, the same man who set off the bomb?"

With no half-truth this time, Aila just shrugs as her response.

"Stay here," Carter says, kissing his niece on the forehead before turning his wrath towards Mica.

Talking to the authorities, Mica finishes his report just before Carter jerks him into the adjacent alley.

"What the hell is your problem? She's my niece, you son of a bitch!"

"I don't know what you're talking about."

Carter nearly loses it and ends Mica's life here on the spot. Rather, he sensors himself, bringing the severity of the situation into one simple phrase. "I trusted you."

Mica has nothing he can say to this. Carter did trust him, and Mica reinforced that assurance when he promised to take care of Aila. This—this is obviously the opposite of that.

"Aila just lied to me, which she hasn't done in years, so you want to tell me why you two were really here?"

"Why'd you try to kill me?" Mica then asks, turning himself into the aggressor.

"What the hell—?" Carter sputters at the wild accusation.

Mica thinks that he's put it all together: the key, Kim's murder, and Carter recruiting him all in the same night. As per Division protocol, agents are not supposed to know the identity of other agents, making this is a rather convenient explanation for the hooded figures on both the night of Kim's death and tonight. Mica has no idea how deep this really goes, not to mention the security ramifications that are intertwined with the compartmentalization of it all.

"You really think that I'd do that?"

"Why was there a bomb placed under my desk?"

"We have enemies, Mica…" Carter feels like this is obvious, but with someone at Mica's level of paranoia, nothing is beyond absurdity.

Avoiding the statement, Mica continues his line of aggressive questioning. "What's in the maintenance room then?"

And like that, Carter figures out the truth. "Where's the key?"

Mica refuses to answer, thinking that Carter's inquiry is the admission of guilt he's been looking for.

"Mica. Were they trying to get into that door?"

"You were in on it, weren't you?"

"Mica, get over yourself! I didn't try to bomb—"

"I'm not talking about the bomb!" Mica yells, his voice reverberating off the alley walls. "I'm talking about Kim!"

Carter throws up his hands, not knowing how else to convince the kid. "This is way more complicated than you realize, Mica."

"I bet it is." And without another word, Mica turns his back on Carter and heads towards the street.

"Where's the key, Mica?"

"I lost it," Mica calls back over his shoulder. "I got you him, though," he says as he points over to someone sprawled out on a stretcher.

This is spiraling out of Carter's control faster by the minute. Running his hands through his hair, Carter makes the decision that could make or break the team.

"I'm Detective Wright," he says, approaching the paramedic. "Can I have a moment? I just want to ask our friend here a few questions."

With a blank expression, the paramedic shrugs her shoulders before walking to the front of the ambulance.

"Hey, boss," the guy coolly says.

"Shut up! You don't work for me anymore…" Carter says, pressing his thumb into a gaping gash on the man's shoulder. "Now, you're going to tell me what I want to hear."

The man winces in pain, but before he can make any sort of audible sound of discomfort, Carter has a hand over his mouth.

"And before you answer," Carter begins, squeezing even harder, reinforcing the thought of future pain, "think very carefully. Do you understand?"

Removing his hand, Carter watches as the man gathers his thoughts, noticing that the two of them are isolated from the rest of the scene. If Carter wanted to, it wouldn't take much effort to shove him into the back of the vehicle and find a place for the two of them to have a lengthier version of this conversation.

Choosing the shorter of the two options, the man simply nods his head.

"Good," Carter says. "Now, what is Harris planning?"

Eleven

Area Thirty-Eight
Spring

"Hands behind your back, buddy."

Turning Jax around, Connor slaps a pair of flex cuffs to his wrists before zipping them tight.

"Easy there!" Jax winces, the skin of his wrist pinching under the plastic vice.

"Sorry. If we want this to work, it's got to look legitimate."

Renn smirks, having very little remorse as she does the same exact thing to another man.

"Come on now…" Jude flirtingly says, licking his scarred lips, trying his best to hide his own discomfort.

The first to volunteer for any dangerous, clandestine mission, is often the last to be selected. In all of Connor's experience, never has he encountered a soldier as oblivious, careless, and seemingly tactless as Jude. He's as self-aware as he is homely, and if it wasn't for the uncanny similarity he has to Jax, he'd be downright hideous. If there were more like him within the Raider tribes, The Government would have won the exhausting war a long time ago. With that being said, trust is in short supply, and since the three are still *earning their keep*, what choice do they have but to take anyone willing to put some faith in their tactics. This mission is far from suicide, but it is risky to say the least and it can't be overlooked that Jude volunteered, putting his life on the line for Connor, Renn, and Jax simply by being here.

"Oi, Jackie boy! What are you complaining about? We're out of the Encampment and have a beautiful set of legs to accompany us. What more can you ask for?"

Jax rolls his eyes, gagging at yet another one of Jude's annoying attempts to exchange saliva with a woman—this woman being Renn. Yes, she got Kip killed, but over the past months, Jax has seen her in a different light.

Like Connor, Renn is highly trained, making her effective and lethal. She saw things that Jax and Kip hadn't—they forced the hand of someone with power and influence that night. He knows if Kip were still breathing, he wouldn't regret what they tried to do, but Jax does. Jax can't help but blame himself for actions that directly led to Kip's death; they forced Renn to do something against her nature in order to protect what she saw as the greater good at the time. She had to keep the upper hand, preserving their ability to overthrow the Oligarchs. The Government has taken from her more than just friends. The cogs within the machine have each taken their turn in stealing her virtue, her sanity, and at times her will to live. From the moment she's taken her first breath, Renn has unwillingly been an asset of the Nine, and Jax can only imagine the fortitude needed to endure what Renn calls her life.

He doesn't need her to say that she regrets her decision to have Kip killed to know that she does—that the execution haunts her. The two still fundamentally disagree on a variety of tactics, methodologies, and particular doctrines they've been implementing with the Raiders, but on the other side of that coin, Jax has also come to understand the intense hatred she has for the Nine. It's the core to everything she does, and from her unique role she's played within the Oligarchs, Renn has a drive that Jax is just becoming privy to. He absolutely loathes it—he loathes her, but his understanding of her actions the night of Kip's death is just another layer wound into the intricacies of their relationship. She's a beautiful woman, and while Jax tries to discern whether it's jealousy, indifference, or a combination of the two, for the moment, Jax would rather just keep Renn where she is in his mind.

"We ready?" she asks, her glance towards Jax not going unnoticed.

Looking around, making one final check, Connor makes the call. "I think so."

Stepping away from their vehicles, the team of four make their way to the edge of the city and into deafening silence. Each crunch of broken glass under their boots shatters through the air, while the crackling of dying embers in the rubble-lined streets sound as a roaring mountainside fire. Every other building stands in ruined abandonment, with bodies irreverently dispersed in the gutters of their foundation, testifying to the fact that ever since Jax stepped foot outside of the PPA's jurisdiction, examples have been made of both worker and citizen alike. With each step sinking into the muddy streets, Jax holds his breath at what a few months can do to a place he once called home, and as he stares at a distant City Hall, what was once familiar is now hauntingly foreign.

"Looks like you're famous, Jackie boy."

Passing the occasional burnt body, propagandistic posters litter the sidewalks and wall space, and while most are tattered remnants stuck face down in the melting snow, Jax is able to find an intact poster that gives clout to his perceived horrors.

Jax Rouge
Residency I.D. 220
Wanted for murder, kidnap of PPA officials, and conspiring against The Government
Dead or Alive: Reward, 10,000 credits

There's some truth to that, but if that needed some context, his photo plastered with a red X and bold letters spelling out *DEAD* is an abject lie.

"Famous, but dead," Jax mumbles. "Any details?" Jax asks Connor and Renn, both of whom shrug their shoulders.

"If I know Caspian, after Connor's little trap, my brother not only tied you with Kip, but since we've all been missing, he took it as an opportunity to link our disappearance to you as well."

"Seems like a stretch," Jude scoffs.

"It doesn't matter," Renn says. "Caspian is all about narrative—about tying things off with a convenient explanation."

"Let me get this straight," Jude begins, still not buying Renn's theory. "They have no idea what happened, and instead of actually expending resources to kill Jax for real, they just publicize his fake death?"

"Killing Jax doesn't explain us missing, and like I said, it's the narrative."

"Which is?"

"That he won," she coldly states. "That his PPA are loyal martyrs." Caspian has no reason to believe that she and Connor betrayed him, but having always been one to sway public opinion, there's no better explanation than the one he has fabricated for the Area.

In the distance, not too far from the four is a pleasantly familiar tone that echoes back to Jax.

"We need to go!" the young voice pleads. Combine that with the woman's sob, and Jax is taken back to the night he left. "Mari, we're not supposed to be outside…"

Jax's heart leaps upon hearing the name, but is it real? As the woman's weeping continues, the party of four rounds the corner where he sees that it is. Mari kneeling in the mud, grasps a crumpled poster, and with Ann standing over her sister, shaking her shoulders relentlessly, Jax's heart pounds against his chest.

Seeing her broken by the paper she holds, as he attempts to shout out to her, any words he might have thought of bunch and stick in his throat as his final, bitter moments with her stand in the back of his mind. Kip's death killed a part of Jax that night, forever changing the meaning of his life. However, Jax never took thought that his absence might leave that same kind of void in Mari.

Ann begins to panic upon hearing their approaching muddy footsteps. Shaking her sister more ferociously, keeping her eyes glued to who she thinks are their executioners, Ann begins shouting.

"Please! Mari, we need to go!"

Panic continues to encompass her tiny frame, and with each step, Ann fixates her gaze on their approach until finally, recognition dawns.

"I don't care anymore," Mari says, the words mirroring her wrenching cry. In a single night, one where Mari saw the two of them building a life together outside of the hell the Nine had them in, Jax vanished. For months, without even a simple reason for his disappearance, she was left with nothing but speculation. Despite this, there'd still been hope that he had a plan and would come back for her, but whatever dream her hope conjured up has been erased by the declaration crumpled in her hands. It was one thing to have Jax missing from her life, but dead—dead is permanent and not a single explanation is left to comfort her.

"Mari?" Jax is finally able to cough out.

In disbelief, her head shoots up towards the familiar timbre and resonance of her spoken name. Her world has been uprooted, turned upside down, and as her eyes meet his, it happens all over again.

Is this really happening? Mari asks herself. Standing, the mud dripping from off her knees, she reaches out. Touching his face, feeling his skin, still in disbelief she moves to every corner of the man's body. Her fingertips glance off his lips and recognize the familiar texture as they move to his chin and down his neck.

With his hands tied behind his back, all Jax can do is lean his head forward, placing it on Mari's, letting her know as best he can that he is real—that he is alive and in front of her.

"I'm sorry," is the first and only thing he can say.

"Jackie!" Ann shouts, rushing up and wrapping her tiny arms around the miracle he embodies. Near tears but holding strong, the little girl just holds Jax in her tight hug, wanting to never let him go again.

"What the hell is going on?" Jude slowly asks, looking around for any awkward attention they might be getting from prying eyes. The streets may be desolate, but that doesn't mean they aren't monitored.

"I've missed you guys," Jax says, trying to hug Ann.

"I love you," Mari finally musters up the courage to say, and like Ann, holds him, never wanting to let go.

"We need to move," Renn hisses to Connor.

"I'm all right," Jax tells the two as he's ushered away. "I'm safe. I promise."

Ann waves, her cheery smile stretched across her face. Wiping tears of sorrow to make room for tears of joy, Mari turns to Ann. "Let's go…"

"Where?" Ann asks, her joyful wave being interrupted.

"After them."

How stupid could he get? Compromising the entire mission, and for what? A hug and a few words? She frets over this, but in the back of Renn's mind she longs for the sentiment of being missed.

"It's a liability waiting to happen," Renn concludes.

"What's done is done," Connor says, keeping his head in the game.

Within a few moments, the company rounds a corner, seeing the extravagant City Hall officially welcoming them into the Area. Outside, thousands of residents await the sorting process to be tried, convicted, and executed all in one swift, efficient judicial ruling. Inside its glass walls, dozens of officials attempt to frantically create order out of their manufactured chaos.

The mission held doubt for Jax, but upon seeing the systematic injustice, all apprehension is erased and replaced by sheer will.

"Where is he?" Jax asks.

Scanning the building, Renn finds him in the middle of the stage, the chief executioner—Caspian.

"There," she says.

"Let's do this thing," Jude declares, and as the four casually walk through the open doors of City Hall, the untamable chaos is instantaneously tempered.

"Renn? Connor?" Caspian shouts, a smile emerging under his heinous eyes.

Jumping off the stage and with open arms, Caspian approaches the two lost siblings. Feigning affection, Connor and Renn allow the embrace, and as soon as they pull away, everything is put in motion.

"We brought you someone," Connor says, presenting Jax to Caspian.

"Splendid!" he shouts, clapping his hands thunderously. "The terrorist himself! And who is this?" Caspian then asks, eyeing the unexpected Jude.

"An associate of his," Connor responds.

With a smile, Caspian throws his arms into the air, and at the top of his lungs shouts, "Stop the executions. You have obtained mercy."

As tears fill the eyes of all residents being shuffled out of City Hall, Caspian looks to both Connor and Renn, gesturing for them to follow.

Together the five make their way to a quiet, secluded room behind the stage where inside, two guards flank either end of the exquisite luxury office. Dark marble embellishes the ground while photos of Caspian and his war medals chronologically decorate the walls in full circle, ending at his desk, marking his achievement as Area Leader of the Thirty-Eighth Area of the North American Union as his greatest success.

"Please," Caspian calmly says, directing both Renn and Connor to two soft, maroon chairs.

Reluctantly, the two warriors sit, casually calculating the threat the flanking guards pose.

"Now tell me," Caspian begins, bringing Jax to the front of his desk as he sits and swivels around in his chair. "Where have you been all this time?"

"Why?" Jax asks.

Pondering the question as if it is a studious and intellectual one, Caspian asks, "What do you think we've been doing out there?"

"Having fun?" Jax shrugs. "Isn't that what murder is to you?"

"I like you. You remind me of someone I used to know," Caspian says with a smile. "To be honest, we've been guessing," he then says, clarifying what the horrendous scene outside entailed. "We've had no idea where it is you could've gone, and with my two top intel advisors missing," he says pointing to Renn and Conner, "what other options did we have? You bombed your own home, bringing us to the assumption that it was a diversion for you to take them! Everyone we've killed, their blood is on your hands, my friend."

Renn gives a slight look to Connor, having a feeling she knows where this conversation is going.

"But," Caspian's tone lightens even more, "it appears they were out hunting the infamous Jax Rouge."

Connor simply nods, reaffirming what Caspian has assumed in his mind.

"And you couldn't have at least told me?"

Quickly, this interrogation has turned from Jax to his family as hostility begins filling the atmosphere. Caspian's no fool. He ordered the fake announcement of Jax's execution in hopes of flushing out any workers that were retaining information, under the guise that they'd be exempt from punishment now that the grand criminal was dead. That obviously wasn't going to happen. Loose ends must always be tied off. However, he finds it strangely curious that not only have his own people come to him with information, but they've also brought the criminal with them.

"Caspian," Connor begins. "We had to act. It was time sensitive."

"Convenient," Caspian chuckles. "I'll ask *you* then. Where were you?" He points to Renn, his eyes instantly shifting back to a dark place. When she doesn't respond, he swivels back to face Connor, and not needing to ask the question a third time, he holds his gaze on the bastard.

"Really? Both of you are just going to—?" Caspian asks, miming the lack of information they are giving him in an annoyed shrug.

"You wanna know where we've been?" Jude asks.

"I really do," Caspian nods, keeping a maniacal smile at bay.

"We can show you…"

"Is that right?" Caspian drawls.

Simultaneously, Connor and Renn kill the two flanking guards with their silenced weapons, catching the bodies before they thud to the ground, and in another flawless second, cut the cuffs from Jax and Jude.

"Lock the door," Connor commands, but as Renn moves to the exit, she begins to hear a slow clap from Caspian.

"Impressive!"

Stretching his wrists for a moment, Jax impatiently takes a silenced firearm from Connor and without hesitating, fires a dart into Caspian's shoulder. "Shut up."

Without any protest, Caspian continues to smile as he sinks into a deep slumber.

From outside of City Hall, Mari and Ann watch as five individuals emerge.

"Is it Jackie?" Ann timidly asks, her gaze fixated on the sole, limp body.

"I don't know," Mari replies, fearing the worst. She vowed he wouldn't leave her sight, but as they entered City Hall, there wasn't much she could do other than wait and watch the glass walls.

"I hope it's not…" Ann whispers, still staring at the unconscious body being carried away.

"What are you two doing?" a booming voice demands from behind.

Startled, Mari turns around to see the three triangles of a young, burly PPA sergeant staring down at them.

"We-we have some friends in there," Mari replies.

"You want to join them?"

"No! We're just worried is all."

"Sounds like you want to join them," he growls, grabbing each by an arm before hauling Mari and Ann towards City Hall.

"Let go!" Ann pounds on the man's hip, nearly punching him in the crotch. Obviously, this doesn't sit well with the sergeant, and in retaliation she's smacked to the muddy ground.

"Hey!"

One of the four distant officers notices the commotion and runs over, despite the protests coming from his three other comrades.

"What are you doing?" he asks.

Noticing the man's face, Ann beams with a smile. Mari, also recognizing him slaps her hand over Ann's mouth before the little girl's enthusiasm gives Jax away.

"They need to be processed," the sergeant coolly states.

"The executions have stopped," Jax informs the oblivious soldier. "So let them go and help return workers to their homes."

Reluctantly, the soldier complies.

Once out of sight, Jax grabs both Ann and Mari. "Come with me," he says, pulling Mari and practically dragging Ann towards the group.

"What are you doing?" Renn asks, irked at this deviation in the mission.

"They're coming with us," Jax states.

About to protest and side with Renn, upon seeing Mari, Jude keeps his mouth shut. It's not every day a beautiful variation comes into the Encampment's gene pool. Renn was his initial focus, but she is the definition of standoffish, and as he continues to examine the way Mari looks at Jax, he concludes that she'll be a far better mark.

"Let's just get going," Jude says, cutting off any further debate on the matter.

Seeing Jude eyeballing Mari, Jax grabs Jude's collar, yanking him to the side.

"What are you thinking?"

"I'm on your side. You want them to come or not?" Jude innocently asks.

"Can we do this later?" Connor asks, looking over his shoulder at a dozen confused PPA guards. They've noticed. "They're coming with us!" he orders. It's not a tactically sound move, but right now they don't have the luxury of choice.

Rapidly weaving their way through the maze of streets, in as casual and official of a manner as possible, the group manages to make their way to their truck unnoticed. Relief is brief though, as a squad-sized element is found searching their vehicle looking for any symbol of identification.

"Damn it," Connor mumbles.

"We took too long," Renn sighs out, glaring at Mari and Ann as the cause.

"We'll make it work," Jax says, taking the initiative and marching forward.

"We're sorry. We can't let you near the vehicle," one of the specialists declares.

"The hell you can't!" Jax shouts, mimicking the officers he's heard.

"It's for your own protection, sir." The specialist glances at the prisoners—one being unconscious and the other two girls. "What do you need it for, sir?"

"It's ours," Renn chimes in, attempting to use her family name to get them out of here quicker.

"But it's an unidentified vehicle—"

"And do you think we need to explain ourselves to you?" Renn burrows her eyes into the specialist's young soul.

Embarrassed, but mostly terrified by her fury, the team lead looks to his squad. "You heard her!"

Hastily, the team recovers their gear and before they are even two steps away, Jax tosses Caspian in the back as the rest of the group jumps into the vehicle.

"What are you doing?!"

As they tear out of the Area, Jax looks back at the protesting officer approaching the *soon-to-be-dead* specialist.

"It was Renn Stone," the specialist answers.

"She just kidnapped Caspian, you dumb sh—" and before the last syllable is heard, a shattering gunshot echoes, killing the young soldier.

—⋆ ★ ⋆—

Raider Encampment

"What's the plan?" Dan Trax asks Kai as he and Connor walk down the path.

"Question him and get information—standard protocol," Kai states.

He hadn't thought that far in advance, though, because he didn't think they'd pull it off to begin with. With his first failure to capture Caspian all those years ago, Kai was doubtful his "white saviors" could do any better.

"I don't think it's enough," Connor adds.

"Why's that?" Kai asks, doubtful of any input Connor can contribute.

"My team has control of the situation, and we need to maintain that integrity. Informing Caspian that any Raiders are involved will only be giving him unnecessary intel. We want to make him think this was an act of subversion, not an act of war."

"An act of subversion is an act of war," Kai scoffs. "You were seen leaving the Area, possibly followed, and not to mention you brought in two outsiders without my consent."

"Your consent?" Dan calmly asks.

"Without the consent of the people," Kai clarifies. "They have no hold on the situation. Not to mention, he has no more right to oversee the prisoner than I do."

"What do you suppose we do then, son?" Dan inquires.

Like every time he says it, the word stings Connor upon hearing Kai being called Dan's son and not him—the man's own flesh and blood. As he was with the Stones, Connor is still a man with no country or family.

"We wait," Kai says, his perpetual smirk plastered on his face from knowing he still outranks this pale-skinned counterpart.

"What do you mean, we wait?" Connor protests, Dan's hand raising up to silence him. Never, not even in the PPA, has Connor been one for customs and courtesies and blatantly ignores Dan's staying hand. "We weren't followed! And as for the two women we brought back with us, what is the point of being a Raider if you don't bring in others from under the Oligarchy's jurisdiction?"

"Those women are painted the same color as every PPA out there," Kai yells.

"Says who? You're no different than they are," Connor snaps, his voice near a breaking point.

Stopping the brawl before it can escalate, Dan turns to the officer.

"What do you propose, Connor?"

"Let us handle this. Let Jax speak to him. Caspian killed Kip—"

Kai scoffs. "I've met Caspian on the battlefield! I have just as much gripe with the man, as do the plenty of Raiders that also knew Kip—"

"Does he know you? Does Caspian know any of them personally?!" Connor yells. "I don't give a damn who knew Kip. He was Jax's best friend, and Caspian knows that…"

"Is Jax emotionally compromised?" Dan asks. "Can he control himself?"

"Can *he*?" Connor asks, gesturing to Kai with nothing more to add to his case.

"My techniques have worked in the past," Kai hastily states, feeling his grasp on the situation waning.

"You're just as cynical as the PPA you fight. There's a reason we found you when we did!" Connor states, stepping up to meet Kai eye to eye.

"What's that supposed to mean?" Kai counters, his nose touching Connor's.

"The Raiders are nearly extinct. You need our help," Connor replies. "Caspian is not like the PPA. He is a Stone. He's part of the Oligarchy and an heir to the Nine. You will not break him; I promise you that."

"You and your team have one chance," Dan says, not letting his son finish the fight. "Get it done or the 'nearly extinct' Raiders will."

"Yes, sir," Connor states. Kai smirks but is humbled by the fact that the white man's real son won.

As the two sons—both soldiers in their own way—turn to leave, Dan is impressed to ask a simple question.

"Kai?"

The Raider turns around in response.

"Have you said your prayers today?" Dan asks, looking Kai in the eyes.

"No, Father," he admits.

"Maybe you should."

Nodding, Kai turns back around, walking past Connor and down the darkened path towards the Encampment.

Yearning for his chance, Connor finds it useless and pathetic to try to talk to Dan, and grabbing the radio on his hip, Connor keeps focused.

"You're up, Jax," he says.

It comes with a jolt, but he's ready. Firmly shutting his father's journal, his gloves tighten as he and a guard step into the makeshift bunker, the wave of emotion being halted by the hooded prisoner's faint, incomprehensible mutters. On approach, Jax rips a tuft of Caspian's hair out as he pulls off the hood, and with awe watches the man continue his unwavering gaze towards the ground below.

"Plan B became the reason," Caspian murmurs. "Plan B became the way."

Thinking of the words from Mica he'd just read, Jax leans on Connor's advice—balance emotion with purpose. He can't dispel Caspian's horrendous acts from his mind, but he can try to leverage them against the history he now knows.

"I have a question," Jax begins.

Caspian ignores Jax, continuing his lifeless recitation, changing the chant as he does. "The Original Nine will reign, The Original Nine will cleanse."

"All are created equal. Ever heard of the idea?"

While Caspian's chanting falls silent, he gives no response and stares into the abyss. Suddenly, a psychotic laugh bursts out, startling Jax as it pierces his ears. The laughter continues, slowly transforming into a beastly bellow before settling back to eerie silence.

"Care to explain what's so funny?"

"Do *you* know where that idea came from?" Caspian asks with a soft cackle.

"From the founders of what this place used to be."

Caspian shrugs his shoulder. "When they said, 'all men,' they didn't really mean all men."

"Explain."

"Do you know what a slave is?" Caspian asks, steering the conversation.

"I was a slave," Jax scoffs out. "The Labor class—they're all slaves."

"Exactly," Caspian cheers out. "The founding fathers that you are trying to praise, they had slaves, did you know this?"

Jax didn't but doesn't make mention of that.

"I didn't think so. Have you heard of the Dred Scott decision?" Caspian asks, throwing yet another historical fact at his interrogator. "I didn't think so," he says again, not giving Jax a chance to respond. "It was a trial of sorts, kind of like what I do at City Hall, only this trial stated very clearly that the founding fathers intended one thing and one thing only," Caspian says, pausing for dramatic effect.

Taking the bait, Jax simply asks, "And what did they intend?"

"They intended to keep this nation clean through racial division—separating the pure from the impure."

The guard at the door grasps the rod underneath his coat, slowly revealing it.

Letting emotion rule for a moment, Jax nods at the Raider who bashes the rod across Caspian's jaw before slamming it into the other side with a backswing. This happens two more times before Jax calls for a stop, handing the Raider a cloth to wipe the blood from his weapon. However, not a mark is left on Caspian's face, let alone blood on the rod.

"Anyway," Caspian says, spitting into the dirt. "Have your little history lessons taught you about the Nazis?"

"What are you trying to do?" Jax asks.

"I'm trying to explain *everything*..." Caspian rolls his eyes. "Now, may I?"

Jax nods, unsure if he should indulge Caspian.

"The Nazis, they saw a natural hierarchy within the world. They then took the initiative with the technology that they had at their disposal... They weren't the first, they weren't the last, but they were the most infamous."

Jax turns his back on Caspian, mustering all his strength to resist spilling Caspian's blood on the ground.

"Let me break it down for you as simply as I can. You're asking me what I am hoping to accomplish, correct?"

Turning back around, Jax nods.

"I'm just trying to restore natural order—the natural separation of society that got lost through amendments, policy changes, and weakened minds."

"You're talking about a pure race?"

"Ideals and symbols corrupted this nation," Caspian says flatly, his eyes hardening into a cold, dark beam creasing across his face. "The American flag—what was supposed to be a symbol of peace and justice—was twisted into meaning democracy and equality. Contextualizing history is key. Contextualizing the history books tells us that equality was never intended."

"It was never intended but was achieved and brought countless blessings nonetheless."

"Wrong!" Caspian yells out. "Equality is a farce that the socialists and Marxists fed off to make others feel good, and while others voted them into power, they used the complaints of the workers to create another type of inequality. Inequality was always intended in America. Free-thinking citizens got caught up in a dream and it fed into their arrogance. Nature will always take back what's hers. Instead of black and white, it became rich and poor—the privileged and those born behind the curve. Once they began solving that issue, it moved back to race and round and round it always goes in liberal society."

"Your view is corrupt."

"My view is corrupt—?" Caspian cackles. "Now that is funny," he says, breathing just slow enough to calm his rising breath. "There's a reason why people look different and think different. It's because nobody was created equal. There are an elite few, and it's only amongst those few that it is fair to make such a bold claim."

"We're done here," Jax says, turning around to leave.

"Don't act like you don't want to know more." Caspian's voice darkens. "You want to know about your father, don't you Jackie?"

Not needing a command this time, the Raider swings the metal rod across the side of Caspian's head.

Without speaking, Jax turns around.

"Your father knew mine," Caspian continues, cracking his own neck back into place. "They planned this dream together."

"I doubt that very much," Jax laughs out, thinking of the box, the journals, and everything he's read from Mica.

"And that box you're thinking about," Caspian smiles. "It was meant for me, not you."

"Again, I doubt that."

"You shouldn't. See for yourself," Caspian says, motioning to the pocket just above his chest.

"If that's true, where is he?"

"Shit happens. You know that. Kip knows that…"

Taking the rod from the Raider, Jax crushes it not once, but three times into Caspian's jaw, dislocating it, but with a quick whip of his neck, Caspian pops it back into place.

"Just look at the photo," Caspian says, exasperated at the lack of commitment he's seeing from Jax.

Carefully, Jax reaches for Caspian's pocket, pulling out a folded photograph.

"Told you," Caspian sighs, watching Jax unfold the image. "I was so pathetic back then. Now look at me. It's all thanks to Mica Rouge and Sullivan Stone!"

In this photo is the awful truth. A smiling Mica Rouge has both arms around a young Sullivan and youthful Bella Stone, holding a crippled kid on his shoulders.

"Caspian?"

Twelve

White's Campaign Office
November 6, 2036

A sweaty hand can only mean one of two things: Mica's nervous, or he's dying right before her very eyes. Aila can't and most certainly won't picture the latter, so naturally she assumes the former.

"You okay?"

A simple nod is all Mica gives, his eyes fixated on the television screen.

"You sure?" she doubtfully asks.

"Yeah… There's just a lot on my mind," Mica states, trying to play it off. It's an understatement, and he's sure Aila knows it. Not only is it election day, the day the Division and Governor White have been working towards, but Mica has no idea how to ask her.

A loud "Huzzah" rumbles their secluded glass office, setting Mica on edge. The last thing Mica can handle is a room full of political nut jobs watching the count of Congressional votes, but despite Mica's prior plans and consistent pleas, the governor needs him at the office. It just got refinished, threats have escalated, and again, it's election day—his election day. Compound all of this with Carter's lack of cooperation with *everything*, and Mica's responsibilities have reached an all-time high. From campaign travel to extra hours at the office, any moment with is Aila sacred.

Letting go of Mica's hand, Aila discreetly wipes it dry before asking, "You want anything to drink?"

"Yeah, a soda," he answers, his eyes still glued to the television.

White is in a dead tie with the competition.

The political game was always Kim's interest, never his. The petty drama from party hacks makes him sick to his stomach because for them, it's just about the vote—their values are bags in the wind. It's a popularity contest, not a political process anymore!

How does the candidate make you feel?

Such a pathos response leads to empty words, and for those actually putting their money where their mouths are, the corporate media's slanderous marketing campaigns destroy their reputations. However, believing in what a man like Governor Reuben G. White can do as President opened Mica's eyes to a real cause—to addressing the real needs of the American people. He's a strong candidate with sound policy propositions, has an affable photogenic persona, and a can-do track record as governor of Massachusetts that shoots his appeal through the roof. He's a modern, but faithful JFK that's loved indiscriminately by the American voters.

"White's campaign to appeal to the people rather than Congress? A tactic like this is unprecedented," the news anchor states. "Congress votes in the President, not the people's electorates—not anymore. But whatever you think of the governor's strategy, clearly it's working."

With Congressional votes being tallied in the lower right-hand corner of the screen, clips of the governor's charm and debating acumen flash on the screen with their campaign motto: *Fixing the Fabricated Change*.

"The platform he and his campaign have been using has had a strange appeal to the public and seems to be pressuring Congress," the dapper anchor continues. "You being the political analyst that you are, I have to know—Alice, what are your thoughts on everything we're seeing?"

"To be honest with you, Hank, I'm impressed," the equally exquisite colleague begins. "Change requires a crisis, and I think that most would agree that the *lack of change* we've seen over the past few years from the current administration has only added to the current economic downturn. Governor White's fearless, blatant attacks towards the Westwood administration having no spine and refusing to address real issues has brought their policy decisions to the forefront of every American mind. White has been very open about how the catastrophic state of our nation has been strategically manufactured by an extremely organized group, and one that President Westwood is allegedly involved with."

"I have to agree with you," Hank says. "Even though a majority of Congress has worked with President Westwood since he took office during President Obama's third term, the governor's campaign has publicized an enormous amount of evidence which again, I think is what's scaring all of them into voting against the sitting President. If we're being honest, what Governor White has revealed about the Twenty-ninth Amendment has made *every* member of Congress look bad because of their private business dealings with Westwood. It's almost reverse blackmail!"

Alice chuckles. "And it is obvious Governor White is not letting his past deter him from what he believes," she says as a bright photo of the governor and his wife holding their five-month-old daughter pops on screen. "It hasn't been the main platform, nor should it be in my opinion, but the obvious social issue of the Fourth Trimester Abortion laws have had an influence on the governor and where he hopes to take this country if elected."

"He's dealt with the attacks and the October surprise rather gracefully."

On cue, a prepared political video clip replaces both Hank and Alice.

"Because it is legally right does not make it morally correct!" White's voice booms from the screen.

The clip then cuts to a stereotypical opponent of the governor stating that, "He is a flip-flopping son of a bitch. Participates in abortion and then fights against it? Is he for women's rights or not?"

"But," a reporter begins asking the bright-haired female interviewee, "is it really women's rights once the baby's born? Is it anyone's right at that point?"

"We still have to raise the child, don't we? What if the entire pregnancy was an accident?"

A screen shot of White cuts to the screen.

"We will fix the fabricated change!" he yells out at a cheering crowd. "Like Dr. King advocated, there are just and unjust laws, and like I am advocating today, there is just and unjust change. Are you a patriot or a useful idiot?"

"I'm back," Aila says, delicately walking in with drinks and snacks in hand, her beaming smile finally detracting Mica's attention from the television.

Grabbing his soda, Mica pops it open before asking himself, *How the hell am I going to ask her?*

"My uncle called, by the way."

Mica's eyes widen as he slowly stops mid-gulp. "And?"

"He still disapproves," Aila says nonchalantly at the old news it is.

And for more than one reason now. After the bombing there was no point in hiding Aila's knowledge about Mica being in the Division and the organization's existence. It blew Carter's lid. When Aila did find out that Mica's "anal retentive" boss was Uncle Carter, it left a sour taste in her mouth. She was quick to forgive, however. She grew up with that anal retentive personality after all. The silver lining in it all is the fact that Mica no longer feels he needs to hide *anything* from Aila—that he can be as open and transparent as possible for the first time since Kim's death.

"The final results are in!" Alice shouts from the television, forcing Mica and Aila to immediately drop their conversation.

"With a close call, the forty-sixth President of the United States of America is the governor from Massachusetts, Reuben G. White!"

The office erupts before White's name is even announced. With President Westwood having served as the forty-fifth President since 2016, all anyone needed to hear was the number forty-six for them to know it was over. They won! Glitter and red, white, and blue plastic explode from the ceiling as the door to the secluded room bursts open with song and laughter. Every one of Mica's colleagues dance around in a fit of celebration, so much so that one actually tries to get handsy with Aila—but is stopped upon Mica's palm hitting the side of his face.

This should all be a relief, but it's not—not for Mica. The governor won and all their hard work has been validated, but there is still one more thing he must do and it's now or never. Managing to find some breathing room in the claustrophobic conditions, Mica squeezes his hand into his pocket, looking directly at Aila.

Her smile is all he needs.

Calming his nerves, Mica finds the courage to drop to one knee, bringing the room to total silence. With the only sound coming from the television in the background, some think he's passing out, while others assume that he's had too much to drink. Most however, see the giant, glimmering rock in his hand.

"Aila Carter," he stutters, the entire office holding their breath. "Will you marry me?"

This was the last thing she expected, and apparently everyone else was out of the loop too. Tears fill her eyes, making it practically impossible to see the perfect ring Mica, her fiancé, is giving her.

"Of course!"

Yet again, the room explodes in jovial celebration as everyone gathers fallen confetti, showering the newly engaged couple in patriotic colors.

※ ※ ★ ※ ※

November 7, 2036
The Pentagon

"You asked her to marry you?" Carter asks, appalled, but doing his absolute best not to show it.

"I did."

Mica knew he'd be having this conversation eventually, but he did not expect it the next day. He's had less than twenty-four hours to come up with something—anything—to say to Carter, and as the two march down the deserted hallway in awkward silence, Carter can't help but bring up the countless conversations he's had with Aila since the bombing.

"I thought I told her to stop seeing you."

"You did."

"And aren't you supposed to ask my permission first?"

"Thought I was supposed to ask the father, not the uncle."

"Wow," Carter mumbles at the low blow.

Rather than antagonizing Carter further, Mica leaves the conversation where it is as their footsteps continue to echo throughout the hallway.

Upon approach, Carter pauses for a brief second.

"Well, Division Agent Rouge. After you."

Opening the door, Carter motions for Mica to enter the dimly lit council room. Showing Mica to his seat, Carter takes his own on the opposite side of the room. Although unaware as to the details, Mica has a strong sense as to why he's been summoned. One by one Mica stares at each member of the council, analyzing every visible detail before looking down at the file in front of him.

"Mr. Rouge," the head councilman begins. "Where is your representation?"

Mica shrugs his shoulders. "You tell me. I found out about this this morning."

"She's on her way," Carter interjects, and the moment he does, in walks a resolute Lisa Rodgers.

Taking her seat next to Mica, she opens her briefcase to pull out a single piece of paper.

"What's that?" Mica asks.

"The only thing I need."

"Are we ready to begin?" the head councilman asks.

Lisa looks to Carter, who gives an approving nod.

"Mica Rouge," the head councilman begins again. "Do you know why we've called you here?"

"From what *little I've been told*," he says, making sure to re-emphasize the brief amount of time he's known about this, "it has to do with the bombing of White's campaign office."

"Why were you there that night? You were in possession of a key, yes?"

Mica pauses to think before answering. Clearly, they know a lot, and if he had to guess, Carter's to thank for that.

"I was. It led me there."

"And where did you get that key?"

"I got it the night my girlfriend and I were attacked by the Ordean Reich back in March."

"Kim, was that her name?" another member asks.

"Yeah." And clearly there is nothing in his private life that they don't know about either.

"She was Mica's fiancée," Lisa adds, clarifying. "She was killed in the attack my client is referring to."

"Can I ask you a question, Council?" Mica then asks, rolling his eyes at the decorum they're projecting.

"Go ahead," the councilman nods, taken aback by the forward remark.

"How do you know about that key?" Mica directs the question more towards Carter but keeps the council in the conversation. "I got it from the Ordeans, after all."

"It was stolen from me," Carter answers, immediately fielding the question.

"Are you saying that you're a member of the Fourth Reich?"

Rodgers places a hand on Mica's arm, shaking her head for him to stop.

"I said it was stolen," Carter slowly says.

Mica jerks his arm away from Lisa and stands up. "Bear with me as I theorize for a moment."

"Mr. Rouge, you are out of line."

"The only reason those Ordeans knew Kim and I were there that night are one, Kim was a part of the Minutemen Division, or two," Mica pauses, thinking of how this could be the only logical reason for Carter's mysterious behavior. "It was a recruiting tactic used by Mr. Carter to get me to join."

"That is enough!" the head councilman shouts.

"A little says a lot," Mica mumbles as he sits back down.

"May I?" Carter asks, all in the council nodding unanimously.

If this pans out, Mica will no longer be a thorn in his foot. He originally had faith in Mica, but he's become a loose cannon—a liability. The council thought he might be when Carter first proposed Mica as a candidate, but he also thought he could change their minds. They ended up changing his.

"Did you ever think, Mr. Rouge," Carter begins, "that the reason they got the key was because they attacked Agent Trax and me while we were on our way to recruit both you *and* Kim?"

That's an absurd question, Mica thinks. How the hell could he have come to that conclusion? Stating a detailed response as an obvious answer always makes the one on the defensive look like a moron.

"No."

Carter continues. "And did you ever think that maybe, just maybe, that that key was a vital factor in maintaining the security of the Division's records?" Carter asks, whipping out a piece of paper from his stack, waving to the guard near the door who in turn opens the door to let in Agent Trax.

"Council, this paper is a contract signed by Agent Trax, stating that he is the Records Keeper for the Division and the only agent authorized to know the identity of other agents—he being the one in charge of each agent's private documents."

Dan takes his place next to Mr. Carter.

"And that key?" a councilmember asks.

"It belongs to the Records Room. I lost it that night, March 27, 2036."

"And do you realize that in that contract you signed, you are subject to extreme punitive measures for losing assets of the Minutemen Division?"

"Yeah, I do," Dan states, his head slightly dropping.

Confused, Mica looks to Lisa for an explanation, but she simply shakes her head. "We'll talk about this later."

"In his defense," Carter says, raising his hand, "we never lost the key for more than twenty-four hours. Agent Rouge obtained it that very same night."

"But you were not aware of that until recently, isn't that correct?" the head councilman states.

"We had suspicions—" Carter begins.

"The judgment of law does not run off of suspicions, Mr. Carter," the councilman says, grabbing the bridge of his nose. Pausing, shifting his gaze to Mica, the councilman addresses the next matter at hand. "The point in question is why did you not present us with your theories about Mr. Carter earlier? If you thought he was part of the Reich all along, why did you not come to us or Ms. Rodgers?"

It's awfully tempting for Mica to be sarcastic, but using better judgment this time, he tells them exactly what was going through his mind.

"I didn't know who to trust. Under the current political climate, I needed to make sure I wasn't being used as a tool in some bigger scheme."

"You trusted Aila. Out of all people, you trusted her," Carter states, throwing out the wild left hook.

The head councilman ignores Carter's emotional outburst and chuckles, appreciating Mica's honesty. "You are a tool, Mr. Rouge—we all are to one extent or another. You're just not one in a big scheme. Do you know where the key is now? Mr. Carter has informed us that you lost it at the bombing."

"I do," Mica reluctantly says, pulling the small skeleton key from his pocket.

"Council, if I may," Carter speaks up.

"You may not, Mr. Carter."

Leaning over to Mica, Rodgers murmurs, "I advise that you be careful about what you say from here on out."

"There are things much more important than your prejudice against Agent Rouge," the head councilman continues, eyeing Carter.

When Mica first was presented as a recruit with Kim's name, Carter advocated for him, and the council fought against it. Now, as the cliché goes, the tables have turned. Mica has proven himself an asset to the Division and to this country, and although the security violations would be astronomical for most agencies, it has worked in their favor—offering plausible deniability, distancing themselves in the public relations realm. How ironic, that the vision Carter had for the Division is coming to pass and yet, the man now vehemently opposes the individual who's made it the success it is. Finding no more reason for debate and discovery, the councilman makes the final ruling.

"I find that since the key was never technically lost, only misplaced, there has been no real harm done. The bombing seems to have had no connection with the Records Room, as this and previous evidence and testimonies have shown. It was just another assassination attempt that again, Agent Rouge stopped. If the council agrees with me, I move to drop all charges against Agent Rouge and Agent Trax, with the warning that although this is not technically a government sanctioned agency, the Division relies on basic security protocols."

As he looks at each member of the council, all say the approving word, "Aye."

"Now, onto more serious matters. Ms. Rodgers, if you please."

Mica thought the single piece of paper Lisa brought with her was to save his ass, but as she stands, taking it to the head councilman, it's obviously not.

"We have been informed," Rodgers begins after handing over the paper, "that there are legitimate insider threats within one of the three branches of the United States government."

"Which one?" Dan asks.

"We don't know," she says. "But we are inclined to assume it is within the legislative or executive branches."

"Where would it be within the White House?" Mica asks.

"Intel is pointing us somewhere within the Presidency's cabinet."

"President Westwood?" a member of the council then asks.

"His and the proposed cabinet of the president-elect," Rodgers states, bringing the room to absolute silence, the information weighing heavy on them. "These insider threats, as you probably have already guessed, are members of the Ordean Reich. That much we know for certain." Lisa paces from one end of the room to the other, as she thinks of how to best present the most recent intelligence. "Sources have shown that what is being termed as 'Plan B' has been put into effect."

"How?" Dan asks.

"It was secretly passed within Congress and is on President Westwood's desk waiting to be signed into law."

"What is Plan B?" Mica asks.

"It's exactly what it sounds like. It's a contingency."

"For what?" Carter asks, having rejoined, putting his emotions in check.

"For the Constitution of the United States."

Again, her words add to the solemn lull in the chamber room. "If ever, at any time, the Constitution is 'hanging by a thread,'" Rodgers says, quoting directly from the bill, "Congress has power to move the executive duties from the President to the nine justices of the Supreme Court."

There's a certain unease that captivates Mica. "Who says that the moles aren't in the judicial branch, or even members of the Supreme Court?"

"Anything is possible at this point, but our analysts have not found any information to support that theory. They *have* found, however, photos and records of certain members of Congress involved in highly illicit activities."

"No surprise there," Carter mumbles. It's what gave them the upper hand in the election.

"Which members of Congress?" the head councilman asks.

"All of those that voted against the president-elect."

And that is no coincidence, Mica thinks. The bastardizing of the Constitution with the Twenty-eighth and Twenty-ninth Amendments, removing presidential terms, giving members of Congress lifelong appointments, and completely reforming the election process—this is when it all began. The real hurdle for White has always been combating media activists and their absurd stories that they projected onto his campaign. The short-sided nature of politics has blinded the public to the far-reaching sight of these subverters, putting the constitutional republic at risk. The former governor had to meet the public where they were, and that was with the great divide that the post-birth abortions and other eugenic-like policies that have been created within the country.

Now that he's in office, the real political fight can begin.

"What do we do, then?" Carter asks.

"That is why we are here," Rodgers says. "We, as the head members and key agents of the Division, need to decide and vote on a course of action."

"I take it you already have a suggested course, Ms. Rodgers?" the head councilman asks.

"I do," she says, pointing to the piece of paper. "As you'll see there, we are recruiting two more agents, ones whose investigational expertise will help us interrogate the corrupted members of Congress and other involved political officials."

"Sounds illegal," Dan states.

"This Division is technically illegal, Agent Trax."

"We need a unanimous vote," Rodgers states, folding her hands, looking at each member of the Division present. "All in favor of the two additions to the Minutemen Division, please raise your right hand." After having analyzed her paper, one by one, every member does. "I'll see to it that the new recruits are informed."

"This council is adjourned," the head councilman states. "We will reconvene the day after the governor's inauguration. Until then, God speed."

White's Campaign Office, Records Room

Mica, having anticipated this moment ever since he and Aila discovered the door, has been picking his brain for what exactly could be so important that they only have a single agent tracking and managing its contents.

Lifting the tiny flap in the lower right-hand corner of the maintenance closet wall, Dan inserts and turns the key where a click sounds from behind the wall. As Dan finishes the key's rotation, a violent hiss of air rushes out from behind the wooden paneling, raising the entire wall and revealing another obstruction.

"What the hell…" Mica slowly mutters, seeing that rather than the relatively small safe he'd been expecting, the entire wall is the door to a rather large security device. With the dial and spindle combination lock that Aila's search uncovered, the mechanism has been repurposed for the door rather than the safe it was originally manufactured on.

"It's old school two-step authentication, my friend," Dan says, stepping up to the combination, and as Mica watches, inputting the combination Aila deciphered: 07-04-76. Another loud metallic click sounds before the door opens, revealing a set of stairs. "Down we go."

Fascinated, Mica follows Dan down the handful of steps. Mica is no engineer, but even he can tell that the room they're walking to is below the first floor and within the foundation. Explains why he didn't find it in his studying of the blueprints.

"Why didn't you tell me about this place?" Mica asks.

"That's a stupid question," Dan chuckles. "I'm the only agent authorized."

"Why am I seeing it now, then?"

Another chuckle from Dan. "Because, like always, you decided to go and do your own thing."

"As if that's a bad thing," Mica mumbles.

Dan can't entirely disagree. Their processes and ways of documenting records were flawed to begin with, and naturally Mica's brash nature exposed every bit of it.

As the two reach the bottom, a faint flickering light illuminates the far end of a hall before expanding into a doorless room for the two to enter.

"This is the Records Room," Dan says. Hundreds of bright red metal boxes, each uniquely coded and named, line every inch of the walls within. "Each box contains specific intel for every agent the Division has recruited, plans to recruit, or couldn't recruit due to unexpected outcomes."

"What kind of intel?" Mica asks as he walks around the room, his fingertips grazing the smooth surface of the boxes.

"Personal records obviously, but anything that defines the owner of the box."

Mica raises his eyebrow. "And who gets to put it in the boxes?"

"I was the primary keeper, Carter was the secondary," Dan states. "However, after your little stunts these past few months, we've determined that maybe this room should be available to all agents. It's their files, after all."

"So, like a bank, but for personal records."

"Exactly," Dan smiles. "We've been testing this with a few agents to see what they deem important for the Division." Dan pulls a random box from a shelf and opens it up to reveal books. "This is what most agents seem to bring. Sometimes it's minted coins or photos, but books seem to be the popular choice."

"I haven't seen one of these in forever," Mica exclaims, picking one up as he does. "*Brave New World* by Aldous Huxley."

"Do you know why?" Dan smiles, knowing this secret piece of trivia.

"Why what?"

"Why nobody sees books anymore?" Dan asks and Mica shakes his head. "It's because in the 2020s, during the whole censorship fiasco, the government began making contracts with publishing companies to have them cease the printing of paper books. An environmental initiative or some bullshit like that. Anyway, by 2027 only e-books became available to the general public, moving physical copies to collectors' markets."

"It wasn't environmental though, was it?" Mica asks.

"How'd you guess?" Dan chuckles. "It actually promoted more censorship. Like when updating a website, the mass digital editing of texts was implemented, and for those texts that were *beyond repair*, it made it easier for mass removal of unapproved books and indirectly, unapproved ideas."

"That's one way to shape public perception," Mica says, in awe at people's ignorance within society.

"Basic propaganda! The mass shifting of public opinions."

Dan pulls out a tablet, opening a digital copy of a *Brave New World*, and finds the first chapter before opening to the same location on the physical copy and handing the two over to Mica.

Mica begins reading, and as he does, he immediately notices that the two copies initially read in the same fashion, but as he continues, he notices subtle adjustments within the e-book version. By the end of the page, it's clear that the story is headed in a direction away from the written author's original intent.

"Wow," Mica mutters.

"Crazy, right? Have you read it?" Dan asks.

Mica shakes his head as he begins swiping through the e-book. "Nope, only heard of it. It's supposedly a classic."

"This one is!" Dan says, pointing at the hardcover. "In it, the author delves into ideas about eugenics, human purity, and totalitarian regimes, forming it all around the theme of control through pleasure, immorality and hiding the truth by flooding people's senses with irrelevance. Conformity through desensitizing society.

"Bernard, the main character, is a social pariah and meets a beautiful young woman by the name of Lenina, the two of whom are incompatible in every way. However, they are sexually attracted to each other and so they decide to go on a retreat to a popular *societal reservation* to appease this desire. In this zoo-like environment the two discover a group of people who live outside their government—the World State. This group of people are not bound by the *pleasures* that Bernard and Lenina's government implements but are allowed to grow old, have disease, experience hunger, treat each other with cruelty while at the same time, create art, fall in love and engage in marriage. The zoo-people even have a powerful religious system. Long story short, Bernard and Lenina start to question the World State when they see people living life as nature intended."

"Okay," Mica slowly responds. "A story of rebels. I like it. Fight the system."

"More or less." Dan grabs the e-book. "In this one, that has all been altered—as you've seen. The characters Bernard and Lenina are simply lovers. No conflict. No questioning. Simply an erotic story in a fictitious future."

"And that's considered classic material?"

"Of course. If people want to believe something is a classic, no matter how bad it is, they'll believe it out of fear of not being part of *sophisticated society*. When they read it, they want so much to not be disappointed that they'll cherish it regardless of the quality. Not to mention, our society is obsessed with sex."

"All because they're told to," Mica says, filling in the blanks himself. "Seems a little out there if I'm being honest…"

"That's just one book, my friend. Imagine that approach with other works of fiction—with ideology and religion. Even political history. If you control the story, you control the culture. If you control the culture, then you control politics, and if control politics, you have control over a nation."

Putting the tablet back before shifting his body, Dan reveals two boxes with names Mica knows.

"Why is Kim's name on that?" Mica asks, moving over to her box lying just adjacent to one in which his own name is inscribed.

"Because she was supposed to be recruited."

"But the Ordeans," Mica whispers.

"Potential recruits still have something to offer, and Kim's research and work in the media fighting against the Fourth Reich has been extremely valuable to the Division. Her research was in fact the foundation for most of your missions."

"She was supposed to be an agent with me?"

"She was going to be involved with analytics on the intelligence side, but yes. Carter was on his way to recruit both you and Kim. She was the primary asset however, while you were secondary."

Mica pauses at this thought. Most arrogance is due to ignorance, making Mica no exception to the rule. If Carter did have a ploy to kill Kim as a catalyst to recruit Mica, it wouldn't make much sense to have an agent box for her.

"What's in it?"

"Mainly her research on the Ordean Reich," Dan says, and as he watches Mica think—as he watches him remember the details of that night—he grabs her box from Mica. "Here," Dan says, handing Mica his. "This one's yours. Store whatever you think is important."

"And then what?"

"And then I'll make sure it's safe. That's my job—to gather and protect vital documents for the security of the United States."

"Like you did with the key, right?" Mica smirks, nudging Dan with his elbow before a deep, interrupting voice booms inside.

"So, this is the Records Room Carter's been making a fuss about!"

Without having to see the owner, Mica smiles at the familiar tone before turning around with open arms.

"Sullivan Stone!" Mica cries, rushing up to embrace his longtime friend. "When they brought up the investigational experts, I had my speculations."

"Dreams do come true now, don't they?" Sullivan laughs before eyeing the room and the countless boxes lining the walls, stopping when seeing the behemoth of a man putting one on the shelf. "Who's this? You gay now, or something?"

"No," Mica chuckles. "Dan this is my buddy, Sullivan. Sulli this is Dan, another Division agent."

"Nice!" Sullivan holds out his hand, grasping Dan's firmly, and as the two alpha males measure the other's fortitude, an all-too-familiar shrill cheer breaks their eye contact.

"Where's my hug?"

"Bell!" Mica yells, practically mirroring her enthusiasm, laughing as he moves to hug his former lover. It's been years, but some bonds can't be broken. "Where's Caspian?" Mica then asks. The moment he does, in waddles a bowl-cut youngster.

"Mikey!" the toddler shouts, raising his arms into the air.

"Casp!" Mica shouts back, picking the kid up.

"Ow!" Caspian proclaims. "You poked my ouch."

"Sorry, buddy." Mica looks over to his parents. "Still on those shots, huh?"

"Unfortunately," Bella begins. "I don't get it, but Sullivan seems to think they're helping with his…" she pouts, struggling to admit his disorder.

It breaks Mica's heart every time it's brought up. The doctors doubted the kid would make it past a year. In fact, some within the fellowships were putting bets in. If it wasn't the disorder itself, they stated the social stigma would do him in. Kids are outright mean and Cerebral Palsy isn't what it used to be.

"Bullies still bothering you?" Mica asks, looking a fragile Caspian in the eyes, the kid shamefully nodding. "I'll teach you how to use these fists as lethal weapons, you got it?"

A slight grin grows on the child's face as he swings a punch.

Dan can't help but smile at the scene in front of him. There is still good out there, and it's moments like these that serve as the small reminder of why he's doing what he's doing—why he's getting his own life back in order.

"Hey, I have an idea."

Running over to one of the boxes, Dan pulls out something that could easily be labeled as an antique. "Let's take a picture," he says, pointing the Polaroid at the group and motioning for everyone to gather.

"Deal!"

Making sure to stay away from the injection sites, Mica lifts Caspian onto his shoulders before putting his arm around Sullivan. Bella, wrapping one arm around her husband, slyly puts her hand in Mica's back pocket, giving a slight, comical squeeze to remind him of the fun they used to have.

"Smile!" Dan calls, clicking the button, blinding everyone with a flash of light. Out of the camera itself, prints the small group photo that Dan waves in the air before handing to Mica.

"There's Mikey!" Caspian bounces on Mica's shoulders. "And Mom and Dad."

"Holy moly!" Sullivan stifles a laugh. "What the hell is going on, Mica?"

"Are you crying?" Bella blurts out in her own fit of laughter.

Mica can't believe the awful sight he's seeing, and despite his appalling face, Mica is fighting off tears of laughter.

"I know just the place for this," he says, walking over to his own metal box and slipping the photo inside. "I can't wait for you guys to meet my fiancée."

THIRTEEN

Raider Encampment

"And David said to Solomon his son, Be strong and of good courage."

Out of all the verses and words in the Bible his father marks, this one cuts the deepest, creating a chasm within the raging battle inside. While one side is fortified with the desire to know why—why the box, why the letters, why the books, and why the Stones—the other end petitions him to forget it and the infectious seed that Caspian has planted. He can't do either, though.

Everything he's read, thought, and felt concerning his father has led Jax to believe that Mica was a good man. The expression of his love for Jax and his mother testify of a wholesome individual. Mica saw the corruption of The Government long before it happened, and he strived to stop it. The impassive behavior of society frustrated him to the core, as he made the ultimate sacrifice for God, family, and freedom.

The Nine were his enemies.

That's what Mica wrote, and a single photograph throws all that virtue into question. Jax wants to believe that there is something more—something he's not seeing, but the simple truth is that through all the pages Jax has read, nothing is mentioned of Caspian's photograph nor of its meaning. Sullivan, Bella, Caspian... Mica writes about none of them, leaving the remaining question: How did he know this family? Why are they smiling together in this picture? Like the journals, it's a beginning with no end—with no conclusion. His records simply end.

Caspian's smart. He's manipulative and has thought things out ten steps ahead and in ten different directions. He must've at least considered the possibility that Jax, the missing fugitive, would come back for him. Why else would he just *happen* to have a photograph of Mica? It could serve as a reminder of his youthful, feeble state, acting as motivation if you will, but if Jax is being honest with himself, that's overly simplistic for someone like Caspian. He knew Mica was Jax's father. He knew the probability of Jax capturing Renn and Connor was next to zero. The only logical conclusion to their simultaneous disappearance is that Caspian also knew that he'd been betrayed, and the only people Renn and Connor could go to at that point would be the Raiders. Rather than continuing the hunt, he'd let Renn and Connor come to him, because tactically speaking, eliminating a general puts an army in disarray, which if Jax is willing to bet, is the very same reasoning Caspian used.

So, if Caspian expected his own capture, he'd have a plan to free himself in order to properly subvert the Raiders from within. This is where Jax gets hung up though. As skilled a threat as the elder Stone sibling is, and as unprofessional as the Raiders are, it's still too much for one man to escape on his own. So, the question of *how* not only remains, but *who?* Who is helping Caspian Stone? Connor and Renn have had the exact same question, and although hypothetical, that small thought has caused apprehension with the possible fact that they were all duped into capturing Caspian.

"Jax," Connor says, stepping into his tent. "We have a problem."

Sliding the photo into the Bible and gently placing the book down, Jax moves to step outside.

"What do you need me for?" Jax asks with a smile and jesting elbow.

"Not my call," Connor shrugs unamused. "It's yours."

None of this was something Jax asked for but ended up getting, nonetheless. All because he found a box with illegal trinkets and knowledge. An immense burden that has taxed Jax, and until that smile, Connor feared his friend would break under the pressure.

The second they were admitted into the Encampment, Dan threw the responsibility of a captain at Jax's feet, not once looking at the former PPA leader despite Connor being far more experienced. The only the admonition given to the young Rouge was to take care of the people like Mica would have. The transfer of power had mixed responses within the clan, most of them negative. Kai for one, saw it as his birthright to lead the Raiders, and when that didn't happen, sour sentiments spread like wildfire throughout the Encampment.

"Where's this *problem?*" Jax asks.

"It's with an Owl," Connor says. "And with Kai and Jude…"

No surprise there, Jax thinks.

Ever since they got their hands on a squad of these aircrafts, they've been accompanied by nothing but trouble, annoyance, and dick-measuring. Being the state-of-the-art pieces of military technology that they are, the whole point was to give the Raiders an uncanny edge and superiority in the sky, but of course, like anything the Raiders acquire, to Kai it's just crude, flawed PPA machinery that offers no strategic advantage because—as Kai's philosophy goes—they've gotten this far without it.

"What is it this time?" Jax asks, stepping onto the crumbling tarmac, approaching what's supposed to be a sleek, jet-black war machine, but instead is Kai's self-fulfilling prophecy of a battle-scarred aircraft.

"It's nothing, pale face. Get back to your books while we figure out this mess for you," Kai states, rounding the aircraft with an armful of tools and gadgets.

"You wish!" Jude states, peeking out from underneath the belly of the beast, his face absolutely covered in caked grease and metal shavings. "Every time we start the engine either the fuel line bursts, or some other hydraulic pump has a class three leak spewing oil and fluid everywhere."

Jax rakes his hands through his hair, gripping it before letting the extended growth slip through his fingertips. "And there is nothing you can do?" he asks.

"You see, that's the motivation I need," Jude sarcastically states.

Jax never has been much of a fan of Jude—he doesn't hate him, but it's like the guy goes out of his way to pry at Jax's ego. Kai is one thing; Jude however is another one entirely.

It became apparent once they got Caspian back to the Encampment that Jax and Mari would never be the same. The damage he'd done by abandoning her and Ann was something neither of them could reconcile with. Being a beautiful new addition to the clan, there were plenty of men and women eager to be the shoulder Mari needed. She could have picked anyone, and Jude was the one who made the cut. Maybe it was his persistence. Maybe it was his *slight* resemblance to Jax. Maybe it was something else. Either way, every time he sees Jude, Jax is reminded of his blundering mistake with Mari... And since he sees Jude daily, Jax is constantly kicking himself in the ass.

"I told you, we've got this, whitey. We don't need you!" *We never have*, Kai then thinks.

"Shut up..." Connor sighs, unamused as he steps in front of Kai.

"Hey, there's Daddy-Issues himself!" Kai chuckles, prying at Connor's insecurities.

And as if this male bravado wasn't enough, Mari runs up and onto the tarmac, adding to the unproductive drama and leaving Ann sulking in the background.

"Jude!" she calls out.

"Mari!" Jude shouts back, causing her to break into a full sprint.

Maybe it's wishful thinking, but it's as if Mari is overcompensating. Jax has known her for a while now and never has she been the giddy type, recklessly infatuated in a relationship.

Then again, we're all different people that change with the times and the individuals we surround ourselves with, he thinks. But as Jax watches Ann through the process, his theory holds ground.

It's clear to everyone that Ann is no fan of Jude. He's like an aftermarket role model to her, and as she broods her way on over, it's a comical sight to see Jude try his damnedest to cheer the girl up. Against her will, Jude pulls Ann into his hip before kissing Mari, all in clear view for Jax to see the entire scene unfold.

It wasn't at all difficult to sweep her off her feet. Nothing is more pathetic than a rebound trying to legitimize itself. All Jude had to do was double down on her fractured relationship with Jax and the coupling practically made itself. Ann, however, has been more authentic and therefore, a tougher case for Jude to crack.

"Give me a break," Jax mumbles.

"Jackie!" Ann yells, squirming until she can pull herself from Jude's embrace, bulldozing right into Jax's hip. "I've missed you!"

"And I've missed you," he says, ruffling her hair. "What are you doing here?"

"We're here to pick Jude up for dinner," Ann says, sticking her tongue out, gagging at the thought. She's having a hard time accepting anything that's happening. In her mind it's a rather uncomplicated matter. One moment Mari's crying, thinking she's lost Jax forever, and then in the blink of an eye, he's alive, but instead of going back to him, Mari and Jude are connected at the lips. The sole conclusion she can muster is that there will be no more blinking.

"He's not living with you guys, is he?" Jax asks, unable to resist the question.

Ann vigorously shakes her head. "Hell no… We're over at his place all the time though. All they do is kiss and cuddle and they sometimes go in the back of the tent to do other things—"

"Yeah, I get it!" Jax waves, regretting even asking.

Damn, he messed up a perfect thing, and having been too busy with his newly appointed role in the Encampment, he's barely had the time to wonder "what if?" What if things were different between Mari and him? If they were, he'd make damn certain that he'd give her both time and attention. But Jax just continues to blame himself for Kip, Mari, and more.

"Hey," Ann says, grabbing his arm and yanking down on it. "She still talks about you…"

Jax frowns at Ann, disbelieving what she's telling him. *How could she?* he thinks. Why would Mari ever think let alone talk about Jax ever again? He's changed since Kip's death—he's not the same Jax he used to be, and he's not alone. Ann herself smiles less, barely laughs, and still, she doesn't blame anyone but Caspian. Mari's numb, like before she met Jax, although she won't admit this to anyone, but even then she masks this with false joy and pseudo contentment.

"I'm serious!" Ann says, yanking down on his arm a second time. "She misses you. I can tell…"

"I don't know what to tell you, kid…"

"Ann, let's go!" Mari calls out.

Dropping her chin to her chest, Ann gives Jax one last hug. "Don't give up on her, Jackie. That's all I'm asking."

Before Jax can respond to Ann's final plea, she is moping her way back over to Mari and Jude who stand arm in arm, lips welded together.

Apparently, you can do whatever the hell you want, Jude, Jax thinks as he waves them away, throwing up in his mouth all the while.

"Are we going to figure this out or what?" Kai yells. "Or should I continue to waste my time for you?"

Connor rams his elbow into Kai's ribcage. "Shut up, man!"

"Can I ask you a question, Kai?" Jax asks, pulling on a pair of gloves before moving to the underbelly of the aircraft.

"Whatever you want, pale ass," Kai says, unable to keep from snickering at the adolescent joke before another one of Connor's forceful elbows finds his side.

"What do you know about Jude?" Jax asks.

"Are you asking because he's sticking it to your woman?"

Jax ignores the crude stab. "No, he seems…odd, is all."

Grabbing a set of tools, Kai begins to fiddle with the tensions on the gears. "I've never particularly enjoyed having him around, he being an outsider and all, but like Kip, he's been reliable. Why?"

"An outsider?" Jax mumbles.

Moving over to where Kai is working, he moves the guy aside to rip open a side panel. Having worked at the Mill his entire adult life, Jax is keenly aware of the simple fact that machines are machines. Whether they be for manufacturing or for war, they function on the same basic principles. Confidently, Jax replaces a fuel line, turns two specific knobs, bleeding the line, and secures a single gear before closing the panel back up.

"Fire it up," Jax tells Connor.

"You can't be serious. Jude and I have been working on this for twelve hours."

Jumping into the cockpit with just as much faith as Kai, Connor hits the ignition where a quick spark ignites and hums, bringing the aircraft from the dead.

Slipping off his gloves and shoving them into Kai's chest, Jax answers Kai.

"That's why!"

"What are you thinking?" Connor asks Jax once they're far enough away from Kai, who is still flabbergasted by what he just witnessed.

"I've been watching Jude and Kai pretty carefully these past weeks."

"You think we have a mole or something?"

"Maybe."

"What do you want to eat, babe?" Mari asks as they enter his tent.

Jude, rather than answering, hastily walks to the far end of the tent, moving behind the divider into what he's explicitly told her is his own space—that she is not to enter under any circumstance. It was a little aggressive at first and is somewhat an uncomfortable idea for her, but anything and everything is unconventional at this point because until now, Jax was her one and only. Mari has appreciated everything about Jude, quirks and all. She's chalked his eccentric behavior up to the simple fact that Jude wants boundaries just as much as she wants to get over Jax.

Kip died, breaking Ann's heart, and Jax left them to endure hell while he figured his own shit out. A small part of her was relieved when she found out he "died." *Serves him right*, she'd thought. Most of her, though, shattered upon hearing the news. Never again would she be able to hold him, punch him, tease him, cry on him. Then, out of nowhere, Jax shows up, reinvigorating her hope in a future life. But again, he let her down. When first getting back to the Encampment, all Mari did was cry. That's all she did for three days and all Jax did was ignore her. Even now, after all that agony and confusion, she still loves that selfish bastard.

Loved him, she tells herself. She deserves better. The question she must ask at this point is if she has the self-respect to not go back to him. Can she resist being with someone who can't even be with himself?

And Jax, he messed up. He knows that there was no fixing what he did. That's why he never tried. Ironic though, because if he *would have* tried to heal the wounds he caused, Mari would have learned to trust him again. She would have been able to put the past behind both of them and move on—she would have been able to start their life over outside the purview of the Nine. But since he didn't try, someone else filled the void he left.

Jude's strict, atypical boundaries are something that she needs. They've oddly grounded her back to the twisted reality she followed Jax into. Yes, the intimacy is forced with Jude, but so is every breath she takes as she experiences life without Jax.

Walking up to the only table in the tent, picking up one of a dozen books, *Rules for Radicals*, Mari calls out. "Jude?"

Unlike most of the Labor class back in Area Thirty-Eight, she is very familiar with reading and with books. It was part of her training in her former life—something Jax has never known about. If he did, maybe he would've acted differently. She sees how he behaves around Renn, barely even fazed by her history and her past associations. Looking at that, Mari regrets every day that she never told him, because nothing is much worse than her current relationship with him.

"Ann?" Mari then calls, realizing that the little one hasn't even come inside.

"Nope!" she yells back.

"Please," Mari begs. Ann's resentment towards Jude is no secret, but it's not up to her who Mari spends her time with. If the kid were older, Ann would understand. She needs to accept that.

Now that's a bunch of bullshit, a voice in the back of her head calls out. Mari laughs because she barely comprehends her own emotions, and as self-aware as any adult can be, mourning is still a process.

"Ann, get your ass in here."

Throwing attitude around like leaves in the wind, Ann whips the flap of the tent open, exasperated beyond belief.

"What is that?" Ann asks in a surly tone upon seeing Mari holding a book—the same type of item that got Kip killed.

"It's a book."

"I know what it is, why do you have it?"

"It's Jude's," Mari says.

"Oh," Ann begins, throwing her arms into the air. "So, he can have one…"

"Just listen," Mari says, placing it back down and lowering her voice. This isn't the first time Ann's pulled a guilt-ridden stunt like this. "I need you to shape up."

Ann opens her mouth to protest, but Mari cuts her off, having none of it.

"I don't want to hear it! Jude hasn't done anything wrong, so stop being a brat. You got it?"

"But—" Ann begins only to be cut off again by a sweeping knife-handed gesture. "Fine… when's dinner?"

"I don't know," Mari mouths, and just as she does, Jude comes back out, apologizing for his weird behavior.

"Food!" he randomly yells out.

"Yes, please!" It's the one thing Ann has ever agreed with him on.

"Before we do though," Jude begins, bringing a very audible sigh from Ann, "I need to deliver dinner to the prisoner. Then," he says in a childish tone, pinching Ann's cheeks, "we can get some tacos or something from the square."

"Whatever," she says, swatting his hand away in complete disgust. "Just let me know when you're done making out." And before Mari can reprimand her, Ann is outside of the tent—having swiped one of Jude's books just because she can.

"Sorry about—" Mari begins only to be silenced from an uncomfortably awkward kiss.

"It's fine. She gave us some privacy. Let's take advantage of that for a minute…"

Before Mari can suggest anything else, his thick tongue is in her mouth, something Jax never would've done so aggressively.

———✦———

Forty-eight days. Caspian chuckles. It's a raw chuckle, his throat dry from the sparse food, water, and high mountain air but maniacal humor and rage is his only semblance of sanity.

He always knew if anyone was to be a disappointment to the family, it'd be Renn. Her involvement in this subversion is something he never saw in her potential though, and yet, Caspian finds a morsel of solace in it all. Yes, she's a traitor. Yes, she's a liar, no better than a cheating whore, but the revelation of her true self is what brings humor to Caspian's despair. After all she's been given—her gifts matching his—Renn has proven to be weak, her emotions and sensitivity being her downfall yet again. Ever since the first raping she's become a Raider sympathizer, trying to "understand" their methods and tactics. For the past three years she's collected her cards, planned her moves, and with Connor gaining intel from the field, the two have become a dangerous pair. Hindsight is a good teacher. It is not something to dwell on. Rhett will be heartbroken upon hearing of her betrayal, but it'll be a much-needed lesson for him as well, he being disposed to the same frailties as Renn.

"Is he in there?" Jax's voice is heard from outside, and right on time.

"Hasn't moved," the guard reports, letting Jax in.

"My brother!" Caspian proclaims with a smile larger and wider than Jax has ever seen. "What brings you to my humble abode?"

"Brother?" Jax asks.

"Most certainly!" Caspian proclaims. "We are brothers in combat now, and like all good siblings, have been matched against each other."

Jax nods to the accompanying guard. The Raider follows Jax's order, making his way towards Caspian before breaking a rod over the side of the prisoner's head. A loud crack resonates on impact, Caspian's jaw popping out of place, and like he has so many times, Caspian whips his head back and forth until a realigning pop puts the joint back into place.

"Feel better?" Caspian asks. "Letting frustration build up is unhealthy."

"Who do you have on the inside?" Jax barks, cutting through the bullshit.

Perplexed, Caspian looks to his interrogator. "Seriously? You think I'd be here as long as I have if I had an insider?"

"Yeah, I do."

"Well," Caspian pauses, letting the dramatic tension build. "I can't tell you what I don't know."

"Sure you can," Jax says.

"I know we don't see eye to eye ideologically," Caspian sighs. "But no, I literally cannot give you information that does not exist within me."

Without hesitation, the guard cracks a second swing over Caspian's head, followed by a third and then a fourth.

Just do it once more, Caspian thinks. All he needs is one more good swing.

"Who is it?"

"Who do *you* think it is? You obviously have someone in mind."

"Jude," Jax responds, having no second thought on the matter.

"Jude?" Caspian thinks about it as if he's trying to recall a lost memory. "The one who brings me my meals?"

Jax nods his head and folds his arms, determined to get the answer he wants.

"I see." Caspian's gaze drops to the floor, where it lingers. "You think he sneaks things to me? It'd be a prime opportunity, now, wouldn't it?" Caspian shrugs. "I mean how would he? In the food? You search the food before he enters, right?"

Jax doesn't reply out of sheer embarrassment.

"You search him, don't you?" Caspian asks, already knowing the answer—seeing one of the many mistakes Jax and his team has made, all of which he's capitalized on.

"Who else could it be, if not him?" Jax asks.

"Renn, for starters." Caspian knows this is an absolute absurdity, but he throws the curve ball, nonetheless, knowing that Jax won't be able to hit it. "She is family, after all."

Jax shakes his head. "It's not her."

"Are you sure?" Caspian sarcastically asks, a light bulb going off the moment he does. "How is she, by the way?"

"Why do you care?"

"I've seen the way men look at her." Caspian smirks, his dark eyes meeting Jax's. "I've seen the way *you* look at her."

"I don't *look* at her."

"Are you sure?" Caspian smiles, having found another fracture in Jax's armor. "You were awfully quick to defend her."

"This is ridiculous…"

Taking the rod from the guard, Jax raises his fist to deliver an emotional, skull-crushing blow, and like always, Caspian sees the event unfold in slow motion. His training, coupled with his genetic capacity for greatness, has prepared him for this moment…

For forty-eight days, he's been playing this scenario out in his mind and has it down to perfection. As the forceful impact comes swinging down, Caspian uses the simple tool from his spy to instantaneously burn through his leather binds. In a simultaneous motion, his right hand smoothly shoots up, catching Jax's wrist while his left hand grips the guard's neck, crushing his trachea with a simple squeeze.

Caspian uses this element of surprise to strike a blow at Jax's jugular vein. However, Jax recovers just enough to slightly shift his shoulder, blocking Caspian's incapacitating hit. Not expecting this contingency, things begin to speed up for Caspian as he recalculates his next move.

Jax doesn't wait. Throwing his hands behind Caspian's head, Jax brings up his knee to deliver a rib-cracking blow that jolts Caspian's system, and for the first time in a long time, Caspian feels what he remembers to be pain. His ribs bend as Jax's knee sinks in, and instead of resisting, he accepts it and by doing so, realizes that Jax just left an opening. With ease, Caspian blocks the predictable second knee, and without hesitation, throws the man back with a strike directly on the underbelly of Jax's chin. Dazed and confused, Jax feels both of his arms grabbed and lifted, and before he can react, Caspian lands his forceful boot on Jax's chest, kicking Jax out of his coat.

Standing with the two torn halves of the thick jacket in each hand, Caspian drops them to the dirt, standing over his prisoner, waiting for his spy to come back.

"Check."

Two more moves and Connor will have check mate. One, if he's lucky and she's stupid.

"I hate this," Renn says with a pout. In all the years they've played together, she has never been able to win. Renn misses Connor's slight smirk as she picks up her knight and moves right into his trap.

"Check and mate!"

"Stupid," Renn mumbles under her breath, flicking over her king in the process. "What's up with you and Kai?" she asks, knowing it'll aggravate him, hopefully making him an easier opponent for the next round.

"Now? You want to talk about this now?" Connor asks, seeing right through her plan.

"Why not?" She's not above psychological warfare.

"You scared you'll lose again?"

"Shut up and just answer the question! What's your problem with him?"

"What's your problem with Jax?" Connor fires back, knowing that his question will have the same effect. "When you going to kiss him?"

"I asked you first," Renn says, not entirely unfazed by the copycat attack as she represses her cheeks from flushing.

As he places the pieces back on the board, he reluctantly accepts her question, answering it in as brief a manner as possible. "He's Dan's son."

"Obviously," she mumbles. It's always come down to that, but this is the first time she's heard him say it. "You are too, you know?" she says, gently placing her queen and king down before putting her hand on top of his.

"If I was" —he pulls his hand out from underneath hers— "I wouldn't have to compete with a tainted man for his attention."

"Don't..." Renn says, disappointment filling her tone.

"Don't what?"

"Don't bring race into this. You of all people should know the value behind this community. It's why we came here in the first place."

"Kai brings it up all the time," he says, looking away, letting his pride step in front of his shame.

"That doesn't matter, Connor. You've read the histories of the world and know that these people are a blessing."

"If they—" Connor begins, but his retaliation is cut short by an earth-shattering explosion.

Like clockwork, the surrounding Raiders seize their firearms, tactically charging in the direction of the explosion.

Knowing an attack was bound to happen, this hardly comes as a surprise to Connor and Renn. They've discussed and trained for the possibility—as much as the Raiders and their stubborn ways would allow. Emerging from the tent, Connor and Renn tune in to their surroundings as they listen to the sporadic gunfire, watching bullets ricochet and burst from barrels in every nonsensible direction.

"Secure Caspian!" Connor barks out the order, but nobody responds. Instead, Raiders continue to return fire at an unseen enemy. If Connor's trained eyes can't see them, the Raiders sure as hell can't either.

"Get to the prisoner, now!" Connor commands, jerking one Raider in the direction of the tent.

Once the Raider and his squad get organized, they cover the short distance, creating a perimeter around Caspian's tent. It's the worst perimeter Connor has ever seen, but it works. Stepping inside, Connor moves in to get eyes on Caspian—only to see a sight that knocks the wind from him.

"Where is he?" Renn shouts as she storms into the tent, finding the same horrific sight. "Jax!" Rushing over to the unconscious, bruised and bleeding man she picks up his head before resting it on her lap.

Stepping outside, Connor analyzes the chaos, trying to find any pattern and rhythm, when his eyes home in on the Owl aircrafts a hundred yards away.

"You two on me!" he orders, pointing to two Raiders before sprinting towards the tarmac.

Casually, Caspian walks towards an aircraft with three guards of his own. Identifying the three traitors, Connor's pursuit is halted as they open fire. Sliding behind a boulder to take cover, the other two with him aren't as agile as a round strikes the head of one Raider, while the other tumbles to the ground, scrambling behind a truck after taking shots to her shoulder and thigh.

Poking his head out from behind his cover, Connor fires a burst that kicks up the dirt just in front of Caspian's feet.

"Cover me!" Caspian orders as he flips open an electric panel. His three bodyguards span out, two laying down suppressive fire with the other moving around to Connor's flank.

Seeing his vulnerability, Connor tosses a grenade towards the two positioned at the point, and as it explodes, he charges the flanking attacker. Panic fills Connor's target, and in less than a second the traitor is dead. Aiming his rifle at the other two defectors, he hears the roaring engine of the fighter jet ignite. With the nose of the Owl aimed in his direction, Connor sees his brother smiling in the cockpit.

Caspian flips a cover, revealing a single red button before pressing it. With a rocket launched towards Connor, against his nature and training, he freezes, his feet rooted as he watches the rocket shoot from the Owl's underbelly. With the missile rapidly inching its way towards him, every detail of Connor's life plays. His regrets, his dreams, hopes, and the numerous opportunities that were given to him all flash through his mind. Despite not being enough, all he's wanted was to make Dan proud. Connor shuts his eyes, accepting his fate. In a senseless gravity, his feet are no longer planted, but rather, it's as if Connor is in mid-air inches above the ground. The intensity of the heat increases as the missile approaches with his death in hand, but when it's within an arm's length, Connor's back slams into the ground.

"Idiot!" Renn shouts, Connor's eyes shooting open as the missile whooshes over the pair, exploding thirty yards behind them in the mountainside.

Raising his head, Connor sees Caspian take off in the Owl, soaring high above the tree line and into the twilight.

FOURTEEN

Washington D.C.
March 31, 2037

Ever since she was little, Aila would give daily updates of her plans and dreams, most of them being about the future Mr. Aila. This girl has always had a confident, optimistic outlook on her life, and never in a million years did Lisa think she'd see her niece this anxious. Staring at the glittering diamond, the young woman's hands uncontrollably shake as she stands in utter awe.

"You ready, honey?" Lisa zips up the back of Aila's dress.

"I think so..." Aila murmurs.

Reflecting on her own relationship status and experience, Lisa says the only thing that might relax the young woman. "I wish I could give you better advice."

"Please," Aila says, turning around. Embracing Lisa in a hug, Aila states the truest thing she knows. "Auntie, you are an amazing woman. I learned what a real woman is from the best."

Lisa smiles, and pulling away before she starts crying, she holds Aila's shoulder, examining her niece's face. Lisa never thought this day would be here this fast. One day Aila's bouncing on her lap and then *blink*. She's now overseas, running around, the only white girl with a dozen Arab children. Another blink and she's standing in the most elegant wedding dress ever put on a bride.

"You are so beautiful."

"You're biased," Aila laughs.

"Doesn't matter... It's the truth."

There's a knock at the door, and before the two can welcome him in, Carter pokes his head in the door.

"Get out of here!" Lisa shouts and shoos.

"Am I not allowed to see my niece before the big moment?" Carter innocently asks.

"Well, when you put it like that..." Lisa then waves him in with a tear-filled hug. "I'm going to go freshen up," she says, dabbing at her mascara before stepping out the door.

The moment Lisa leaves, the two stand in a long, solemn silence. With Aila refusing to turn from the mirror, Carter is at a complete loss for words as he stares at the beautiful woman she's become. Before his brother died, Carter saw Aila maybe twice a year but by the age of three, she was an orphan that never left his side.

"Hey there, beautiful," Carter hopefully says, opening his arms.

Aila thinks about it for a moment—about the months of annoying heartache he's caused both her and Mica, but upon realizing that her uncle has never been perfect, nor has she, Aila halfheartedly gives in and walks towards her uncle's outstretched embrace. In a long hug, the two stand, reflecting on the years they've had together. From the deserts of Southeast Asia to the coasts of the United States, it'll take a lot more than some boyfriend drama to break the relationship she's forged with her uncle.

Aila is the first to pull away, feeling that she's done her part to mend the wounds but as she attempts it, Carter brings her back in with a small squeeze. He's sorry. So sorry for making things difficult—for fracturing the trust she had in him. Out of all the times to abandon her, it was in a time that should've been her happiest, but not once was he there. Floral arrangements, venues, food, guest invites, none of it. No support from him, her guardian—the only blood family she has. And for what? A perceived prejudice.

When he finally musters the courage to do so, Carter opens his mouth, but finds himself choking on his words. Rather than expressing his remorse or even having words of advice, a quiet sob is all Carter has to offer.

"What is it?" Aila asks, shifting her head to look into his eyes.

"Do you forgive me?" he barely is able to ask.

In hopes that it will save the mascara and eyeliner, Aila rests her forehead on her uncle's shoulder, knowing that if she doesn't, all the custom makeup she had done will be ruined with waves of tears.

"Don't beat yourself up. I had Lisa there every step of the way."

"It should've been me, though."

The second he found out that she was dating Mica, Aila noticed a dramatic change in her Uncle Carter, and after learning about the convoluted relationship between the two, she empathized to a certain degree. The mixing of personal and professional is never something someone should actively seek out, especially in their line of work. It happens though, and her understanding stopped the moment she saw the unfair judgement and harsh scrutiny her uncle put Mica through.

"I forgive you," she says. "But this thing with Mica, it's got to stop…"

"Yeah," Carter nods, squeezing his niece even tighter, reinforcing his commitment. "You two are making promises to each other to be one and the same. If I don't approve of him, I don't approve of you."

"Thank you," she sniffles, bursting into tears. So much for saving her makeup. "Can you go get Aunt Lisa? I need some help fixing my face."

"Bro! You ready?" Sullivan shouts, grabbing Mica's shoulders in violent enthusiasm.

"I am so nervous!" Mica mumbles, waving his hands around as if he's trying to shake the angst out through his fingertips.

"You'll do fine. Just stand there and don't be an ass. Everyone will be looking at Aila anyway."

These men have had a rollercoaster relationship, and Bella's tangled tie between the two never made things any easier. Despite Mica and Sullivan's rivalry, Sullivan was devastated when he read about what happened to Kim. Mica went off the grid. From Mica's radio silence, Sullivan had no choice but to assume the worst—that Mica was dead. The only reason Sullivan found out anything was because of the nationwide media coverage of Kim's death. Politicized murder always goes viral.

"Where's Dan?" Mica asks, his question immediately being answered.

"I got it!" Dan exclaims as he flies into the room, out of breath and holding the night-blue bow tie. But before he can give it to Mica, Sullivan snatches it from his hand, the menacing gesture not going unnoticed. "It's a mad house out there…"

"Excuses and assholes," Sullivan states, throwing the tie around Mica's neck.

"Not sure if that's the saying…" Dan mumbles before rolling his eyes and walking back out the door.

"Thanks, Dan!" Mica tries shouting out, the appreciation going unheard.

Mica should be taken back by Sullivan's harsh demeanor towards Dan, but he's always equated Sullivan to grabbing a rose by its thorny stem just to smell it. Sullivan's the funny, cynical, sadistic asshole that everyone wants to be with, and if you don't, it's because you're the one with the problem, not Sullivan. It's not an ideal way to describe your best friend, but Mica and Sullivan are like fire and water. They always go together, just not in the most harmonious of fashions.

"Why'd you have to do that?" Mica adds quietly.

"Do what?" Sullivan innocently asks before quickly changing the subject as he finishes the final touches of the tie. "You got something on your chin…"

Shifting to the mirror, Mica is immediately appalled by what he sees. "What the hell is that?" The pimple smack dab in the middle of his chin grew within the last two hours, and there is nothing Mica can do about it now.

"Does it hurt?" Sullivan asks, prodding the cherry protrusion.

"Damn it…" Mica growls, recoiling to slug his friend in the chest.

Laughing, Sulli comically adds, "Relax. your chin isn't what Aila will be looking at later tonight."

"*That* I am nervous for," Mica slowly admits, standing up and examining the rest of his appearance in the mirror.

"Really? Even with all the practice you've had with Bella?"

It's an awkward comment, but Mica takes it as the joke Sullivan intended.

"Aila's nothing like your wife." Mica laughingly blushes. Yes, Bella's always had the *ideal woman's* body—lean build, perfectly proportioned hips and chest, and a movie star face, all of which have only gotten better with time it seems—but even with all that going for her, she could never look past her own mirror, and when they were together, he didn't care that she couldn't.

"Just make sure you don't—you know, get any of the black on you," Sullivan then coldly remarks.

"That was an odd thing to say…" Mica nervously chuckles, the out-of-the-blue comment completely changing Sullivan's demeanor.

"Not really, if you think about it. Rodgers, she is the one getting Aila ready, isn't she?"

"You can't be serious?" Mica asks in disbelief.

"You know what black people are like!" Sullivan responds, doubling down on his stance.

"Do you?" Mica snarls back, staring down Sullivan into an awkward, long silence. Again, this comment should surprise Mica, but unfortunately it doesn't. If nothing else tells Mica that he made the right choice in breaking things off with Bella when he did, it's in this moment that he realizes just how far his values are removed from the Stones'. Mica's never thought about Lisa's "racial status." He's always been highly aware of the extreme critical theorists that can only see the world through the lenses of appearances and power structures—but having never subscribed to the fringe idea, Mica's obviously overlooked the fact that not everyone can see people for the content of their character.

"It's a joke, dude," Sullivan backtracks, attempting to cut the tension from the room. "Just forget it, man. Sorry I said anything. This day is about you."

※ ★ ※

Exhausted, relieved, and anxious, Mica carries Aila to the hotel room wondering how in the world he managed to score a woman like her.

Aila notices the butterflies in his stomach because she's feeling the exact same way. The hallway seems to double with each step he takes, and for the only thing she's had on her mind all day, the waiting is about to pay off.

Early on they promised each other that they wanted to save intimacy until after they were married. They both had promiscuous histories and experiences, making it that much harder and unconventional. Aila wasn't always the faith-based individual she is now, but when that all changed, her Christian values had a forgiving influence on her, which she knows isn't always the case with those that find God. As far as Mica's past is concerned, the details never mattered to Aila, so she's never asked. All she knows is that there were others before Kim. What's important to her is that the two of them have something special—something that neither of them has had before, and the last thing they wanted to do was repeat the lust-filled cycle.

On and on the deprecating comments came from friends and colleagues on both sides of the aisle. They each had their own graceful way of responding to each unique judgment, but what it really came down to for Aila was faith. Ever since reuniting with him in Lisa's class that day, she's had the feeling that nothing can or will take him from her again, no matter what the standards of society.

Mica's hand slips on the handle twice before finally getting a grasp on it.

"Come on, butterfingers!" Aila teases.

"Keep your panties on!"

Opening the door, Mica carries his wife into the room before kicking it closed behind them.

"What if I told you I wasn't wearing any?" she teases, hopping out of his arms, her nerves practically moving her towards the bed.

"Wait," Mica says, tenderly grabbing her shoulder.

Before he knows it however, his knees buckle, and he's shoved face down into the carpet.

"So romantic," his muffled, sarcastic comment going unheard as his lips are smashed into the floor.

"I am so sorry!" Aila is so uptight that her instincts kickstarted what her uncle taught her over the years. Combine that with what little training she's gotten from Mica, and you get a badass kissing the carpet of a hotel room.

Helping her husband to his feet, she knows Mica is wondering if teaching her *anything* was the best course of action. In theory it was. After the bombing, both she and Mica realized that something had to change if he was to ever get on Carter's good side—that and the flashbacks he had of Kim's death brought a sense of urgency. So naturally, Mica trained Aila. He couldn't protect Kim, and he won't make that mistake with Aila. In his current condition, Mica is second guessing that decision.

"Not bad," he says, rolling out his shoulder.

"Well, you know, I had a good teacher!" Aila retorts, giving a flirty smile and a wink to match. Finding no better time to lighten the mood, Aila makes her way to the bed. "I think I might have hurt my back though…" she says, arching across the sheets. "Could you do me a favor and check?" Without any other warning, she slips off her shirt, revealing fair, smooth, flawless, and delicate skin.

"Hell yeah, I can!"

April 1, 2037

Time has a way of meshing together. Days can feel like weeks, the weeks like days, and the years feel like both the more of them you accumulate. If she were still alive, Tiffany would be coming to that same realization as she would be entering her twelfth year. She also would have loved every second spent in the halls of the ultimate presidential suite. He can imagine the jokes she would come up with about the Whites in the White House, and the food—he bets that she would've been a daughter after his own heart, enjoying every piece of cuisine the chefs could muster. It's all speculation though, as Reuben never allowed for her personality to thrive in this world. Ironically, if he would have—if Tiffany lived today—White never would have campaigned for the presidency to begin with. The tragic inspiration of Tiffany's death would be just as fictional as are his very real musings about her sense of humor and her love of food.

It's been three months. Three months since the troubles of the nation were piled on top of him and he took up the mantle to be the leader of the free world. Never has he tried to replace Tiffany, but at times he does wonder if the title of President of the United States is just compensating for the life he refused to have with his daughter. In the ninety days he's spent here in Washington, the only real burden he's bore is the void Tiffany left.

Stretching underneath the ridiculously expensive silk sheets, President White breathes in the fresh spring air. A renewed season for what he hopes is a renewed country. Happiness has evaded him for twelve years, but today—today feels different as he reaches across to his sleeping wife, gently rubbing his fingertips over her cheek.

Grabbing the intercom phone, Reuben presses the speed dial for his head of security, Special Agent Bryant picking up on the other end.

"Good morning, Mr. President. How may I help?"

White, noticing a particular stress and concern in the voice asks, "Is everything all right, Alex?"

"Of course, Mr. President. Everything is fine."

White chalks up the uneasiness in the agent's voice as nervousness. He's still getting to know everyone, after all. If he's not mistaken, Alex is new himself.

"Okay. Well, can you have my morning briefs brought in?"

"Will do, Mr. President."

Before setting down his phone, White is suddenly reminded of something that's been on his mind. "Wait, before you go, are Sullivan and Bella Stone on shift this morning?"

There's no immediate response, so White pulls the phone away from his ear, checking to see if Alex hung up before he could ask.

"Alex?"

"Sorry," he abruptly responds. "Yes, yes they are, Mr. President."

"Good, could you send them up in about thirty minutes? There's something I've been meaning to talk with them about."

"Of course, Mr. President. Is there anything else I can do for you?" he asks, the stress still thick in his voice.

"No. That should be all. Thank you—" And before White can say good-bye, the line goes dead.

White shakes his head at the odd behavior. He needs coffee. That's the conclusion he comes to before reflecting on heavier matters.

With the quick changes in the United States Government, the Children of the Ordean Reich virtually disappeared. White teamed with the Division, battling the Reich for nearly a decade, meeting them on countless battlefields. From the political arena to legitimate firefights, it makes it that much more of a mystery that the moment he's elected, they go incognito. He would be asking Mica his opinions on the matter, but since he's on his honeymoon, that's not a viable option—not for another two weeks anyway. Dan would be the next on his list, but he's had some family emergency, and with Carter out who-knows-where doing who-knows-what, Lisa is probably right alongside him. Naturally, Sullivan and Bella are his next best options. Rather, they're his only options.

Shaking any doubtful thoughts he has on the Stones, White begins focusing on the second item on his agenda. He'll most definitely lose the feminist vote, but he never had a lot of their support to begin with—

"What was that?" his wife shouts, shooting up out of bed as a loud crack sounds in the corridors.

Knowing exactly what it was, White reaches for his bedside gun, but he's too late. His bedroom door bursts open, and in steps an ominous hooded figure.

"Don't!" the figure commands and White reluctantly obeys, noticing the dead agents in the hallway.

"Who are—?" White begins, but his question is answered as he studies the figure more closely. "Why?"

⸺⸻★⸻⸺

Morning comes with a rude awakening as the high-pitched ring echoes throughout the hotel suite. "Who the hell—?" Mica asks, prying himself loose from Aila's naked body. He shakes her but there is no sign of consciousness. "Aila!"

"Morning," she finally stirs, stretching under the silky sheets. She always told him she was a deep sleeper, but never did she tell him that she was a brick in the morning.

"Why's your phone ringing?" Aila asks, the phone still going unanswered.

"It's not mine, it's yours."

"No, it's not—wait," she stops, listening for another ring. "Yep!"

Jumping from the bed in search of her phone, Aila hesitates at the same time. She thought being naked in front of Mica would come naturally, but as she searches for her phone, she self-consciously tries using the bedsheets to stay somewhat modest. "Hello?"

Her answer begins with a smile, but slowly, it fades as she listens a moment longer before holding the phone towards Mica.

Confused, Mica grabs it. "Hello?"

"Why is your phone off?" Carter shouts from the other end.

"I got married yesterday… Honeymoons are still a thing, aren't they?"

"The Pentagon has been bombed… We're under attack."

"What?" Mica runs up to the window to see if he can see the smoke from their D.C. hotel.

"The council is dead," Carter finishes.

Off in the distance, black smoke rises from a variety of locations, most barely visible from how far away the couple's hotel is, and down below, thousands of panicking people try to make sense out of the news Mica's staring at in disbelief.

———⋆★⋆———

"Mica! We have our orders!" Aila desperately shouts over the racing wind, her husband weaving in and out of traffic.

"I know!" *We've got to do this, though,* he thinks.

He must. He can't let White die. The council is gone, and it is only a matter of time before the Ordeans move in on the President. Carter wants his niece protected more than the Commander in Chief? Carter's gotten better, but Mica can see that he's still emotionally compromised. Leaving Aila at the hotel room by herself is out of the question, so this is the best of the worst options.

Within two minutes Mica and Aila pull up to the opening gate.

"Put your mask on," Mica states before slipping on his own deviled appearance and proceeding forward.

"Stop!" an armed agent demands, holding out his hand.

"Division agents!" Mica says.

"I said stop!" the agent commands, grasping Mica's handlebars. "No one is permitted in or out until the building is secure."

Spoken like a true rule follower. "There's been a bombing at the Pentagon, and the President," Mica jabs his finger into the agent's chest, "needs us here if he doesn't want to be the next one on the Reich's hit list."

"I said no!"

Reaching back, Mica squeezes Aila's thigh, signaling for her to get ready.

"Yeah, I heard you," Mica says. "And I'll say again, I'm a Minuteman that's been assigned to protect the President."

"We have all the Minutemen we need," the agent says dismissively, looking into Mica's bicolor eyes and not budging from his stance.

It's in that moment that the red flag pops up. Mica knows every member on the White House security detail, and he has never met this agent.

Before the man can react, Mica knocks the mystery agent unconscious and throws down a smoke pellet at each of the three other guards. Aila hugs his torso as Mica races forward to the front doors, dodging bullets and attacks the entire way. One guy even attempts to get his hands on Aila, but she clubs his teeth in before he's able to lay a finger on her.

"Hang on!" Mica shouts.

Slamming his hand onto the front brakes, Mica abruptly tilts the bike forward. Instinctively shifting his weight to the left, Mica brings the bike's rear tire into an arcing swing towards the handful of guards rushing them, sending their broken bodies to the side.

"I hope you're ready, love," Mica says.

"Ready as I'll ever be," Aila quips, throwing three more smoke pellets down, masking their entrance into the White House.

As soon as they step into the building, agents from every corner rush forward to eliminate the threat. Mica, expecting this, takes out two in a single second. Aila is shot at, but narrowly the bullet misses, hitting the wall directly behind her, and before he can get off a second shot, Aila pulls out her taser and shoots, the prongs piercing the inner thigh and chest of the agent, buckling him over.

"That was—" Aila begins but is choked from behind. Instantly, and like Mica taught her, she turns her hips, jabs her thumbs into the attacker's eyes, and picks her favorite of a dozen methods to incapacitate him: the throat.

"That was easy," Aila mumbles, finishing her previous thought.

"Who are they?" Mica wonders, still not recognizing a single person.

"They're not Secret Service?" Aila asks, shrugging her shoulders.

"No. I've trained with the Secret Service, and they are not them."

"Maybe they—" Aila begins.

"No, hun. I've met every single one of them. It was part of my assignment to know *all* of them in case—" Mica stops, realizing a dreadful truth.

Flying up the stairs three at a time, Mica rounds half a dozen corners as he makes his way to the President's bedroom.

"Mr. President!" Mica shouts, seeing White's bedroom door agape. "Mr. President, it's Agent Rouge." Slowly he approaches, hatchet in one hand and a club in the other as he makes his way down the barren hallway.

"Help!" a woman's voice shouts back.

Running forward, Mica kicks his way into the room only to see the First Lady kneeling over her bleeding husband.

"Who did this?" he asks, looking to Mrs. White.

White tries to respond, but a puddle of blood replaces his words, pouring from his lips and down to the gaping hole in his chest. His wife, in an uncontrollable panic, pushes down on the wounds, desperately trying to stop the bleeding.

"I've got you, Mr. President," Mica states, his hope quickly fading.

"Mica!" Aila rushes in, out of breath, and upon seeing the President dying on the floor, drops her weapons, slowly raising her hands to her mouth.

"Get something!" Mica shouts, not taking his eyes from White's gaze.

Aila rushes to the bathroom and a split second later is back, pressing a towel to the President's chest.

"It happened so fast…" the First Lady mutters, putting her arms firmly around Aila. "They were about to shoot me when they heard you guys coming in downstairs…"

"Who. Who is *they*?" Mica asks.

"I-I don't know… They were gone before I could see their face."

With only seconds left, Mica begins to feel the historical gravity of this moment. The President—who he and everyone else thought was going to be the one to turn this country around—is dying right in front of him. As the light in White's eyes dwindles, the President lets out his last breath, the future of the country fading with him.

Sullivan and Bella suddenly rush in to see the tragic scene before them.

"Oh my—" Bella says, her hands covering her mouth in utter shock.

"Mica," Sullivan says urgently. "We have to go. The Secret Service are on their way…"

"One day. I was gone one day!" Mica stands, facing Sullivan.

"We were at the Pentagon—" Sullivan tries explaining but is cut off before getting the chance.

"Mica," Bella is the one who steps forward this time. "We do need to go. Everyone's going to think that you did this. There's footage in the media that caught you attacking the Secret Service at the front gate."

"They were not the Secret Service!" Mica shouts.

"We know, but the truth doesn't matter to the media," Bella says.

"We can't just leave the First Lady," Aila says.

"I'll be fine," Mrs. White quietly states. "I know it wasn't you, Mica…"

Conflicted between his loyalty to this woman and self-preservation, Mica yields to the First Lady's words.

"Let's go, Mica," Aila says, helping her husband up before the two quickly leave with Bella.

Sullivan, kneeling beside the President he swore to protect, takes Mrs. White's hand in his, and with both eyes, he looks into hers.

"I'm sorry."

"He was a good man," she says, kissing Reuben's hand. Ever since AP American History, the story of Jacqueline Kennedy holding her husband's lifeless body in her arms broke her heart. How terrible that must have been for a woman to endure. Now, in this moment, she can truly empathize with that great American.

"Go, before they get here."

Sullivan stands, reaching into his vest. "You misunderstand my apology."

And without hesitation, Sullivan pulls out a silenced pistol, shooting her right through the head.

III
ORIGINS

Fifteen

Area Thirty-Eight
Five Years Ago

"Will work for food," he says, the wrinkled sign in his hands mirroring the words. "Will work for—"

"Look what we have here." Like clockwork, the PPA patrol makes its rounds to the corner of Franklin and Thirteenth, instantly spotting the decrepit man.

"The old timer back at it!" the young squad leader mocks, ignorant to the fact that he is two years his senior.

"Will work for food..." the beggar slowly repeats, ignoring their taunts.

"You know what you're doing is illegal, don't you?" another PPA private spits out, crouching down.

Three days this guy has been begging and nothing's been done about it. They just hoped he'd die, placing bets on it. Tomorrow will be day four, which means that for this private he'll lose a lot of money if the guy lives that long. It might piss his comrades off, but if he plays it right, he'll be justified in ending the beggar's life today. Nothing in their verbal agreement states that he can't force an outcome in his favor.

"What is the law, you piece of shit?"

"Will work for food..."

"'Praise the Nine by our actions.' Is begging praiseworthy of The Government?" the private asks, the question yielding a handful of chuckles from PPA soldiers and passing workers alike.

The beggar continues his mantra. "Will work for food..."

"'Live, work, and if needs be *die*, so that the Nine and their Government may continue to prosper and bless.'"

"Will work for food..."

"You hear that, fellas? He's not working. He's *barely* living, so it seems like the only good he'll do the Nine is die. He's a leech on the system."

Seeing what the newbie is doing, the others begin mumbling protests. They have just as much money—if not more—riding on the beggar's timely death. The squad leader in particular has an enormous amount riding on a desired outcome.

"You'll be on shit detail for a month if you win—" he states, pulling the private aside.

The threat is an empty one though. In a vice-like grip the squad leader feels his testicles compressed before they are pulled out and sliced from his body. In a cry of agony and terror, the sergeant drops to his knees while his squad freezes in abject horror.

"Will work for food…" the beggar repeats, standing and holding his bloody trophy out to them.

"The report says that you…" Caspian stops himself, in disbelief as he laughingly reads the statement. "Squeezed and cut off the sergeant's balls."

The beggar, just wanting a warm meal, ignores the Area Leader's interrogation.

Having no choice than to use the pun, Caspian is impressed by the size of the pair on this guy. What's a fitting judgment for someone who blatantly defied his PPA officers in such an iconic manner?

"Is that true?" Caspian asks.

Again, the homeless man ignores the inquiry.

"Listen, I get it," Caspian continues. "You're hungry. Nobody's giving you a break and you've got some aggression built up. I'm not here to judge. I would've done the same thing."

Still no response. It's getting annoying, but again, this guy doesn't give a shit. It's this kind of attitude that Caspian needs to foster within his ranks!

"What's your name?"

Silence.

"Listen, I'm the only one who can help you out at this point, and after what you did, you can either take that help, or I've got to kill you at the Gathering."

More silence.

Not wanting an asset like this to go to waste, Caspian tries one more thing. It's clear that the guy is starving—at his wits' end for anything to eat. It was going to be a reward, but what good is a reward if the recipient is dead? Snapping his fingers, Caspian's guard steps just outside the office.

"Have you heard of the Legacy class?" Caspian asks, and as expected, the beggar is unresponsive. "It's a class system we've set up to ensure that The Government's employees are taken care of—that those loyal to the Nine but outside of the Oligarchy, they won't go hungry, so to speak."

The beggar's ears twitch.

"I can enroll you. I can get you a reliable job. Steady wage." And then pausing for dramatic effect, Caspian holds his last offer until he hears his office door open back up. "I can make sure you never go hungry again."

The aroma is the first thing the beggar notices as the scent of warm beef, gravied potatoes, and a side of buttery vegetables fills the room. Sure enough, as the guard enters, that's exactly what is on the plate. The only thing the starving beggar didn't smell was the glass of clean, filtered, ice water.

"What's your name?" Caspian asks.

Smacking his lips, the beggar thinks before answering, contemplating the offer he's being presented.

"What's the job?" he asks, his eyes fixated on the warm plate of food.

"It's whatever I want it to be," Caspian says. "Now, what's your name?"

"Jude," the beggar says.

"Well, Jude, I'll have some paperwork for you to sign. But while you eat," Caspian says, pushing the plate of food forward before standing and moving over to the filing cabinet, "let me brief you on the Raiders."

Raider Encampment
Present Day

"Jude, what's going on?" Mari asks, listening to the dying peppered gun fire.

"You two need to leave," he says, stuffing a jacket into a bag.

"What are you talking about—Jude, what happened?" Mari asks, tired of his vague explanations.

She's always had an attention to detail. It's no coincidence that Jude came waltzing into her life when he did, and as awkwardly charming as he's been, the sickening feeling she's been having has only continued to grow these past weeks.

"Caspian got away!" he growls. Dashing over to the cot, he pulls out a second bag, throwing it to Mari. "It's not safe here anymore."

"Why?" Ann chimes in, having felt the tension from outside.

Ignoring the little girl, Jude continues to pack. If Jax gets his hands back on Caspian, his cover is blown. He's already on bad terms; that was by design. If he's compromised, though, who knows what will happen to Mari and Ann.

His controlled rage towards the Raiders is how he's been able to infiltrate as deep as he has—it's how he's been able to sabotage Jax emotionally—but rather than keeping his own sentiments in check, Mari and Ann have become like family. They remind Jude of a nostalgic time when life wasn't ideal, but where he was happy. For so long, all he had was his investment in Caspian, and he forgot what it was like to feel love. Now that he does, that choice he made five years ago comes to haunt him.

The Raiders took his family—they took Lauren and his daughters. "Collateral damage" was the explanation he got from the PPA when he filed a complaint. That ire is what drove him for so long, and unless Mari and Ann leave, they'll be more than just civilian casualties in this instance. He's seen the Raiders' justice system, their way of processing evidence—it's all broken and will guarantee their slow executions. They'll be guilty by some messed up version of association, and with his cover most likely already in shambles, he must find a way to protect them from the Raiders. He couldn't with Lauren or his little girls, but he might be able to for Mari and Ann.

"Jude!" Mari grabs his arm, stopping him from his frantic packing. "What did you do?"

"I-I..." he stutters out, hanging his head as he does.

Mari's gaze hardens. Picking up the bag in front of him, she shoves it in his arms, and while her hand raises, ready to delve out a vicious slap, Mari stops, a tear trickling down her cheek. "Out!"

"You don't understand..." he slowly says.

"Jude!" Jax rushes into the tent. "Jude, we've got to go!" And as quickly as he came, Jax leaves to shout off other orders.

Dropping the bag to the dirt, Jude reaches out to Mari, wanting to touch her face one last time.

"I'm going to fix this," he says. If he does, the secret dies with Caspian.

Recoiling from his outreached hand, Mari protectively takes Ann under her arm, and with one final look, Jude walks out of the tent and out of their lives.

All this for a plate of food.

"Get it running, now!" Jax orders.

Renn, not thinking twice, grabs Jax's arm. "What are you doing?"

"What do you think I'm doing? We can't let him get away!"

Renn shakes her head, reiterating her question. "Why? Why are you doing this? The camp is in a panic. The Owls haven't been field tested, and we should focus on getting out of here, not attack—"

"We're not attacking," Jax counters. "It's a retrieval."

"However you want to label it, it's reckless." Renn jabs her finger into his chest. "Look around. These people need a leader... At the very least, we should use the Owls to patrol our relocation. Abandoning the camp for this mission will leave the Encampment vulnerable."

"Hey!" Kai shouts, jerking Jax's shoulder back.

"Not now, Kai."

"Look at this!" Kai insists. "Twelve women and children dead, and we're still counting."

"I said not now!"

"You're the one that brought Caspian in, and you are the one that let him get away. Their deaths are on you!"

"Let Caspian go. We got him once, we can—" Renn pleads.

"We're going after Caspian, there's no debate here." Jax puts his foot down, tired of the circle of bullshit they're in. "Renn, you're my advisor. That's it."

"We never should have let white people in…" Kai coldly states.

Before Jax can respond, one of the mechanics runs up to the three.

"The fuel line needs more tension. If we don't take care of it now, it could burst in mid-flight. The Owls simply aren't ready—"

"How long will that take?" Jax asks, cutting him off.

"Thirty, forty minutes?"

"We don't have time for that," Jax growls out. "If the line bursts mid-flight, can it be fixed?"

Pausing, the Raider thinks about it. "I think so, but I'm not going to lie, it'll be tough and there's the strong possibility it can't."

"Get it fired up. Run the pre-flight checks."

"Jax!" Renn shouts out, but before she can let out another one of her protestations, he issues the ultimatum.

"Either get in the jet with Connor or get out of the way!"

Biting her tongue, Renn jogs towards her plane, knowing full well the odds are against them. If he's to stand a chance, though, she needs to be in the cockpit.

Out of the corner of his eye, Connor sees Renn, furious and annoyed, jogging up to their aircraft.

"I take it he didn't listen," Connor mumbles.

"Bingo," Renn throws off her officer's jacket and zips up her flight suit.

"We'll do what we can." Connor knew he wouldn't listen, but they had to try.

"I hate protecting stupid people," Renn coldly states. She's been doing it her entire life. It was naïve to think here in the Encampment it'd be any different.

"We've dealt with worse."

Renn sighs. "You should have become the leader of the Resistance."

Connor rolls his eyes as he continues to flip switches. "That's rather flattering, but we've been through this."

"Yeah, yeah." And she doesn't believe one word of it.

Connor says it's because he's not leadership material, but that's clearly a lie. They go round and round, but it always concludes with the fact that people naturally follow Jax—an extremely rare trait in any leader. Clearly, Dan agrees due to his decision in appointing Jax. Despite this, Renn thinks it's an excuse Connor's using to avoid the truth—the truth being that he fears that he's a disappointment to Dan. She knows it's the reason why he gave up back there with the missile, but if Connor never admits it, all Renn has is her theoretical explanation as to the complex father-son relationship.

"Diagnostics check," Connor shouts.

Renn hops into the cockpit, quickly checking the weapons systems. "You sure you want to fly this time?"

"I am a better pilot than you," Connor laughs.

"Shut up," she scoffs, punching the back of his seat.

Firing up the Owl's engine, listening to the roar and hums of the aircraft's deep idling rhythm, Renn flips a switch before putting on her headset and checking the night vision.

"Night Owl One, this is Night Owl Two. Radio check, over."

There's a crackle before Jude's voice comes on loud and clear. "I read you five by five. How me, over?"

"I read you five by five," Renn echoes.

"You doing all right, Night Owl Two?" Jude asks.

"I've been better."

"You and me both," he says with a heavy hint of anxiety. "Looks like it's the two of us along for the ride."

"Let's keep our pilots alive, yeah?" Renn says. Even though she's furious with Jax, she's glad he and Connor are flying together. Out of all the logged flight hours from everyone, with these two on the same team, they were unbeatable in every battlefield scenario.

"We'll take point, and you'll follow a hundred yards back on our left. Copy?"

"Roger. Ready when you are."

With that, Renn looks out to see Jax lifting the beast off the ground, and as Night Owl One rises into the air, Renn can't help but admire the sleek, dark blue hue of the war machine. Three powerful engines propel the craft into the night sky, and once above the tree line, the engines rotate to thrust the bird forward, slowly at first, but in a matter of seconds the aircraft is clear of the Encampment.

"We're clear," Connor says as he begins to lift their bird off the ground, and within moments, they are chasing down Night Owl One.

Down below and still in the Encampment, Kai and Dan watch in despair at the warriors flying off to battle.

"Idiots!" Kai declares. "They don't give a damn about us."

Dan no longer has a say in the matter. "It's his call."

"It shouldn't be," Kai says. *It should be mine*, he thinks. He was promised that when he came of age, he would take up his father's responsibilities. "He should not be leading the Resistance. We've made so much progress, and the second he comes in, this kind of shit happens."

"It more complicated than that, son."

"How?"

Trying to find the right answer, Dan reflects on his old friend Mica and the promise they made to each other at the beginning of the fight twenty-four years ago.

"Do you remember when I first found you?"

"Of course. How could I forget?" Even though he was young, Kai remembers every detail with vivid exactness.

The violence. The pain. The death.

"Do you remember what I told you?"

"You said that you'd take care of me."

"And I stand by that, even if it means you disagree or don't understand what I think are in your best interest."

───※★※───

"We're at altitude," Jax says, scanning the night horizon while doubt still weighs on his mind. "Can I trust you, Jude?"

Surprised by the sudden, direct question, Jude sits silent for a moment as he ponders on an answer. *I can still fix this...*

"Why do you ask, sir?"

"If I'm being honest, I ask because I've had my doubts about you..."

Jude's thoughts divert first to Mari and Ann before shifting to Caspian. "I really haven't given you a reason to trust me, have I?"

"Mari has nothing to do with this..." Jax slowly says, his eyes still fixated on the night's horizon. "Do you think it's possible that somebody helped Caspian?"

"I'm almost certain of it."

"I mean from within the Raiders?"

"I know what you meant." Jude looks away from the radar and reaches into his pocket. His gloves make it difficult, but with some effort he's able to pull out the only picture of him and Mari there is—a reminder of his dark truth.

"Can I ask you a question now?" Jude asks.

"Seems fair enough," Jax replies.

"How close are you and Mari?"

There's a fair amount of pain that comes with that question, and every answer Jax has tried to find stings. "Before all of this, we were really close."

"She said that you changed after Kip's death."

"I did..."

"I liked Kip," Jude slowly states, and then picking his next words carefully, tentatively adds, "I was there you know—when Kip died."

That's the night when he'd thought Caspian's ideology was right—when it all culminated, and Jude had everything figured out. However, Caspian was wrong about everything. He'd lied, used him; and all there is to show for Jude's absolute loyalty are dead men, women, and children. Jude's legacy is nothing but collateral damage.

"I was there too," Jax scoffs. "What's your point?"

"I get why you want Caspian so bad."

Finding the conversation too painful to continue, Jax refocuses on the task at hand outside; the crescent moon the only vivid detail he can see.

Suddenly a tiny blip appears on the radar.

"I've got something," Jude reports, flipping on his radio. "Night Owl Two, do you guys see anything up ahead?"

After a second or so, Renn comes back with her reply. "Connor can't, but I'm picking up something moving fast on my radar."

The realization instantly hits Jax. Without another word from either Jude or Night Owl Two, he takes the jet into a sharp turn just as a red glow zooms past them.

Connor, having the same immediate intuition, follows Jax into the sharp turn.

"Masks on!" Renn shouts over the radio.

Looking down at the once-blank radar, Jax and Connor take their aircrafts up to Mach 3, zooming ahead at an enemy group.

"We've got five up ahead and closing in fast," Jude reports.

Flipping his visor down, Jax reveals a thermal image of the night, confirming Jude's assessment. In perfect formation, five enemy fighters charge their way. Knowing what his wingman is thinking, Jax dives down and to the right while Connor pulls up and veers left, and just as expected the group of five splits: three chasing Jax and two after Connor.

"Why do I always get the bigger group?" Jax mumbles. "Weapons armed?"

Hitting three buttons, Jude gives Jax three groups of two missiles. "Yes, sir. Happy hunting!"

Jax takes careful aim and fires at the three assaulting jets. With the missile screaming forward, within four hundred yards of it leaving their aircraft, the rocket splits into three as it continues towards the enemy cluster. Veering left and hitting their flares, two successfully evade. The third isn't so lucky as it is obliterated in a fiery glow where it hurtles to the earth.

Banking right, Jax narrowly misses a barrage of bullets. "How's Night Owl Two doing?" he asks.

"Better than us," Jude retorts, looking down to see Night Owl Two in pursuit of only one other bird.

"Good for him…" Jax curses, having spotted the newly acquired tail. Hitting a button, Jax switches the direction of the Owl's missile system, and with a simple press of another, two missiles shoot out from behind to obliterate their tailing target.

"Do your job, Jude! That happens again, we're dead."

"Got it," Jude says, calming his breathing. "Last one is dead ahead. Watch the rear missile system—"

Jude's words are thrown into the back of his throat as Jax hits his flares and jerks the aircraft into a dive, avoiding the oncoming missile from the back of the enemy jet. Releasing the brake, Jax hits the thrusters into a hard acceleration. Just then, Jax is splattered in the face by a warm, black liquid.

"The fuel line burst!"

Flipping up his visor, the spitting hose throws fuel and oil over every inch of window space, blinding them from the fight.

"Night Owl Two, we have a situation."

Renn's voice immediately comes up on the radio. "We see you. You've got a bird directly behind you."

"Take care of it!" Jude frantically shouts, attempting to wipe the window clean.

Jax finds it just as futile as he smears the oily mess. "Get that line fixed, Jude!" And then, flipping a switch, Jax hopes that thermal imaging will help him see through the smudging, but the heat from the liquid proves it pointless, forcing Jax to solely rely on the instruments on his dashboard.

"Keep it steady!" Jude yells out. Every time he has a grasp on the spewing line, Jax jerks the jet, forcing him to lose his hold on the problem.

"If I do, we die!"

Shaking his head, Jude shouts to Renn. "This is impossible. Night Owl Two, kill this bird behind us and we'll try to land until—"

Jude's voice is abruptly cut off. Looking down at a blank radar, Renn tries locating Night Owl One, but neither Jax nor enemy aircraft can be seen.

"Connor, go to their last position," she shouts. "Night Owl One?"

Turning the bird around, all Connor and Renn face is the horrid sight of falling, glowing debris hitting the forest treetops.

―⟩·★·⟨―

Two hours have elapsed and nothing. Mari's never this fretful and scared.

"They'll be back," Ann says, hugging Mari's waist.

Wanting to believe and have Ann's natural hope, Mari struggles to hold back an impending flood of tears. *How could he*, she thinks. The warning signs were there, and she was blinded by the simple-minded urge to move on, thinking Jude could provide the means of healing.

Just when Mari feels her dam is breaking, the deep hum of an aircraft in the distance sounds throughout the camp. Running out of her tent, she sprints for the runway as she sees the joyous sight of one of the landing jets.

"They're back," she whispers.

"If you just listened," Ann mumbles. "That's what I was trying to say…"

Stopping short of the safety zone, Mari folds her arms in her best attempt to contain her excitement. The second he steps off that plane she's going to make sure Jax knows how much she's missed him. Whatever Jude did, whatever he said to sabotage what little threads Mari and Jax had between them, she will stop at nothing to weld them back together. Both have been used as pawns and she can't hold any of that against him.

She can't because she loves him.

The aircraft lands and the cockpit opens, but neither Jax nor Jude step out. It's not their plane, and as Connor jumps down, he's quickly followed by Renn Stone.

"Where's Jackie?" Ann calls.

Mari listens for the second Owl, but finds no deep hum, just crackling fires, quiet conversations, and the engine of the first aircraft cooling down. As calmly as possible, Mari walks up to Connor, where she encounters an emotion that she's seen only once—in herself, not too long ago.

Fearfully, she asks what she needs to know. "Where's Jax?"

Mari's the one person he can't bear to see, but Connor steps her way anyway. He knows the history she's had with Jax, and despite her situation with Jude, Jax admitted that he still loved Mari.

"They were shot down..." Connor slowly says.

Mari's dam bursts and as tears roll down her cheeks, whatever will Mari had is lost as she falls to her knees, defeated by the news.

Ann, not being a stranger to growing up fast, wraps Mari in a tight embrace, not allowing a single tear to fall from her own eyes.

Emerging from the solemn crowd, Dan and Kai quickly infer the mission's outcome, and instead of ambling forward, Dan instantly turns his back on Connor.

"Dan!" Connor runs up, grabbing his father's shoulder.

"Don't!" he hisses out. "This was your chance!"

"My chance? My chance for what?" Connor steps back, fearing his next words.

"It was your chance to prove your worth as a member of the Resistance. Now who is to stop the Nine from killing us once and for all?"

"We can still do this. We still have the box—"

"Caspian knows!" Dan shouts, his voice echoing throughout the Encampment. "He knows everything now!"

"We'll relocate. That's still the plan, isn't it?"

Dan, refusing to see the logic, simply states, "You've put us all in danger."

"But, Dad," Connor pleads.

"You do not get to call me that. I didn't raise you... You're no son of mine," Dan says, his final words turning with him as he and Kai walk away.

Connor takes a step forward, but Renn holds him back, unable to see her brother take any more embarrassment.

"From day one, all he's seen is the PPA uniform I've worn."

"Don't think like that." Renn gives his shoulders a shake. "He's outside of your control, just like everyone else is. Now, let's find Jax."

"Is Jax dead?" Mari asks, having overheard their conversation.

"There's a good chance that he is," Renn apprehensively says.

"I said they got shot down," Connor blares out, his anger getting the best of him. "We both saw it!"

"The truth is, we don't know, Mari," Renn solemnly says. "We flew over the crash site multiple times, but it's still possible that Jax ejected. We had to come back for fuel, but we're headed right back out."

With her enthusiasm revived and a small amount of hope restored, Mari stands as she looks to the two soldiers. "Let's go get him then!"

Sixteen

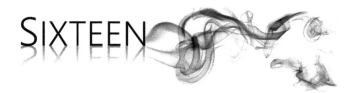

Origins

Phoenix Arizona
November 26, 2017

"What happened exactly?" Lisa asks the lawyer.

"They were stopping at a gas station on their way back from California when they were mugged."

Mugged. That's a sugarcoated way of putting it, Carter scoffs and thinks to himself. Just say murdered. They were held at gun point and shot in the face.

"Did they catch the person?" Lisa then asks.

Carter doesn't need to look away from the carpet he's been staring at for the past twenty minutes to know the lawyer's answer. California is already a shit show of a state, but San Francisco...

Damn his brother.

If Jim wasn't such a goody two shoes, then he would've had his gun on him, but thanks to Pelosi and her progressive goon squad, their "common sense" firearms regulation took the gun from his brother and put one in the hand of that low life criminal. Thanks to the narrative of safety, inclusion, and whatever bullshit bureaucratic policy, his brother and his wife are dead.

"Why were they in California?" This question is more hushed as Lisa asks it, but again, although Carter has been silent since stepping into the conference room, this does not mean he's been oblivious—quite the opposite in fact.

"She had family there?" Carter mumbles, startling both Lisa and the lawyer.

"They were visiting her family for the holidays. Rachel's parents had plans to move to Arizona to be closer to their granddaughter and they were helping them sort things out logistically speaking."

Swinging open the door, Carter and Lisa's stateside supervisor bursts inside. Immediately the six-foot-five former tight end rushes over as he finds Lisa, giving her a hug before moving over to Carter.

"I'm so sorry I'm late," Reuben says.

Standing, Carter shakes his head before embracing his boss. "Don't worry about it. We're just waiting…"

"It's no excuse," White argues, shaking his head and catching his breath. "I'll get caught up later, but you doing alright?"

"I'm great," Carter replies sardonically.

The casual response and tone catches Reuben off guard. "Could you give us a minute?" he asks the lawyer.

"Of course! I'll just be next door and I'll come back when she gets here."

Once the lawyer gathers his personal belongings and steps out, White turns back to Carter and sits down next to his friend.

"Listen man, if you need some time off, Afghanistan isn't going anywhere. Their minerals sure as hell aren't, and we can handle the Chinese and Russians for now while you get things sorted out—"

"Reuben, I said I'm good. I appreciate you coming by, but I know you got a lot on your plate with Harris and Huck. Lisa's just here for the weekend and I'll be back next week."

White isn't doubtful, but he is more than concerned. Not letting that show, he pats Carter on the back as he pulls out a flask from the inside of his jacket.

"Really?" Lisa chuckles in disbelief.

"What? It's not just for me," he says, unscrewing the lid and handing it over to Carter.

"Thanks, but I'll pass. I want to be sober when she gets here."

Turning to Lisa and offering her the same invitation, she too rejects it.

"Maybe it is just for me," Reuben mumbles, taking a swig. "Is there *anything* either of you need?"

Shrugging, Carter looks to his friend. "A flight back to Afghanistan, housing and a good school once this is all sorted out here."

"That's easy! I've already got people working on it. I'm talking about you…" Reuben states, jabbing Carter in the arm.

"I'm good. Honestly!" Carter has to add this last part because from the look both White and Lisa just gave him, they're calling bullshit.

But, finding it pointless to argue or convince Carter otherwise, White finds no other choice but to just take what his friend is giving him on pure faith. He knows Carter won't let the mission fail and he'll be more than capable in the field no matter the stress. That's not the point White's been trying—but failing—to get at. His friend *is not* doing well at all and if Carter is going to admit that himself, the only person capable of accomplishing this is Lisa.

"Well," Reuben sighs out. "I'll just be talking to the fine piece of ass at the front desk if you need me."

"Thanks, Reuben," Lisa says softly, walking him to the door and closing it behind him.

As the two then sit in silence, Lisa refuses to be the first to engage in conversation. She more than wants to, but it won't do her or Carter any good to talk just for the sake of having a conversation. It'll only piss him off. As a man of few words, Carter responds better to touch, so that's what Lisa does. Moving over to him, she takes the seat next to her best friend and simply places her palm on top of his folded hands. For a moment or two, Carter doesn't respond. He just sits there, letting the continuing silence grow as his mind sorts through both the facts and hypothetical details that brought him to sit here in this room. However, as the warmth from Lisa's touch grows, the intertwining hold his fingers have on one another loosen. With Lisa's grip finding his, it is here where she gives her friend's hand a slight squeeze telling him everything he's been needing to know.

"I don't know if I'm ready, Lisa," Carter softly whispers.

"I know, John," she whispers back. "But you have to be. That little girl's got no one else. She's just got you and God."

"God..." Carter scoffs, not having the energy to engage in this kind of conversation.

He wonders if God was there that night, watching as the bullet entered and exited the back of their skulls. Jim was the man of faith, and Carter is willing to bet that he was praying up until the moment that shit bag pulled the trigger on him and his wife. Two bullets, three point two seconds and what good did a prayer do then? This isn't even taking into account the gross travesties against women and children he's seen terrorist groups engage in, because after all, it is their "God" who condones such actions.

"Alhamdulillah," Carter mumbles, sneering at Lisa's advice. *Praise be to God.*

"Yarhamuk Allah," she mocks back, not taking offense to his emotional lash. *May God have mercy on you.* Yes, the term is used as more of a *bless you* after someone sneezes, but by how mature Carter acted just now, the direct translation seemed fitting.

"Fair enough," Carter laughs.

Just then, a light knocking is heard at the door. A moment later, the lawyer pokes his head in.

"She's here," he says.

Without saying a word, both Lisa and Carter stand to greet the little girl and nod to the lawyer. Carefully, he pushes the door open as he walks in holding the hand of a three-year-old toddler. Shy and timid and with puffy red eyes, in walks Jim's little girl, a picture of pink holding her well-loved stuffed fawn.

"She's been crying," Lisa whispers.

"Aila," the lawyer calmly says. "Do you remember your Uncle Carter?"

The toddler doesn't respond but rather begins fighting off another wave of tears as she looks to Carter, Lisa, and back to the lawyer, unsure who any of these people are.

"Hey," Carter gently says, catching the girl's attention before she cries. He could count on one hand the number of times he's seen his niece, and although she was apprehensive each encounter, he was able to win her over in a matter of seconds.

With a slight wink, Carter crouches down to the little girl's eye level before immediately puffing his cheeks out. It works. Aila's cry is halted, and before she can make too much sense of it, Carter then begins to slowly and obnoxiously let the air out of his cheeks. In a bashful smile, Aila purses her lips together as she refuses to laugh. Not satisfied with the reaction he's getting, Carter repeats the juvenile joke, this time receiving a minute giggle as payment.

"Come here," he then whispers, holding out his arms to his niece. Not needing any more convincing, Aila releases her hold on the lawyer's hand before pattering her way over to Carter.

Any and all apprehension that Carter has been carrying with him this past week instantly fades as he embraces his little niece, the doubt and anger put on pause as he stands and whispers into Aila's little ear.

"God or not, I'll always be here for you."

———⋆ ⋆ ★ ⋆ ⋆———

Colorado Springs
June 6, 2037

"Dan!"

The sound of her reverberating shriek bouncing off his ear drums and making him wince—that he could do without.

"Yes?" he patiently responds, simply continuing to unpack his things.

"Dan!" her shrill tone continues cursing out.

"Yes?" he repeats, more to himself at this point than to her. Then, in the delicate voice he fell in love with, his wife enters, her demand still unmet. "Have you seen the kitchen knives?"

"Wow," he mumbles, his eyes still on his own task.

"Wow what?"

"Wow, was that necessary—?" Dan asks, finally looking up from the box. Whatever annoyance he had flees, his gaze following the curve of her long, golden legs to bring back countless fond memories.

"Was what necessary?" Victoria asks.

"Have you looked in the kitchen?" he asks, shaking the lingering exasperation.

"Yes…" she states, poking her tongue out.

"I don't know what to tell you then, Tori."

"A lot of help you are!" And then before she doubles down on this premise of her husband's apathy, she stops as the obvious thought pops in her mind. "Connor!"

Dan shakes his head. That woman's determination has always been able to put a smile on his face, no matter how dramatic the antics.

Looking back down, Dan finally finds what he's been searching for.

Victoria is back, and Dan is more than grateful for that, but when she first left, she took everything. His books, his table, his tv. She even took his socks, leaving his life in the same manner this box is in—in utter disarray! However, Dan couldn't hold it against her. He won't. Raising a family as a cop isn't easy, as personal and professional lifestyles often mix, which to her credit, was something Tori vowed she would never tolerate all those years ago.

Pulling out his antique, Dan is amazed at the resilient technology as the disc player boots right up, and rushing to his backpack, out comes his treasured copy of *Continuum*. Signed by John Mayer, the third—and by far the best studio-released album—changed Dan's life. As a ten-year-old, its 2006 September release transformed the way he would see the world. He'll sound like a hippy, but Dan began viewing life through a lens of optimism and love rather than the cynical nature he was brought up in. Rather than "waiting on the world to change" as Mayer puts it, the little boy Dan made it a goal to be the change he wanted to see. It all culminated as his proudest moment being when the Las Vegas Police Department sponsored him to go to their academy. One of the most efficient and well-structured departments wanted him, and Dan knew he'd be getting some of the best experience working in the City of Sin. Despite the anti-police rhetoric that was plaguing the nation, he saw through the political bullshit and hoped to change problems from within. He learned and accepted the depth of issues like the improvement of training and hiring standards of the different departments, while he saw others, like the systemic targeting of minorities, being blown out of proportion.

It all prepared him for the day Carter found him.

Kissing the case, Dan gently places the disc into the player where, after a moment, the theme of his life begins playing. Shit just gets in the way. It shouldn't, but it does, and humans have a natural knack for passively sucking the joyful simplicity from one's own existence simply through apathetic behavior. This and many more of life's truths echo to Dan as he's taken back to his first playthrough of the album, and like he did then, he stands, eyes closed, and embraces the music.

"And when you trust your television,
What you get is what you got,
Cause when they own the information, oh,
They can bend it all they want."

He forgot that—he forgot why he started his journey to begin with. After Victoria and Connor left, there wasn't a bitter day that went by that they weren't on his mind. After all he sacrificed for family and their community, she left. At the time, it didn't compute. He was supposed to be rewarded, not punished for his service, and yet, something always must give. In this case it was his family.

"Nothing changes if nothing changes," he was once told at a group therapy session. "Two plus two will always equal four, no matter how much we want it to equal five or more."

Something from a canceled Dr. Seuss book, Dan thought. When did his determination to change a broken system become a bad thing? When it turned to stubborn addictive behaviors, that's when, and no matter how much he fought to stay the course, he was under the false belief that everyone else needed to alter their world views, not him. He was addicted to drugs, but for a good cause! What could be better than taking down a criminal from within their own circle of influence? That was just as much a rush as the physical dependency of the substances. *She just refused to see it*, he thought. Naturally, that kind of mindset led to compounding disaster. His wife left, taking their child with her. Friends abandoned him. Dan lost his badge, the landlord complained, and on and on it went. That's when he was reminded.

On the street, outside the door of some hole-in-the-wall café, he re-heard this song and the light bulb turned back on. An epiphany. A revelation. Whatever you want to call it, somewhere along the way, the simple concepts that he so easily understood at the age of ten were lost as the life he built crumbled. If he wanted the summation of two and two to equal five or more, he had to fundamentally change all concepts of natural law—which he'd tried, and broke himself in the attempt. He was in the wrong. That's the cold, hard truth. His addictions were supported by his profession, not his wife, nor his son, and he was immoral for thinking that they too were to accept a lifestyle that was "part of the job."

This—this is where Carter found him. In that group therapy session, damaged, adrift, and useless to society. The same night he re-heard the song became the same night he was offered a chance by both God and man to correct his course...

"She gone?" Connor asks, poking his dark, almond eyes out from underneath the bed, carefully pushing a box to the side and revealing his hiding spot, and pulling Dan back to the present.

"For now," Dan smiles before putting on a sterner face. "Did you?"

"No!" is the kid's immediate reply, and with Dan's apparent doubt, Connor backtracks, flopping face down on the bed. "Well kind of."

"Kind of?" Dan's voice doesn't waver.

Connor lets out a timid sigh before finding the courage to respond. Disappointment is something he never wants to give his dad. "Caspian took them."

"Did he take them, or did you give them to him?" Dan asks, filling in the blanks to the incomplete confession.

Slowly, Connor nods.

"Well, you have two options then," Dan says, holding up a finger. "You can either get them from Caspian before Mom finds out." Dan holds up his second finger. "Or you can tell your mom where they are."

"I'll go get them!" Connor states, sitting up and hopping off the bed. Cautiously making his way to the door and peeking into the hall, leave it to a kid to find the path of least resistance.

"What did he want with them anyway?" Dan whispers before his son leaves.

Without looking from the hall Connor whispers back, "He found a rat."

Having all the information he needs, Dan begins to devise ways to sterilize the kitchen knives without Victoria finding out.

"What the hell?" Dan mumbles. Where does Caspian get these ideas? He can't be more than five—not much younger than Connor. Before Dan can delve too far into the dark mind of that child, his phone dings.

"BBQ?" is all Mica's text says. "Time?" the next line asks as it comes in.

"Hell yes! 1700," Dan replies, and after hitting send, in walks his lovely wife.

"Dan? My love?"

"Yes," he says, lovingly dragging out the S. *It'll blend sarcasm with love*, he thinks.

"Try that again..." Tori states, snapping her fingers. Apparently, all she heard was the sarcasm.

"Yes, dear," Dan then says, all sarcasm, no love this time just because he can.

Victoria rolls her eyes, not having time for the banter. "Where's your son?"

"I sent him on an errand." Dan shrugs.

Shooting him one of those looks, Tori begins ranting in her native tongue. Tongan if Dan remembers correctly. He should be able to, but damn, right now he can't help but admire her sexy figure. Having yet another epiphany, he realizes that he has hit two birds with one stone.

"He'll be back. You can interrogate him then." Slowly, lifting his eyebrow, Dan seductively adds, "In the meantime, I have some questions of my own."

"You think that'll work?" she asks, trying but failing to hide the creeping smirk growing on her face.

"I do," Dan states, standing up, turning around, and ripping off his shirt, the rippling muscles in his back practically bursting from his skin.

Wow, Tori thinks, having to let out a tiny sigh. She forgot how much she missed having a man's man. Muscles have always been her weakness, especially the back of the male physique. After leaving him, she completely went the other direction, thinking that the body type had an association with personality. It didn't. Call it vanity, but she's glad muscles are back on the menu!

"Ask away," she states, slamming the door closed and moving to the bed.

"Seventeen hundred hours," Mica tosses his phone onto the couch.

Aila lets out the heaviest sigh he's ever heard. "What?"

"The barbeque," he says, treading carefully with his tone. "Tonight, at seventeen—"

"Damn it. Just tell me the real time!"

"Five," he quickly states. Never thought that using a twenty-four-hour clock cycle would be something to put him in the doghouse.

"I'm sorry," Aila slowly says, seeing the land mines she ambushed him with. She opens her mouth in hopes of elaborating on her apology, but before she can, her head begins to whirl.

"You okay?" Mica asks, walking over to Aila, taking her in his arms.

"Yeah. Just don't squeeze—" Before she can finish though, Mica flexes his muscles, crushing her body into his. Her back crackles as the world spirals, bringing up this morning's omelet. Before it makes its way out her mouth, Aila forcefully pries herself from her moronic husband and leans into a dead sprint for the sanctuary of the bathroom. A long moment later, one filled with gags and splashes, a whooshing flush sounds before Aila comes trudging back, her mouth full of Listerine.

"What was that?" Mica belts out.

With a glare, Aila says all she needs to, and spews the burning green liquid out in the kitchen sink. "You squeezed me, you idiot!"

Mica knew it'd be difficult dealing with a pregnant woman, but this is ridiculous. He can't joke, but he can't be boring. He must be spontaneous, but too much and it pisses her off and/or makes her throw up. She wants him to cook, but can't use meat on Tuesday, Thursday, Sunday and sometimes Monday, Wednesday, Friday, and Saturday. Monthly cycles are one thing, but this is something else entirely.

"Fine," Mica mumbles, silently moving to unpack. Now that everything of hers is out and set up, he can start on his own things, filling in what gaps she left open for him.

"I'm sorry," she again sighs out, walking back in with a remorseful expression. There's no way she's making things easier. They weren't ready for *any* of this. The assassination, the move, the we-used-birth-control-but-still-got-pregnant honeymoon baby. It's all collapsing into this nightmare.

"It's fine," Mica says, shrugging his shoulders indifferently.

She misses gazing into his blue and brown eyes like she used to. Nothing else mattered then—nothing but the two of them and their ambitions.

"No, it's not—" she says, but again, before she can fully explain herself, Aila slaps her hand back over her mouth before rushing back to the porcelain safe haven.

With a heavy sigh of his own, from within a cardboard box Mica pulls out two of the red metal containers from the Records Room—Kim's and his. Placing Kim's empty box down, he flips the clamps up, opening his own where inside lies the solitary picture of the sonogram. It's only been a few months, but it seems so long ago since the soon-to-be-parents fled their homes in Boston.

This baby is going to change everything. They're not even through the first trimester and Mica is already seeing the future in a whole new light—the possibilities it yields for their child. The meaning of historical records and personal history is that much more impactful. The ability to record and interpret life events is a key factor in humankind. Human nature, societal structures, ideological discoveries, all of this allows for us to witness evolution and progression. The good, the bad, the ugly, and the beautiful; this child will grow up in an America that Mica and Aila were not born in, and these histories of the world will help him navigate the unprecedented future.

Taking out the photograph, Mica looks to the shelf and begins to fill his red metal box, starting with one of his dark blue journals. Then, upon finding a pen, Mica rips out a piece of paper from a notebook to write the first letter of what he's hoping will be many to his future child.

As he seals it inside an envelope, there's another flush in the background, followed shortly by his wife with another mouthful of mouth wash. Mica smiles this time, the expression being the only apology Aila needs for his lack of patience. Aila returns the sentiment, smiling back, relieved her husband has forgiven her—that they are somewhat back to normal. She winks, he winks back and in that moment, they forget the tragic, dark, and life-altering events that brought them to Colorado.

A knock at the door snaps Mica back into reality. Running over and whipping it open, both Sullivan and Bella greet him with exuberant grins.

"How's the future daddy?" Sullivan asks, throwing his arms around his friend before inviting himself in.

Bella, who is much more affectionate in her embrace with Mica. "You've always been a daddy to me," she whispers into his ear, the joke forcing an uncomfortable chuckle from Mica. "Where's the wife?" she then asks as she lets go of her former lover. "I have some cute ideas for the baby's room!"

"She was just here. Maybe she got sick again?" he says, unsure as he points down the hall towards the bathroom.

"Poor baby. I remember..." Bella pouts, skipping her way towards Aila.

"Where's Caspian?" Mica asks.

"At our place with Connor," Sullivan replies, pausing before looking to the ceiling. "He's doing great, by the way."

"I was about to ask. So, the palsy isn't giving him any more trouble?"

Sullivan shrugs. "It's still there, but barely noticeable. I'm telling you; I am on to something with these treatments."

Sullivan's odd fascination with genetics has always created an unsettling feeling for Mica. It's part of the reason he's stayed clear of any of the research and development. He can't put his finger on what it is exactly, only that the ideologies Sullivan ties into science and that come up in his rants are ones that Mica disagrees with on a fundamental level. Sullivan has always been a supporter of radical hierarchy, and now that he has science backing up these "power structures," Mica can't help but think that in the hands of an unhinged individual, it could be implemented within society. Mica might be overthinking it, but what it really comes down to is that there is a cynicism behind any sort of postmodern critical theory Sullivan advocates for in his research, and cynics have never built anything wholesome.

From the sound of it though, some of that obsession has paid off.

"You guys done unpacking?" Sullivan enthusiastically asks.

"I still have my things, but after that, yeah!" Mica says, walking over to the fridge. "You want a drink?"

"Beer?"

"We don't have any, I've told you that."

"Damn, forgot. Soda's fine."

How has the guy stopped drinking? Sullivan asks himself. Despite all the parties he, Mica, and Bella used to attend together... And now that Aila is pregnant, there's no hope in returning Mica to the guy Sullivan used to share everything with.

Walking in, Mica tosses a can of Sprite over before sitting down. "So, what brings you to our humble abode?"

"Just wanted to check and see how you guys were doing," Sullivan says, popping open and taking a swig of his drink.

"Sure... Since when do you just *visit*?"

"Sue me, why don't you?"

"Can't!" Mica declares before letting out a sad chuckle.

Over the past two months, Congress has been busy. While Americans have been distracted with the minutiae of pop culture, through legal gymnastics and sleight of hand, Congress has completely reformed the justice system. Vast legal protections have been offered for allied public figures, civil servants, big tech firms, and contracted corporations. While the right hand of government has been accomplishing this, the left hand has simultaneously stripped public and private opponents of legal rights, forcing households and companies like Smith & Wesson into bankruptcy and into "government repayment programs."

The presumption of innocence has been thrown out the window as mob rule floods the court of public opinion, trying, convicting, and pressuring judges to make rulings without a shred of evidence. With President White dead, his wife missing, and the most spineless vice president in American history, it's not an exaggeration to say that their country is un-American.

"There's actually something I wanted to talk to you about."

Before Sullivan can though, an abrupt vibration in his pocket cuts him off. On the other side of the room, Mica's phone dings and rattles on the kitchen counter.

"Lisa?" Mica asks.

"Yep," Sullivan says, annoyed at the timing. "Bella!"

"Yeah! We're coming," she shouts from the other room, and within seconds, the four head out.

—— * ★ * ——

"Hey Sulli!" Connor shouts as he opens the door of *Grandma* Lisa's house. Throwing a punch into Sullivan's gut, the guy chuckles before running his hand through Connor's bushy hair.

"Hey there, buddy!" However, Sullivan's cheery demeanor quickly fades.

"Where is everyone?" Mica asks Connor.

"Watching the news," the kid sighs, sticking his tongue out at the activity.

"The Congressional Statement is about to start!" Carter states, pulling out chairs and making room for the late arrivals.

On the television, a gorgeous news anchor and her handsome assistant shine their camera-perfect smiles as the obnoxious station theme music fades. In a quick cut, the Speaker of the House steps up to a podium. Christine Pelosi—daughter of infamous Nancy Pelosi—stands as a testament of another political dynasty as she readies herself to address the nation. Regimes seem to always abide by the mantra of "rules for thee, not for me," and as the nation watches, every citizen knows that this moment won't be any different—that the apple has not fallen far from the tree.

"Good afternoon," Madame Speaker Pelosi begins. "Fellow Americans. After the tumult and confusion in Washington these past months, we all continue to mourn the loss of the President."

Lisa scoffs.

She doesn't believe that. Pelosi and her possie slandered Reuben's name, throwing false accusations left and right before *and* after he was elected, all the while using emotional manipulation to further her political image. She couldn't be happier that he's sitting six feet under. If Vice President Ryan wasn't incognito and did his damn job, none of this would be happening—this statement, the hearings, the political witch trials, all of it would've been squashed by the simple transition of power within the executive branch. Not to mention, the Supreme Court's hands-off approach to the bastardization of the document they are supposed to defend through the courts. Like they are infamously known for not touching any sort of voting case brought to them, here seems to be no different as they ignore what Congress has done to decide the fate of the executive branch in an unprecedented course of action. What separation of power? Maybe the Children of the Ordean Reich have corrupted all three branches of government, not just one as she and Carter believed.

"After numerous hearings and countless investigations from both the FBI, CIA, and DOJ, Congress is pleased to announce that the treasonous individuals known as the Minutemen have been apprehended. These usurpers of our democracy are being questioned about their treasonous actions to assassinate President White."

"Have we now?" Mica asks.

"They do have some Minutemen, just not us," Sullivan says.

"And last I checked, we're a constitutional republic," Dan throws out.

"Shut up!" Carter hushes, his hope hanging on by a thread.

Speaker Pelosi continues. "The founders of this nation have made it clear that 'in the course of human events, it may become necessary for one people to dissolve the political bands which have connected them with another in order to secure rights of life, liberty, and the pursuit of happiness.'"

"Is she really—?" Lisa mumbles, fearing that she is using the Declaration of Independence to ironically justify tyranny.

"However," Pelosi continues, "'when a government cannot fulfill these rights,' and might I add 'needs,' there is an obligation to alter or abolish it."

And there it is, Lisa thinks as she and the rest of the country are about to watch the nullification of the Constitution.

"These United States have proven yet again to the world that we will not be defeated—that we will not go silently into the night. We will not negotiate with terrorists. These foreign and domestic enemies of ours, they will be the ones that will be defeated. They are the ones that *will* go silently into the night. The trait that makes us a successful people has been our ability to adapt. We have the technology. We have the know-how and above all, we have the heart to do so. Because of the tragic death of our President, we as your elected officials have found it necessary to adapt once more. I am pleased to announce that effective immediately, a policy known as 'Plan B' will be initiated, merging the three branches of government into one, in the name of efficiency and progress. Instead of one head as Commander-in-Chief, we will have nine. Instead of five hundred thirty-five lawmakers, we will have nine."

Lisa shakes her head, disappointed that she didn't see it earlier. There's a reason the Supreme Court has been eerily quiet during the previous administration and particularly since Reuben's death.

"Nine Presidents of these United States," the Speaker continues. "With the Prime Minister of Canada and the President of Mexico, these nine will work in harmony for the good of the citizens of this great country, this great continent, and the world which we all inhabit. Congress has deemed it necessary to have our nine presidents come from the already-appointed officials of the Supreme Court. Their wisdom has prepared them to take up this mantle and bear the burden of this national amendment for solidarity within the North American Union that will branch into a more united world order under the Union of Continents. They will serve you; they will serve me. If you have one, may your God comfort you in this time."

Thunderous applause follows as useful idiots cheer the annihilation of what was known as the greatest country on Earth. Flipping off the television, not a single word is spoken as everyone somberly sits. Not only have the Minutemen failed the President, but they have failed the United States. The Fourth Reich is victorious.

"We all love this country," Carter begins.

"This is not the country any of us fought for," Mica counters.

"So that's it then?" Carter asks, a tear dripping down his cheek. He has had dreams fall apart before, but like any patriot, Carter admits failure, stands back up, and tries something new. "What are we doing here? Why did we move here?!"

"We had to," Aila quietly says. "We were being hunted."

"We don't give up." Carter hates the truth behind what his niece has said, but that hard truth doesn't change anything. Not only does it go against each of their natures to just lie down, grit is an American value. "Out of all the states in the nation, why Colorado?"

Everyone made the move on a leap of faith, not fully understanding the reasoning. The only thing they knew was that they had to eliminate their proximity to D.C. and leave the East Coast.

"It was my idea," Sullivan says, raising his hand.

"Our idea," Bella immediately clarifies.

"Why?" Carter asks, knowing the reason, but wanting to finally communicate it to his team. The announcement they all just watched... Carter saw this coming after the assassinations of the council and his friend Reuben. He didn't think it would happen this soon, but Carter has always believed that it is better to plan for the worst and hope for the best.

"Because we have a plan—a plan that can be carried out only in Colorado."

"Get to the point," Dan sighs out, his patience wearing thin.

"We own a construction company," Sullivan begins. "And we've been working on an in-depth 'Armageddon Project.'"

"What's that supposed to mean?" Mica asks, asking what everyone's thinking.

"At the Denver International Airport, we have been working on a secret project. The original target market was paranoid rich people—the doomsday survivalist with a heavy bank account."

"An expensive bomb shelter? That's why we're here?" Mica exclaims.

"Yes and no," Bella says, inserting herself into Sullivan's conversation. *Damn men can never just let a woman have a moment.* "The Denver International Airport has been the center of some pretty crazy conspiracy theories since about 1995. Years ago, when the airport was originally under construction, the architects mapped out five distinct buildings. However, after reviewing the initial build, it was concluded that the construction company and engineers screwed up."

"Screwed up? How?" Aila asks.

"The foundation, framing, wiring, everything was built incorrectly. But," she emphasizes, "instead of starting from scratch, wasting millions of dollars, Sullivan's father, Sullivan Sr. had them bury the old buildings and build over them."

"I'm assuming they weren't actually built wrong," Victoria chimes in, becoming intrigued by all this conspiracy planning.

"Actually, they were," Bella smiles. "As the one funding most of the project, Sullivan's father saw an opportunity for the government, and in particular, the military, to make an underground base. However, because of all the conspiracy theories about a secret army and the bad PR the secretly repurposed buildings were receiving, the military canceled their contract, scrapping the entire project, leaving Sullivan's father with an absurd amount of debt. For years it sat, until Sullivan and I eventually bought the place, turning it into the bomb shelter business that it's been.

At first" —she shrugs her shoulders— "we saw it as an investment and asset. Once the military lost interest in it, we figured that we'd use it in the private sector."

"And this is where we come in," Mica realizes, having put the dots together.

"Correct!" Bella again smiles. "Once we were recruited by the council, we completely restructured the business to be a failsafe for the Minutemen."

"In case the Division ever failed, which it has," Sullivan concludes.

Having watched Connor play with Caspian this entire time, a mysterious, weighty sentiment has grown in Dan's stomach. It could be the convenience and timing of the situation. It could also be the fact that he just lost his country. Either way, there are questions that still need answering.

"I don't like it," Dan quietly says.

Perplexed, but not surprised, Sullivan shows neither as he asks, "Why?"

With his eyes still on his son, Dan is brought back to the conversation they had not more than an hour ago. Caspian—a kid—wanted to cut into a dead animal for fun. Unable to fully justify this gut-wrenching feeling, he just looks to Sullivan before saying, "Too many people know about your Armageddon project."

"I agree with Dan," Lisa speaks up.

"Of course, you do," Sullivan cynically states, his snide tone not going unnoticed. The "people of color" have always banded together against *white* policy and ideas. It cuts deep that the only kid Sullivan's son knows is nothing more than a half-breed disgrace. He's never liked Dan—didn't expect much from him—but he never thought Dan would go as far as dishonoring his own people. Upon seeing Dan take Victoria back, Sullivan no longer has any loyalty to the man.

"I'm not stupid, Mr. Stone!" Lisa stands from the couch. "You're a racist son of a bitch. Every time you look at Victoria, Connor, or me, your eyes burn with hatred."

Racism goes both ways, he snidely thinks.

"You have any suggestions?" Bella stands, folding her arms, sternly bringing everyone back to focus on what really matters.

Dan stands, mirrors her defiance. "Yeah, what about guerrilla warfare? It was successful with the Minutemen. We modify it to our current situation, starting out with small raids and scale it from there—Fabian tactics."

"Was it? Was it successful? Because the President is dead!"

In a matter of seconds, everything falls apart. Having been unified in sorrow over the destruction of their nation, that moment quickly fades as their common ground is taken from them. This is an unconventional war, and as tragic as the battlefield is, conflict can yield fruitful results—it can have a just cause. It's a controversial idea, but look at what the Civil War did for this nation. Slavery was a millennium-old tradition that spanned continents and political dynasties; in less than half a decade that tradition was questioned to the point of abolishment, virtually wiping it from the face of the earth. How can one refute the inspiration of such a war that progressed human civilization tenfold? World War II—the Good War—has made it very clear that the world would not tolerate the spreading wildfire known as Hitlerism—a militaristic movement inspired by Marxist Socialists—and that great men and women sacrificed to extinguish the global threat to humanity.

Those wars were scores of years before anyone here actually experienced any patriotic sentiments. In the Five-Year War with Russia, Carter and Lisa learned firsthand that underneath the blood, politics, propaganda and ethics of war, they helped kill terrorists, war lords, and conventional military forces led by dictators and haven't lost an ounce of sleep. They did it for the love of Americans and for their brothers and sisters on the battlefield.

Carter would do it all again if it means this nation could continue to live.

As the two look into the eyes of each of their agents, Carter and Lisa can't help but wonder if this is the start of another "good war." Grabbing each other's hands, the two watch those they have come to love rip each other apart as they feel the lessons of a lost battle. No unity. No harmony among them. If this is the start of another shift for righteousness, then something must change here and now.

"Shut up!" Carter bellows, the yelling and bickering subsiding. Nervously, Carter turns to everyone before asking something he hasn't done in years. "Can we all kneel for a minute?"

"Prayer. Are you seriously suggesting that right now?" Dan raises his voice.

"I'm with Trax on this one," Sullivan says.

"Please," Carter begins. "Things are out of our control and clearly, we need help. At the very least, we need a moment to think and where we can come together."

"God helps those that help themselves," Bella mutters under her breath.

"I'm not forcing any of you to participate. If you would like to leave, then leave," and as Carter says this, he folds his hands, waiting for each person to make their decision.

"What a waste of time!" Sullivan mumbles, grabbing Caspian's hand.

"I want to stay, Daddy!"

"No," he says, flicking his son in the forehead and jerking him toward the door. Just before the family leaves, Bella turns and shoots the group a stabbing look of insolence, slamming the door behind her.

"Anyone else?" Carter calmly asks.

Looking to his wife, Dan motions towards the front door, but she simply shakes her head and kneels. Surprised, Dan's sight shifts to his son Connor, who is following his mother's example. Mica, Aila, and Lisa all follow suit, and as Dan is hit with humility, he faithfully kneels next to his family.

He can't lose them again, and if this is what it takes, then so be it.

Seventeen

Area Thirty-Eight

Darkness weighs on his mind, the breeze numbing his senses and the glow of the distant burning debris offering little relief. But he's alive. In a matter of seconds the Owl went from four thousand feet to ground level in a single burning free fall, and with just enough power within the safety systems, the aircraft auto-ejected Jax and Jude before its destructive landing.

Having been thrown into a cluster of trees, Jax finds himself suspended and fighting to reach the buckle of his parachute. Keeping one arm looped, once able, he unclips, catching himself from an immediate fall. For a moment he dangles, but a sharp pain in his shoulder makes it impossible to hold on. Wincing under the discomfort, Jax's shoulder tears further as his hold breaks, dropping him twenty-five feet. Snatching at a flimsy branch only slows the violent decent as it snaps under the sudden weight, and after hitting three other limbs, Jax slams into the forest floor a split second later. Miraculously, he's left with just bruises and scratches, and as he slowly stands, Jax stares in awe at the crash site and the freshly charred path the aircraft took through the trees.

"Jude?" he shouts out, unable to remember if he even saw him land.

"Over here!" Jude calls back, his voice carrying in the wind.

Jax heads towards Jude's voice, and five hundred meters away, finds his breathing and smiling copilot. The relief is short lived, however. In a muddy pool of blood, Jude sits, his right leg pinned under an aircraft's wing.

Seeing the shock in Jax's eyes, Jude simply and calmly coughs out, "Don't."

"Don't what?" Jax asks, attempting to find a silver lining in the gory scene.

"Don't bullshit me. It's bad," Jude huffs out, shifting his body to the right, unveiling another visceral sight in a raspy breath. "After I landed, I was taking off my chute when this damn thing"—he punches the hunk of metal pinning him down— "comes flying out of nowhere, yanking me from my tangled chute!"

"That's not our aircraft then," Jax says.

"Nope," Jude smiles. "Either we were able to shoot him down or Connor and Renn got the bastard."

Never having been one to sit around and wait, Jax crouches down to examine Jude's injuries. His broken leg isn't compounded, so there's less risk of infection, and a missing arm can easily be replaced if the Raiders can get their hands on the tech—which after the acquisition of the Owls, shouldn't be a problem. None of this will do any good though, if Jude bleeds out before the operations can take place. Hitting a single button on his vest, a beep sounds as it links up with the emergency beacon frequency.

"They'll be looking for us," Jax says as he removes his belt and moves to put the makeshift tourniquet on the bleeding stump.

"Yeah." Jude chuckles again, shifting his head to the tree line as if looking for something or someone.

"We've got to stop the bleeding before we can move you—"

"Jax?" Jude interrupts.

Having heard this tone from Grandma Lisa a long time ago, Jax simply but firmly states, "We're going to get you home—"

"No, we're not. I'm not stupid." He motions to the bloody slush he's sitting in. "I can't move, my arm is who knows where, and I'm pretty sure I've got some major internal bleeding." Leaning back, whatever fight Jude had to survive fades in this moment as he begins accepting the inevitable outcome of death. The only positive spin that can be had is at least he won't die alone. "Can ya do me a favor?"

"Yeah, sure thing."

"Tell Mari that I'm sorry," he says, his breath more labored.

Jax raises his eyebrow. "For what?"

Jude lets out a heavy sigh. He's been aware of Jax's suspicions of him, none of which are untrue. So, it's not a matter of if, but when and how Jax will learn of why Jude's a Raider to begin with. It'll either be the truth from Jude's mouth, or it'll be the truth according to Jax; either way, the only real protection to offer Mari is to tell Jax the facts and not let Jax's convoluted emotions endanger her.

"I'm sorry for getting her involved. I was under orders..." Jude begins. "Orders to stop—"

Before Jude finishes his confession, a cracking gun shot is fired, his head jolting to the side as it catches the bullet in the temple.

Instinctively, Jax dives away from the direction of the projectile, and rolling behind the fighter jet's wing, Jax draws his sidearm, ready to return fire.

"That was close," a familiar voice shouts out, echoing from within the black forest. "Jax, in the interest of time, just put it down and slowly walk out."

Raider Encampment

"Let me help," she asks, for the fifth time in an hour.

Calmly, Renn takes in a breath before letting it out as she walks by Mari. "I told you that things will go a lot smoother if you just let us work."

"My ass!" Mari yells out, yanking Renn's shoulder back, forcing eye contact.

All the logic inside tells Renn to ignore the pleas and the expressive tactics. Mari's emotionally compromised. Anyone can see that, but as she examines someone aching for their lost love, there's a demeanor that very few women have, Renn being all too familiar with it. Mari wants to help because she knows she can. On a hunch, Renn glances at Mari's grasp on her shoulder, the skin on her forearm slightly exposed from her outreached hold.

"Are those scars?" Renn asks, knowing full well that they are. They're less methodical and precise compared to Renn's tallies, but wounds on the soul have a way of being expressed on the body in one form or another.

Shocked by the blunt observation, Mari removes her hand from Renn's shoulder. "Everyone has scars."

Finding the irony almost uncanny, Renn rolls up her own sleeve to reveal her own, and then bringing the collar of her neck down, Renn shows Mari the rest of the forty-eight self-inflicted tallies.

"Not everyone," Renn says. "I was PPA too."

It's rare to find someone who shares her burden, let alone expresses it in a similar fashion. Mari stands in awe, seeing Renn—the Princess of the Nine—in a whole new light, their shared trials, vexations, and horrors being no respecter of rank.

"I stopped when I met Jax," Mari chokes out.

"Me too," Renn says, the man having made an akin impression on her. Jax's rage, his ire against The Government—against her—it all gave her purpose. It validated all her prejudices towards the Nine, giving her strength to make a stand. From the moment they met, with him standing in front of her after being ambushed by a handful of PPA grunts, she knew he was different. If a member of the Labor class can take that kind of beating, she has no reason not to rise to her own potential.

"Please, let me help—" Mari begins before stopping, her thoughts of the *what if's* suffocating her hope.

Renn's never lost anyone that she's cared about. In her life there are only two that could be on the same pedestal as Jax is for Mari, and both men do a pretty good job at handling themselves around danger. With that being said, Renn lets out a heavy sigh as she empathizes more than she'd like to, and without a word, Renn moves aside, letting Mari into the tent.

"Stay quiet and listen. If we need you, I'll tell you."

Mari nods in agreement before stepping inside the chaos.

"Where's that beeping coming from?" Kai shouts out, another Raider responding promptly.

"It's the EMF device we give to the pilots," he says, hammering away on a digital keyboard, bringing up a hologram of the geographical location.

"Impossible." Kai picks up his tablet and swipes, stopping at a particular point on screen. "What's the frequency number?"

"It's them," Connor states, not needing any more proof. What other EMF device would it be? They've recalled every patrol and active mission and have a hundred percent accountability within the Encampment.

"We don't know that!" Kai snaps, matching the frequency with pilot and aircraft information.

"We do!" Connor says before putting his hand on his earpiece. "Get a team prepped and ready."

"No!" Kai shouts, abruptly stopping everyone from their assignment. "We will give no such order until we can one hundred percent verify the information. They could be dead and I'm not putting any more of my people at risk."

"They're not dead!" Connor turns towards the exit of the tent, but as he moves to leave, Kai makes a grab at the soldier. A split second later, Kai is face down on the dirt with Connor on top, ready to snap his arm. "There's a reason why Dan didn't put you in charge," Connor hisses.

Kai scoffs. "Says the brainwashed white man with daddy issues."

"That is enough!" Renn yells. "Get it together! You know he's right, Kai."

Standing, Kai brushes himself off. "And if he is? Give me one reason why we should let Jax back into the Encampment."

"He's a key leader of the Resistance!" Connor retorts.

Kai throws his arms up in the air, pointing an aggressive finger at both Connor and Renn. "It was an arbitrary decision. We were doing just fine before you three came here. And that's beside the point. What if they're dead and the PPA found their bodies and hit the beacon, knowing we'd come for Jax and Jude?"

"And what if they're alive?" Renn snaps, having to throw herself into the argument now. "You had a nonexistent pilot program, let alone a fleet of aircraft. Your people were starving before Jax and Connor helped strategize and improve the efficiency of raids. Basic filtration and farming equipment was unusable. We've recruited more effective combatants and have helped train and make your people deadlier. Arbitrary or not, Jax has been a key figure in helping get the Encampment back on its feet, and you owe it to him to at least go out there after him."

Kai grits his teeth as she spouts these facts, and even if none of them were true, morale at the absolute least has increased. Yes, something like that can't be measured, but it can be felt, and he—along with every other Raider—can perceive their refined purpose. That doesn't change anything though. The oppression of his people—the Unapproved status that Connor, Renn, the PPA, and the Nine have given his people—can never be forgiven. Blatant oppression can never be atoned for.

Pulling back his dreadlocks, Kai looks Connor dead in the eyes as he says, "You are no better than all those other white skins out there."

Kai's deep seeded hatred is a mutual sentiment the two groups have and ignites blind uproar as soldiers from both classes quickly lose sight of the mission.

They're broken, Mari thinks, watching them get nowhere with finding her Jax. She couldn't give a damn about personal or collective conflicts. Jax may still be alive, and the fact that he has key intel on the Encampment should be enough for Kai to put aside prejudices and expend resources to find him. But it isn't, and just because her personal feelings on the matter align with the strategic logic of it all does not make the point any less valid.

"You think this is about race?" Mari asks. At first, her question falls on deaf ears. "Hey!" she shouts out, this time grabbing the attention of both Renn and Kai, and once she has their focus, the rest of the room falls in line. "What's everyone's problem? You honestly think this is about race or even class?" she asks, directing her gaze to Kai.

Instead of accepting the blows this random woman just gave his ego, Kai moves to drag Mari out of the tent. To everyone's surprise though, she breaks the man's grip with ease, shoving her finger into his face.

"Get your hand off me," Mari states, holding her ground with the alpha male.

"I'll ask you one question," Kai says, folding his arms across his chest. "What was the point in bringing Caspian here?" He stares down Mari for a second before opening his question to the room. "Out of all we've done, why does Caspian matter?"

Still, nobody answers.

"Who was Jax's best friend? Kip! And who killed Kip? Caspian..." Staring Mari back down, Kai closes his distance with her. "It was his personal vendetta and his personal crusade to kill Caspian. Nothing more."

The premise of his argument is flawed from the beginning, Mari thinks, and as she smirks at his bravado, she looks past Kai and towards everyone else to ask a simple question. "Wasn't Kip a Raider?"

Kai doesn't move, and neither does anyone else.

"He was one of you," Mari says. "He was *white* and yet he was still one of you, was he not?"

With mumbles of agreement, Kai feels his grip on the situation falter.

"It's clear you don't trust anyone without burnt skin," Mari says, jabbing Kai in the chest. "And it's also clear that none of you see the overall picture."

"What overall picture?" Kai scoffs.

"No wonder Dan lost confidence in you," Mari says. She's observed way more than anyone could fathom an outsider would, and she's about to prove it. "Let me lay this out plain and simple. Caspian is the Area Leader, which means he has key information on the Area you are desperately trying to overrun. He's also the son of not one, but two of the Nine, which could not only give you control over the Area but could possibly give you a hold on The Government. At the very least it'd put them in a very difficult position. Even if you do manage to take over the Area without Caspian, the other forty-nine Areas will destroy you in a matter of days unless you have leverage. Finally, Jax has information about you, and if,"—she stresses this condition—"*if* he's alive, then you better pray that you get to him before they do."

As the tent falls silent, in the back, a solitary individual begins to applaud.

Dan chuckles, stepping out from the crowd and slapping Kai on the shoulder. "What's your name, miss?"

"Mari," she says. Grabbing his rugged, outreached hand, Mari expects his grasp to crush her palm, but is instead surprised by the man's delicate grip.

"I knew a Mari once. What's your last name?"

"Carter, Mari Carter."

"I thought I recognized that tone," Dan smirks, turning to the Raiders. "Well... You heard her, let's go get Jax!"

―――***―――

Area Thirty-Eight

"You haven't answered any of my questions. Where are your manners?"

A fist slams into Jax's face for the eighth time.

"Why are you with the Raiders? What's your mission?" Caspian questions. Jerking Jax up by his hair, staring into his swollen eyes, a maniacal idea comes to mind. Drawing his blade, Caspian points to the thick, crusted laceration lining his face just underneath his eye and all the way to his upper lip. After tracing the healing scar, Caspian vengefully slices into Jax's cheek, mirroring his own wound and letting dark red blood ooze down and drip rapidly onto the white tile.

"Ouch," Jax deadpans.

Caspian's lost his ruthless advantage. The only thing Jax found remotely unbearable was the burning sensation that accompanied the thick needle stabbed in his arm.

Sensing that it might be time for an escalation of sorts, Caspian ignores the feeble attempt to illicit an emotional reaction as he sheathes his knife and turns to the table behind him. Picking up his favorite tool, Caspian forces the shiny hinges of the pliers open, before turning back around and quickly clamping down on Jax's fingernail. Prying, Caspian twists, savoring the joy from the elongated moment. Jax winces. No longer can he keep a shrill of pain from sounding as the nail clings by the last bit of thready flesh before a flick of Caspian's wrist leaves Jax's nailbed bare. In a continued breath of fire, Caspian moves to the adjacent finger, where in another slow pull, removes it as well. He continues this process three more times, slightly prolonging it as he does until the tip of each finger of Jax's right hand is bare and bleeding. Moving to the left hand, Caspian relishes in Jax's labored breath knowing that it won't stop until all ten fingers and toes are in the same condition.

"Caspian?" From out of the corner of the bright room, Rhett's voice echoes. "Can I talk with you?"

In a long sigh, Caspian tries to contain his outrage as the homicidal aura in the room suddenly changes. Not seeing any other choice, Caspian motions for Rhett to follow him out.

"This isn't working," Rhett says, the door clanging behind him.

"That depends on your definition of 'working,'" Caspian retorts, flicking a fingernail from his pliers and wiping off any remaining blood.

"At this rate, he's not going to survive the experiments."

"I doubt that," Caspian says, lifting his shirt, revealing his bony, bruised ribcage. "He did this."

Shocked, Rhett examines the contusion more closely. "Do you think he's—?" Rhett begins, stifling his own intrigue.

"You'd think so. His blood work doesn't show any modifications though."

"Then he's just strong?" Rhett slowly thinks aloud.

"Maybe. I've seen strong. This is something different."

"Has he said anything about Renn and Connor?" Rhett asks. "Does he know where they are?"

What is vexing you, brother? Caspian then wonders, his mind wandering from Jax and towards the pained expression upon Rhett's face.

Caspian knows exactly where Renn and Connor are and who they've been associating with. He practically smelled it on them the moment they stepped into his office in their feigned attempt to offer the infamous Jax Rouge over to him.

Inclined to speak his mind and say no, Caspian isn't sure of who he can trust as of right now. Unlike the naïvety Rhett is projecting, Caspian knows to keep certain things close to the chest. The powerful always have a healthy sense of paranoia. Progress comes at a price and does not go without opposition. The speed at which the elder Stone was pushing humanity within Area Thirty-Eight was something bound to attract attention and that would lead to an attempt on his life—or at the very least his capture—hence the contingency plans.

Not only have they apprehended a legitimate threat to the Area within the Labor class, but Caspian's forethought has also unveiled the true nature of his sister and that bastard Connor. Caspian and Connor were friends before Rhett was even a thought. He's always wondered how much that half-breed remembers, but as for Caspian, every moment they spent together is a vivid memory. He remembers being weaker—less of a person—than Connor, who ideologically should have been the inferior individual. As Caspian grew stronger, the experimentation eradicating the imperfections encoded inside him, his relationship with Connor in turn began to change. He copied the physicality that defined Connor, making himself the literal utopian superior being, which Connor noticed. By the time the Nine completely took over, Sullivan and Bella found use for Connor, overlooking the filthy gene pool he came from. They made him part of the Legacy class, but no matter what Connor did, he would never be an Oligarch, something Caspian would ensure. If he was willing to bet, it was in these formative moments that Connor made the conscious decision to plan a coup.

Despite the blood Caspian and Renn shared, she always had an attraction to Connor that superseded Caspian's own relationship with his sister. When Caspian first noticed, he thought it was sexual in nature, but the more he observed, the more it was clearly fraternal. They had a bond forged in the arena, making it less of a mystery and more of hard truth as to why she followed Connor down his path. As Caspian looks at Rhett, he wonders what road his younger brother will take. He was mentored by Connor and has always put Renn on a pedestal, but Rhett has been a pupil of Caspian's as well, leaving the greater influence yet to be determined.

Keeping his own malice and bigotry at bay, Caspian puts his hand on Rhett's shoulder, not finding it sound to tell him the truth about their fallen siblings.

"We'll find them," he tells Rhett. "We must be patient though. First, we break him, then we can ask anything we want."

"There are other ways to break a subject," he says, knowing that Caspian has yet to utilize these methods.

"I know, brother," Caspian says, a sense of pride growing inside. "You'll make a great leader. I mean it. You have something I never will."

As much as it pains Caspian to admit this, truth is truth. If Rhett can stay focused on his heritage, the younger brother will be the greater being. Never has he had the genetic palsy that Caspian did, setting his progress back more than half a decade. Rhett has never dealt with the frailty of doubt and the demoralizing nature of physical weakness. When school was an institution, their parents removed Caspian because of the sadistic nature of his peers. For years, those scars have stayed with him, forever haunting his soul, creating doubt that constantly must be overcome. Rhett does not have to fear failure; rather he can set his sights solely on success.

"I'm not ready," Rhett says, thinking specifically of Kip's execution and his weak will to not fully participate.

"You will be," Caspian says, hugging his brother, knowing exactly what Rhett's thinking. "It's in your blood." After a long embrace, praying that he said something of value to his younger brother, Caspian releases him. "I'm headed back in there. You coming?"

Rhett thinks about it—thinks about this conversation and everything he's felt these past months. He's battled with the memory of sympathizing with a lesser form of life, making him an embarrassment to his parents. He's also been in a lifelong war with his conscious, questioning the value of any human life.

"No. I've got some things to mull over."

"See you at lunch then?"

"Of course," he says, forcing a smile, the doubt creeping back.

Caspian has tried. At one point he wished he could share the same remorse that Rhett has for Renn and Connor, but he can't. He won't allow himself to be that weak ever again.

"I know you miss them," Caspian says. "But they're alive. I can feel it."

With a knowing nod, Rhett marches away from the interrogation room, and giving a proud, hopeful smile, Caspian turns, walking back inside. Upon seeing his bleeding subject, Caspian decides that maybe a different course of action is needed—that Rhett's right. There are other ways. His fingers and toes aren't going anywhere.

"Would you like a drink?" Caspian asks, opening his jacket and pulling from it a small flask. Taking a swig, the burn drips down into his stomach, fueling him for the immediate task at hand. Tilting the flask towards Jax, Jax shakes his head. "You sure? It'll help with the pain."

Jax holds his ground, refusing the offer.

"Are you going to take me out to the Gathering?"

"You do speak." Caspian chokes and coughs, spitting out his drink. "I was worried that you hit your head a little too hard in that crash. What else can you say?"

He knows Jax won't say anything else, and instead of pressing too hard in that direction, Caspian takes one last drink of the brown liquid before sliding the flask back in his pocket.

"No, I'm not taking you out to the Gathering. You're supposed to be dead, remember? And since everyone in the Thirty-Eight believes that, don't you think it'd make us look like we didn't know what we were doing if I brought a supposedly dead guy on stage?"

"Would've fooled me," Jax mumbles.

"Oh, how I have missed your uneducated wit," Caspian deadpans, sitting on the ground next to Jax. "You want to know something?"

Jax doesn't respond, and Caspian doesn't offer him time to anyway.

"I know your father," he purrs.

"You *knew* my father," Jax quietly clarifies.

"If you're implying that I misspoke, I didn't." Caspian smirks. "The fact is, I actually met him."

"You showed me the picture."

"You mean this one?" And like a kid eagerly waiting to show a magic trick, Caspian reveals a photo, an exact copy of the one Jax has looked at so many times inside his box.

"Where did you get that?" Jax asks, the concern apparent in his voice.

"Relax, I don't have your box. I wish I did, believe me. It's dangerous information, but I don't." He points to the little version of himself sitting on top of Mica's shoulders. "We were buds, Jax. That's what I've been trying to say…"

"Why are you telling me this?"

The question Caspian was hoping he would ask.

"To enlighten you. Maybe there's more to your father than you think. So, I'll ask you again, why do you fight with the Raiders? What do you hope to accomplish with this war that you've started? You use the box like some sort of exalted model and guide, but what has it gotten you? It's like looking through a pinhole; you're missing most of the picture."

For a long moment, Jax thinks about this. Why go to war with the Nine? Their Government is the most powerful force this world has known, and sitting as a prisoner of that war, what good has the cause done? Workers in the Area are worse off. There's discord within the Encampment, and the fatalities on the battlefield have been disproportionally against the Raiders.

"It feels like the right thing to do," Jax finally says.

"The *right* thing to do," Caspian scoffs, hopping to his feet. "That must mean that I'm doing the *wrong* thing. And what makes you think that, Jackie? Because you read it in a book your dad left you?"

"Yeah," Jax says, his conviction waning.

"You sure? Are you sure you're not fighting for your dead dad? Are you sure you're not trying to fill a void deep within, trying to make him proud from the distant chasm time has created?"

Confused, Jax looks to Caspian, not fully understanding what he's saying. Letting out a sigh, Caspian rewords his questioning.

"Are you sure that this war is what your father wanted?"

Caspian lets the question simmer, giving Jax time to digest the information later. In the meantime, he'll get to the meat of the matter.

"Do you know why those boxes are so important? To you? To me? To the Nine? To the Raiders?"

At this point, Jax has grown tired of the endless hoops Caspian is forcing him through, and letting his head fall forward, Jax stares at the growing puddle of blood his gashed face has created.

"Look at me!" Caspian yells, his demeanor completely changing upon witnessing his subject's disrespect. Slamming his boot into Jax's chest, Jax lands ten feet backwards on his back, staring at the bright white artificial light overhead. Dispassionately, Caspian approaches, stepping down on Jax's head, the treads of his boot widening the bleeding cut on his face.

"Ask me why?" is all Caspian asks. "And be specific, Jax."

Lifting his boot, Caspian kicks his cheek bone with his steel-toe boot.

"Why are the boxes so important?" Jax asks, feeling fresh blood dripping down his cheek.

"I'm glad you asked," Caspian says in a cheery tone. "Because it's history." Caspian then rolls his hand through the air, implying that Jax needs to ask an elaborating question.

Jax reluctantly gives in. "Why is history so important?"

"An excellent question! How do you know where to go if you don't know where you have been? How do you know what to do if you don't know what's been done?" Caspian smiles, the vision of his parents glittering in his mind. "History is knowledge, and if knowledge is power then…what?"

"If you control history, you control power."

"You see it now? The masses squandered this knowledge! When the nations of the world had unlimited information at their fingertips, how did they use it? They indulged in lusts and insignificant content that had little to absolutely no value. Access to libraries of knowledge within seconds. You know what a library is, don't you?"

Jax nods.

"Then you understand their sin."

"They took it for granted," Jax says.

"That's an understatement. They let the gift they were given rot. Instead of envisioning a brighter future, they died in front of their flickering screens, molding in their chairs rather than shaping the world in their hands."

"And you—are you creating a brighter, greater world?"

"I am. Your friends keep getting in the way, though." Time for Caspian to take this home and to the heart. Holding up the photo of his parents with Jax's father, Caspian says, "Our parents started something long ago, and it's our destiny to be the ones to finish it."

"And what is that?" Jax asks. "What are we *destined* to finish?"

"Perfecting humanity."

"How the hell do you plan on doing that? Genocide?"

"Alone, that's too slow. The only way to accelerate the process is through science. Instead of waiting years for evolution to take hold, we shape evolution to our societal needs." Again, he pulls out his flask of brown liquid. "It's not a perfect solution, but it's as state-of-the-art as ever before. You sure you don't want a drink?"

"No."

"If you're trying to keep your blood untainted or whatever, forget it. You already have some version of it inside of you. It's been watered down essentially as you haven't been taking it regularly, but there are lingering, lasting effects."

"How?"

"That—that is the real question. Your bloodwork doesn't show it, again, probably because you haven't taken it in so long, but clearly, you've been modified," Caspian says, thinking of his bruised ribs. Rather than dwelling on that however, Caspian crouches down to crush any glimmer of hope Jax may be holding on to. "The truth of your father will betray you, just like your friend Jude and his girlfriend have."

"What does that mean?" Jax mumbles, shocked by the words Caspian just spoke.

Not needing a second more, Caspian begins to walk out, leaving his subject with the seed he planted in his thoughts, chuckling as he approaches the exit.

"We both know of the power and influence women can have on a man."

———✧✦✧———

Prodding the tender steak, separating the once live muscle fibers, Caspian watches the bloody juices seep from the cooked pores, steam lifting from the meat on his plate. There's clarity, but Jax has turned out to be more interesting than expected, especially when his aggression started coming to the surface. Still, there's something that puzzles him though. With no formal training, mentorship, or military assets, how has Jax been such a formidable force? How has he been the one who practically reinvented the Raiders—completely reforming their combative processes. Yes, he has Renn and Connor, but why rally behind Jax?

If it wasn't for Jude, Caspian doesn't know how long he would have been in the Encampment, which is a sobering new reality. Before, they were flies on a horse's ass, now, the Raiders are becoming hunters. One out of three PPA patrols that go out don't return—they are completely wiped off the maps, nowhere to be found. The Raiders are now armed heavier than ever. Artillery, weaponized aircraft, and mass casualty-producing firearms—they now have the ability to protect and expand their supply chains that the PPA can no longer cut off. Connor and Renn are phenomenal tacticians, but on a small unit level; they've never been able to see the bigger picture and it's hard to imagine the probability of someone from the Labor class having that capability. There must be someone behind the scenes that Caspian just isn't seeing.

He must break Jax, and he fears the girlfriend ploy won't be enough. Caspian knows it's hurting like hell to grapple with the fact that a lover might be a double agent, but he needs something more to truly crush him. Shifting his head to the left, Caspian rests his eyes on the display case—his first kills. It was important to Caspian to have the taxidermist shape hatred into the eyes and brow lines, reminding him of how his life hung in the balance that day.

His first patrol mission nearly became his last as Caspian's platoon was chopped in half by a roadside bomb. It was in the early days of the Transition War where the freedom fighters, which later became the Raiders, had more conventional forces at their disposal. The placement of the initial explosive separated their convoy in two, and as two more bombs went off at either end, the platoon was bookended by heavy machine gun fire. In a single minute, Caspian, Rhett, and two other PPA sergeants were left bunkered down behind one of the upended armored trucks. As the fighting died down, the freedom fighters thought they had control of the battlefield, revealing their one advantage. Caspian saw how many attacked them as the smoke and dust settled. Five freedom fighters did this to his entire platoon—five plus one.

Caspian smirks as he sees the five of them behind that glass display in the order both he and Rhett eliminated them. He then grits his teeth upon remembering the one that got away. There was no way he nor Rhett could have gotten to him. With six being a nicer number than five, that one Raider who managed to elude capture will forever be a demerit on Caspian's impeccable kill record.

"What are you sneering at?" Bella coldly asks, dropping her fork to her plate, startling Caspian back to the present.

"Do you remember that perfect future you told me about?" Caspian asks his father, ignoring his mother's inquiry.

Methodically cutting a piece from his own steak, Sullivan takes a bite before gently taking a napkin to the corners of his lips. "Your mother asked you a question," he says, his one eye bearing down on his son.

"I'm fine," he quickly states.

"That's not what she asked you," Sullivan says, the intensity in his voice rising.

"Can't I smile just to smile?" Caspian retorts.

"You seem frustrated," Bella says gleefully, scooping a mouthful of creamy mashed potatoes.

"I'm just working through some things is all, and I think—"

"He got to you, didn't he?" Bella assumes, and not so much because she thinks she's properly assessed her son, but rather because she knows it'll get a reaction.

Caspian looks down at his plate, barely able to resist the urge to point out that he just returned home from being a prisoner of war less than three hours ago. For the last forty-eight days his world was confined to a dusty brown tent, mushy grey food, and torture by the man who is now *his* subject of study. If she's implying that Jax is the center of his focus, then yeah, that may be an understatement.

"Was she there?" Bella asks.

"Renn? No," Caspian lies, putting his knife down to again gaze at his trophies. Like he was patient in acting then, he won't play the Renn and Connor card just yet. More needs to be fleshed out before he can present his parents with this information.

"Can I talk with Father now?" Caspian sighs out, done with her yapping interrogation.

"Son, you are being disrespectful," Sullivan says, noticing Caspian's tone.

He sighs again, and with reluctance apologizes. "Sorry, Mother."

Having noticed the flippant attitude, Bella sticks her nose in the air. Wiping her mouth clean and storming out of the dining hall, she leaves a trail of broken dishes and injured servants in her path.

"I do," Sullivan says, the doors slamming behind Bella.

"You do what?" Caspian asks.

"I do remember that day we talked about a perfect future," Sullivan says, taking another bite of raw steak. "Why?"

Pausing for a moment, Caspian takes a sip of wine. "I'm just wondering what happened?"

"Don't be vague."

"Are we moving to that perfect society?" Caspian asks. "Because if we are, why did we have the Transition War? Why do the Raiders resist?"

"You know the answer, Caspian," Sullivan replies, taking another bite before sipping his own wine. "Change…it's painful, especially when one's life is rooted in what will no longer be."

Caspian did know this, from firsthand experience. His body had been weak and destined to always be that way, and when the solution to cure his palsy came, a strange thing happened. Yes, the scientific process is a painful one. His physical body rejected serum after serum, until finally there was a solution that took, recoding his damaged brain, causing literal growing pains as his muscles had to then learn to forget and reprogram a new way of functioning. That was the easy part. Unexpectedly, Caspian identified with his condition, despite him being so young. It was all he knew. The psychological barrier of being a new person not only made him nervous, he was terrified that it could make his condition worse, and therefore worsening the identity he already had. It's no wonder ideological enlightenments have a resistance.

"Jax is not what I thought he was," Caspian sighs as he searches for the right word. "He's strong. Not only is he resolute in what he believes, physically he is nothing like I've encountered before on the battlefield."

Sullivan adjusts his eye patch, looking to his son. "And what's your analysis?"

For a third time, Caspian looks over to his trophies that he and his brother procured. "There's something that I'm missing—that there's more to the story."

"That's a fact of life. Nobody can see everything," Sullivan drawls, gesturing to his missing eye.

Caspian looks around the elegant room. The lights, the walls, the dirty dishes, even the plants all have a fabricated sheen to them—everything adding to the unnatural atmosphere. All except for the five dead trophies.

"I think there's something you're not telling me."

"You sound like him." Sullivan takes another sip, swirling the beverage in the crystal glass.

"Like who?"

"Mica. He was a false dreamer too, and in the end what good did it do him?" Sullivan brings the cup back to his lips, tossing the rest down.

Caspian slides his chair from underneath the table and stands, approaching his trophies, the middle one in particular catching his attention. If Rhett had hesitated for a second longer, than Caspian's role could very well have been switched with this Raider.

Immediately his eyes widen as he comes to a sudden realization. "Where's Rhett, Father?"

"Where are we going?" Jax asks, being picked up with ease and gently laid down onto a floating medical bed. The bed activates as his weight is placed on it, a light humming increasing as it calculates and adjusts for the added mass.

"You tell me," Rhett says, handing Jax a sidearm. "Where are Renn and Connor?"

Jax is oblivious to the question as his focus rests on the firearm. He can barely see straight, let alone handle a weapon. "I don't think that's a good idea."

"Are you serious?" Rhett asks, not waiting for an answer as he shoves the gun into Jax's chest. How did someone from the Labor class become one of the most effective Resistance fighters Rhett has ever heard of, and yet he doesn't even know an opportunity when it's given to him? He's supposed to believe that Jax had the expertise and skill to shoot down two Owls? Rhett expected at least some effort from Jax to try and kill him—he did help take Kip's life after all. "If we do run into any trouble, stab this into your leg and press down here," he orders, handing Jax a syringe.

"What is it?"

"Adrenalin, but don't use it unless you absolutely have to. It is a heavy dose. For now, just lay down."

Rhett puts his broad hand on Jax's chest, pushing him down onto the medical bed. Punching several buttons on a side panel, the floating bed shifts and points directly at Rhett, following his every move. He darts to the door, the bed slowly following suit. Cautiously opening it, Rhett looks to the left and then the right. Once clear, Rhett walks out and heads straight.

If Rhett thought this through as well as he thinks he did, they have approximately seven minutes before Caspian figures it out, and then another two before the alarm is sounded, locking the entire facility down. Nine minutes is plenty of time to get to the tarmac and loaded into an Owl.

"You doing all right?" Rhett murmurs, glancing over his shoulder.

Holding up two thumbs, Jax can't help but wonder. This man kills Kip, aids in the hunt for Jax and once captured, breaks him out. "Why are you doing this?"

Before Rhett can answer, he glances down the right hallway to see a PPA officer blocking their way. Having heard their whispers, the officer begins searching the hall for the source of the noise. Whipping back around the corner, Rhett holds his finger to his mouth, and Jax nods. Drawing his silenced firearm, Rhett hears the officer's radio click to life.

"Calling all channels, we have a twenty-seven sixteen. Say again, we have a twenty-seven sixteen. Officer Rhett Stone—"

The guard doesn't hear the rest of the transmission as a silenced bullet slices through the back of his head and he flops to the ground.

"Sounds like he's figured it out."

"Who?" Jax hisses. "Caspian?"

The alarm went out sooner than expected, but Rhett figured that was a possibility. The contingency plan will be a bit more difficult, but not impossible.

"Why are you doing this?" Jax repeats.

"Listen!" Rhett snaps. "I want to know where Renn and Connor are, and if you're not going to help with that, then you're dead weight—"

But before he can finish, a bullet whips by his head, exploding on impact into the far wall. On instinct, Rhett throws himself to the right and fires a single shot that finds its place in the middle of the target's head. Two more PPA privates round the corner, but before they can properly engage, they are both on the ground with matching holes in their foreheads.

"Be ready to shoot that into your leg," Rhett orders.

"How are we getting out of here?" Jax asks, looking down at the syringe.

"You ask too many damn questions," Rhett snaps before jogging down to the end of the hallway, swiftly clearing it. As the medical bed slowly catches up, Rhett turns to Jax. "I've got an Owl fueled and ready to go. We've just got to get to the tarmac."

Having the rest of his questions answered, Jax jams the syringe into his thigh and pushes the button, releasing a rush of chemicals throughout his bloodstream that jolts him off the bed and onto his feet.

Two shots are then fired from behind and Jax engages. He misses the head, but the shots still find flesh to bury into, dropping the PPA privates to the ground as they scream into their radios. Red lights flare up along with a high-pitched screech that echoes throughout the halls.

"How far to the tarmac?" Jax yells.

"Just here!" Rhett calls, rounding one last corner before barging through the outside doors and into the bright noonday sun. The intensity of the sirens lessens in the chilled mountain air, but the pace of their urgency doesn't.

"The Owl is just over there. Get it fired up."

"Where are you going to be?" Jax then asks.

Another damn question that Rhett ignores. Pulling out a dozen small metal magnets from his cargo vest, Rhett takes one, hits the single button on it before throwing it towards the nearest unmanned Owl. It flies through the air, and as it nears the metal armor, it increases speed, sticking into the side of the aircraft. Repeating this process three more times on adjacent Owls, Rhett tosses the rest towards barrels of fuel and an anti-aircraft turret. As he returns to Jax, Rhett begins climbing the ladder into the Owl just as a bullet finds its way into his left calf, the impact throwing him down to the asphalt.

"Over here!" Caspian's command echoes, his eyes meeting with his brother's.

Regret. When Rhett saved his life that day, that is what Caspian saw in his eyes, and what he sees now. The bitterness Rhett has always seemed to have made little sense until today, where Rhett seeks to correct that mistake.

Ignoring the betrayal within Caspian's eyes and the pain in his leg, Rhett pushes a button on his wrist, igniting the entire tarmac into flames, the heated pressure whooshing through the mountain breeze.

"As far as the Resistance is concerned, we shouldn't have any trouble from here on out!" the vibrant man proclaims, blowing a party whistle over fabricated applause.

Stan Braithsworth aka Cackling Stan. As a little girl, Renn found his voice "funny like a clown." But as she matured and started to question, the news he reported in his broadcasts went from comical to maniacal, until they were eventually horrifying. Just like a clown.

Stifling giggles, Braithsworth continues the news. "The Resistance leader's second in command is in custody right this very second, and as far as I know, our Area Leader Caspian Stone has some tricks up his sleeves," he cackles out.

"Why do you listen to that shit?" Connor asks, his question earning himself a smack on the head.

"Shush!" Renn states, turning up the volume.

"If you remember, some months back the treasonous worker known as Jax Rouge was killed in a standoff with local PPA officers. And welp, you know…" Toy guns go off in the background laced with hollers and screams of pain.

"It's all just propaganda from the Nine," Connor says stating the obvious.

"I'm not stupid!" She turns to her brother. "You of all people should know that we can still get some intel from monitoring their radio waves."

"Not this—"

Renn shakes her head. Everything—and that is no exaggeration—*everything* that Cackling Stan says has an opposite twist to it. He tells the truth through his lies.

"Just shut up!" she says before turning back to the radio.

"Now that we have the—hold on!" Cackling Stan stops abruptly as light static is heard. Two seconds later he's back on, panic-stricken and hysterical. "Ladies and gentlemen, there's some breaking and tragic news," he begins, his given script filling their ears. "Twenty minutes ago, one of our beloved leaders, Rhett Stone, was tragically killed in a daring escape by a group of Raiders, all of whom were apprehended and executed on the spot. Funeral services will be held—"

Renn flips the switch, cutting off Cackling Stan's voice. With a knowing grin on her face and a tear trickling down her cheek, she listens for the sound of her brother coming home.

Receiving a transmission at that precise moment, Connor places his hand over his ear to block out Renn's over-joyful rambling. After a moment, he grabs Renn by the arm. "Where's Mari?"

Renn, shocked by the intensity in his eyes, stutters as she tries to find the answer. "I-I don't know. Last I checked she was in HQ talking with Dan."

Without waiting to answer the next impending question, Connor is out of the tent and sprinting towards HQ, dodging dozens of Raiders as he searches the skies for the deep thunder of an approaching Owl. As Renn steps out of the tent, she sees the dark aircraft hovering above the tarmac, finishing its landing pattern. Slowly it lowers onto the dirt, and as the hatch pops open Rhett is the first to step out and stumble down the ladder. Searching the masses for his sister, Rhett's eyes find hers just as she slams into him with a hug, burying her face into his shoulder.

"It's about time!" Her joyous shout muffled by his jacket.

"You're telling me," Rhett says, gently running his hand through his sister's hair, relieved that it's all over. "We almost didn't make it."

"Cackling Stan said you were killed."

"Obviously that was a load of shit." He smiles.

Lifting her face from his shoulder, Renn kisses Rhett's cheek. "I knew it would work!"

"How'd you know it would work?"

"Because you're my younger brother."

"By like two minutes!" he laughs out, shoving Renn away.

Renn, almost stumbling into Jax as he steps down onto earth, turns to give him a returning hug as well. "And I've missed you!"

Immediately, Jax pushes her away, the violent energy being an utter shock to Renn. Aside from the bruises that paint his face and the bandages on his fingertips and hands, the long cut under his eye matches an emanating darkness that Renn can't quite place.

"Let's get out of here," Rhett says, attempting to turn Renn away.

"In a second," she shrugs, ignoring Rhett and looking at the fire in Jax's eyes one more time.

"What's wrong?" she asks.

"Where's Mari?"

Eighteen

Area Eleven

With the overwhelming darkness weighing down on her, an unbearable chaotic screeching thunders throughout the muffled turmoil. Buried in gritty, wet mud, Mari tries to block out the harrowing siren, but her arms are unmovable and the harder she strains in her attempts, the more her shoulders feel as if they are being internally shredded and dislocated. In a scream for release, her mouth floods with cold, grainy mud, and before she can regurgitate any of the grimy winter earth, a sharp pain rips through the middle of her scalp.

Jerking his commander's head up from the ground, the specialist sees the incoming attack out of the corner of his eye.

"Sergeant Carter!" he shouts, slapping her across the face.

Mari coughs, spitting out the putrid wet dirt, her eyes fluttering open as slushy snow pelts her face, washing away the muck and mire.

"Report!" she manages to finally shout.

"Two units are down," the specialist replies, the commotion of the battle growing. "They cut our convoy in two and are flanking on the left!"

Bunkering down behind the remnants of the storefront, Mari peeks from around the corner of some concrete debris for a better perspective.

"Sergeant..."

The Unapproved are becoming bolder, making this convoy assault more of a norm, not an exception. Ignoring the spiraling panic in her specialist's voice, Mari scans the urban battlefield for anything that will tip the balance back in their favor. With the left flank out of the question and the right losing ground fast, Mari takes her assault bag from off her back, scouring the contents.

"Sergeant Carter!"

Grabbing her specialist by his coat collars, Mari makes sure his eyes meet her stoic demeanor. "Jones, we're fine." And then finding the device of her own making, picks up the improvised explosive and points the mounted infrared laser at the various targets on the right before punching a series of numbers into the keypad. Grabbing Jones's weapons, she clears it of its jam, reloads a fresh magazine, and hands it back to its owner.

"I'm going to move in on their mobile turret on the left flank—"

"The left? But the left—"

"Jones!" Mari snaps, gritting her teeth with aggravated patience. "Just listen. I'm going to move in on the turret," she explains, pointing at the heavy machine gun, "and what I need you to do is cover me while I move. Draw their fire—"

"But Sergeant, what if—"

"Jones," she then says, placing her hand on his shoulder. "I only need thirty seconds. You give me thirty seconds, and this will all be over."

After three quick breaths, the specialist nods, having finally taken up some courage. Charging his weapon, Jones moves into position. Taking swift aim, Mari sees the soldier that she's invested so much time in training open fire. In four successive three-round bursts, Jones easily draws the Raiders' attention as they take cover and shift his direction. Before they can pinpoint his exact position, the specialist has already repositioned for another series of shots. In his movement, one enemy combatant does manage to get a well-aimed shot that finds Jones's shoulder. For a moment, Mari's heart drops as she watches, but immediately her specialist pops right back up and returns fire.

Make the one feel like many, Mari thinks to herself. As a path to the turret opens, Mari takes this one opportunity and sprints down the clearing, killing two guarding the rear of the heavy machine gun. Placing her device next to the front wheels of the mobile turret, Mari arms it and kills one last Raider before diving behind a fallen brick wall. Having seen his sergeant arm the weapon and bunker down for cover, Jones takes one final shot before ducking behind a corner wall himself.

In a matter of two seconds, a bright blue blinding flash shines from the device before a massive explosion erupts. From out of the bellowing fire shoots seven more explosives, each landing on the predesignated targets Mari marked prior to her assault. With only the sounds of a distant battle, its peppered bullets echoing from the isolated firefight, Mari keeps her head low while she peeks from around her concrete barrier.

"Clear?" Jones shouts out from his bunkered position. .

"All clear!" Mari responds, standing up, taking one last scan of the battlefield as she smirks at the damage her improvised explosive did.

———※ ٭ ★ ٭ ※———

"Damn, Sergeant! I mean…what the hell?" Jones asks, drifting into a sharp turn on their way back to City Hall. "I was freaking out when I saw you go down."

"That's putting it mildly," Mari jokes, prodding at his ribs. "You sure you didn't piss yourself?"

"What? Hell, no I didn't piss myself!"

"Then what is that?" And before Jones has the time to react, Mari unscrews the lid to her canteen and dumps the remaining contents into his lap.

"Nice," he mumbles, not surprised in the least bit at her juvenile behavior. "Was that really necessary?"

"Of course!" she giggles. "How's your shoulder, by the way?"

"It's nothing," Jones says as he rolls the joint around, feeling the small protrusion the wound left. "It missed the armor, but it was a small caliber, I think. Barely felt it."

"You want me to look at it?"

"Nah." Jones shrugs. "I'll head over to med bay once we unload."

Pulling up to Area Eleven's City Hall, Jones brings their truck to an abrupt halt before stepping out. "By the way, why hasn't the section leader approved any of your explosives for unit production? Clearly, they work!"

"Because he's a dick," she scoffs. Closing her door, Mari slings her weapon before moving to the bed of the truck for the rest of her equipment.

"You'd think he's given enough of his dick to you already…" Jones jests, not thinking about the ramifications behind the offhanded comment.

Playing it off as best she can, Mari shrugs, glancing down at her scarred arm.

"Sarg," Jones sighs out. "I didn't mean anything by it. I-I wasn't thinking…"

"Don't worry about it. I know what you meant."

Jones is the little brother she never had. After her dad died, she had nowhere to turn but to the Legacy class and enlist, and in a very similar situation, the two found themselves attached at the hip throughout the brutal training regimen of the PPA. With that being said, there were some hazings that Mari had to endure alone—some that she still must weather.

"You want to grab some lunch after I—" Jones begins, but before he can finish, drops to his knees in sheer agony.

"Jones, you good?" Mari asks, shocked at the abrupt movement.

"Sergeant!" Clasping his shoulder, Jones screams as an intense burning begins coursing down his shoulder and throughout his arm. "I think—"

"Shut up!" Having seen this before, Mari pulls out her knife and cuts the straps to his vest for a better look at the entry wound. "We don't have a lot of time. Medic!"

"What is it?" Jones cries.

"It's not a small bullet, that's for damn certain."

Taking the tip of her knife, Mari prods around until she feels the metal projectile.

"What's going on?" the medic asks as he and his team rush over.

"He's got an explosive dart embedded in his shoulder," Mari states.

"Let me see—"

"I can get it," Mari then says, pulling out her knife. "I just need—"

"We've got it from here," the medic hastily states, rolling Jones onto the gurney. "I just need to get him to our truck, and I'll be able to get it out."

"We don't have a lot of time—" Mari frantically begins.

"I know, which is why you need to let me handle it."

Before Mari can argue further, the medical team lifts Jones up and begins jogging towards their truck.

I could have—

But before Mari can even finish her thought, Jones's shoulder bursts in a violent blast that throws the medical team to the dirt and rips his head from his body. In utter shock at the visceral scene she just witnessed, Mari stands, and as she turns around, she spots off on the horizon a squadron of Unapproved combatants moving in on the Area.

―――・★・―――

Area Thirty-Eight

Shooting her eyes open from the dream, electric torches reveal a dim tent space to Mari. With her wrists bound, every part of her aches as she is brought into sudden remembrance of the exposed flesh of her fingertips and toes. In a sudden spasm, Mari's body locks up as a violent voltage is sent coursing through her body, while the vile taste of the moist rag in her mouth begins to gag and suffocate every breathing effort.

"That's enough!" a shadowy, chill voice declares, the painful spasms ceasing as he speaks.

She can't remember who—if anyone—was assigned to keep watch, and as time begins to blur itself together, it becomes more difficult to make sense of her current situation, let alone the rotation of guards. Squinting, she strains her eyes to match the voice to an exact face, and just when she is about to give up, his silhouette comes into focus.

"What do you want, Jax?" Mari manages to mutter through the gag, and if it hadn't been the hundredth time she'd asked the question, it would have just sounded like disgruntled nonsense.

"You want to go over this again?" Jax asks as he steps into the artificial light.

Mari manages to hide the bone shaking shiver his response gives her. Her basic human instinct to love was stolen and replaced with pain and torture—violence to an intimate degree.

What did Caspian do to you, Jax? she asks herself.

"You know what I want. You and Jude—" Jax says, stepping forward. A sharp pain cuts him off however, as it courses through Jax's elbow. Since his escape, the annoying ache has only escalated, but since there are more pressing matters at hand, his focus must be on Mari.

His words are filled with disdain, but Mari can also hear the remnants of a broken, bleeding heart. Shoving his hand in her face, Jax rips out the wet rag and a loose tooth in the process.

"How long have you been PPA?" Jax asks, recalling his debriefing with Renn.

"I've told you…" she mumbles. None of the countless explanations will change the conclusion that Jax has already made, and answering any more questions will only feed into his biased perspective. Rather than digging herself into a darker hole, she looks down to the dirt as if hoping to find another answer scratched out. She's been trained to endure far worse than an interrogator's enraged, emotional beating. Nobody, however, trained her to endure a lover's wrath.

"How long were you working with Jude?" Jax asks, his tone reflecting his desperation. It is still unknown what intelligence the two of them managed to smuggle out, and there could still be other insider threats lurking within the Encampment.

"No!" Mari responds vehemently. *I'm not even part of it…*

"Then tell me what I need to know!"

"Need to know, or want to hear?" Mari sighs out.

"Tell me, or I'll give the order and have Ann in here next to you."

"Do it and you'll see what I'm truly capable of!" she growls, the tone of her slow, methodical nature solidifying her motherly instincts with rage and resolve.

Having nothing to say, Jax scoffs and smirks before exiting the tent.

Where is the man I once loved? Mari asks herself. *Where is my Jax?*

The panel sits, some in belief and gratitude while others remain skeptical, not sure of how to look at the man before them. *Two* Stones in their cause? Where Renn and even Connor were once unworthy of his trust, their determination in getting the results they have with Jax has made Dan—and many others—believers. And now Rhett... Dan would like to think that he's seen stranger things, but the usefulness of his experience has run out at this point.

"Rhett," Dan begins, "what makes you think we'll trust you?"

Glancing at each Raider in front of him, Rhett looks first to the black one with dreadlocks on the far left, quickly analyzing each member until his gaze ends with his sister on the far right, Renn's smile giving him the courage to smile back.

"I brought you Jax," Rhett says, letting the blunt truth speak for itself.

"That doesn't mean shit," Kai scoffs. "You know how many people we thought we could trust because they did us *favors*? Your undercover comrade, for starters..."

"I was not briefed on Jude's mission," Rhett replies.

Opening his mouth to argue against the claim, Dan simply holds out his hand to Kai. "Have we scanned him for any tracking signal or device?" Dan asks the rest of the elders on the board.

"Of course," another Raider says.

"Have we scanned Jax?" Kai blurts out.

"That is enough!" Dan bellows out.

A Raider on the panel raises his hand, and Dan acknowledges the request.

"The only way to see his true intentions is to put him through a thorough debrief and process."

Renn laughs to herself because she knows how genuine Rhett being here is. Both she and Mari were planning a rescue of their own when Rhett got word to her of his own design. From that alone it seems obvious that Rhett's motives are pure. Renn's not naïve though. She is aware that the Raiders need to see her brother the way she has always seen him. Mari's situation on the other hand, that is out of Renn's control. There's simply not enough information to know if Mari helped Jude, or if her rescue plan for Jax was part of a bigger whole to do more damage to the Raiders or not. Time is the only remedy Mari has right now.

Dan briefly thinks about the request. "Let's start with how you knew where to find him."

"I'm a Stone," Rhett laughs. "If I want something, I get it."

"How did you know where to bring him? How did you know we even wanted him back?"

Again, Rhett scoffs. "What kind of questions are these? Jax told me! And yeah, we didn't know if we'd be shot down or not. Call it an act of faith if you will."

Dan ignores Rhett's attitude, continuing his line of questioning. "Mari Carter, does that name mean anything to you?"

Rhett shakes his head. "Should it?"

"We've been recruiting a number of your PPA agents to our cause," Dan says, folding his hands. "And despite the cultural differences between them and us, they've added value and training to the Encampment as we've properly vetted them as potential threats. Mari Carter, thought to have been a civilian at the time of her being admitted into the Encampment, was recently discovered to be a member of Area Eleven's PPA and was not part of this original vetting process."

"She's not PPA anymore," Rhett says. "If she's here in Thirty-Eight then she abandoned her unit and by definition is no longer loyal to the Nine's PPA."

There are a handful of scattered mumbles upon Rhett announcing this. It's something that Renn brought up with Jax after he put her in that tent, but again, without proper questioning her true motives have yet to be revealed. Jude's actions shocked everyone in the Encampment when Jax brought it to light. Even worse, it made Connor, Renn, and Jax look incompetent as they often brought him in on their missions. If the three are to gain their lost trust back, they cannot let anything like that happen again.

"Why is this the first I'm hearing of this?" Kai shouts, enraged as he stands.

"Few were briefed," Renn speaks up. "We just found out she was PPA and since she was in close contact with Jude, we are still unsure of her loyalty."

"She's the one you picked up from Area Thirty-Eight, isn't she?" Kai asks, feeling more betrayed by the second.

"She was." As Renn answers, more scattered discussions sound.

"That was Jax's call. How do we know he's not with her?" Kai yells out.

"If she is a traitor, we'll know shortly," Renn says, her solemn tone saying everything that needs to be said about the situation.

She is no traitor, Dan thinks. Patriotism runs in her blood.

He remembers back to when Carter left for Vermont after things fell apart—after Aila was killed. He didn't know Lisa—the mother of their newborn child—survived the explosion, but being left with no choice, Carter took their daughter with him in order to escape the hostility of Area Thirty-Eight. He had a network back in his home state, and although he was grieved for the loss of Aila and apparent death of Lisa, Carter was a patriot and thought it'd be a good place to start another cell to fight in the Nine in the war.

Now, when the hell he died and how his daughter ended up in the PPA, is yet to be determined. What little contact their group in Colorado had with Carter's Vermont cell was lost about twelve months into the operation, the war ending shortly after, so intelligence is scarce on the matter. Dan tries to fight the idea that Carter defected, but ultimately Dan silently succumbs to the fact that he has been wrong about a person before...

"As soon as I found out Mari was former PPA, I monitored her every move," Renn says.

"And how do we know we can trust you?" Kai accuses. "There are too many unknowns. The fact of the matter is we don't know if we can trust anything from any Stone, let alone the PPA. We should be questioning everyone we've recruited again. How do we know Jax and Rhett weren't followed? Everything is under this guise—"

"Get to your point," Renn says.

"I want proof," Kai says flatly. "No more testimonies. Evidence and proof need to be admitted in this hearing." As Kai says this, everyone can't help but agree. From the sudden transition of power from Dan to

Jax to two Legacies now making tactical calls, the unease is quickly growing unbearable; whatever trust Jax, Connor, and Renn had is quickly unraveling.

"The Program," Rhett speaks up, silencing all commotion. "December 25, 2037. I have files on this day and of the decade-long Program my family has been working on."

The beginning of the end, Dan vividly recalls.

What the Minutemen Division sought to accomplish was to resurrect American principles and values, but on that day— December 25, 2037—the country's fate was sealed as the American experiment and the world's hope died, being buried in that bunker underneath the Denver International Airport. With Dan being the only one there and who can validate Rhett's claim, everyone else on the panel mutters questions that none but Dan and the files Rhett has can answer.

"Can you confirm this?" one Raider asks Dan.

"I will need to talk with Rhett, Renn, and Connor in a private session. We are finished." As he adjourns the hearing, and before Kai can protest that his name was not on that list, Dan turns to his son. "Kai, keep an eye on Rhett. For now, he stays."

Dan orders this all with confidence, but there is still something he's not seeing. Determined to figure out what, Dan makes the mental note to at least pray, and for Mari in particular.

Everyone leaves the tent, some more pleasantly than others, but waiting until the last exits, Renn rushes forward, bulldozing into Rhett.

"Looks like it's going to work out!"

"Does it? I'll admit, things have fared better than I expected, but I'm still doubtful," he scoffs, eyeing Kai as the last one to leave the tent. "Renn?"

"Yes?" Renn gleefully replies, oblivious to the solemnity in her twin's voice.

Rhett doesn't immediately answer, his heart in conflict with his next words. Reflecting on the day of his first kills, Rhett can't help but connect them to the night he reluctantly held Kip on stage, allowing for Caspian to brutally murder the man under false pretenses. He also can't help but advocate for the opportunity to better the future of humankind. Rhett understands the sacrifices that must be made in order to bring to pass a greater good. That's not where the conflict within him lies. It comes from the subjective nature of "good." For years his parents—the Nine—have defined it as "collective progression of their country." That collective pursuit under their definition completely disregards what is good for any individual—what is needed for a singular citizen. Kip…the reason for his death was a necessary lie to help propagate The Government's narrative in their ambitions to create their perfect, unified society.

Caspian is not a bad man. Rhett sees the love his brother has for him, the vision of their parents, and the Nine, but does that justify the horrendous nature of Caspian's actions? That is something Rhett cannot answer, nor can he determine the balance of collective progress with an individual's freedom of choice. If he's being honest, the question must be asked if anyone should have that liberty to choose? As a soldier, Rhett is highly sensitive to the nature of putting the needs of the mission above his person. If Rhett had let Caspian die on the day of their first kills, would he be standing where he is today? Would he have been the one to kill Kip instead? Would he be pushing the vision of the Nine in as ambitious of a way as Caspian is? He'd like to say no. Rhett would like to think that he is nothing like Caspian, but in all reality, he is fully aware of his love for both his brother and for Renn—even if they are in conflict and literal battle with one another.

"Do you remember your first kill, Renn?" Rhett asks.

"I do…" she responds, the sobering question forcing whatever joy she had to be wiped from her face. "Do you not?"

He shakes his head. "I wish I didn't, but I do. It's all I've been thinking about lately. Every day I see those trophies at breakfast, lunch, and dinner, constantly reminding me of the choice I made that day to save Caspian's life."

Bella and Sullivan have proudly told the story many times, and in each retelling of it, Renn's had the question of "why" in the back of her mind—why did Rhett pull the trigger then? Why didn't he wait a fraction of a second longer? Apparently, she's not the only one.

Not knowing what to say, Renn simply takes her brother's hand in hers.

"Did I make the right decision?" Rhett asks.

Squeezing his hand, Renn responds with what little comfort she can. "Right or wrong, the choice was made, and we must live to deal with the consequences."

"And that night I helped kill Kip?"

Both choices, if made differently, would have changed the trajectory of the impending war between Raiders and the Nine. Who knows what could have been done if the individual sanctity of Kip's life was held intact—if Rhett would have used his own agency to allow for Caspian to be killed first before killing the Raider. Jax would never have left because Caspian never would have pulled the trigger—meaning Kip would still be alive.

Vigorously shaking her head, Renn grabs Rhett's face and looks him right in the eyes. "Don't. You can't change the past. You're a good man—"

"But am I a coward? I was then. I feared what Father would've done to me if he found out I let Caspian die—"

"No!" Renn snarls, knocking some sense into Rhett with an open palm to his chest. "You weren't back then, and you aren't now."

And what she doesn't say is if they are truly twins, then they share the closest kind of bond any person can have. If Rhett's evil, then how could she not be? That night she was just as complicit if not more. She not only turned Kip in, but she also just sat there and watched—waiting for Kip to die so the pain she caused him and herself would stop. The greatest irony of all is while Kip's pain died, hers has not only persisted but has metastasized.

"Are you both being serious right now?" Connor's bass voice booms as he enters the tent.

Unable to keep a smile from growing across his face, Rhett looks over to his brother just before the freight train comes rolling towards him. Picking Rhett up off the ground, Connor embraces his little brother, squeezing him until his back pops.

"It's been a long time," Connor bellows. Breaking away and looking Rhett straight in the eyes—making sure he clearly understands this next part—Connor says what an older brother should. "Stop feeling sorry for yourself, or I'll have to beat it out of you." And then turning to Renn, says, "Both of you. I'll kick both of your asses right here, right now. We're all standing on the right side of history here."

Stepping out of the tent, the shock of pain returns, coursing through Jax's arm as if someone has taken pliers to twist and pull the ligaments of his elbow.

"Jackie?"

Doubled over, Jax is unaware of Ann's presence. After a few quick seconds of massaging the inflamed bulge in his arm, he looks up to find the little girl's concerned face staring up at him. It's like she hasn't slept in days. A girl her age shouldn't have anything to lose sleep over, but as he looks back to the tent he just exited, thoughts of Mari haunt both Jax and Ann. With a feeble smile that does little to revive the child's happy demeanor, Ann's hardened gaze is a reminder that she is no longer the young woman he remembers. With feathers and beads and flowers in her hair, Ann fits the mold of most girls her age around the Encampment, but emotionally, she dwarfs them all.

"Where's Mari?" Ann asks, tears welling up.

Raising his hand to smooth out her hair in a gesture of comfort, Jax stops himself upon seeing Mari's caked blood on his fingers. This does not go unnoticed by Ann as she sees both the blood and Jax's sudden change in expression. Secretly, she knows the truth of everything. She also knows that Jax is wrong about her sister.

"Mari's in a lot of trouble, Ann." It's all Jax can think to say. He could go into all the details of betrayal and the technicalities of war, spy craft, and deceit, but in the end, it boils down to the concept of trouble.

"What'd she do?" Ann asks solely for the sake of formality.

"She's not a good person…" He put her in that tent immediately upon his return but battled with it for days before he ever laid a hand on her. Mari's past came back to haunt her, and the more Jax learned, the quicker his confidence in her waned.

"Not a good person?" Ann's voice raises as she asks this rhetorical question. "She's the best person I know!"

Jax ignores the dried blood on his hands this time and reaches out for Ann, but she just slaps it away, the force of it awakening the dull pain within his elbow. He tries his best to ignore it, but Ann sees the agony and relishes in his pain.

"She's better than you," Ann retorts, hitting his arm a second time. "She's better than Renn. She's better than everyone! Now tell me, what did you do with her? Why did you take her from me?" Again, Ann hits him, only this time with a closed fist. "Do you know what she did for you?"

"Did for me?" Jax spits, appalled by Ann's audacity. She's nothing more than an angry child who knows nothing about what's at stake. She swings again but is stopped by Jax's open palm. "What do you know?" he shouts back.

Ann isn't fazed in the least bit by Jax's aggression, testifying of the emotional fortitude she's gained these past weeks, and although the welled-up tears pour down her cheeks, Ann stands defiant.

"I know that she loved you! Or loves you if she's still alive. I know she did everything she could to get you home—to bring you back so she could hold you one more time… Damn you, Jax," Ann shouts. "Damn you! I know that she cried for you every time she thought I was sleeping. She cried and I heard her pray like everyone else does around here, only she wasn't praying for the cause or some bullshit war! She was praying for you!" she screams, jabbing her finger into his stomach.

Jax's heart is in his throat as he watches Ann's tears patter the dirt below. Is it true? He can't tell what is real and what is coming from a narrative that's being used to break him. Caspian planted a dark seed, and it grew so quickly—in such a bizarre manner that his entire perception of reality has become distorted.

"Don't 'Ann' me! Where's my sister?" Ann shouts, her words echoing. "Where is she?!"

"What is going on?" Renn asks, both her and Rhett walking up to the scene.

"Where is Mari?!" Ann screams yet again.

"Ann..." Renn says, trying to place her hand on the distraught girl's shoulder, but Ann just shrugs it off as she punches Jax one more time before running off in tears and sorrow.

"I've got her," Rhett quickly says, dashing after her before Renn can react.

Jax drops to his knees.

"What happened?" Renn asks as she kneels beside him.

"Why?" is all Jax can manage to ask.

She's been where Mari has. They are sisters of the uniform. It makes it that much harder for Renn to reconcile what needs to be done in order to find the truth. Is Renn better than Mari? Is rank the sole deciding difference between the two women?

"With new information comes a new situation," is all she can think to say as she stares at his blood-stained hands.

In the distance a light, rapid thumping draws Renn's attention from him, and as it grows, so does the familiarity of the rhythm, bringing her to her feet. Grabbing Jax's elbow in sudden urgency, she feels the protrusion that was exactly what everyone feared, but rather than it being in Rhett it was in Jax.

"You brought them here..."

━━◥ ⋆★⋆ ◤━━

"Ann!" Rhett shouts out. "Ann, c'mon, let's go back and talk about this."

"Get away from me!" she yells in her continued sprint. A little girl can run only so long, though, before beginning to slow down. At a casual jog, Rhett catches up, gently tackling Ann to the ground.

"Get off of me!" Ann fights back, ferociously swinging and kicking her limbs.

"Hold up! Be quiet…" Rhett says, afraid at what he's hearing in the distance.

"Get away from me!" Ann continues to kick and scream.

"Shut up!" Rhett bellows, and Ann does, taken off guard by his sudden hostility. "You hear that?"

Nodding, knowing exactly what it is she's hearing, Ann finds immediate trust as she looks to the stoicism Rhett is donning.

"Stay with me, okay? Now, get up."

He pulls Ann to her feet when the thuds of the incoming Helos emerge overhead. Some zoom past and land on tents and people while others simply hover, creating chaos as they whip dirt into the air, spitting out bullets and soldiers. Throwing on his goggles to block out the flying gravel, without warning or hesitation, Rhett snaps the neck of a PPA specialist that lands right next to them, shouldering the soldier's weapon in one smooth motion. Before the body of the dead soldier collapses to the ground, Rhett takes aim at a Helo's engine, firing a single shot that brings the airframe crashing down.

"They're taking people!" Ann shouts out over the battle.

Having seen and participated in this practice before, Rhett shoots two dead in the head who were in the process of loading women for Caspian's experiments. Aiming for a third soldier, Rhett misses as the aircraft takes off over the tree line.

"Ann! I'm going to need you to get out of here!" he shouts, shooting another Helo down before turning to see if she heard what he said. "Ann?"

She's gone, and looking up, Rhett sees an aircraft right above him, a soldier pulling Ann up and into the cabin.

"Rhett!"

Taking aim at the zip line's engine, an easy shot from this distance, as Rhett places his finger on the trigger, a sharp pain is felt at the base of his neck and his whole world goes black.

It must have been installed while in captivity. That is the only plausible answer. Why else would Jax have a tracker embedded in him? Catching Jax before he collapses, Renn lays him down on the ground.

"How's your arm?" she asks.

"It's on fire!" The second the aircrafts came in, it was like a switch was flipped with ten thousand volts coursing through his veins, powering the transmitter.

"I don't know how to do this," Renn says more to herself than to Jax, looking at the pulsating bulge in the crux of his arm.

"I do!"

Renn's gaze whips to the tent and voice coming from it.

"I promise!" Mari continues, almost as if she sees Renn's speculation. "I specialized in explosives!"

"Are you sure?" Renn shouts back.

"Yes! We don't have a lot of time."

Renn looks to Jax and back to the tent, unsure of what to do.

"Do it!" he screams, unable to bear the pain.

Quickly Renn rushes into the tent, cuts Mari free, and helps bring her outside.

"Do you need any tools?"

"A knife. I need to get it out of him before I can disable it."

Unsheathing her blade, Renn hands it to Mari. "You sure about this?"

"Unless whoever has the switch hits the button, I am positive that I can do this. It can't be triggered any other way."

"Just get it out of me!" Jax screams as Mari digs the knife into his arm.

With bullets kicking up the dirt surrounding the trio, Renn draws her sidearm and returns two shots, killing two PPA.

"I'll draw their fire; you just worry about getting that thing out!" Renn then takes two more shots, only killing one this time around before rushing to the border of the forest with an aircraft in pursuit.

"Hold still!" Mari orders. "I know this hurts, but there's no other way."

"Mari?"

She sees the blinking lights underneath a thin layer of tissue. "Almost there."

"Mari?"

"I can feel it." The metal bulge is masked in slippery blood, but it's exactly what Mari was expecting as she grabs it between her fingers. "It attached to the ligaments, Jax. I'm going to have to cut it out."

He doesn't care what she has to do. He just wants her to listen. "Mari!"

"What?"

"I'm sorry…" he sighs out. "You were with Jude and—and Jude was a—"

Mari just places her hand over his mouth before quickly replacing it with her lips in a soft kiss.

"Let's take care of this first," she says, turning her face back to his elbow, ready to extract the device. "We'll talk about this after—"

Renn sees the entire scene unfold. After she draws away the Helo, she has no problem bringing it down. Swinging her way onto the aircraft, clearing the cabin, it takes just a few more well-placed shots in the back of the pilot's head before the aircraft hits the ground hard. When it does, she's tossed from the tumbling metal like a rag doll across the dirt and rocks of the mountain floor. Slowly pushing herself up from the ground, her bones and joints popping in the process, as she lifts her head, she sees him. Standing less than ten feet away from her is Caspian.

"What's the matter, sister? Aren't you glad to see me?" Little by little he approaches, taking each step methodically and carefully. "Nifty little device from the Raiders, isn't it? I'm disappointed that you didn't catch it earlier. Thought a couple of days would be plenty of time for you to find it. Figured I trained you better than that. But it offers this learning opportunity, now doesn't it?" Reaching inside his coat, Caspian pulls out a small, metallic button.

Shifting her gaze in the direction her brother faces, Renn is a hundred feet away from Mari digging into Jax's elbow. Bit by bit the violent event unfolds. Mari kisses Jax, moves her focus back to the device, and boom. There's a flash of light with a simultaneous blast that rips Mari from Jax, obliterating his arm from off his body. Tossing the metallic switch in front of Renn, Caspian waltzes off towards his aircraft, killing a handful of Raiders as he does.

Nineteen

Area Thirty-Eight
October 13, 2037

No more than a college puke, this private has grown up with having never known sacrifice, and therefore true victory—having been given everything from The Government , earning nothing on his own. Every industry has bad apples—this man is old enough to have the wisdom to understand this—however, when there are no standards and ethics in an organization, the opportunity for power and control is within anyone's grasp, making bad apples the rule rather than the exception.

"Get in line!"

Forcefully pushed forward, the scraggly old man barely catches his footing, stumbling with his cane as his only support.

"You okay, Pops?" his grandson asks, the young man glancing over to the brutish private.

"I'm fine," Pops says. "How are you holding up, Junior?"

The elderly man is in colossal denial. This boy is no longer a toddler on the ranch's tire swing. It's been a year since his parents died on the islands, and oh how their son has grown in that time. Every boy needs a moment that cultivates him into a man. The death of his parents was only the first. This moment in their nation's history is another.

"Not sure," Junior responds as he grips the only thing he has left of his father, thinking of what Dad would do if he were here beside him.

"Don't even think about it," Pops growls. Being a Middle East War vet, he sees the contemplation in Junior's eyes. "With the armor these guys are wearing, the most you'll do is make their stomachs itch."

"I know," Junior says, wishing there was another way.

This Smith and Wesson .223 caliber rifle, by the standard of today's technology, is the equivalent of a twenty-two in Pops's time. So, it's damn near useless if you'd want to plan an assault or coup. That doesn't matter though. It's the "spirit of the law" they say. *Sure*, the kid thinks. North Korea, China, Russia, those citizens all followed the spirit of their law too. The theft of individual liberties will always be under the guise of collective safety.

"Hundreds of shootings have occurred within the past week. Our citizens have the right to safety and security. The Government will provide this."

Junior scoffs every time he hears the "public safety announcement." Everyone knows these events are fabrications of the Nine's narrative—that people were paid to commit them. Even if they were *authentic,* the media grossly misrepresented the events, taking some details out of context while completely omitting others.

Junior shakes his head. President White was right: "Fix the fabricated change." Every U.S. citizen is in uncharted territory. Looking around at the newly appointed PPA, he can't help but wonder how they came to the logic that anything they are doing is moral and just. State-sponsored security just following orders… Maybe that's the difference between a soldier and warrior—one who defended the old Constitution versus those in desperation for a paycheck.

"Service. Loyalty. Order—The People-Protection Agency."

The only thing the knock-off Uncle Sam is missing is a burning flag in the background.

"Do you think things will get better—that this is all just a precaution?"

"Yeah," Pops lies, and Junior sees right through it. There's no coming back from this. It always starts with guns, and it may move to knives, slingshots, or whatever The Government finds "threatening." The true genius is in that subjective standard, and if there's one thing Pops knows, when you give people an inch, they most always take a mile.

Bowing his head, the old man says a soft prayer—one for Junior and one for his country. Whispering a soft "amen," when looking up, to his surprise, he spots a man perched on the rooftop across the street. Nudging his grandson, Pops points over to the angelic spectacle with his nose, and Junior's eyes widen. More conspicuously than not, Junior then darts his gaze from PPA soldiers to the rooftop and back and forth until his grandpa has to slap the back of his head.

"Stay cool…" Pops chides.

"Sorry. It just seems—you know…"

"Yeah, I do," Pops says, and glancing back up, finds that the rooftop man is gone. "Just keep quiet and be ready."

———✦✦✦———

Hitting the gravel, Dan checks in. "I've taken out the overwatch, but I'm changing positions. Somebody spotted me."

"Seriously?" Bella's witchy voice cracks over the transmission. "Dumbass—"

"Stand down," Mica chimes in. "It was just some kid and his old man. No Ordeans saw your position."

"You mean PPA," Bella states as if annoyed by the synonym.

"Whatever. The fact is, you're good. We don't have time to readjust."

Dan contemplates for a moment. He hates the fact that he got spotted, especially by people not even on the lookout.

"All right, give me forty-five seconds and then engage."

"Roger. Patriot Two, keep close to Patriot Four and wait for my signal."

Sullivan acknowledges the order, homing in on his wife's position and covering every possible angle she could be compromised. He knows he has orders to keep things "manageable." But, if she's in any danger all hell is going to break loose. The mission is of little importance compared to the safety of his wife and future posterity.

Dan is back up on the roof in thirty seconds flat and in another nine, he's putting Mica and Sullivan in his sights.

"In position," Dan says.

Finding the small button on his wrist, Mica makes one final sweep, ensuring civilians are clear of their target.

"Patriot Four, draw him in. Patriot Two, wait sixty seconds before engaging."

Up ahead and as planned, Bella does what she does best. Approaching the PPA leadership, slightly raising her hand, she traces the zipper of her jacket with the back of her fingertips, motioning for the commanding PPA officer to follow her into his office. Without looking away from Bella's breasts, he tries to stifle his excitement and goofy ass grin as she begins undressing him before the door of the office is even open. Unprofessionalism coupled with the aptitude of lascivious men...

That's when it happens.

At the top of his lungs, Sullivan begins shouting like a madman with nothing coherent or anything that follows a logical thought track. At first people back away, uncertain of his mental stability, but as the hysteria continues, some begin to laugh. As the team knows, it's not within the PPA's standard operating procedures to handle a situation like this, but a single PPA private approaches, nonetheless.

"Sir," the private barks, but Sullivan just continues to freak. "Sir. Please, I need you to calm down!"

With an outreached hand, the private poorly tries to subdue Sullivan. Without hesitation Sullivan breaks the private's arm the second his collar is touched. In a painfully panicked grab, the young soldier accidently clicks a button on Sullivan's wrist, and in an agonizing holler, the soldier's yelp is masked by a thunderous explosion from the very office Bella seduced her victim to.

Chaos ensues, scattering the citizens while the PPA desperately tries to keep order. Their pitiful attempts are only exacerbated as they lock away the confiscated firearms while simultaneously attempting to smother the raging fire. Capitalizing on the chaos, Mica picks off PPA guards one by one; however, his confidence in the plan momentarily ceases as he finds himself staring down the barrels of five guns.

Pausing, Mica studies the soldiers, seeing the fear that is quickly overtaking the untrained boys. Without moving, Mica waits for the closest officer to approach.

"You-you are under arrest for—"

Sliding his head underneath the pointed firearm, Mica jams his knife into the gap just beneath the armpit of the soldier's armor, leveraging the body as a human shield. Amidst the pandemonium, Dan's gunshots are disguised, and counting off one at a time, he pops each in the head from his nest, the last one hitting the ground three seconds after the first was killed.

"Patriot One, you're all clear."

Mica drops his PPA shield. "Patriot Four, what's your status?"

There's no response. On cue, both Mica and Sullivan rush the small group of PPA guards carrying away the confiscated firearms. Without hesitation, Mica and Sullivan swiftly dismantle the squad without a scratch or bruise.

"Area clear," Dan calls over the radio, continuing to scan the outskirts for a counterattack.

Mica sighs with relief. "Any civilian casualties?"

Dan scans the battlefield briefly and replies, "Negative. We've got some lingering eyes, though."

Mica looks to Sullivan who, as calm as he appears, is in a state of outright fear. Wiping the blood off his blades, Sullivan puts his hand to his ear.

"Bella!" Mica gives him a look for using her real name, but Sullivan couldn't give a damn. "Bella, where are you?"

There's a faint crackle followed by a loud pop before a pissed off Bella crackles over the frequency. "What the hell!"

"I'm so sorry," Sullivan lets out a great sigh of relief. "The kid grabbed my arm and hit the button."

"That won't be a story to tell our kids anytime soon, now, will it?"

Mica picks up on the plurality of what she said. "You pregnant?"

"Not now," Sullivan says, slugging Mica in the arm as an elated smile spreads across his face. "Let's go see what these people want first, yeah?"

———✦✦✦———

Denver International Airport: Minutemen Headquarters

After the emergence of the Nine, as imperfect and incomplete as it was, the Denver International Airport became the only place to hide.

The Constitution and the Division became relics of the past, and what remained had to be preserved by any means necessary. The *official story*, according to the Division archives, is that years ago, when the airport was built, it was constructed incorrectly, and instead of tearing it down—starting completely over—Sullivan's father had the contractors and engineers carefully build the legitimate airport over what was already there. The reasons were twofold: one, it was simply more economical and timely to not have to start from ground level. Two, there was a huge financial incentive as a market opportunity was seen to repurpose the "mistake" for the United States military. This entire shift in scope didn't go unnoticed, however, as the blueprints got leaked to the press by a partisan contractor looking for their fifteen minutes of fame. This PR stunt was nipped in the bud for the most part, but as the airport was nearing completion, members of the public began to notice that the pace of construction was not slowing down as personnel, equipment and supplies were still being funneled underground.

Conspiracy theorists had a heyday, quickly coining the term the "DIA Conspiracy" which quickly caught the ears of honest investigators who then began to look into the secret underground army fort. This chain reaction led religious zealots and political nut jobs down a freeway of dead-end theories and explanations that their imaginations thrived on in their desperate attempts to explain the underground tunnels and secret warehouses. The most popular of these was mass genocide. At first, Sullivan's father found it comical. It was great marketing for his company, and to amuse himself even further, Sullivan Sr. ended up hiring an artist to paint symbolic murals depicting exactly what the theorists were claiming—that in the last days there will be one government to rule with an iron fist. It all backfired however, thanks to platforms like Google and YouTube, and with more eyes on it than he intended, the military had to back out of the contract.

Official stories aren't always complete truths though. The truth is this:

Sullivan's father *did* work for the government, and did, in fact, buy the old airport to build the new one over it for the military, all as a place where the Department of Defense could perform secret tests on upcoming and promising technology—another Area Fifty-One. Like Area Fifty-One, it would be immune to any sort of conspiracy theory because the name alone was almost a deterrent for the average individual. But *unlike* Area Fifty-One, this underground facility was within walking distance of the public. Propaganda and psychological campaigns were implemented to try and mitigate this issue, projecting the conspiracy theories, further confusing the public as they subtly marketed the bunkers as an Armageddon Project for the paranoid rich, all of which created a smoke screen for the actual intent. It was a feedback loop that was fed from the simple psychological tactic that the truth was just too crazy to be real. In other words, the military was planning on hiding in plain sight with this one.

Lobbyists and government officials became heavily involved in the unofficial "Area Fifty-Two" Project, blending government and corporate power, and with the Ordean Reich having infiltrated both. This was their opportunity for progressive weapon development and "super soldier" experiments. Sullivan inherited the project and everything that came with it when his father died. Because of the secrecy and corruption of the project, his clearance was "above" Top Secret, therefore making this nefarious agenda unknown to the Division when they recruited him and Bella. After the Nine came down hard on the Minutemen Division, agents everywhere had nowhere to go. The agency lost too many to count, but those who did survive were told by the Stones to fly to the Denver International Airport as a place of refuge to fight another day.

Deep down in one of the many reinforced rooms of the DIA, Aila contemplates how they came to be here as she attempts to lift a metal box. Out of sheer fear of shooting the baby out on the spot, she immediately drops the massive weight of it back down before plopping herself against one of the shelves—where Aila begins loathing both her fatigue and cravings.

Yogurt and pickles…again.

"You okay?" Victoria asks, stepping into the room after hearing the crash.

"Yeah," Aila lies. She didn't need babying before. She doesn't need it now.

"Well, what are you doing in here?"

"I'm looking for my husband's box. They were all transferred here, weren't they?" Aila asks, scooting another hefty box to the side with no help.

"Easy there," Tori urges, grabbing her friend's shoulder.

"Do you know where it is?" Aila cries, on the verge of frantic behavior.

"Why?" she asks, eyeing the black book in Aila's hand.

"Because I've got to put this in it!"

Realizing what she's walked into, Tori's eyes widen as she searches amongst the various metal boxes.

"The first one is always the hardest," Tori chuckles, finding Mica's red box stuffed in an impossible corner. Frowning, Aila takes the box from Tori and flips it open, gently laying her only copy of the Bible on top of the various other artifacts that Mica has already collected.

Apparently, people are beginning to notice her naïvety. Aila never thought she would be this bad at being pregnant because she always wanted kids, therefore having a baby would be easy in her mind.

"It's nothing to be ashamed of. I remember when I was pregnant with Connor. It seemed like it would never end—the mood swings, bizarre cravings, not to mention the swollen ankles." Tori sits, grabbing her feet to shudder off the awful memories.

Glancing down at her own water-filled ankles, Aila lets a small smile loose. She's not the first, nor will she be the last woman to get pregnant. The only hope she can cling onto is the possibility that she'll look as good as Victoria when all is said and done. Everything about the woman is perfect. Her tan, foreign body, carved legs, thick brown hair. Aila is even willing to bet that her mid-section is the chiseled fantasy of every man.

"Can I ask you a question?" Aila abruptly asks.

"Sure!" she smiles, revealing another one of her perfections.

"Why did you leave Dan?" Aila asks, picking at her own teeth.

Although she's anticipated the question for months now, it doesn't make answering it any easier.

"I was stupid," Tori says.

Aila nods her head as if she understands the short, vague answer.

Tori knows the white lie is putting it lightly, but how else is she supposed to say it? She could go into this prolonged story of how her relationship with Dan was rocky from the get-go, and with the addictions his job encouraged, once the steamy passion cooled off, Tori's eyes opened to the man's many weaknesses. Don't get her wrong, she's flawed! No one knows this better than her, but some weaknesses are not ones to raise a family around, which, as ironically as it may seem, is the only reason they stayed together. All that passionate steam got her pregnant, and something in the back of her mind told her the kid would change the man, who at the time, she regretted marrying. At the very least, a kid has the right to a father, no matter how flawed. Dan didn't change however, and when Connor was two, she was sick and tired of the excuses from both her and Dan for the addictions. Being the arrogant woman that she was—and still is at times—Tori thought she could find a better father for her son.

"Seriously, I was stupid."

That, Tori tells herself, is the truth. Impatience, lack of understanding, and most of all arrogance taught her there was no better man for her and her son than Daniel Anthony Trax. The second she left it was a reality check for him, and straightaway he got his life back in order. Sure, there's been stumbles since, but once she saw him changed at her front door, she knew things would be different. Working for President White was the finishing touch on his fractured life. Reuben saw a younger version of himself in Dan, which is what she believes ultimately inspired Dan's reformation. He needed mentorship.

In hindsight, "stupid" may be a harsh thing to say—causes have effects after all—but to say that she was lucky he came back at all, that is anything but an understatement. They just needed time. Now, Connor has the father he needs.

Attempting to avoid another prying question, Tori blurts out, "You hungry?"

Aila bursts into a fit of laughter, nearly toppling over as she grabs her stomach, trying not to pee.

"Yeah," she finally says, her emotions somewhat under control. "Sorry…"

"No need to be sorry," Tori chuckles. "I've been there."

Before either of them can make the decision of what to eat though, the ground and walls begin to slowly rumble. After ten seconds it all stops as if it never happened and once it does, smiles stretching from ear to ear appear on the women.

They're home!

Shooting from off the balls of her feet, Tori lands delicately on her toes.

Show off, Aila thinks. It takes three attempts before she can get up, and even then, Victoria has to help her. Once both are up, they race to welcome their husbands. Victoria travels in a hybrid skip and angelic float, while Aila feels more like an aged penguin.

Up ahead, the growing cheers and shouts of hundreds of people can be heard.

"I can see them!" Victoria squeals, gliding to a stop on the edge of the crowd before wiggling her way closer to the front.

"Good for you," Aila mutters. *You want a medal or something*, she thinks—then quickly realizes how badly she is now craving one of those cheap chocolate coins.

When Aila arrives, she stumbles to a halt at one of the various pillars, taking a second to catch her breath. Despite her annoyance at her feeble state, it's impossible for her not to stand in awe at the engineering marvel of this facility. Thousands of tons of concrete would bury everyone in seconds if not for the pillared structure. It's a wonder how Sullivan's crew managed such an engineering feat.

Finally, under control, Aila straightens her posture as the team and refugees continue down the descending auto-ramp. Mica is barely discernable, and the only reason Aila can spot him is that he, unlike Dan,

Bella, and Sullivan, is the only one not waving to the mass of people. He's told her on a few occasions that never will he let what he is doing for the country go to his head. The moment he does will be the moment he loses himself.

As the ramp approaches the basement floor, it grinds to a halt, dispersing dust in every direction as it hits rock bottom. The few closest to the landing zone begin to frantically cough as they inhale the particles, Victoria being one of them. Aila says a little prayer of thanks for the tender mercy, for this is one of the only times when her awkward waddle-jog has been a blessing.

As the dust settles, in a matter of seconds, Aila spots her man. It's been over a week since she's been able to be in her husband's arms, and each second that he was gone, the image of him being killed haunted her every thought.

"Hey, beautiful," Mica says.

Aila begins choking on her tears as she throws herself in his arms.

"How's the little man holding up?" Mica asks, still in disbelief at how close he is to holding his boy. It's all been inconvenient timing, but he's finally concluded that no timing is ideal in today's world when it comes to anything, let alone having a baby.

"He's good." Aila smiles, not letting go of her husband. "How are you?" she then asks, glancing up and gazing into his bicolor eyes. She's especially missed those.

"I'm good now that I'm home," Mica says. Making sure to keep her close, he carefully pries free from Aila's embrace, reaching into his pocket. "I wrote him a letter."

"You what?" Aila asks, snatching the outreached envelope from his hand. "That's a little weird, don't you think?"

"Is it?" Mica shrugs. "Something could happen out there…"

"Don't like hearing that," Aila mumbles. Mica's always been a prepper, no matter how dark or bright the future is. "Can I read it?"

"Sure," he smiles.

Jax,

Our history is ours to write. Don't ever forget that. Your ancestors have shaped your past, we as your parents will help shape your present, but only you can shape the future. There will be times when you aren't sure what to do, and that is okay. All you need to know is who you are, never forgetting your potential.

I have seen many men fall away from their core beliefs through small and simple means. They dwell on insignificant details, hyper focusing on only that, losing sight of their surroundings and the bigger picture. In contrast, by small and simple things have great and marvelous things happened.

Your mother and I both love you more than we can express, and although I am writing this letter before you are born, it feels like I've known you all my life. You will accomplish great things, I know it. I can feel it. I hope to give this letter to you one day, but if that's not possible then as your mother would say: May God be with you until we meet again.

Your father,
Mica

"Jax, huh? You naming our son without me?"

"That's what you got out of that?" he teases, taking the letter back. "Do you not like it, the name?"

"Ask him," she retorts, looking down at her protruding stomach. The second she suggests it, her stomach flips and turns.

"You okay?" Mica asks, catching her before she falls.

"I think he likes it!" she laughs.

October 14, 2037

"Smile!"

Mica unsuccessfully tries dodging the incoming video camera. With a full-blown shot of a mouth stuffed with cheeseburger and chips, it's ironic that he can evade bullets and slip past knives, probably even a missile if one was ever shot at him, but never in a million years will he be able to get away from his wife holding a camera.

"You kidding me?" Mica sputters, burger particles spewing from his mouth.

"Nope!" Aila's smile widens as she turns the camera at herself for a beaming selfie. "Come on sweetie, these are memories you'll want to look back on."

"Yeah, sweetie!" Dan elbows him before chomping down on his own burger.

"Doubt it." Staring at his wife, Mica has a vengeful thought. "Did you get a shot of Victoria?"

"Nope!" She's been avoiding that bombshell all morning. The last thing she needs is another reason to hate her whale-like body.

"Well, here she comes!"

Whipping around, Aila tries getting eyes on the angel so she knows which way to run, but as she searches, she's gently taken to the ground in a swarm of tickles.

"Payback!"

Mica is relentless, and the only reason he doesn't let up is because he knows how much she hates the tickling sensation. Aila shouts and kicks, trying to buck her husband off, but with no success. The torment lasts for less than a minute, but to Aila it is an eternity, and once released, she slams a clenched fist right into Mica's chest, knocking him from his knees to his ass.

"Ouch!"

"Yeah, ouch!" she mocks. "Dumbass…" She grabs the video camera and attempts to get up from off the ground, but just topples around. She tries a second time with the same result before finally turning to her husband.

"Help me up so I can get away from you!"

Mica rolls his eyes, does as his wife wishes and sure enough, she storms off after one more slug to his arm.

He looks over to Dan, but all his friend does is shrug.

"You better go fix that," Dan states, taking another juicy bite of his burger.

"Holler at me when Carter gets here, will ya?"

Dan nods as he watches Mica leave to go save his marriage for what seems like the thousandth time this week. Those were the days. The only difference between Mica's current situation and Dan's previous one is that Dan's marriage *was* in jeopardy.

"Hey there, hot stuff," Tori says, waltzing up to Dan before sitting down and biting into what Dan knows to be the most putrid-smelling burger ever grilled.

"Is that—?"

"An impossible burger? Yes, it is!" she proudly states.

"Didn't your people like invent meat, or whatever?" Dan asks. Upon examination of her plate, he notices other abhorrent "healthy" food choices. What kind of woman has he gotten involved with—?

"Hey Dad!"

"What are you doing to him?" Dan suddenly protests, his son approaching with the exact same anti-American abominations littering his plate. "This is abuse!"

"Hamburgers are good, Dad…"

Dan motions for his son to come to him. As Connor gets close enough, Dan picks up the sorry excuse for patriotism and tosses the faux burger to the ground.

"Hey!" Connor whines.

"Relax." Dan turns and grabs the second hamburger from off his own plate. He was looking forward to it, but desperate times call for desperate measures. "Try that one!"

Tentatively, Connor picks up the juicy burger, eyeballing the greasy, salty concoction before looking over to his mom.

Tori rolls her eyes. "If you don't like it, blame your dad."

Glancing down at his veggie burger, which at this point is swarming with ants, Connor slowly takes a bite of the new burger, nibbling at the American classic. It takes a moment, but eventually the flavor registers, lighting the boy's eyes as he attacks the meaty sandwich, finishing it in a handful of bites.

Never having been prouder of his son, Dan throws his hands in the air triumphantly. "Voilà!" he shouts before turning to Tori.

"Whatever," she sighs, sticking her tongue out at both of them.

Enjoying his small victory, Dan looks over to his beautiful wife, realizing that he's never once questioned why. It's such a vague query, but all the same, there most definitely is a specific answer.

"Why did you take me back?" he asks.

Apparently, this is the topic of the week, she thinks, recalling yesterday's talk with Aila. She could say love, but then he'd continue to ask why until it was no longer an affectionate question. So, like the question was posed, Tori is simple and direct.

"Because you changed."

It's fair, but it stings, nonetheless. "It's not because you love me?"

Great, she thinks. *Just what I was trying to avoid—a downward spiral.* "Of course, I love you!"

Dan isn't one for self-deprecation, but when it comes to his family and his temptations, he is as vulnerable as a child.

"Do you feel like you settled?"

"Dan," she calmly but firmly begins. "You're ruining the day. I love you, Connor needs his real father, and it's as simple as that."

"Trax!" Carter shouts out over the party's commotion.

"Try this while you're at it," Dan says, standing and handing his boy his can of Sprite before turning to Tori for a kiss. "I'm sorry. You know how insecure I am about stuff like this."

She's sympathetic, which is why she gives him a big mustard-filled smooch.

"Disgusting!"

"I love you, Dan Trax!"

Connor echoes the affection, and turning from his jog towards Carter, Dan shouts his love back.

The three men step into a secluded part of the party and out of range of the numerous ears.

"Any word from Texas?" Mica begins.

Carter nods his head proudly. "They're on board."

"You can always rely on the Lone Star," Dan says.

Texas, better known these days as Area Twenty-Eight, was the last to accept and ratify the Nine as official presidents. Even then, everybody thought they were going to secede and fight as an independent nation, but like every other state, they caved—they just did it last. It wasn't until the Division started making headlines that they decided to jump back on the revolution wagon. It took some persuasion, but with Colorado on their side, Texans were more than eager to start a war.

"We still have a problem though," Carter says. "There is at least one state separating us from them. We have no physical connection to Texas. Any convoy or transfer of information must go through one of two different Areas."

"I'm not worried!" Dan practically shouts. "There's what, New Mexico and a sliver of Oklahoma between us and them? Oklahoma you know is good, and New Mexico can get there."

"All The Government needs is a little bit of doubt and they have more than that," Carter says. "The Nine knows the Division is here, and they figured we'd go for the next strongest state."

"Which we did," Mica adds.

"They've fortified the borders of those Areas, making it a territorial Fort Knox. I nearly got caught both ways."

"So, what do we do?" Mica asks. "We can't let that stop us."

"No, we can't," Carter says, thinking for a moment. This is only a contingency plan, but it's something they can work with if Texas is too dangerous. "I know this is a stretch, but I still have a lot of contacts in Vermont."

Mica's eyes widen. "We just left the East Coast, and you want to go back?"

"It's not ideal, but it can be something we could work with. Just because it's on that side of the country doesn't mean it's a lost cause. Yes, it's across multiple state lines, but for that very reason, it's not something the Nine thinks we'd be looking into. If played right, it'd be a diversion away from Texas."

Both Mica and Dan shrug, seeing Carter's point.

"All I'm saying is that it's an option worth considering."

"I have a question," Dan then says.

"Is it relevant to the dilemma?" Mica asks.

"Not sure," Dan shrugs. "It's been bothering me ever since we got here."

Carter nods. "Sounds relevant to me."

"There have been talks of a eugenics program."

"What kind of eugenics?" Mica slowly asks.

"A genetic modification program to eliminate undesired genes that will target specific races and ethnicities."

"Thank you for the definition," Mica sighs out. "The point?"

"I don't trust the Stones," Dan says bluntly.

"Of course you don't." Mica throws his arms up as if this is no surprise. "He hates your wife."

"And why does he hate my wife?" Dan asks. "And Lisa?"

"Because he's racist." Carter states the obvious. "Hard core, old school racist. It's nothing new and he does a poor job of hiding it."

"Exactly!" Dan blurts, holding out his arms in hopes that this insight will yield a new perspective on the concrete walls of the DIA. "He brought us here, but why? Do you honestly believe what he says about this place—about *why* he brought us here?"

"I've known him a long time," Mica says. "And Bella even longer, and yeah, he may be a dick sometimes but he's loyal, that I know for certain. Not to mention, we need both him and Bella to pull this off."

Carter points at him. "I have to agree with Mica."

"Loyal to who?" Dan asks.

Mica shakes his head. "What are you saying?"

"Are the Stones loyal to us or the Nine?" Dan questions, bringing Mica's suppressed fears to the surface. "I've done some digging and found out that some of the genocide theories about this place may be true."

"And where did you get your information?" Mica demands.

"From locals. I've gone out and asked around. I've also noticed how liberal this state is." He holds up his hand, ready to tally off more things to support his case. "It was the first state to legalize cocaine, heroin, and all previously illicit drugs; it was the first state to implement strict gun control laws and limit one gun per household—not California or New York—and to top it all off, it was the first state to ratify its Area status. I'm willing to bet that the official story the Stones sold to the Division is only partly true."

"That is quite the stretch," Mica argues, not wanting to hear of this possible truth—not about Bella or Sullivan.

"At least I'm asking!" Dan growls, his retort reaching some other ears at the party. "What if we're here because this is the easiest place to eliminate the Division, and by proxy, the United States? We've put all our eggs in this basket…"

It sounds farfetched. Dan's theory is too thin, but in an effort of sounding reasonable, Carter offers some reassurance. "We have an emergency drill in the works in case anything does happen."

"Which Bella oversees. You guys keep proving my point!" Dan throws his hand up in exasperation.

Mica, slowly seeing Dan's perspective, looks to Carter. "We could have a team look into it."

Stewing on the influx of info, Carter can't come to an immediate definitive conclusion. "I'll talk with Lisa, and we'll go from there."

"Thank you," Dan says. He can't ask for much more than that.

"Next order of business is City Hall," Carter begins.

"That glass building?" Mica asks for clarification.

"Yeah. But before I forget," Carter says, folding his hands, "let's pray." Turning to Dan, Carter asks him to lead them.

With a grimace, Dan hesitantly states, "Still think it's weird…"

"Fair," Carter chuckles at Dan's honesty. Carter himself was there not too long ago.

TWENTY

Raider Encampment

With only faint mechanical clicks and electronic whirs trickling in the background, Jax's eyes slowly flutter open. Scattered medical supplies and bloody engine parts create a hybrid horror show, and as he makes strenuous efforts to simply rotate his aching neck from left to right, Jax searches for the origin to the elusive sounds. Against his right leg, Jax sees the mechanism as it hums and processes data, and unsure of what to make of the slab of metal gears, tentatively reaches out with his right hand. To his surprise, the metal object twitches—not as if it was bumped or nudged, but as if on its own accord. The moment he thought to touch it, the machine contracted much like an arm would have.

Again, Jax attempts to investigate with the same lively result.

"What the hell?"

Upon closer examination, a theory begins to formulate in his mind, the frightening details becoming apparent. The metal-beamed machine has a hand—a hand with four detailed fingers and an opposable thumb, and every intricate hinge, tiny rod, and minute piston are both fascinating and horrifying.

Slowly, Jax thinks, but as the thought crosses the synapses in his brain, the metal prosthetic is brought to life. Reaching forward and grasping thin air, bit by bit Jax's eyes follow the metal fingertips to the artificial wrist and then from the wrist to the pistons in the elbow. The elbow connects what should be a fleshy bicep until finally the mechanical muscle connects to the tissue of Jax's shoulder.

Part of Jax hopes this is just a dream—that it's a way his brain is processing trauma—but as the memory begins to flutter back, he realizes that this is in fact reality. First there was pain—agony—as he bends his arm, recalling the sentiment. Then, noise. Helicopters, aircraft, explosions and gunfire. Finally, his memory reminds him of the apology—but for what?

"Wanna switch?" a raspy, hoarse chuckle asks from the corner of the tent.

Origins

Bruised, beaten, and bleeding, Rhett Stone lies face up on a bed, hanging onto life by a wire running from his heart into a generator not two feet away. Searching his memory for anything that can clue him into where, what, why and how the surreal scene was painted, no memory yields itself to Jax.

"What happened?"

"You got the lucky end of the bargain, that's what happened," Rhett scoffs, coughing multiple times, each one creating a digital statistic on the monitor next to him. "Look at that thing. You're a literal cyborg now."

"Why?" Jax asks, not sure how to fully pose the question as he looks to his mechanical arm.

"Because Dan told them to," Rhett replies, chalking up the question as daft to say the least. "Just be grateful. A lot of resources were expended on your behalf."

"Kill the bastards!" a mass chant erupts from outside the shabby tent. "Kill, kill, kill the white bastards!"

"Soothing, isn't it?" Rhett closes his eyes as if actually finding solace in the death hymn. "How long do you think you've been out?"

"Rhett, what is going on?"

"Three days," Rhett mumbles. "You've been out for three days."

"Three days?"

"Yep," Rhett coughs. "You want a recap, because I really don't want to give you one?"

"Kill, kill, kill the white bastards."

Three days since what? Jax asks himself, his eyes widening as the floodgates to his memory suddenly open.

"Mari!"

"Looks like it's coming back," Rhett says, his eyes still peacefully closed.

"Where's Mari?" Jax asks, the details becoming more vivid by the second.

"Kill, kill, kill."

"I already said that I don't want to fill you in…" Rhett sighs out.

"Where's Mari?" Jax then shouts, the crowd silencing for a moment as they listen in to the tent.

"Listen man... the high-level overview is that she's gone."

"Gone?" Jax groans, disbelieving the simplistic answer.

"Yeah," Rhett coughs. "And not just her. Dozens of others were killed and taken by the PPA; the Encampment is divided because of everything you, Renn, Connor have done here..." He's seen it a hundred times within the PPA and has read about it countless more. Division creates confusion, and confusion primes the pump for a power vacuum, and it's here where opportunists graciously show their faces. If there is one thing Rhett is willing to bet whatever life he has left on, it's that Kai will try something before this all comes to an end.

"Kill, kill, kill," the crowd starts back up.

"Where is she?" Jax then yells. *She can't be dead,* he thinks to himself. *That's not how—it's not supposed to be like this.* "Where is she?"

"Buddy, you need to calm down or the docs are going to—"

"WHERE IS SHE?! WHERE IS SHE?! WHERE IS SHE?!" Repeatedly shouting the question, each time Jax's voice rises, signaling to the monitor at his bedside of the rise in vital measurements.

Jax attempts to stand, but is stopped by seven leather belts binding him from feet to chest. Reaching with his newly equipped arm, Jax tears through the first like wrapping paper before reaching for the second, where it too tears with ease. Taking hold of the third strap, Jax is stopped as six Raiders rush inside, pinning him back down on the table.

"I tried telling you," Rhett coolly states.

"Hold him!" one Raider commands as another attempts to re-strap one of the leather belts. The moment he lets go to readjust though, Jax's arm thrashes forward, knocking the Raider unconscious.

"Get me a tranquilizer!" another shouts, desperately trying to compete with Jax's strength. From across the tent a medic rushes to a set of cabinets, pulling out a small bottle and needle before running back over. While four others each pin a limb, the doctor hastily measures out a dose of the sedative before plunging the syringe into Jax's thigh. The violent writhing doesn't stop however, and as Jax lurches forward, his mechanical arm knocks another to the other side of the tent where he stumbles and crashes into the medical supplies. The doctor, moving to prepare another dose, stops as he watches Jax begin to slur his words, his swings and kicks immediately becoming uncoordinated.

"Grab him before he falls," the doctor shouts out.

Catching him, the three remaining Raiders move Jax back over to a bed where they strap him down.

"Where is Mari?" Jax mumbles, the question further softened as the image of her smile and the kiss they shared moves to the forefront of his memory.

"Your body needs rest," the doctor says, injecting one last dose into Jax's leg as he does.

As sleep begins to overtake him, the serenity of their intimate moment is interrupted. Moving her lips away, Mari looks down at his arm where the memory is swiftly erased by a white, blinding, explosive heat.

★

"Do you remember the time when Mother and Father went to Area Thirteen, leaving us home alone for the first time?" Rhett's raspy voice asks.

"Yeah, we got in so much trouble," Renn chuckles.

Jax's eyes open, but as they do, he keeps as still as he possibly can. The sedative left a lethargic wave as it passed through his system, and to avoid a spinning scene, Jax keeps from abrupt movements and just listens to the voices that woke him.

Rhett then makes a mocking impression of what Jax thinks to be Caspian. "I told you not to go into the warehouse, didn't I?"

"Where was Connor again?" Renn asks as she scours her memory.

Rhett thinks on it for a moment. "I don't know. There's no way he left with them, did he?"

Before any of them can figure it out though, Connor's booming voice enters the tent. "I was reading in my room."

"He was reading in his room," Renn snaps her fingers as if remembering on her own.

Kneeling next to his sister, Connor looks from Rhett to Renn, subtly answering her concerning question before she can ask it.

"Oi!" Rhett blurts out. "I'm not stupid!"

Gently, Renn places her hand on Rhett's and with more tears than intended asks, "Remember that fight Connor and Casp got into?"

"How could I forget?" Rhett replies and is thrown into a coughing fit as he remembers the terrific memory, weakly swinging his arms in his reenactment of the fight. "Connor had him pinned in two seconds flat."

"It was ten," Connor corrects.

"Whatever." Rhett shrugs. "Once you had his face in the ground, he began to cry, I swear."

Renn laughs as she too recalls the fight. "I thought Casp was going to win!"

"Your vote of confidence goes a long way…" Connor scoffs.

"What were you guys even fighting about?"

"Caspian was going to rape a girl."

As abrupt as the answer is, an awkward silence fills the room, killing all laughter on the spot, the gravity of the current situation spilling in to the happy void.

"Nothing like good old family memories to sober us up," Rhett remarks.

Not being one for emotionally cramped settings, Connor stands.

"I'll be back. Keep an eye on his vitals," he says, patting Rhett on the shin and kissing the top of Renn's head.

"I wish Connor had been there when this happened," Renn says, looking down, firmly grasping her twin's hand. Caspian wouldn't have dared attack Rhett if he had been.

"He's just misunderstood," Rhett quietly says.

"Who? Caspian? How can you say that? After what he did to you? After he took Ann?"

"He's my brother."

"And what is Connor? If Caspian's *your* brother, what does that make me?"

Rhett chuckles at the silly question. "It makes you my sister. Just because—"

"He's evil!" Renn interrupts. "How can you not see that?"

When your flesh and blood are at war with each other, how can you not suffer with both causes? Can't there be a balance? Can't Rhett be that equilibrium? He understands where Caspian is coming from. He empathizes with the man, which has only allowed him to see the irony of the Raiders' own cause. While their sentiments are just, divided or not, their ideals are no different from Caspian and the Nine. This war is nothing more than a power struggle between extreme ends, the pendulum swinging from one radical to another.

"This isn't fair," Renn whispers.

"Life isn't fair," Rhett counters, his hand touching her soft cheek before lifting her chin. "Renn?"

She can't… She won't open her eyes. As much as she wants to believe he'll pull through, she's seen people die from lesser injuries. Out of fear of regret, though, she moves her gaze to his.

"Renn, you can't trust the Raiders."

"How can you say that?" Renn sputters out.

"You've read Marx," Rhett says. "This power shift is nothing new to human nature. They want exactly what the Nine wants."

"Not all of them," she softly whispers.

"No, but they are few and far between…"

This is something Renn has been willfully blind to, but feared, nonetheless. Radicalism is humanity's endless loop of self-correction, and it doesn't matter if some side with Jax and the rest of them. More and more of the majority are becoming sympathetic to the duality of Kai's cynical ideology that there are Raiders or there are PPA—there are allies and enemies and nothing more.

This is an inevitable outcome, unless of course there's a catalyst from within.

"Get Ann back..." Rhett urges, wiping her tears away. "Whether you fight with the Raiders or not, get that little girl back. Make something right in this world."

Renn nods, more tears trickling down her cheeks.

"And take care of Connor. I have no idea who's going to once I'm gone."

Renn knows he's trying to lighten the mood, but the morbid joke falls flat. Instead, she lets her head fall to her loving brother's chest, the sound of his beating heart and labored breath echoing in her ears.

"Renn?"

She hears Rhett but continues to wallow, her growing cries muffled in the blanket.

"Renn. I need you to focus." It takes some effort on Rhett's part, but eventually he's able to lift her puffy and swollen eyes up from off his chest. "They have a plan."

"Who?" Renn asks.

"Everyone," he says. "Everyone has an agenda. The Nine. The Raiders. Everyone wants their piece of the pie." As Rhett says this, he runs his fingertips over the tallied scars on her wrist. "*Everyone* wants to control someone."

"What the hell am I supposed to do with that, Rhett?" Renn asks, flustered by his ambiguity.

"You remember the lessons we had in genetic engineering and modification?"

"Of course. Mother and Father seemed to have an abnormal fascination with the subject."

"That's because they created a program—a program that will shape the world as we know it," he says, looking to the shadows of the countless protesting Raiders outside. "Everyone wants their piece..."

"How will the world change?"

A heavy, raspy sigh, the last one Rhett will yield, is released. "The super soldier myth. Sounds stupid, but it's real. They've created an army, each soldier as strong if not stronger than you, me, and Caspian. We were just tests."

"I don't understand. Why the army?"

Rhett pulls his sister towards him and lays his head down on top of hers, noticing as he does that across the way, Jax is awake and attentive. Without moving or shifting his weight in acknowledgment, Rhett just continues to stare at him dead in the eyes, making sure he understands what's at stake. With a reassuring nod from Jax, Rhett gives his last gesture: a simple wink of gratitude.

"Renn. Save Ann. Stop being a pawn—for the Nine, the Raiders, or anyone…" Rhett's eyes shut, and without warning the machine at his bedside beeps. The first beep goes unnoticed, but as they continue, they jolt Renn to her senses.

"Rhett?" she cries, her voice filled with concern.

The beeps grow louder and more rapid, and as they do, Rhett slowly rests his head back on his bed.

"Don't do this, Rhett!" Renn pleads, but the beeps mercilessly continue to grow faster and louder.

She searches for something, anything to keep him with her.

"Remember that time when—?" she begins, unable to finish the thought, her words mixing with her growing sense of dread. "I'll get Ann back!"

The beeps are at an uncomfortably intense pace, matching each pattering tear that drips from off Renn's cheeks until finally they abruptly merge into one continuous tone.

"Rhett?" Renn shakes her brother. "Rhett!"

She continues to shake him, but of course, there's no response, and once she finally accepts his passing, she buries her head back into his chest to find what little comfort she can in his diminishing warmth.

Before she can fully come to terms with losing her other half, a dozen Raiders from outside rush in, yanking her from Rhett's body. Hitting one in the crotch with a sharp elbow, Renn then kicks the knee of another backwards as she fights to stay by her brother's side. With seven more entering the tent, her combative spirit is smothered as a rag is shoved into her face, putting her to sleep in a matter of seconds.

"Renn!" Jax shoots up from his bed, tearing through the straps holding him down as he charges their attackers. Utilizing the newly equipped metal arm, Jax sends one flying ten feet backwards and out the entrance of the tent. It takes four men to wrangle down his one mechanical arm and another three for the rest of his body, but once under enough control, the same rag that rendered Renn unconscious muffles Jax's shouts of protestation, until he too becomes limp and useless.

As the Raiders catch their breath and begin tending to those wounded in the brief encounter, in walks Kai, casually observing the scene before him.

"Burn the dead one's body. Take the other two out to the clearing with Connor…"

"Little girl?" the old lady asks, praying that the child is not dead this time. There has been enough death these past few hours to last a lifetime. "Ann!"

Finally, Ann hears the old lady's petitioning pleas as she's jarred awake. With her eyes still focusing, the only stark detail is the bleak, grim atmosphere of her iron surroundings. Packed in a single metal room, dozens of people captured from the Encampment cluster together as far away as they can from the massive, locked entryway on the other end.

Shoved in the far corner with an elderly woman, Ann gets to her feet as their prison doors are heaved open, permitting three beastly PPA officers to walk in.

With guns aimed, trained to kill anyone daring enough to move, the one who appears to be in charge shouts, "All of you! On your feet!"

Conditioned by death and pain, the surviving Raiders jump up, their hands behind their heads. Scoping her surroundings, Ann can't help but let out a soft chuckle. These soldiers act like they're in front of armed and hostile savages. There's not a single man—Ann can only assume they've been killed—and as for the women and children, it's not like any of them can usurp the Nine all by themselves.

"You think this is funny?" the one in charge asks.

A little surprised he noticed her snickering, Ann doesn't let it show as she faces the direct question.

"No sir," she says, naturally mocking the man by comically erecting her body and standing at the position of military attention.

"Then why do you have a stupid smile on your face?" And without waiting for Ann to respond, the PPA officer gives Ann a fierce backhand, knocking her back three feet, instantly wiping her smirk away. Bouncing off the far wall, Ann stumbles right back into the PPA officer's vicinity. "Huh?!" he shouts, the one-word retort echoing in the tiny concrete and iron room, everybody falling silent as it does.

"Didn't have a chance to answer you, sir," Ann simply says. "You smacked me before I could."

"A smart ass…" the man mumbles, smacking Ann a second time across the face. Looking the frail little girl up and down, he then whispers something to Ann that only she can hear. "You're almost old enough, you know?"

Ann gags at the grotesque remark. Being intimidated is the furthest thing from her thought process. She can thank Mari for her indifferent outlook on death, she being the tough cookie that she is, but it wasn't until finding the Raiders that Ann began applying this unwavering courage. If she's going to die, she's going to die and there's nothing she can do about it. Everybody dies, every regime falls, and it'll only be a matter of time before the Nine and The Government must face their own inevitable end. This is the hope and liberating perspective some of the Raiders gave her, and she'll be damned if she gives that up because of some guy who measures the size of his dick by how hard he hits a child.

"You have no idea what I could do to you," the officer says.

"You really think I care?"

Whatever commotion was left in the room, it truly falls silent upon hearing Ann's bold David and Goliath statement.

"What did you say?"

"You heard me, you prick," she says, stating each word with bold emphasis.

For a moment, the PPA officer is speechless, resorting to his sole pathological response, delivering another heavy backhand that again sends Ann backwards.

"Do you even know why you're here?" the officer chuckles out, his rage masked by a delirious tone. He waits for a moment, letting the rhetorical question set in, Ann's heavy breathing the only audible human sound. "Why are you here?" he then asks, gripping Ann's hair and standing her on her feet.

"For pleasure?" she grimaces, and although her smile is puffy and bleeding, it's managed to find its way back onto her face.

"You're lab rats." The officer smirks. "You are tests, and after every one of you are dead, we can hand your bodies over to your families and friends in separate bags. There'll be a bag for your arms, one for your legs, and I'll personally deliver the ones your heads are in."

Then, dropping Ann to her knees, the officer grabs the young woman just next to her before motioning to his two other minions to do the same. After each has picked out a sufficient female, the three brutes leave, locking the door behind them.

"Yeah, right," Ann mumbles. If they were going to cut them up into little pieces, they would have done it by now.

The old lady Ann has vaguely gotten to know as Mihi, approaches and examines the fresh cuts and bruises.

"You're a different one," Mihi says, helping Ann to her feet.

"Is that a good or bad thing?" Ann smiles.

"Only time will tell, young one," Mihi shrugs and with surprising strength, carries her over to a corner of other women.

"How old are you?" Ann asks Mihi.

"Old enough to have seen children and grandchildren grow up and die."

"I'm sorry." Ann blushes, having not expected such an abrasive response.

"Don't be. They all died fighting the good fight, and for that, I'm proud."

"I wish I could say the same…"

"Wish you could say the same about who?"

"No one…" Ann quietly says, her thoughts going back to Mari in the tent, bruised and bleeding worse than Ann's current condition, the image forever seared in her young mind. Rancid water, molding food, no fingernails, cuts and burns in unimaginable places, and of all people it was him. *Jackie* did that to her sister.

Mihi, seeing an all-too-familiar look sagging on Ann's young face, takes the little girl's chin in her hand. "War does things to people—it changes them. It's changed some of us Raiders."

"And that makes it okay?"

"Of course not! It doesn't mean you can't still love them. Although their works may be dark, it doesn't mean their hearts aren't yearning to be in the light."

"Good intentions," Ann scoffs. She would very much like to disagree, but her exhaustion wins the debate. "Maybe you're right…"

"I know I am," Mihi chuckles, gently touching Ann's face. "I used to be one of them." And then before Ann can respond or inquire any further, Mihi raises her head to the crowd of women and children. "Let us pray."

Not a single protest is heard because in times like these, there is nothing else one can do. Those who are able, kneel, and those who aren't all reverently bow their heads where they lay.

"Oh God, our loving God in heaven to whom we pray…"

———·★·———

Denver International Airport
December 25, 2037

Nothing is more terrifying than to have a missing child amidst violent chaos…

Finishing his business, the little boy flushes the urinal. Squeamish from the water splashing out at his hands, Kai stumbles backwards and bumps into an older gentleman, scuffing the shiniest shoes he's seen outside of his cousin's Air Jordans.

"You little prick," the man states. "I just got these polished..." Who cares if it was just a child! All he needed was to take a piss before the meetup, and apparently, that was a mistake.

"Sorry," Kai mumbles, trying to move past the man. Being broke and from the inner city, Kai hasn't had very many opportunities to travel, and on the few occasions he has, it's never been by plane. So, to say that he isn't entirely aware of the social etiquette in a situation like this is an understatement.

"Is your *sorry* going to keep me from looking like a piece of shit in front of a future client?"

"Hey!" From around the corner, Kai's dad pokes his head out from behind the wall dividing the sinks and toilets. "You mind watching your language?"

The businessman, first looking to Kai and then back to his father, just gives a miffed click of the tongue. He's already late. Without an apology or demanding one himself, he simply picks up his carryon and walks out.

"Freaking disgusting," Dad says, waving his hand underneath the paper towel dispenser. "Whitey didn't even wash his hands."

"Sorry, Dad," Kai then says to his father, the guilt of the whole encounter weighing on him.

"You just got to watch where you're going. Not saying the pale face was in the right, but you just gotta pay attention."

"Yeah," Kai says, stepping up to the kids' sink.

"I'll be outside," his dad says, throwing away the used, moist paper towel.

He doesn't have much, but at least he has two parents, Kai thinks as he watches his dad leave. Most, if not all, of his friends have just their mom, and most, if not all, of their older siblings have issues with law enforcement and gang violence. Peers is probably a better word... The only time he's allowed to associate with them is at school. Once he gets into football and basketball, Kai knows he'll be able to see them more, and *maybe* become their friends, but even then, he's doubtful. With the strict academic regiment his parents have him on, Kai has little confidence that he'll ever be able to "hang out with the boys." But if he's being honest, he's okay with that. Kai's okay if it's just him and his mom and dad. He's still got his cousins that he sees at least once a month, if not more, and with what he wants to do when he grows up, Kai's grateful that he has parents who care about his dreams as much as he does. Owning a car repair and detailing shop, his parents work extremely hard and make sure that he has the same work ethic in school.

His peers—well they can't say the same…

Even before Plan B, riots were commonplace where he lives. As much as his parents try to shield him from the woes and biases of the world, they themselves are imperfect and the internet and social platforms can infect anyone. Yes, Kai's parents make sure to monitor his internet activity, but again, his peers' parents don't have the same standards and expectations, and the race riots are all they talk about these days. That and porn, but Kai is more interested in the riots, knowing *for a fact* his dad would murder him if he ever found out he was looking at girls the way his peers do. He's also had a natural interest in politics despite his age. While everyone at school talks about the cool new tv or phone their brother got from looting, Kai notices the dynamics of the different groups involved—white people in particular. Not only do they try to tell his parents how to vote, where to vote, how to run their business, and ultimately what to think, they do so with absolutely no context about their situation.

He's heard the term "Uncle Tom" on more than one occasion, and again, as young as Kai is, his talent for discernment of what "the whitey" wants is eerily accurate. The Democrat, as his dad would say before the United States disappeared, is one that wants to suppress the black community; they always have. Infamously known for implementing poll taxes, supporting the KKK, and creating a welfare system, that's old news, but the ways they backhandedly offer their help with continued and renewed socialistic policies and reparation programs, it's as if the Dems want them to want the government's money. Money is a form of ownership, after all.

Kai still is sorting through the intricacies of the cultural situation, but from what he's heard his parents talk about—and from his own observations within his community—white Liberals seem to treat black people like they're stupid and ignorant rather than expecting them to pull their own weight. That's a gross generalization, but as someone who comes from a family that owns their own business, he identifies with the latter point of view. Yes, he is convinced that no one party is the answer to all his people's problems, but the Progressives seem to be the cause of them, the white ones in particular. What does a kid like him know though?

Like his dad, Kai waves his hand underneath the towel dispenser. When nothing happens, he jumps to see if the height will help trigger the sensor, and as he lands, the earth beneath him quakes in a powerful rumble. Kai keeps his balance, but when he hears the screams and shouts of terror outside, he begins to panic.

"Mom!" he calls out. "Dad," he then screams, slipping and exiting the bathroom as fast as his little legs will allow. Continuing to shout, Kai's crying pleas of confusion are drowned out by the sheer uproar the airport is in. With three more shattering explosions, the madness only grows, adding to his disorientation, and before he can hope to find his mom or dad, a fourth blast shakes through the terminal followed by a fifth, sixth, seventh, and then eighth.

Area Thirty-Eight
Twenty Years Later

"In position," Kai whispers into the microphone. "How long do you want me to hold?"

"Until we need you," the voice on the other end states.

"Obviously. I'm asking when the hell that will be?" Kai demands, but there's no reply. In fact, there's a brief mic pop which tells Kai that his team just cut off communication with him. "Asshole..."

Kai wants in on the action, but for some reason, everyone else has other plans. Sitting on the outskirts of the convoy's route and in the shadows of the tree line, Kai can't help but be a little annoyed Dan didn't have him spearhead the operation. With a simple divide and conquer approach, it's going to be an easy operation, let alone, if their intel is half correct, they'll have one of the Stone children in custody by the end of the night—something that has the potential of changing the Raiders' fate in the ongoing fight.

He's not a kid anymore! Why can't Dan see that? Kai tries and tries to be grateful for what the father figure has done for him over the years, but sometimes he just can't see deeper than Dan's white skin. His wife Céleste, the only person that's grounding him at the moment, keeps telling him to let it go. She keeps telling him to be patient. Dan isn't a bad man, but, if Kai's being honest, he hasn't trusted anyone in a long time, especially those that look like his surrogate father.

Glancing at the bracelet and the dangling charms his wife made him, Kai refocuses on the mission—on getting himself and the team back home safely.

It's only a couple minutes of radio silence before the convoy rounds the bend at the point of the mountain. About five kilometers out, Kai picks up his rifle and aims down the scope at the lead vehicle, counting back seven to the rear. *A standard convoy*, Kai thinks. Nothing heavily armed, which will make their approach that much faster, and if the PPA soldiers are following SOP, the target should be in the second or third vehicle. Shifting his aim to the team, Kai spots them patiently waiting, strategically dispersed on both sides of the road—three on the north and two on the south. As Kai moves his aim back and forth from the convoy to the team, he visualizes the plan, trying to find any sort of last-minute weakness within it.

Detonating the charge on the fourth vehicle, Sergeant Brekken cuts the PPA convoy in half, making them an easier force to handle. The second and third charges then ignite on the lead and rear vehicles, blockading the entire line on the choke point, isolating the second and third trucks. At only eleven hundred meters now, with his long rifle, Kai takes out the heavy gunners on vehicles five, six, and seven. It wasn't in the brief, but rarely are these things verbatim. As he watches Brekken and his group secure the two lead vehicles from the north, from the south Bravo team cleans up the remaining PPA soldiers in the rear before the operation takes a drastic and unprecedented turn.

In the third vehicle, out pops the two Stone boys—first Caspian, and then the younger Rhett. Before Kai can get a bead on them, Caspian kills Brekken's second-in-command before Rhett takes out the other Raider from the north. Firing off a chain of suppressive fire, Brekken links up with the remaining two Raiders where they quickly coordinate before attempting to flank Caspian and Rhett. The two Stones must have a tactical suspicion about Kai's sniper position, because instinctively, they move behind one of the burning vehicles that acts as both cover and concealment.

"Damn it to hell," Kai swears before abandoning his position and sprinting to the fight. "Brekken, do you read? Do not advance on the target. I do not have eyes on. Say again, do not advance!"

As expected, Kai's advice is only met with radio silence. Moron probably never turned his radio back on after he cut off the transmission. Regardless, Kai continues his move on the battle, tactically checking in on Brekken's team from what cover he can find along the way. When Kai is a two hundred meters out, gunshots begin to reemerge as the Raiders then advance on Caspian and Rhett. Kai is still unable to see the two Stones but watches as both of Brekken's remaining men are shot in the head. Throwing out a smoke grenade, Brekken screens his flank on what Kai believes to be Caspian and Rhett's position. Brekken then quickly falls out of Kai's sight before a long silence fills the battlefield. Figuring the Stones are fixated on Brekken's move, Kai begins to make his way forward, cautiously closing the two-hundred-meter distance between him and the burning vehicles. With nothing to fix his sights on, Kai keeps his gun trained on Caspian and Rhett's last known position. As he gets closer, Kai hears the roaring, crackling fires before a short three-round burst shatters the stillness in the air.

Dropping to a knee, Kai waits for a second three-round burst, but doesn't hear one.

"Shit," he whispers, knowing that Brekken was just killed, leaving him the lone Raider on the field of battle with two children of the Nine.

Being way too close to engage with the Stones, Kai has no choice but to retreat. With two options at his disposal—speed or silence—Kai opts for the former. He may not completely disappear unnoticed, but Kai's fast and he can at least be out of effective firing range before they spot his retreat. Drawing two smoke grenades and frag, Kai pops the smokes ten meters in front of him before throwing the frag up and over the fiery vehicle. Just as the smoke begins to hiss out and up, the explosion from his frag grenade bursts, adding to the confusion of his retreat. With the failed ambush seventy-five meters behind him, Kai begins hearing gunshots that are followed by whistles past his head and the zip of ricocheting bullets. Tossing a second and third smoke grenade down behind him, Kai continues to sprint back to the tree line as he increases the distance by another hundred meters.

With the sounds of shots ceasing, Kai stumbles into the foothills before looking back. In the distance and behind the heat of the burning trucks, Kai sees both Caspian and Rhett looking in his direction. They don't advance, knowing he now has the upper hand, but rather, bunker back down. For a split second, Kai thinks to make one final attack, but the thought is quickly cut off at the sound of an approaching aircraft. Knowing that he has only a few minutes before the Owl has a potential thermal reading, Kai starts up his mountain motorcycle and hauls ass out of the area, cursing God that the Stones will live to fight another day.

—\·★·/—

Raider Encampment
Present Day

"Justice—this is why we are here," Kai yells out, the multitude erupting in a roar of cheers.

As the instigator of the rage, Kai looks to the white traitors, his imagination reveling in the thoughts of every one of their deaths. While it's more than easy to picture each of their heads on a pole, mouths agape and eyes rolled into their skulls, he relishes in doing things right and making that vision a reality.

"Son! What are you doing?" Dan shouts out, seeing the bastardized trial before him. He sensed division within the Encampment, but never did he think that it would escalate to this mob justice. Dan moves to stop the abomination before him, gesturing for other surrounding Raiders to help, but the former leader is blatantly ignored. After all he's done, in blind, emotional outrage they are willing to dismantle what they've built together.

"What you lacked the spine to do..." Kai mumbles, in a pathetic attempt to avoid Dan's gaze. Rather than taking them to trial, risking their acquittal, Kai took matters into his own hands. It's the only way he can finish what he always wanted to start. "Does anyone wish to state their testimony before the gathering vote?"

"The gathering?" Renn whispers on her knees, shaking her head at the irony. Rhett was right. They are the very thing they deplore.

"Kai!" Dan shouts back out as he forces his way through the crowd. "Stop this madness!" Once to the front, Dan approaches Kai in a demand for reason, but before he can say anything more, Kai throws a wild punch, connecting with the side of Dan's head.

As the man drops to his knees in utter shock, the mumbling crowd is momentarily silenced before scattered chuckles begin to move throughout the horde. Some even have the audacity to threateningly approach the downed, former leader, but as Connor stands up and steps next to Dan, their advance is immediately halted.

"Death or exile!" Kai blares out, roaring laughter growing from the crowd and accenting his declaration. "Now again, is there anyone willing to state a testimony?" No one steps forward, and for a long moment, Jax, Connor, Renn, and now Dan await the next fixed condemnation.

Dan's heart breaks as he watches Kai be the catalyst for the seeping corruption that is now within the tribe. He brought that boy and every one of these individuals together in hopes of getting away from the crony collectivism that brought down the United States in the first place. Now it seems that only emotion is the primary ruling force at play.

However, in an act that reignites hope, Kai's smug crowing is cut off by a single elderly woman speaking up and raising her hand.

"Aye, I wish to state a testimony."

Emotions begin to boil as she steps forward, everyone knowing what her intentions are. Allowing order to overrule his cynicism, Kai knows that there is nothing this woman can do to change the predetermined fate, and as a grin creeps across his face, the populist judicial process he's manufactured plays the role it's been designed to. Pure democracy is a beautiful thing in moments like these, and as murmurs turn into shouts, not a single person allows room for her to speak.

The woman, however, stands resolute in her conviction, barely resting on the cane by her side, and once in front of the mobbed assembly, she turns without waiting for silence. These enraged protestations will be their demise.

"Enough blood has been spilt in this country—on our land!" the woman shouts out, her combative tone an unsettling one to the most hostile Raiders present. While some reach for her shoulder, their hands being swiftly smacked away by her cane, others take exception to her words with vitriol and fiery rhetoric.

"Race traitor!" one shouts out. "Those white, filthy pigs deserve to die! They ruined our land. They brought the PPA here to kill us!"

"No!" the woman shouts back, stabbing her cane in the air at the man. "No, Dajun! Our land, this land has been polluted by us, not these four! Look at you, wanting death over mercy? Your mother would be ashamed of you. And you Kai, condemning your own father?"

The commotion dies down, all eyes waiting for him to meet the accusation.

"The white man is not my father," Kai mutters.

"He raised you, did he not?"

"The people did!" His shout of contempt slowly stirs the masses back into outrage. "The white man is *nobody's* father!"

"Wrong again, my boy. He found you orphaned and took you in when you had no one else."

"My real father was killed by the same government that these four brought into our Encampment."

"And Céleste?" she calmly asks, looking to the charmed bracelet around Kai's wrist. "What would she think?"

"She's dead," Kai grits out, the weight of the decorated ornament heavy on his wrist.

"You don't know that," she continues, her resolve unwavering. "Dan took care of you. Dan raised you, he raised her, and everyone here that condemns him."

"And what of the other three?" Kai snaps, stepping toe to toe with the woman. "Let's say you're right about Dan. Do *they* deserve my trust as well?"

"Yes," she defiantly states. "Your father trusts them and so should you."

Kai smirks. "And what of Kip Wright?" He turns to the crowd. "Do you remember what he was sworn to bring to us?"

"A box," hundreds shout out. "The box!"

"And what was in this box?"

Mumbling silence follows the question. Nobody says anything because nobody ever really knew what the box contained. Kip was killed, failing to bring them back what their leader swore would change the world, none of them having the chance to see the coveted crimson trinket. Rumors say it's inside the Encampment—that Jax is the one who actually has it. But, box or no box, it is of little importance because its alleged contents are nothing more than a fairy tale—a fantasy Dan has used to concoct false hope. For years they chased and protected these red chests to no avail, and to think that this one was supposed to be different. This box was to be the saving grace of the Raiders. These "records" that Dan has been obsessed with have been nothing more than a bloody, wild goose chase unnecessarily shedding the blood of his people and distracting them from their true purpose. It is time for the Raiders to rise and take what is owed them.

"All our dead, they are all dead because of them! He hid the box from us," Kai yells, pointing out to the surrounding crowd before moving his finger first to Dan and then over to Jax. "*He* hid the very item Dan said would turn this war around, and what has it done? We are worse off than ever, all because of these four *white* liars."

The woman looks on Kai with saddened eyes, knowing that *he* knows of the truth but refuses to see it based solely on skin-surface prejudices. He can justify it all away with rhetoric that appeals to an enraged mob, but she knows it is nothing more than white and black in Kai's eyes.

"We agreed to let them in," the woman states. "It was *our* choice that Dan offered to us, and we took it. We wanted to fight with them because deep down we knew something had to change if we were to start winning. We weren't afraid then, so why are we now? Why are you letting Kai impose his will on you?"

Kai grits his teeth. As the crowd has progressively gotten quieter, the stark reality that he is losing control of the storm takes hold of him. Jax, Connor, Renn, and Dan—they need to die. They need to be made into examples that different is unwanted. That it is unacceptable, because different will not give the Raiders power over the Nine. Fire can only be fought with a stronger fire. If he is going to defeat Caspian, he too must do the unthinkable…

"My will. Dan's will," Kai intones, his hand gripping his holstered sidearm. "None of that matters anymore. What matters is justice."

With no more time to waste on trivial debate and semantics, the opposition must be eliminated. Kai draws his weapon. Pointing it at the woman's head, Kai pulls the trigger without hesitation, and before her body hits the earth, the crowd is silenced as he shifts his aim to the next closest target.

"You made me do this…" Kai spits out, pressing the metal barrel of the gun to Dan's head as his eyes well up with rage. "I wish you never would have saved me. I would have been better off dead all those years ago…"

Dan closes his eyes, accepting death. Connor, on the other hand, is anything but compliant as his hand swiftly rises, sweeping the gun up to the sky just as a bullet exits the gun.

"Run!" he shouts out to the other three. "Get an Owl and get out—"

But before he can finish, Kai has recovered and hits the side of Connor's head with a closed fist. Although dazed, Connor keeps his hold on the firearm, and in their struggle, the gun is pointed from the sky to the crowd where another round is fired. Striking the stomach of a young woman, most in the crowd erupt in panic while others join the fight and draw their own weapons.

"Move! Now!" Renn shouts. Pushing Dan aside, a bullet strikes the dirt where he knelt, but as she stands, Renn finds herself staring down the barrel of a rifle. To her surprise, Jax rushes forward and bends his metal arm up and in front of Renn's face where the fired round ricochets off its surface.

Having seen the origin of the shot, Connor elbows the underbelly of Kai's chin before yanking the gun from his grip. Aiming, he shoots the rifleman and three others that have their guns drawn, neutralizing all immediate threats. By now the massive crowd has scattered into absolute chaos, and taking advantage of the crisis at hand, Connor kicks Kai backwards where he is trampled by a handful of frantic people rushing to safety.

Fighting to his feet, Kai reaches for one of the downed rifles, gripping it and chambering a fresh round. He takes aim and shoots into the rushing crowd, striking a man in his thigh, only to see that the four white traitors have disappeared.

Twenty-One

Area Thirty-Eight
December 25, 2037

"We're eager to begin. So, if everyone could find a seat we can get started." Few heed the proclamation, but standing at the pulpit, the announcer piously waits.

From within the flurry of people finding the *perfect* seat, Mica whispers into the hidden mic within his lapel.

"The governor is up." Amongst all the agitation and commotion, the duo intentionally finds seats towards the right of the stage and near the edge of the aisle.

"Mandatory gathering..." Dan scoffs. People-Protection Agency or not, if Dan and Mica have any say in the matter, this will be the first and last. "This better work."

"It'll work. Give me a sitrep," Mica murmurs, putting his chin back into his shoulder as if to cough.

Across the room and up in the rafters, Sullivan sits perched as the spotter. "I've got eyes on both of you."

"Good," Dan states, looking up past the intricate chandelier and transparent supports beams and towards Sullivan.

"Hey, dumbass, you're going to give me away!"

"Shut up," Dan hums out. "I'm just admiring the architecture."

"You start admiring and then everyone else will start admiring—"

"Keep the frequencies clear," Mica chimes in before the bickering escalates.

With a slow inhale, Sullivan exhales a calming breath. It's times like these that he wishes he had his other half, but they're at a point where the two will be more effective if she handles what needs to be done back at headquarters and he does the necessary tasks here in the field.

As far as *this operation* is concerned, Mica has felt an all-too-familiar uneasiness gradually grow. In the past it's been his gut warning him moments before an operation was about to become fubarred, but based on the singular fact that Mica has never failed a mission to date, no matter how many broken pieces he's had to patch together, he chooses to ignore the cautionary sentiment.

For the past week, they've been tailing the newly appointed Area Leader, formally elected Governor of Colorado, and the job couldn't be any simpler. Former SPEC-OPs or not, this guy is as corrupt as they come and is about as arrogant as his tailored suit suggests. Hardly any security outside of public events made the decision to extract him as he exited City Hall a no brainer, and even then, security is so light in here that if they wanted to, Mica's willing to bet that he and his team could take him out right on that stage. He's most likely wearing light Kevlar and has *maybe* two handguns concealed on him. It'd be too easy, but for obvious reasons the cost-benefit analysis made this option a last case scenario.

The Area Leader stands, and as he does the American national anthem begins to play. Only a measure or two, and as it concludes, Area Leader Milley coughs three times, allowing for the commotion to settle down and cease entirely.

"Thank you for coming to the first of what we hope will be many wonderful Gatherings," he says, pausing and waiting for the scripted accolade. It takes a moment, but once people catch on, the applause trickles in before immediately fading. "I'd first like to thank all of you for making this possible. The Nine would like me to express their love and concern for every one of you."

Dan barks a laugh that turns a few heads.

"As they have been in office, they have become fully aware of a scientific problem that is infecting our culture and society," Milley continues. "Inspired by the Bale Act in the European Union and as a response to the ever-growing civil threat that plagues this newly formed nation, the Nine have passed The North American Union Purification Act of 2037."

Dan leans over to Mica. "Is he talking about what I think he is?"

"I think so…"

Carter was right. Physically and intellectually disarm the citizenry. Stage one, create a collective belief. Stage two, remove firearms. Stage three, silence opposition through systematic extermination, and in this case, all done in the form of an ethically presented eugenics program. That's what the Bale Act is, and if patterned after that, then this will be no different. In fact, Mica's willing to bet it will be more radical.

It's the same pattern as any Marxist, socialist, communist movement. This isn't simply a political ideology, but rather a world shaping, dynamic power and class shifting movement. Mao Zedong's Cultural Revolution, the National Socialist German Workers party, the Communist Party of Kampuchea in the Cambodian Civil War, Romania in the wake of World War II, Zimbabwe in the 1980s, and even the Democratic Socialists of the United States in the late 2010s and early 2020s, all were movements that hijacked political systems for fascistic power grabs. All were also abject failures, and it wasn't until the Children of the Ordean Reich took their turn that this destructive world view worked on a global scale.

Mica decides to listen to his gut after all; it's not just a warning. None of them are equipped to handle what's coming, and even if they could grit through the mission, it's an admonishment for him to get his ass up and out of his chair.

Mica turns to Dan. "We're leaving."

"Negative," Sullivan firmly states, overhearing the anxiety in Mica's voice. "They'll pick you out like a sore thumb if you try to get up now."

"Killing Milley won't do anything. We've got to abort and reassess. The target shouldn't be the Area Leader, it should be the Nine—"

"Mica!" Sullivan snaps, stopping him before things get out of his control. "Finish the mission, and then we can reevaluate."

"This act," Area Leader Milley continues, "is in direct response to the fugitives many have come to call the Minutemen. They are poisoning our society…" Removing the mic from off the pulpit, Milley walks stage right, motioning with his free hand to a pair of PPA specialists. Following orders, the soldiers march up, carrying what clearly is an individual, and upon closer examination is a woman. With her head covered in a canvas bag and dressed in a baggy, grey prison jumpsuit, the woman's identity remains a mystery.

It's in this very moment that Dan nudges Mica. Fearing that the wrong ears will overhear, Dan simply hands Mica his cell with an open text for him to read.

"Impossible," Mica whispers.

Dan, staring his partner dead in the eyes, shakes his head ever so slightly, motioning his eyes up to the rafters.

"Mica?" Sullivan asks over the radio, the unexpected uncertainty being heard by both Dan and Mica.

"Standby," Mica simply says. "What do we do then? We can't call Carter with this until we know for certain…"

"Call Lisa then," Dan whispers. "She's the only one that'll believe it."

Looking from the specialists dropping the woman to her knees and back at Dan's phone, Mica makes the executive decision. "Call her and make it quick. We don't have a lot of time."

Whipping open his contact list, Dan scrolls down until his cursor highlights the name Lisa Rodgers. Touching the send button, once the line connects, a quiet ring sounds on stage.

"What is this?" the Area Leader proclaims, reaching into his pocket, pulling out a cell phone. "It looks as if our example is getting a call from—Dan Trax."

"What the hell…" Dan mumbles, terrified by what is taking place.

"Should I answer it, Ms. Rodgers?" Milley asks, ripping the bag off her head.

With countless cuts and bruises, Lisa struggles to catch her breath as blinding lights fill her dilated eyes. Watching in horror, and with absolute rage filling his lungs, Mica moves his gaze from Lisa's beaten body to Dan's eyes.

It's in this moment where Mica realizes that this is one more mission where he'll have to lean on his improvisation and instinct, whether he should or not.

"Move!" Mica shouts.

Standing, he charges down the aisle with Dan directly on his heels. Immediate panic engulfs the PPA specialists as the two warriors each pull out a blade and club. By the time the young soldiers come to their senses and react, Mica and Dan viciously beat them down to the stage's surface. Two shots are then fired from afar, both hitting Mica in the back, thudding into his body armor and forcing him into a stumble. Turning around, he easily identifies the undercover PPA officer on the front row five feet away, and with a flip of his wrist, one of Mica's knives flies towards the officer, striking him just below the chin.

"Get Lisa out of here!" Dan shouts, pivoting to face another five oncoming PPA soldiers. The first makes the foolish mistake of attacking straight on. Dan simply boots him square in the chest, sending him backwards and crashing down the stairs headfirst. The next two are slightly wiser, but still stupid as they both tentatively approach with their rifles at the ready. Dan just dodges the timid shots and subdues each with a well-placed punch to their throats.

Mica picks Lisa up and cradles her in his arms, pivoting to exit the stage. "Let's go, Dan—!"

A burst of three shots rings out, cutting off Mica's words.

"Mica, stop!"

From out of the glass-beamed rafters, Sullivan Stone rappels down, landing directly in front of a wounded Dan. As Mica moves to draw his next weapon with his free hand, Sullivan takes aim directly at Mica's head. "I said stop, damn it!"

"What are you doing, Sullivan?"

"What's necessary."

"And what's that?"

"We're purifying society."

"We?" Mica asks, looking to the bruised and beaten Lisa. "Did you do this?"

"Someone had to," Sullivan says. "Someone has to do what progress requires."

Before Sullivan can even start his monologue, there's a loud crack next to Dan where a suffocating amount of grey smoke hisses and scatters, enveloping Sullivan, Dan, and the remaining PPA guards. Smiling at his friend for what very well may be the last time, Dan looks to Mica before tossing a second pellet down at Mica's feet, creating the same masking result. Half a dozen more pellets are thrown throughout the entire floor of City Hall, and in the time it takes for the smoke to clear, Mica and Lisa are long gone.

"Shit..." Sullivan can't believe he didn't see that coming. Kicking Dan in the ribs, Sullivan digs his toe into the gunshot wound he'd made in the middle of Dan's calf. "You and I need to have a talk..."

✦ ✦ ✦

Pulling up a chair, Sullivan sits himself in front of Dan, prodding the hole in Dan's leg with the tip of his rifle.

"Pretty good, huh?" Sullivan chuckles.

"It took you three shots," Dan mumbles, antagonizing Sullivan's ego like Sullivan is his leg.

"Well, you were moving all over the place. I'm still impressed with myself."

Dan shakes his head. "Trust me, you shouldn't be."

Dan's tough but he will break. Sullivan has experience with *tough* people, long before he was even considered by Carter and the Division.

Without warning, Sullivan bats an open palm across the side of Dan's head. Over the high-pitched ring in Dan's ear, Sullivan continues without skipping a beat. "And what about that? Was that a good shot?"

"Meh," Dan mumbles, unfazed by the interrogation. He'd expect nothing less than macro aggressions from Sullivan. The guy is at best predictable.

"You want to know something I read about you?"

Shrugging, Dan could care less what intel this son of a bitch has on him.

"I read about your son," Sullivan chuckles.

Dan stares straight into his enemy's eyes, keeping his mouth shut.

"What I can't understand is why Victoria would leave and then come back?" Sullivan contemplates.

Again, Dan fixates his gaze on Sullivan and continues to ignore the premise of the interrogation.

"Did she just want some time to whore around—to unleash some of her *feminine rights*?"

"I'd stop right there if I were you," Dan snarls.

Sullivan stares back, a sly smile of satisfaction growing. "Why did you let her come back? Were you really that desperate, to let a brown bitch like that leave and then return like nothing ever happened? I'm completely sympathetic to people like us asserting dominance over someone like Tori, especially in the bedroom, but it's like you begged her back... Just thinking about what she is, how could you *want* someone like her? It's disgusting to say the least."

"What do you want?"

Sullivan grins from ear to ear upon hearing the question. "Do you remember your first fight?"

"Why does that matter?"

"Just answer the question," Sullivan sighs.

"No, I can't say that I can."

"Well, I do," Sullivan sneers. "It was some black kid in elementary school. Kid was a nobody—no one, and I mean no one liked this kid, and yet nobody was doing anything about it. So, I decided to take matters into my own hand. Every day I would beat his weak little ass. Over and over, day after day, until finally he ended up killing himself. It was three years later, but persistence favors the bold, am I right?" Sullivan chuckles. "That day—that's when I first witnessed the fragility of colored people. They all pride themselves with this bottom punching up approach—their harsh and cruel history, demanding reparations for something that happened over a hundred years ago. Polynesians, Blacks, Mexicans. Indigenous Americans. They're all the same, but let's take Hawaiians for example. On the islands, the natives absolutely hate white people, and why?"

"You're sick..."

"They hate us because we won! They hate us because ideologically, they know they are a weaker and less intelligent race, and they lost the war against Western technology and ideals. That's when I had my next revelation: what if we could eliminate weakness? It's not unheard of or untried and untested. History is littered with attempts, but the one fallacy they all had was that they got too political and it turned them to greed."

"And you think history is on your side?" Dan laughs. All dictators think they have the equation of power figured out.

"You do have a point there, my friend. But…what if we could control history? Alter it just like the human genome?" He pauses, savoring the thought, cherishing the clarity this idea has brought him throughout his life. "That's when I came across the Denver Airport and conveniently the Minutemen Division."

"The Division's a haven—"

"Is it?" Sullivan asks. From out of his pocket Sullivan pulls out a small tablet and with a few quick swipes, the digital images in his hand project onto the wall. "Do you recognize any of this?"

Dan stares at the hundreds of tiny images, immediately recognizing the tunnels within the DIA.

"Let's see if this helps." Sullivan clicks a single cell where it zooms in, taking up the entire wall. In it are Victoria, Connor, Bella, and Caspian.

"Is this—?"

"A live feed? Yes—yes, it is. As we speak, our wives and kids are playing and having a good time…"

"Connor…"

"I have a proposition for you," Sullivan slyly states, bringing it back to Dan's son. "Since your son is part white, why don't I take him off your hands for you? We still have a lot of room to expand the testing of those with mixed blood, and he's a prime candidate—"

"What do you want!" Dan yells, the rage in his voice echoing off the small, barren room.

Continuing to pace, Sullivan states the price he's asking. "I want Connor."

"He is *my* son…" Dan sighs, defeated. After all of this. After everything he did to get them back—to get Connor back—is he going to lose them all over again?

"At his age, there could still be some alterations done to his DNA. It'll give us another opportunity to experiment with variances," Sullivan hums. "He could be a valuable asset to the Stone family legacy. By the way, Bella is pregnant—with twins!"

"And?"

"And I'm waiting on a few details from Five in London, but pending you giving me your son, everything should work out just fine."

"Leave my son ALONE!"

"WHY?!" Sullivan yells, immediately matching Dan's intensity, dropping the playful banter. "I have never liked you nor your shit brown wife. Despite that, I'm still willing to give your son a chance!"

It's not the first time that Dan has been confronted by a madman, but even with experience on his side, it doesn't stop a tear from sliding down Dan's cheek.

"Pathetic. Some of us are just as weak as they are. If you befriend the enemy, you become the enemy. The Division has befriended the weak and filthy. They don't have what it takes to survive in my world."

Sneering, Sullivan pulls up his phone to call Bella.

On screen, the live feed plays out as Bella stands up and walks to the corner of the room, placing her own phone to her ear.

"Hey, honey," Dan hears Bella say on the other end.

"How's it going?" Sullivan tenderly asks.

"Meh," Bella forcefully giggles. "Casp is having fun. How about you?"

"Good. Everything should be ready to go. Bring Connor and Tori with you."

On camera, Bella gives a disgusted look. "Why her?"

"It might make the kid more compliant. Obviously Connor is the priority, so if she is making things difficult, don't hesitate—"

"TORI!" Dan yells at the top of his lungs. "RUN! GET—" but before he can get any sort of coherent warning out, Sullivan punches Dan in the jaw, flipping Dan backwards on his chair, knocking the wind out of him and shutting him right up.

"Please," Sullivan coolly says. "I'm trying to talk to my wife."

Lying face up and helpless, Dan tries to remember the last conversation he had with Tori and Connor. There was no argument. No resentment. There were just hugs, kisses, and affectionate words, none of which he can give them now. With nothing but prayer at his disposal, Dan begins like he's heard Tori and Conner do many times before and closes his eyes, whispering his sorrowful plea.

<hr>

"What about Aila?" Bella asks in a softer voice. "Okay. I'll hurry."

"How'd it go?" Tori asks, not looking up from her knitting—an old lady hobby that she's had to pick up simply to pass the time around here, and one that she definitely prejudged.

"They're on their way home," Bella says with a smile.

"Dad's on his way home?" Connor asks hopefully.

"That's what it sounds like," Tori says, her relief not fully surfacing.

"Awesome. I can show him my new back flip."

"And *your* father wanted me to remind you to take your vitamins, Caspian."

"Yuck," Casp mumbles, turning his back towards his mother. "I'm sick of those shots."

"I know sweetie, but they're good for you. Look how much stronger you've already become!"

A slight grin grows across Caspian's face as he flexes his muscles. Bella wasn't much of a believer at first, but Sullivan is a literal genius. He has figured something out that will not only propel their son forward, but it will be the catalyst that moves the world into the next age of progress and evolution. And it's not just on the biological level either. Her faith in Sullivan has given her access to an immortal technology, one that she is eager to showcase to her enemies.

Slipping the phone back in her pocket, she simultaneously hits the button that initiates the evacuation drill. In a shrieking siren, both Connor and Caspian slap their hands over their ears, attempting to blot out the painful echo.

"Is that what I think it is?" Tori asks, shouting over the alarm.

Bella fiercely nods her head. "Where's Aila?"

Tori shrugs. "I don't know. I think she's with Carter."

Grabbing her son, Bella motions for Tori and Connor to follow. "Come on, let's go to the tunnel. Just like we practiced, kids!"

Tori takes her own son by the hand. "Where's Dad?"

"He'll meet us in the tunnel," Bella says, answering for Tori.

"Come on, Connor," Caspian then shouts, holding out his hand to his friend.

"Are you sure they'll be there?" Tori asks, feeling that there's something she's not seeing. "I mean, isn't this alarm system for something going wrong?"

"It'll be fine," Bella states. "We've got to get going though. The tunnels are shutting, and we'll be stuck if we don't get there in time."

Not liking any of this, Tori pulls out her phone. "I'm calling Dan!" Tori says, holding her son back from going with Bella and Caspian.

"We don't have time for that!" Bella snaps. The more time they wait, the greater the chances are they'll die down here like everyone else.

"Go ahead. Connor and I will catch up! I want to make sure he's all right."

"Call him on the way!"

Shaking her head, Tori dials her husband's number and puts her hand over her other ear. It rings three times, and on the fourth he picks up. "Dan? Is everything all right?"

Nothing but silence on the other end, the siren making it nearly impossible to hear anything.

"Dan? Dan, what's going on?"

Without a single word spoken, the line goes dead.

Dan had this theory that Carter and Mica were in denial over, and he would talk about it for hours in bed at night. Every waking moment it was on his mind. He even brought it up while they were being intimate, which drove her absolutely insane. Sleep, fine. She's been an insomniac all her life, but she's no nun and if there was one thing his conspiracy theory would not disrupt it was sex. However, now that it appears he's been right all along, she might never have the chance to be upset with him about it again.

"Connor," Tori grabs her son's hand. "We've got to—"

In that instant, Connor takes it all in as he watches his mom's head whip to the side, the splitting gunshot overpowering the screeching alarm. The firmness of her grip instantly becomes limp, her eyes rolling into the back of her head, and as she lands against the blood-stained wall, never again will she speak his name.

"Mom?"

"I'm your mom now," Bella yells, holstering her firearm and grabbing Connor's hand. "Let's go."

"What did you do?" Connor yells. "Mom!"

"Come on, Connor," Caspian tentatively says, just going along with what his mother is doing.

"MOM!"

With the searing image of his mother's lifeless body, Connor will be taught that she was just some woman who tried to take him away from his destiny. As he's pulled from the room kicking and screaming, he will never forget those dead, sunken eyes as they are the last things he sees of his mother.

Twenty-Two

DIA Headquarters
December 25, 2037

The painful screech—the bursts of excruciating reverberation from the sirens—vibrates Carter to the core.

Something's wrong, he thinks. These emergency procedures have never been rehearsed, and with no live drill on the schedule, especially on Christmas, the only justified conclusion is real-world. But what? Not only was the team supposed to be back, but according to his contacts on the outside, nothing eventful occurred at the Gathering. That was not supposed to be the case. Eliminating Governor Milley was the extreme circumstance, but the primary objective was to apprehend him; either scenario would have spread news like a shot heard around the world. So, either nothing transpired, or intel is being silenced and suppressed—making Carter's sources unreliable. Regardless, the only logical outcome is that the mission failed, making the timing of this evacuation far from coincidental.

"Aila, let's go!" Carter yells out.

"We can't leave," Aila pleads, holding her uncle's hand. "Mica's not back."

"Mica's fine," Carter lies. Urgency is the priority here. Crisis management is their only option. Grabbing the emergency kit, Carter shuffles her out the door. "He'll meet us at the rendezvous like we planned in our contingency."

Hustling down the claustrophobic concrete corridors, Carter keeps as fast a pace as Aila's body can handle. The doctors told her to keep the stress levels to a minimum in these last weeks, but they clearly didn't know who they were talking to.

"What is going on, Uncle?"

"I'm not sure," he replies, shoving a group of frantic teens out of the way. "It can't be good though," he then mumbles, unable to keep the lie entirely suppressed.

"Where are we supposed to go?" Aila asks, her anxiety rising to the surface.

"This way," he says, confidently moving to the right. Truthfully, he has no idea, and rather than spiraling down the dark rabbit hole himself, he moves them into a corner room. Assessing the situation and catching their breath, the two watch the panic evolve and unfold in front of them. Lost children crying for their parents, hordes of people dropping and tripping over bags and boxes. No one has any idea what is going on. It's the kind of chaos their enemies would want.

Before Carter can dwell any longer on the depressing scene, he gets a phone call. Looking to the screen, a wave of relief rushes over him.

"Mica! What happened?"

"Sullivan!" Mica manages to blurt out before gasping for air.

"What?" Carter asks, already piecing the puzzle together, scraping together a conclusion that he hopes is wrong. "Did you kill him?"

"Negative. I'll explain in a minute. I've got Lisa and we're on our way. Get to the Records Room."

"How will you—"

"Just get there. Is Aila with you?" Mica then asks.

"Of course."

"Good. What about Tori and Connor?"

"I have no idea where they are. Should I go find them?"

"No. Just get to the Records Room and we'll figure—"

The line goes dead.

"Mica?"

Hopefully, Aila looks up to her uncle. "Is he okay?"

"He's fine. We're meeting him and Lisa in a few minutes."

"Lisa? How is she with Mica? I was with her this morning—"

I was too, he thinks. Again, grabbing the emergency kit, Carter is about to shuffle Aila back into the chaos, but stops as he sees her aching expression.

"You okay?"

Before answering, she takes in a couple of deep breaths. "I think so." She has a pretty good idea what just happened, but she decides to push on and ignore it.

"Are you sure?" he asks, still looking to his niece.

Aila nods her head confidently. If they're on their way to see Mica, she is more than okay.

Stepping back into the hysteria, Carter and Aila push and shove, delivering a few deliberate punches in order to bypass the mainstream crowds. Stumbling into a more secluded corridor, within a matter of minutes, they're at the Records Room door. To Carter's surprise, Aila beats him there, and as she begins pounding on its metal surface, it immediately swings open where Aila falls into her husband's arms, squeezing Mica as if trying to pull herself through him.

"Aila," Mica soothes, the concern in his voice the heaviest Carter's ever heard. Looking to Carter, he motions for them to get inside. Bolting the door behind them, Carter turns to Mica, but before he can ask anything, his eyes catch Lisa's. Astonished, Carter tentatively steps forward, tenderly grabbing her battered and bleeding face, his eyes welling with tears.

"It looks worse than it is," is the first thing that comes to Lisa's mind. To be honest, she has no idea what she should say. She's still trying to process the last ten hours that came without warning.

"The Stones," Mica quietly says, still holding his wife.

"Dan was right then…" Carter mumbles, the conversation he had with Dan and Mica a couple months ago stepping out from the back of his mind.

Mica nods, regretting the fact that none of them took their friend's warning to heart. All the signs were there for everyone to see, and for Mica, the red flags have always been blatantly waving. Out of denial, Mica ignored them on the premise that Sullivan was the lesser of two evils. He took the blue pill over the red. He was blinded by his past with Bella. Their history not only clouded his judgment with Sullivan, but it continues to haunt his life.

"He's yours," she says.

"You're telling me this now? Why? After how many years, why now?" he asks, unable to know if there's truth in anything she's telling him.

"It wasn't relevant until now…" is her only response.

"Relevant," Mica scoffs. "Since when do you care about relevance?" and before Mica can let her answer and ascertain Bella's true intentions, he leaves for the mission.

"Where's Dan?" Carter asks.

"Sullivan's got him," Lisa says.

"Alive?"

Mica slowly shakes his head. "I don't see a reason to just off him—"

"Why not? Why wouldn't Sullivan just kill him?" Carter demands.

"Pride," Mica quickly says. *He likes to relish in his victories.*

Turning to the shelves of boxes, amongst the empty slots, Mica finds his own metal container, pulls it out, and flips it open. Everything's here—the journal, Bible, music, home video, iPod, and key. After all is said and done, what he holds may be the only history that anyone will have left. Reaching in, Mica pulls out the one thing he regrets.

Looking at the picture once more—at Caspian and the Stone family, Mica's thoughts return to Bella.

"He's yours," she says.

Then, unsure if it's an impulse or inspiration, Mica hastily begins searching the shelves for Kim's box. Upon finding it, he opens it, dumping the contents of his own box inside.

"Here," he says, locking up Kim's box and handing it to Aila.

The Stones and the Nine will be looking for Mica, wanting to erase him from history, so, as a middle-fingered gesture, he places the traitorous photo in his own box along with his devil mask. This is all they'll find of him.

"We need to get out of here," Aila says, holding Kim's box to her chest.

"I can't," Mica shakes his head. "I have to get Dan."

"No," she says, a tear falling down her cheek as she stares into his brown and blue eyes.

"I have to," Mica says. Placing his hands on Aila's face, he kisses her for what she fears could be the last time. "I can't just leave him—"

"No!" Aila shrieks. "You can't! I won't let—" Aila begins, but abruptly stops and collapses to her knees in pain as she throws her arms around her stomach.

Mica's eyes widen. "Is she going into labor?"

"Yes!" Carter says, irritated that she didn't say something sooner when he asked. "Get a towel or something!"

As if the last ten torturous hours were merely a bad dream, Lisa shoots to her feet, ripping her jacket off and throwing it to Carter.

"Go, get Dan," she says, turning to Mica. "We'll take care of her."

"I can't. My son…"

"Go!" Lisa orders, grabbing his collar and tossing him towards the door.

Taking one last look at his wife, Aila stares right back before mouthing, "I love you."

Mica echoes the sentiment, and before he gives in to the need to stay, he exits the door, leaving to go after Dan.

———⋆⋆★⋆⋆———

"Amen."

As he opens his eyes, staring at the artificial lights on the ceiling, an unfamiliar and overwhelming peace fills his soul to capacity, completely enveloping Dan. It's a serenity that Tori always told him existed, but never did he believe until this very moment. For a brief instant the fog lifts and Dan forgets the inevitable future, the haunting past, and the destructive present. From Victoria leaving, taking their son, to her coming back, restoring the chasm that was left in his life. From the moment he met Mica on Governor White's campaign, to the second they were all betrayed by Sullivan and Bella, in this split second, Dan sees his life from the beginning to the end, understanding what he's done, what he must now do, and he'll be damned if his fight ends here as a prisoner of war.

The first slam goes unheard, but the second and third don't. It's as if God pushes play on the present moment, rushing Dan back to reality. Shooting his head up from off the ground, Dan's mind wakes. Rolling onto his side for better leverage, he raises his arms back and up before swiftly bringing them down in an attempt to force his wrists free from the thin plastic cuffs. However, the binding just cuts into his wrists, and trying two more times, the rigid band only carves deeper into his flesh. As the banging continues, and with blood dripping from off his fingertips, Dan tries one more time. Exerting all the force he can muster, in an excruciating effort, Dan pulls his wrists apart, his shoulders firing as the thin plastic band continues to carve into his wrists. Miraculously, the band breaks and his hands are finally free. Moving to his feet, Dan stops as he hears the constant banging cease. Holding his breath, he then listens to what appears to be the sounds of claws scratching the door.

Quickly realizing what is really happening, Dan rolls to the side as an earth-shattering explosion rips the metal barrier from its hinges and across the room where it cracks the concrete wall. Dust, rubble, and debris fills the small room, but Dan is still able to make out the approaching silhouette.

"What the hell?" he yells out.

"So, you are here," a relieved Mica says. Stepping forward and whipping out a small knife, Mica cuts the rest of Dan free. "I'm just lucky the door didn't take your head off."

"You're lucky? It's my head we're talking about!" Dan chuckles as he stands, brushing off the dust and cracking every joint up his spine.

"Where is he?" Mica asks. "I thought he would be with you."

"He left me here to rot."

"Any idea of where he's going?"

"Oh yeah. That guy has a mouth on him."

"That he does," Mica mumbles.

Pausing, Dan looks around as he analyzes the next steps. "Is Lisa safe?"

"Yeah, she's with Carter and Aila," Mica says, his tone changing the instant he says his wife's name.

"What's wrong?"

"Aila's in labor."

"Now?"

Mica nods his head and takes in a deep breath. "It's crazy over there."

"The emergency drill…" Dan whispers, context revealing itself by the minute.

The drill was never planned as a safety precaution. It was never even about creating mass mayhem. It was Bella's brainchild, and the mere fact they haven't amended or reevaluated any aspect of the plan, assigned an oversight committee, or done anything but implement the actual alarm system, proves now that security was never the goal. It's a purge. No matter how many times Sullivan tried to refute the conspiracy theories about the Denver International Airport, they were all true. The engineers specifically designed it as an underground trap with the sole purpose of genocide for its occupants.

One way in. One way out.

"Where are we, Mica?" Dan asks as they step outside the room.

Pulling out his tablet, Mica opens the GPS. "We're in the underground units beneath City Hall."

Rounding a corner, the two make a sudden halt and turn back.

Up ahead, half a dozen PPA guards block the solitary hallway. Concealing their approach, Mica slides out his hatchet and hands it to Dan before taking a club in his right hand and his whip in his left.

Mica is the first to advance into the narrow hallway. Without warning, Mica's whip lashes onto the neck of the soldier in the back, and yanking him forward, Mica pulls the man through his comrades. As the entire squad stumbles against the walls, Dan rushes forward, the hatchet finding its first victim as it is buried into the center of the soldier's chest. Quickly, a second is sought out, Dan digging his blade in the soldier's shoulder just below the neck. Releasing the whip, Mica pulls out a second club, and as a PPA private reaches for his firearm, his hand is shattered. Another is smart enough to realize there is no time for a gun, but he's not skilled enough to take on Mica hand to hand. Throwing a slack right cross, Mica easily dodges, and before the soldier can recover, three of his ribs are broken and his jaw shattered. One of the last standing soldiers manages to raise a rifle at Mica's head, but before the trigger can be pulled, Dan brutishly slams the private into the wall. Reacquiring his whip, Mica grabs and breaks the knee of the final obstacle before he and Dan continue.

Clicking the receiver in his ear, Mica dials Carter's number.

"Do you have Dan?" Carter asks.

"Yeah, but we've run into some trouble."

"No surprise there," Carter says.

"How is she?" Mica asks, hearing Aila's agonizing cry in the background.

"Have the PPA informed others of you and Dan?" he asks, ignoring Mica's query. The kid needs to stay focused. That's the only way Mica will make it back to Aila alive. "Does Sullivan know?"

"How is she?" Mica repeats.

"Mica, do they know?" Carter's forceful tone erupts.

Closing his bicolor eyes, Mica does his best to concentrate on the task at hand. "I don't think so."

"Are Tori and Connor with them?" Dan then prods.

He holds out his hand towards Dan and listens to Carter.

"Get here as fast as you possibly can," Carter orders. "The doors are about to close and once they do, you'll be locked out."

"No!" Mica yells.

Unseen to the two warriors, a small squad hears Mica's echoing shout.

"Dan was right," Mica continues. "The airport was a mistake. Bella organized the evacuation plan and it's meant to kill everyone caught inside."

In a matter of seconds, Carter's morale dies. With the mass panic outside, they are trapped. How could he be so foolish and not consider *all* factors? Societies, organizations, countries…they all collapse eventually, as has the Division. The only thing that was salvageable were their lives, and now there is uncertainty in even that as the paralyzing fear sinks in—their escape blockaded by explosives and hysteria.

"Give it to me," Dan says. Keeping the earpiece in, Mica hands the phone to Dan. "Carter, you need to listen. You're in the Records Room, correct?"

"Yeah," Carter slowly says, trying to hold on to some sort of fight.

"Good," Dan sighs out. "On the shelves, there should be a box labeled Kip Wright. It'll be on the bottom row in the far-left corner. Tell me when you find it."

Rushing over to the shelves, Carter finds the box.

"Got it."

"Open it. Inside should be a transmitter with a single red button. Is it there?" As soon as Dan asks, the squad of PPA soldiers rounds the corner, spotting the two agents. "Do you see it?" he repeats, motioning to Mica at the approaching threat.

Masking their retreat up a flight of stairs, Mica throws three round metal balls that explode into asphyxiating clouds of smoke.

"Yeah, I see it," Carter says, pulling out the small, simple transmitter.

"Push the button. When you do, someone named Kip Wright will get the signal and will meet you in the Records Room."

"Kip? How can I trust this guy?"

"Because," Dan replies, "he helped me build a secondary exit."

Despite nobody believing his theories, the entire DIA was tactically asinine with a single outlet for the entire Division and every American refugee.

"You paranoid bastard," Carter mumbles, a smile creeping across his face. Pushing the button, the transmitter lights up with a solid signal for five seconds before it begins to blink.

"It's pretty straightforward and will blink once the signal is received." Slowly and tentatively, fearing the answer, Dan takes a slow breath, a sense of hope compelling him to ask anyway. "Where are Tori and Connor?"

"I don't know," Carter sighs. He doesn't want to say it, but he also knows that there is no point in lying. "Last I heard, they were with Bella and Caspian."

Dan's fears begin to unravel. What was the last thing he said to her before he left? What were his last words to Connor? He'd like to think they were words of encouragement, or maybe they were just plain repetitious phrases that every husband and father says before leaving home for a bit.

Reaching the top, Mica opens the hatch that leads out of City Hall.

"Commander Stone!" A PPA grunt shouts into his receiver from the bottom of the stairs. "We have eyes on the prisoner. He's with someone—"

Mica and Dan don't wait to hear the rest of the conversation. Seeing that their exit is clear, the duo pulls themselves up from out of the underground tunnel, locking the hatch behind them.

The silence of the outside air offers both peace and anxiety. On one front, Mica can think more clearly, filling his lungs with real air rather than the circulated oxygen of the underground tunnels. On the other end of the spectrum, there is a calm before the storm in the atmosphere that he simply cannot shake.

"Mica," Dan says, turning to his friend.

Mica holds up his hand to Dan. "Carter?"

"Where are you?" Carter's voice crackles.

"Just outside City Hall."

"Mica!" Dan bellows, shoving him this time.

"Just a second, Carter. What?"

"I need to go. I can't lose them," Dan whispers, his eyes showing the overall angst Mica feels. "Tori and Connor were with Bella. Sullivan said—" He can't finish the thought, the very idea choking him, his perceived fears transpiring into reality.

The only thing keeping Mica sane in this moment is knowing that Carter and Lisa are with his wife and soon-to-be baby boy. How can he deny Dan from having that same peace of mind?

Tossing him the backup key to his bike, Mica says, "Meet up in the mountains outside the district."

Catching it, Dan briefly feels that maybe it's a better idea to find another means of transportation. "Nah," he says, tossing it back. "I've got this."

As Mica watches his friend leave, he turns and heads towards his motorcycle.

"Carter," he says. "Put my wife on the line."

Dan worrying for the safety of his family has caused Mica to reflect on the dark truth of his own situation. For now, Aila and his baby are safe. Mica will do everything in his power to prevent what he fears is coming and make it back to them. In the end though, Mica's a realist.

Jogging his way around the corner and towards his escape, Mica slows, his heart dropping as he stops. He counts two dozen PPA soldiers surrounding his motorcycle and blocking the route that leads to his only escape.

"He's arrived!" Slipping off Mica's bike, Sullivan steps forward, rubbing his hands together.

"Mica?" Aila's voice finally comes into his earpiece. As exhausted as she sounds, his name spoken from her mouth puts Mica into a more composed state.

"How's it going, love?" he asks, studying every possible angle, but only finding one. One is all he needs.

"I wish you were here!" Aila cries out.

"I will be. Just keep breathing," Mica says, verifying the details of his sole option. "Lisa and Carter know what they're doing."

"Is that Aila? I can't believe the luck I'm having today!" Sullivan crows. "Tell her I say hi."

Briefly contemplating Sullivan's request, Mica decides to go with it—a few words can offer a lot of information and time. "Aila, Sullivan says hi."

"Where are you, Mica?" Aila asks, the panic in her voice rising.

"Everything's all right. I'm just talking with Sullivan."

Pulling out his sidearm and pointing it at Mica's head, Sullivan motions towards the ground. "Knees. Now…"

Defiantly, Mica stays on his feet.

"Are you okay with the name we talked about?" he asks his wife.

"Mica, I need you!" *How can I do this*, she thinks. *I can't do this alone.*

"Aila, are you okay with the name?"

"Yes," she breathes out, a heavy contraction on its way. "It's perfect, but I need you with me. I can't do this by myself."

"Down!" Sullivan repeats, his commanding yell echoing off the surrounding buildings and concrete structures.

Slowly, Mica kneels, formulating and perfecting his plan. "You're not alone, Aila," he says. "You have Carter and Lisa—your uncle and aunt."

"I'll keep this real simple, Mica," Sullivan begins, stepping closer, the barrel of his pistol touching Mica's head. "Join us or die."

"But I need you, Mica," Aila cries out. "I need *you* here…"

Mica stares his enemy in both his eyes, and Sullivan loves it. Seeing defeat and anger in the eyes of a formidable foe is a rare opportunity. Dan, he's nothing to shy away from, but Mica, he's the prize any hunter wants. The corners of Sullivan's lips turn up ever-so-slightly as he imagines the kind of pain he'll be causing Aila, taking away her boy's father before he's even entered the world.

"Is she pleading for you?" he asks, pulling back the hammer of his firearm, placing the cold metal tip of the barrel between Mica's brown and blue eyes. "Hope you said your goodbyes…"

"Aila, I love—"

———⋆✦⋆———

In a loud pop, the line goes dead. With his last words being incomplete, Aila holds back a flood of tears, using the agony to engage her core and push their child out into the world.

"I can see him!" Lisa exclaims, grabbing a towel and canteen of water. "Come on, dear. Keep pushing!"

There's a sudden knock on the door, and before Carter can get up to answer, the entrance slides open where a young kid who appears no older than ten walks in.

"Who the hell are you?" Carter yanks the boy inside, slamming the door behind him.

"Kip!" the boy states in a surprisingly calm manner, holding up an exact replica of the blinking transmitter.

"You're a kid!"

"Teenager! I'm fourteen, thank ya very much!"

"Dan sent a fourteen-year-old boy?"

"Oi!" Kip yells out. "Back off, old man. I'm a freaking genius, all right? I helped build that second exit—" Kip abruptly stops, realizing he might have just leaked sensitive information. "Dan told ya 'bout the exit, right?"

Carter nods his head. "Yeah, he did."

"Good! Listen, I helped Dan the buff man build that—"

"Dan the buff man?" Carter can't believe what he's dealing with right now.

"I helped him, all right!" Kip throws his arms up in the air. "Cut me some slack? This brain did all the heavy lifting," he then says, jabbing his finger into the side of his head.

"Carter!" Lisa shouts. "I need your help!"

"What's goin' on?" Kip asks.

"My niece is having a baby!" Carter says, rushing to Lisa's aid and grabbing the towel. Expecting to help coach or calm Aila down, to his complete surprise, Lisa gently hands him the crying newborn.

Having no kids of his own, Carter has never had the experience of seeing and holding something so new and miraculous. His eyes, his face, his tiny fingers and rising chest, everything about Aila's little boy is working, breathing, and living on his own. Tenderly, Carter proudly squeezes the boy to his chest, and as he does, the baby stops crying, feeling the love and security of Great-Uncle Carter.

"Hi, Jax," Carter whispers, the infant locking eyes with him, and as a tear trickles down Carter's cheek, the chaos of the day—the tragedy of the country—is far from his thoughts. The only thing that matters is that this child feels loved.

"Wait, what's going on?!" Kip blurts out, nearly losing his lunch upon spotting the bloody baby in Carter's arms.

"Here," Carter says, gesturing for Kip to hold the baby.

"Nuh uh! Nope. No way in hell am I touching that thing. Frickin' gross!"

"Just do it! I've got to make sure my niece is okay." Carter's booming command shocks Kip into going against his instinct to avoid anything as grotesque as the gore-covered baby is. However, Kip awkwardly extends his arms where Carter lays Jax.

"What's his name?" Kip gags as he asks.

"Jax," Aila manages to say.

"Well, Jax," Kip begins, looking down at the putrid infant. "Ya stink, buddy."

Rushing over to Aila's side, Carter grabs her hand.

"Mica?" he asks, needing to know what happened, having seen her pain change after her conversation with him.

Shaking her head, Aila shrugs. "I don't know…"

"What do you—you don't know?"

Rather than repeating her uncertainty, Aila just wipes her eyes with the back of her hands before reaching out for her boy. "I'm okay, Uncle, really. I just want to hold my baby."

Jumping on Aila's offer, Kip practically tosses the child into her arms, wiping his hands free of the permeating smell. "Nasty…"

"He's beautiful," Aila tenderly corrects as she looks into Jax's eyes for the first time, affectionately kissing the top of her son's head. Nodding his head in agreement, Carter takes his niece's hand.

Kip rolls his eyes. "These people are frickin' blind," he mumbles. "Listen, I hate to break up the family bonding, but we got to get outta here."

"What about Mica?" Lisa asks.

Aila opens her mouth but clamps it shut as the tears make a resurgence.

"He didn't make it," Carter whispers.

With her words just as frozen as Aila's, Lisa's hands shoot across her mouth, her gaze resting on the fatherless child.

"Who's Mica?" Kip asks.

"He's my husband," Aila manages to say, making sure she uses present tense. She still has hope.

The gears in Kip's head begin to turn before clicking together. "That famous devil dude?"

"That'd be him," Carter affirms.

"That guy is my freaking hero!" Kip hollers, his eyes lighting up. "I don't believe it. Nothin' could kill that guy!"

With too much disappointment for Carter, he grabs the metal box Mica left and tosses it to Kip, the weight alone nearly knocking the kid over. Then, together, Carter and Lisa help a weak but very alive Aila to her feet.

"So, Kip Wright," Carter begins, "where is this exit?"

―――\ ⋅ ★ ⋅ /―――

Out of breath, Dan approaches the entrance of the burning airport, the entire facility being destroyed before his very eyes and before the eyes of the entire nation. Panic ensues everywhere as fire explodes out of windows, doors, and the underground crevices that he knows leads to the tunnels.

"Oi, Dan the Buff Man!" That stupid name is music to Dan's ears. Kip's smart. There was never a doubt in Dan's mind that he would get them out safely.

"Kip, where's Tori and Connor?" Dan asks.

"I haven't got the slightest clue. I got them out though!" Kip says with an exhausted Lisa, Carter, Aila, and baby Jax in tow.

"Carter," Dan says, turning to his mentor. "Where are my wife and son?"

"I don't know," Carter says, just as defeated by the question as he was when Dan asked the first time.

Enraged and disappointed beyond repair, Dan grips Carter by the throat, ready to break every limb. However, in the chaotic masses, the bobbing hair of his son rustles in the crowd and freezes Dan in place.

"Connor!"

"Dad!" Connor jerks his head towards the sound of his dad's voice, reaching out before his arms are slapped down.

"Shut up!" Bella shrieks.

"Don't, Mommy, don't hurt Connor!"

"Dad!" Connor repeats, ignoring Bella's violence.

"I said shut up!" A wild slap whooshes only to be abruptly stopped inches from Connor's cheek.

"Don't you dare touch my son."

In a solitary punch, Dan collapses Bella's rib cage, and for good measure, kicks her knee backwards, dropping her to the ground. As Dan picks his son up in his arms, before he can even turn to run back to Carter and the group, the all-too-familiar cackle sounds above the panicked mass.

"You really don't know what you're doing, do you?" Bella asks, realigning her ribs and cracking her knee back into place, standing as if Dan had done nothing. Finally, she can show the world what she is really capable of. Her surviving that explosion of Sullivan's back on that mission was not a mere coincidence, but rather, a marvel of science as she stands here now, unbroken and stronger than any natural man.

From within her coat, Bella whips out a six-inch blade and slashes at Dan. Dropping Connor out of harm's way, a gaping gash opens across Dan's chest, blood spitting out onto the concrete. She slashes again in an aim towards his throat. Dan barely blocks the kill shot, and with his wrist against her, he throws Bella's arm down, bringing an arching elbow up into her jaw. The cracking blow is as soft as a pillow, and rotating her body, Bella flanks an unsuspecting Dan, hitting three precise spots with her free hand: the floating rib, the pressure points inside his armpit, and his neck where the sternum and clavicle meet.

"Daddy!" Connor shouts, seeing his father drop to his knees.

Looking to his son, Dan attempts to call out and tell him that everything will be okay, but before he can, Dan's words are swiftly cut short as the world around him goes black.

━━━ ⋆ ★ ⋆ ━━━

"Dad?" a little boy calls out.

Get up, Dan, he tells himself. *Get up and off your ass.*

With his eyes shooting open, Dan gasps, charred air and burnt dust filling his lungs.

"Tori…" he mumbles, coughing as he pushes himself up to a sitting position.

"Dad?" the little boy cries again.

"Connor!" Ignoring the weight of his body's agony, Dan gets to his feet, scanning the charred horizon for his son. "Where are you?"

"Dad!"

Unable to see anything or anyone, Dan gazes on the bodies of countless victims under concrete and metal, fearing that the supplication he's hearing is just a haunting echo. Falling back to the earth, he begins crying. It's softly at first, but as the agonizing, flashing images of his son being taken showcase his mind, his audible weep begins accenting the festering fires of the debris.

"Tori," he then tries calling out, knowing that this too is a futile plea. If she wasn't with Connor, that's explanation enough that whatever Dan's parting words were for her, they were the last ones she heard from her husband.

"Dad…"

Sitting back up, Dan is shocked into reality, recognizing that the call isn't a ghost tormenting his failures as a father and husband, but rather is the call of a real-life child.

"Hello?" he calls back.

"Dad!" the boy cries, more urgent than ever.

Searching the carnage before him, in the distance, Dan spots a lost little black child. "Over here!"

Whipping his head around, the boy doesn't see his dad, but a rather muscular white guy waving him down. Hesitant towards the frighteningly large white man, the fear of being alone weighs heavier than his prejudices and is enough of a motivator for Kai to run over to the only living individual he's seen in hours.

"Hey buddy," Dan says, grabbing the frightened kid. "You okay?"

Kai shakes his head. "No. Where's my dad?"

Not having the heart to tell the kid the truth quite yet, Dan looks up from the child's gaze and out to the destruction of the airport.

"I'm not sure, son. Let's go see if we can find him…"

Twenty-Three

Area Thirty-Eight

"Drop off, retrieve. Drop off and retrieve," Renn whispers, the silent petition her best attempt to smother the growing anxiety.

Looking over, Jax places his hand onto hers. "We've got this." *What choice do we have?* he then thinks. "I'll be with you the whole time."

As his fingers interlock with hers and squeeze her shaking hand, Renn's repetitious rehearsal skips a beat as she is flooded with euphoric guilt. Mari's dead and she isn't. Jax was not Caspian's solitary target. Her brother knew that there were two others willing and able to remove the device from his arm—Renn and Connor. Either one would have been a sufficient sacrifice for Caspian's bloodlust, bringing some semblance of justice to the family betrayal. But instead, Mari became nothing more than collateral damage within their feud. There was never any romantic competition between the two women, but if Renn had kept at the task of extracting the explosive from Jax's arm, then she would not be holding his hand here in this moment.

Then there's Rhett…

With everything she has yet to process from these past twenty-four hours, Renn grips Jax's hand back and leans in, placing her forehead on his chest.

"What are we doing, Jax?" she whispers into his shirt. Refugees from Area Thirty-Eight and now the Encampment, Jax, Renn, Connor, and Dan barely escaped with their lives, having left with no army, belonging to no community.

With just as much pain and confusion whirling around in his own head, all Jax can do is continue to feel the warmth of her palm, using his mechanized arm to press against the small of her back and pull Renn closer.

"We're staying in the fight," Jax whispers back.

"What fight? Us four against the PPA? The Government? Against the Nine?"

What can Jax say to that? The first thing he learned about Renn is that she likes to have a well-thought-out plan—one that she can look at from as many angles as possible. It's what led her to kill Kip and his brash personality all those months ago, and it's exactly what's leading her to drown in the apprehension of their current situation. He heard Rhett's final words to his sister, and yes, it seems like they are worse off than ever with no army and some patched-together mission, but allegiance to anything but what is right will only lead to enslavement and regret. Raiders or not, Jax has to believe—he has to hope that what they've strived in hasn't been for nothing.

"We're getting Ann back," Jax ends up saying.

"Whether you fight with the Raiders or not, get that little girl back," Rhett's words echo in the back of her mind. *"Make something right in this world."*

"We're getting Ann back..." Renn repeats. "Drop off, retrieve. Drop off and retrieve."

"We're on approach. Sixty seconds," Connor shouts out, breaking Jax's thoughts and recentering Renn's resolve. "You ready to take the bird, Renn?"

She breathes in and exhales twice before responding. "Yeah, I think so."

Before moving back to help Dan with the gear, Jax frees her hand from his and kisses her forehead, an act that both shocks and calms her.

"When does Renn Stone only *think* so?" Connor asks.

"When she's flying an Owl G6 into a hostile Area," she scoffs, finding her seat next to Connor, timidly grasping the controls.

"You good?" Connor looks over to his sister.

"Yeah..." *It's simple,* she thinks. Suck it up. It doesn't matter how impossible it is, they have the moral high ground. They are on the right side of history. She feels it. Jax feels it. Renn's even tried experimenting, talking with "God" to see if He feels it, but at the end of the day, no matter how many times she tries to talk or con her way out, she knows what must be done.

"Dan needs you back there," Jax states, tapping Connor on his shoulder and gesturing towards the rear of the aircraft before taking his seat next to Renn.

Slapping the two of them on the shoulder, Connor heads to the back and takes up his position with Dan.

Donning a chute before handing one to his son, Dan looks to Connor as he approaches. "She looks nervous as hell."

"Aren't you? We're on a suicide mission…" Connor scoffs.

"I stopped feeling things like that a long time ago…"

Buckling his parachute across his chest, Connor is taken aback by the solemn tone in which Dan says this, and looking into the old man's eyes, Connor realizes that it's been twenty-seven years. Twenty-seven years since seeing the man he looked up to beaten down, his pride shattered as his wife was murdered and his kid was taken to be raised by wolves.

"Is that why you've been an asshole?" Connor asks. It's a slight jest, but there's dark truth in every joke.

Dan tries not to read too much into his son's comment; it's a fair question after all. What he can't do though is look past his paternal intuition and guilt. For so long, Dan was forced to face two dark futures for his son. At best, Connor would have been brainwashed about who his father really was. Tori raised a tough kid, but no matter how hard one contests against abject deceits, with the Fabian strategy of constant, mundane pressure, propagandized distortions still weave themselves within the truth. At worst, Dan saw his boy's life cut short—killed by Sullivan and Bella as an annoyance and half-bred disease. In order to survive, Dan had to consolidate it in his mind, and either be dead to his son or accept that his son was dead to him, shutting out the love he had for Connor.

"Connor," he slowly begins. "About your mother. I—I can't help—"

"DIA Headquarters dead ahead," Renn shouts out over the intercom, cutting off any amends Dan was thinking of making.

"Opening the hatch," Jax calls back.

In a slow opening, the cargo ramp drops, letting in the cold winter night as gusts of snow shoot around both Dan and Connor on the loading dock.

"Jump in five," Jax says.

The father and son tighten the final latches and straps of their gear.

"Dad?"

"Four."

"Yeah?"

"Three."

"Good luck."

"Two."

"You too, son."

"One. Jump, jump, jump!"

The gunshot sounds, echoing throughout the silent chambers of City Hall, mops sloshing across the stage as another failed experiment is summoned.

"Next!"

"Don't go," Ann pleads, gripping Mihi's weathered hand.

Gently, the elderly woman caresses Ann's face with the back of her fingertips. "And do what? Ignore them?"

"Yes! Stand up against them."

"I am," Mihi then says, the smile across her face emanating resolve.

"Next!" the officer repeats, ripping Mihi away from the little girl's grasp.

"No!" Ann shouts, her hands reaching out for Mihi. "Let her go!"

Being squished in line leaves no room for Ann's arms to flail, and as a result, Ann's elbow finds the PPA officer's crotch. Doubling over, the officer immediately regains composure, throwing a wild backhand across Ann's jaw that knocks her backwards into the mass of Raiders awaiting their own execution.

These guys have no originality, Ann thinks. Slapping, shouting. Rinse and repeat.

"Put her back in line!" he orders.

"She hasn't done anything!" Ann repeats, standing up and throwing a rapid volley of fists.

"Ann..." Mihi's delicate voice calls out over the commotion.

"Shut her up!" the officer repeats, swinging his rifle at her head, the butt of the gun missing its intended target as it grazes the girl's scalp.

"I'll kill you all!" Ann screams, her penetrating shriek having just as much ferocity as the fight inside her heart.

"Ann..." Mihi echoes, the affection in her voice finally reaching the little girl.

"What?!" Ann cries out, her eyes meeting a smiling Mihi staring back at her.

"Be at peace, little one—everything is going to be okay."

"No..." Ann's voice muffles, her tears flowing freely as an overwhelming sense of dread fills her little soul. Reaching out to Mihi, the memory of Kip crawls its way to the surface. "Not you too..."

Shrugging off her PPA escorts, Mihi continues to look to Ann. "I'm not going anywhere," she says, her fingertips grazing Ann's reaching palm. "As long as you remember me, I will always be with you."

Attempting to regain control of the situation, Mihi's escort grabs the elderly woman's shoulder, where it is defiantly rejected. Mihi's dignity won't allow for her to be dragged on stage kicking and screaming like every other one of her people. No, she will stand with steady hands and her head held high. Her gaze will not waiver from the ones she loves, and until her last dying breath is taken, Ann will be in her thoughts, calming and strengthening her final moments.

"No," Ann whispers, her hushed tone touching everyone's ears as each step Mihi takes resonates in the vast room of City Hall.

"Do not fear," Mihi mouths, her eyes meeting Ann's gaze one last time, the cold metal tip of what will end her life hovering inches away. "I am going home—"

With a simple squeeze of the finger, it is done. The gunshot sounds, echoing through the silent chambers of City Hall, mops sloshing across the stage, as another failed experiment is summoned.

"Next!"

Ann steps forward. *Be strong and of good courage, like Mihi was*, she tells herself. *Like Kip was.* If everything Mihi said is real, Ann will be seeing the both of them here very soon. Whether it be true or not, this little thought brings comfort to the girl's soul. Her breathing slows as she steps up, making it a point to stand exactly where Mihi stood, the gun hovering in front of Ann's young eyes.

Closing her eyes, an idea is sparked in Ann's mind that miracles are not impossible events. If they were, nobody would talk about them. They only border fiction because unbelievers cannot accept perfectly timed events meeting individual needs—that the will of something greater looks after our interests whether we understand or accept it.

This thought brings enough peace for Ann to open her eyes and witness the final moments of her life. Taking one last inhale, she watches the young soldier's hand tense around the pistol's grip before moving her gaze to meet his. It's in this brief period of time that all rage is dispersed and the fire inside her heart is smothered as she watches the young eyes of the boy in front of her fill with fear—they fill with regret for the orders he has no will to resist.

"I'm sorry," she whispers to him before the room goes black.

No gunshot sounds, the mops stop sloshing, and the execution of failed experiments ceases. Slowly, the vast room grows from abject darkness to a dark crimson that shadows everyone and everything in red.

"There has been an unauthorized flight into Area Thirty-Eight," a loud voice calls out over the intercom system.

"What's that mean?" Ann turns and asks the officer by her side.

"Shut up," he says, shoving Ann off stage and back into the crowd before turning to the private holding the gun. "Get them back in their stalls and then get your ass to your battle post."

───※★★※───

Looking from the half-moon lit sky to her radar, Renn watches as two blips hold position.

"The angels have landed," she says.

"You think they were spotted?" Jax asks, worrying that the moonlight could give anyone away.

"No, but we have," she says, seeing the glow from City Hall change from white to black to red. "They'll be scanning the horizon any minute." And before Jax can even have a say, Renn takes the Owl into a dive, bringing the aircraft fifteen feet above the shabby shacks of the outskirts and just below scanning altitude. Carefully, Renn then maneuvers the bird through a silent hover over to the biggest clearing in the Mill before softly landing and powering down.

"You think this is close enough?" Jax asks.

Unbuckling herself from the pilot seat, Renn tosses Jax a small pouch. "It's going to have to be."

Pulling on his own jumpsuit, Jax clips the rest of his gear on his back before grabbing a number of weapons, holstering and slinging them to his person. Renn arms and loads two rifles and a pair of pistols, readying her mind for the mission.

Flipping the switch for the back hatch, it slowly lowers to the icy ground.

Turning to Renn, Jax asks, "How long do you think we have before—"

His single question is cut off by a bombardment of bullets shooting into the inside of the airframe's cabin. Rounds ricochet and riddle the inside of the aircraft as both he and Renn narrowly take cover and wait for an opening to return fire. But there isn't one. The thuds and cracks of metal bouncing off metal don't subside in the least bit.

"I'll draw their fire," Jax yells out. "When they follow, get to City Hall—get to those prisoners!"

Renn doesn't like it, but she sees no other option. Waiting for Jax's lead, she racks the slides of her dual sidearms and slings the two rifles over her back before giving a readying nod. Blindly tossing two fragmentation grenades, Jax repeats the sequence. The four explosives take their turn rolling down the ramp and into the blaring night. Three seconds later, a bright white flash illuminates and is followed by an erupting boom sending shrapnel in every direction which is quickly followed by a second violent and deafening explosion. Whipping from cover, Jax rushes down the ramp and charges the stunned and battered PPA soldiers. Pulling the trigger twice, he fires two three-round bursts that finds one soldier in the chest and the other in his right leg.

"Jax," a maniacal voice calls out. "I've been expecting you."

Hearing his name causes Jax to stumble a step before bolting to the left where a volley of fire follows his fleeing direction.

From within the Owl, still bunkered down in secret, Renn grits her teeth as she listens to her brother and his ensuing battle with Jax.

"I just want to talk," Caspian yells out, firing a line that kicks dirt up inches from Jax's sprinting heels.

"Sir," a soldier whines, grabbing his bleeding thigh as he looks up to his Area Leader. "Call for med—"

Without even looking, Caspian fires a round in the top of his head with the bullet exiting the bottom of the sergeant's jaw.

"After him!" Caspian shouts.

As the gunfire fades and the rapping of boots are in pursuit, Renn waits until only the sounds of distant commands and peppered pops remain before moving out of the aircraft's cockpit. Cautiously, she makes her way down the ramp, instantly taking note of the two dead soldiers. Taking a knee next to the nearest one, she waits and listens, homing in on her surroundings. Whistles of air howl past her ears while the sound of Jax's outlying battle bursts in the background. That's when she hears it. In the foreground, the foreign crunch of dry cold dirt twisting underneath a leather boot is as loud as thunder. Renn angles her body off to the left and pulls out one of her sidearms in less than half a second, the other half consisting of her pulling the trigger. The single shot claps and then quickly fades.

"Impressive," a familiar voice calls out. "But you missed the rest of us."

In a sudden panic, Renn turns to fire a second shot, but a quick blow to the side of her head drops her unconscious.

━━╲ ✦ ★ ✦ ╱━━

From the ground, there's only one way in and out. What was once the DIA, bordering the most highly sophisticated militarized medical and laboratory facilities within the Areas of The Government, the entire landmass is surrounded by a reinforced concrete wall, and like the surrounding air space, the entrance is heavily guarded and monitored. Where traffic control towers once stood are military oversight and protection sites. Each runway and tarmac, save a few, have been replaced with countless rows of buildings that hide unknown human biological horrors and experimental warfare, while miles of asphalt and tracks have been laid to connect the various projects throughout the footprint of the facility.

Having landed ten clicks from the perimeter, both Dan and Connor slowly make their way to the east portion of the securing wall. Upon approach, they take a knee to evaluate the next objective. The stillness in the air is unnerving and it is uncertain as to whether the inactivity is good fortune or not, but as always, Dan expects the worst. With no immediate threat, Dan turns to Connor, tapping him on the shoulder before advancing on the wall. Silently, the two warriors systematically begin distributing two blocks of P14 explosive vaporizer on the surface of the concrete barrier and within thirty seconds, they are ready to make the breach.

"There's no knowing what's behind the wall," Dan states, readying the detonator.

"We know enough," Connor responds.

Sullivan and Bella's experiments with their children were only the beginning. From a genetically enhanced super fighting force to the most novel weapons of mass destruction, whatever is behind this wall is an established institution the Nine relies on to retain the power they've stolen through their agenda to eradicate weakness in both physical and ideological forms. This is more than just winning Area Thirty-Eight. It's about laying a foundation for something more—something that Connor has only begun to start seeing and believing—and if the Raiders won't help, then damn it, he'll do it himself.

"Hit it," Connor states.

Dan punches the button on his wrist, and as a hiss comes from the right, a flash of light zooms to the left twenty feet. The wall doesn't explode like one would expect; it simply crumbles, and as each slab of concrete hits the ground, it silently puffs to dust. As the powdered debris settles, the skeleton structure of the rebar in the wall remains, but the father and son easily climb over, stepping on the other side of the wall.

"Nothing," Dan whispers, the still quiet air continuing to hold its tongue. No alarm system thus far announces their entrance, and no swarm of PPA or hybrid army charges out to greet them.

"Which building is it?" Connor whispers back.

Dan searches his memory as he tries to recall what the civilian layout looked like all those years ago. Through his binoculars he studies the silhouettes, terminal after terminal, building after new building until finally he recognizes the rigid, distinct shape of the tent-like roofing of what was once the main building, the flood of terrorizing memories welling up in his heart.

"There."

"You sure?" Connor asks.

Dan scoffs at the thought. "Without a doubt. It's where I lost you."

The only way any of this will work is from below—from beneath the surface and at the foundation. Dan remembers the structure vividly, and if it wasn't for Kip's help all those years ago with the secret exit, he never would have noticed the opportunity. Once inside, the eerie silence they've encountered only intensifies. No more wind, no more distant aircraft or vehicles, only the sound of their own movements echoing off concrete walls.

"Are you sure this is it?" Connor questions, squinting as he attempts to see through the black. "The way Renn was describing the entrance made it sound—"

"I'm positive..." As Dan moves to a barren wall, he flips open a hidden panel and hits a single switch that sounds a loud screech. Aged, rebuilt gears grind into place, the entire floor beneath them sliding downwards, and like it was yesterday, Dan recalls each return home that he and Mica made side by side in their decent below the earth's surface.

The only difference this time being that the deeper they travel, the fouler the air grows.

"Is that what I think it is?" Connor asks, sniffing the sulfuric air.

The burnt, charred air has a haunting aroma, recalling far too many vile memories, and as the metal ramp hits rock bottom, pounds of dusty ash are kicked up.

"Put on your goggles," Dan says, strapping his own on over his eyes. Once secured, both hit the switch on the side of the lens to illuminate the mysterious, genocidal scene. It takes a second for the brain to connect the dots, but once the synapses sync, Connor's heart drops to his stomach. Crouching down, he picks up a petite skeletal hand, black and charred, the tiny bones fused to what he can only think is a deformed plastic action figure.

"What happened?" he asks, horrified as his own memories surface.

Slowly, Dan drops to his knee and picks up the remnants of a single book. *This is our brave new world*, Dan thinks. The idea that started a genocide of the last free people on Earth. It was in this moment that the Union of the Continents was complete, North America being the last to join the accords. What was his greatest failure as a father and husband— losing both son and wife in the same day—was also his greatest patriotic defeat, having no control as the last organized resistance of the old free world died in a sweeping fire.

"Didn't we teach you anything, son?" the cold voice calls out, reverberating off the bunkered concrete tunnel walls. Whipping around, Dan draws his weapon, aiming it directly at Bella's porcelain face.

"Hello, Dan," she says, her artificial smile stretching ear to ear across her dollish visage and into a morbid portrait. "I've missed you."

"As have I, old friend."

Sullivan Stone, the man who started it all, steps forward, taking his place at Bella's side. Adjusting his eye patch, he asks something that frankly has been bothering him all these years. "How's Lisa these days?"

"Couldn't tell you. What happened to your eye?"

"Another story for another day," Sullivan smirks, holding out his arms as if welcoming them in.

Feeling precious time slipping from their fingers, Connor covertly slides out a brick of the vaporizing explosive and begins glancing around in search of the support structures.

"Ah," Sullivan throws his hands together in a clap, "that is why you are here. I figured it was for something, but this—this is bold."

Tilting her head ever so slightly, Bella tiptoes her way towards Dan. "If memory serves me correctly, Dan, Connor was much smaller—"

Not having the patience that he did back then, Dan just squeezes the trigger, the sharp echoing gunshot masking all other noise.

Bella sees the sly shot coming, and tipping into a forward roll, the bullet flies through her hair. Coming up and out of the tumble, her fist cracks forward and up in the back of Dan's elbow. As his arm breaks, she catches the falling firearm, kicking Dan back another three feet with ease. Spinning around, ready to aim for Connor, she is caught off guard with a vicious right hook that drops her to the left.

"That is your mother!" Sullivan growls, leaping forward. His charge is cut short though as Dan recovers, ramming his shoulder into Sullivan's ribs and rushing until Sullivan's back slams into the nearest concrete wall.

"Find the pillars," Dan yells out, kicking the bag of P14 over to his son.

Bella lets loose a frustrated shriek, bringing her heel to the inside of Connor's leg. Connor drops and narrowly deflects a second oncoming heel aimed at his temple, before Bella attempts a third that also comes up short as Connor regains his footing. Snagging the bag, he uses it as a temporary shield from her attack and shifts to go on the offensive.

Two gunshots suddenly sound, taking Connor's breath away.

"Drop the bag, and I'll let you two talk before he bleeds out."

Turning around, fearing the gun is pointed in his direction, Connor sees the barrel of the gun pressed up against the side of Dan's head as two wounds profusely bleed from his chest.

A shrill giggle erupts from Bella's lips. "Same old Dan," she sing-songs.

Reaching out for the bag, to her surprise, Connor jerks it out of her reach.

"What did I just say, Connor?" Sullivan snaps, jabbing the barrel into Dan's temple. "Drop the bag and give it to your mother."

With her outreaching hand still in the air, Bella impatiently waits for Connor's obedience. Over the years, Connor has closely observed the soft spot Sullivan has for his wife and his own blood. For such an insensitive creature with no respect for life, in the end, that's what he cares most about. Sullivan attacks family, friends, and anyone dear to someone else because if he were in the shoes of his enemies, his family's safety is exactly what he wouldn't want compromised.

Without hesitation, Connor swiftly draws his sidearm and fires three rapid rounds, leading his target with all three. The first one narrowly misses as Bella yet again sees the oncoming projectile. The second grazes her cheek though, and while she isn't quick enough for the third, Connor's last leading round nestles deep in her skull, quickly exiting the back.

"NO!" Sullivan's grasp fails, and as Dan falls forward, Connor takes a second aim, firing three more leading shots. Like Bella, Sullivan leans and two of them miss, but the third finds a place and strikes his shoulder.

"I'm going to kill you, you son of a bitch!"

With caution and care thrown to the wind, Sullivan hits a button on his wrist. He then reaches for his own gun but is unsuccessful at finding a viable target as Connor continues to fire shot after shot at the fleeing Stone.

Connor rushes to his dad's side, fearing the worst. "Dad—!"

"I'm fine," Dan sighs out, looking to Bella's body lying prostrate and twitching on the cold concrete. "Nothing I can't handle."

Before Connor can respond, the ground begins to quake. Starting as a slow rumble, the concrete around them tentatively and rhythmically moves.

"What is that?"

"It's exactly what we need to stop," Dan says, pushing himself up and grabbing the bag of P14. "We've got to find those pillars."

"Give it up, Jackie!" Caspian shouts, firing off a volley of bullets, obliterating the edge of Jax's stone cover.

Having moved the fight inside city limits, Jax has more cover and a variety of tactical funnels to lessen the effects of Caspian's numbers. However, it's all for naught as he's bunkered behind a concrete fountain in the middle of a town square. Jax returns fire, sending out a burst, barely missing his intended target but killing the PPA officer just to the left of Caspian. Dropping back down, more shots are fired in Jax's direction, diminishing the edges of his cover even further.

"You're surrounded, Rouge!" Motioning for one of his officers to flank, Caspian fires another burst of cover fire. "What was your plan exactly? Fly in, save your friends, and fly out?"

Jax blind fires from around the edge of his rock with no success. His options, time, and ammunition are running low, and with nothing at his immediate disposal, Jax must figure out a way to regain one of these resources.

"I have to admit, I'm impressed you actually made it to City Hall," Caspian continues, gesturing to another soldier, sending him around the opposite side.

"What are you going to do? Kill me?" Jax taunts. "I thought I was too valuable, you said it yourself."

"It's true, but when did I say that?"

"You just did." Jax pops out and kills one of the flanking officers, mortally wounding the other.

"Wow," Caspian drawls. As stupid as it was, for the first time he feels like Jax's wit has accomplished something. "Okay," he then says, casually calling over to Jax. "So, I'm not going to kill you, but why would I keep you around?"

"For sport," he retorts, going along with the banter, keeping his eyes peeled for any unseen PPA troops. If he can't get any time back for himself, at least he can try to give more to Renn.

"*You are* quite the specimen…" Caspian mumbles, looking around at all available angles. He knows Jax is just stalling for Renn. She can have all the time she wants! He just got a notification that his father activated the army. So, no one is going anywhere. Counting his remaining underlings, Caspian snaps his fingers at a dozen before holding up his own hands for surrender.

"Hear me out," Caspian slowly says, standing in the open, his arms up. "You seem tough enough. You survived that explosion after all, and if it's sport we're talking about, let's settle this fair and square. You and me, no guns, no knives, just fists and bones."

Time is all he needed, and it seems like Caspian is handing it over on a silver platter. Moving from behind his own cover, Jax stands, taking Caspian up on the offer.

"Kai, what are you doing?" Renn asks, his firearm digging deeper into her stomach.

"Isn't it obvious? After your escape, I knew exactly what you were planning, and my team and I followed."

"What is it then? What are we planning?" Renn hisses out.

"You're here for people," Kai quickly responds. "To bolster your rebellion."

"Your people! We're here to save *your* people!"

Without warning, Kai slaps Renn across the face. "*My people* died the moment you pale faced pieces of shit walked into the Encampment. I'd rather have them die than be recruited by you."

"Then save them yourself. You're here!"

"They're already dead," Kai scoffs.

Astonished, Renn looks to the rest of the Raiders that joined Kai on his vendetta-suicide mission. "You can't tell me you believe any of this?"

"Hey!" Kai yells, smacking another open palm across her face. "They listen to me. Now that Dan's gone, I'm in charge."

The second slap across her face was just the distraction she needed. Without anyone noticing, Renn loosens the bonds wrapped around her wrists.

"Speaking of which, where is that old deadbeat?"

"He's doing what you didn't have the balls to do!" Renn sneers.

"And what would that be?"

Renn smiles, letting out a small chuckle, looking to the bracelet and the charms dangling from Kai's wrist. "I just figured out why you hate me so much."

Kai raises his eyebrow at the sudden change in the conversation. "Enlighten me then, why don't you."

"I remind you of her—the woman that took your wife," Renn says with a growing smile.

"I'd be careful at what you say next," Kai threatens, his gaze hardening.

Forgoing the warning, Renn dives deeper. "I saw it. I was a junior officer when she was taken—"

Raising a closed fist this time, in perfect form, Renn grabs his wrist, nearly breaking it in two as she twirls him around into a human shield.

"Drop your weapons!" she yells out.

No one moves as they keep their aim fixed in her direction. Unsheathing her hidden blade, Renn digs it into the side of Kai's neck, making sure they're aware of the fatal leverage she has.

"I will kill him!"

"Put them down!" Kai orders, knowing they won't if he doesn't.

Once the last weapon is dropped, Renn rewards herself and breaks Kai's wrist. Shoving him forward into the dirt, his agonizing cries of pain are muffled as she sprints to City Hall—the one place she knows she'll find Ann.

———⋆★⋆———

Dead ahead, Connor rushes up to the pillar, takes out a block of P14 and attaches it to the base.

Like cutting the feet from underneath a giant, he thinks.

"Five more," Dan yells. Looking back, the shadows of the approaching army meld in a horrific fashion as the overwhelming rumble of their march echoes through the wide concrete hall. "Move faster!"

"No shit!"

Lifting his dad onto his shoulders, Connor slams Dan back down as they approach another support structure. Like he has on all the others, Connor hastily programs the explosive before syncing it to the detonator.

"Ready?" Connor asks, picking his father back up.

In that very moment, hundreds of distinct clicks sound from the army's shadow, and without needing to decipher its meaning, Connor begins sprinting as thousands of bullets obliterate the concrete around them.

"The bag!"

Bouncing from side to side under the fragmenting ground, their remaining two bricks of P14 inside narrowly avoid being struck by the oncoming projectiles. Tossing two smoke grenades, Connor whips around from their cover into the masking haze, firing a blind barrage towards the oncoming army as he rushes to retrieve the explosives. A few of the elite soldiers drop, and when they do, Connor lunges for the bag just as a bullet strikes his knee, bursting it open. Falling just out of reach, Connor pushes himself up, before a second shot strikes his shoulder, forcing him into a crawl, his fingertips forward, grasping the strap. With continual flying shrapnel, Dan grasps onto his son's ankle and drags him back behind the pillar.

"Stupid kid!"

"I got it though!" Connor states, forcing a smile.

Exerting every ounce of effort he can muster, Dan presses against the wounds in his own chest as he gets to his feet, firing a blind hail of bullets from behind the pillar. "Get up!"

"I can't," Connor sighs, looking at splayed flesh where his knee once was.

"Suck it up, son!" Dan wrenches Connor to his one good leg. "You see that room up ahead?"

"Yeah," Connor says, lifting his eyes to read the sign that says Records Room.

"Inside, there's a tunnel that leads out of here," Dan says, firing another volley before an explosion shakes the ground. "It's the only other way out."

"Okay, but—"

"Son, I'll be right behind you. Trust me."

Before either of them can say anything more, Dan throws his arms around Connor for what he knows to be the last time. He wasted so much energy hating both himself and the man the Stones turned Connor into. Yes, Bella took him—the Stones manipulated his son, but when Connor came walking into the Encampment the cynic inside him arrogantly refused to see that something from both he and Tori must have resided with their little boy. Why else would Connor turn from the path he was led down? Why else would this man fight against the Nine? Connor *is* Dan's son. It's time he be proud of his son once more.

Letting his dad go, Connor limps his way towards the room before turning back. Seeing Dan shooting into the massive army, straightaway, Connor is struck four more times: two in his shoulder and two in his thigh.

"Connor!"

Ignoring all his pain, Dan throws two grenades before sliding next to Connor, helping him finish the remaining three feet.

"The exit's right there, son."

Seeing the aged tunnel, Connor looks from it to his father. "I can't do it…"

"When you get to the top, hit the button," Dan says, ignoring Connor's doubt and handing over the detonator.

Confused, Connor looks to Dan. "You said that—"

"I lied. Someone has to place the other two devices," Dan calmly states. Gripping the back of his son's head, he brings his forehead to touch Connor's. "I love you."

Before Connor can offer any protestations, Dan picks him up and pushes him into the room, slamming the door shut, leaving and locking his son inside.

"Dad!" Connor shouts, trying but failing to get to his feet.

Ignoring the urge to stay and wait for his dad, Connor puts his emotions aside and crawls his way to the tunneled exit. Throwing himself onto the ramp, he hits the only switch he sees. At a breakneck speed, the ramp rises faster with each surpassed meter, until it comes to an abrupt and violent stop at the top, twenty-five hundred meters above the surface. Pulling himself from off the platform, without further thought, Connor hits the trigger, feeling the ground below him mildly shake, and then, as subtly as it started, the quaking stops.

※ ※ ★ ※ ※

His mechanical arm does what it's designed to do and halts the forceful blow of Caspian's powerful mass, but with a swift kick, Caspian crushes Jax's open ribs.

"That's it?" Caspian asks, standing Jax back on his feet, the mocking tone hissing between his teeth.

Three more powerful blows follow. The first, Jax easily blocks, however, the second and third find the underside of his fleshy arm and the soft tissue just beneath his sternum. Caspian attacks with a fourth and a fifth strike at Jax's hip joint and his diaphragm.

"How was it?" Caspian begins, watching Jax crumble to his knees. "To see her die? Mari, was that her name?"

Standing right back up, Jax throws a flurry of hits. As one of his uppercuts narrowly misses, he grips Caspian's hair—which is immediately used against him as Caspian first headbutts one of Jax's punches before throwing the crown of his head into the center line of Jax's chest.

"I saw it, you know," Caspian huffs, wiping his bloody forehead.

Jax attempts to crawl away from Caspian's advance but finds nowhere else to go as he's backed up against the walls of City Hall.

"Ann," he whispers, praying that Renn is doing her job.

"And yes, Ann. I know all about her too," Caspian mocks, pointing to the transparent building. "She told me everything, right up until the moment I killed her."

"You didn't—"

"I did! I crushed her throat and felt it collapse in my grip."

"Liar!"

"Am I?" Caspian stomps on Jax's exposed, fleshy fist, breaking a variety of bones in his hand. In a futile attempt, Jax swings his mechanical arm at Caspian's knee, but by simply lifting his leg, Caspian kicks the crux of Jax's machined elbow, halting the blow with his heel. "Look in there! Do you see anyone—anyone alive?"

It's not true, Jax thinks. *It can't be... we did not come all this way for this...*

"Hey, Casp!"

"Renn?" Caspian slowly turns, his attention immediately distracted from Jax.

With a slight smile, Renn fires a burst that Caspian dodges, allowing the three rounds to bounce off the wall of City Hall. Lifting his own gun, Caspian misses his shot as Renn rolls behind a corner of an abandoned building.

"Kill her—" Caspian begins to order, but his words quickly fall short.

Rounding an alleyway corner, dozens of Raiders enter the battlespace firing mad, wild shots. Shocked by the sudden turn of events, Caspian turns to the remaining PPA and orders them to attack.

"Kill them all!"

Four Raiders drop dead before they know what hits them. Realizing what Renn Stone led them into, one Raider sees the opportunity and rushes Caspian, managing to slam the butt of his rifle into his jaw. Unfazed by the attack, and with a wide smile, Caspian collapses the Raider's facial structure in a single punch.

They're not alone, Jax thinks, running towards his allies for cover. But to his despair, Jax finds Kai among them. Jax sees Kai's aim directly between his eyes, and not needing any more evidence that the Raiders are not here for the reasons he thinks, Jax tilts his head, dodging the shot.

"Over here!" Renn calls out from the doors of City Hall, killing one Raider and one PPA soldier. Scrambling every which way, Jax dashes around the corner and through the entrance, the bulletproof walls all the protection he and Renn need.

"That makes a lot of sense," he gasps.

"What does?" Renn asks, her breath just as heavy as Jax's.

"Why I didn't see you inside earlier. You had a run-in with Kai."

She rolls her eyes. "Let's just get Ann and everyone else."

"They're not here," Jax quickly says, terrified that what Caspian was telling him was the truth.

"Yes, they are."

Rushing towards the far end of the stage, Renn finds a partially hidden latch. Squeezing the handle in her hands, she pulls with all her might, and as the lever slowly lifts, she manages to muscle the trapdoor open. With a loud hiss of air seeping out, the latch clicks before slowly rising.

"Let us out of here!" the little girl's familiar voice sounds out.

"Ann?" Rushing downward and leaving Renn above to stand guard, Jax peeks his head into the dark stalls below.

"Jackie?" she calls out.

Throwing himself inside the underground prison, Jax begins searching every cage before finding her huddled in the back.

Quivering in the arms of the mysterious woman, Ann avoids his gaze, the memories of him torturing Mari the last she has of him.

"Did you kill her?" she asks.

"No..." he slowly says, knowing the truth isn't any better. "But she—she—" he stutters, unable to find the right words. Rather than try, he raises his mechanical arm, showing Ann the carefully placed surgical incisions. Noticing the minute details, she looks up and down the medical masterpiece as questions flood her mind.

"Did she do this?" Ann solemnly asks.

"No," Jax quickly states, trying to redeem what dignity he can while exalting Mari as high as possible. "Caspian did and she—" He tries again to explain to Ann why Mari is no longer with any of them, but to no avail.

Ann doesn't need to know the details. Mari's gone, and Jax isn't. It's not fair. In fact, it's the furthest thing from actual justice, but hate is all this little girl has known these past few weeks. Hate for Jude. Hate for Jax. Hate for the life they both built for her, and there is nothing hindsight or any further analyzation of her orphaned situation can do to offer peace.

"Just get us out of here," the little girl demands, her icy tone cutting deep into Jax.

Slowly, he approaches the cage, and throwing his mechanical arm down, Jax rips open the door with ease. At first, nobody moves, astonished that their rescue was that simple. There is a reverence they also feel will be disturbed by them exiting the cell, and so they hold still, waiting and watching the little girl.

Debating in her mind as to whether it's worth leaving at all—weighing the kind of life she'll have from this moment on—Ann holds her ground. Looking up to the man she once saw as a brother—as a father—Ann says the only thing her heart can express.

"It should have been you on that stage. Not Kip…" she whispers, a glaring rage in her young eyes.

With no other recourse but to simply accept the loathing words, Jax stands as his heart breaks a little more, the words simmering and burning his soul.

A roaring explosion sounds up top, shaking the underground room. With a burst of gunfire sounding, Renn suddenly jumps down below, sealing the door shut behind her.

"Well, the front door is out of the question," she announces before noticing everyone still in their cages. "Why aren't they out?"

With just as much ease as before, Jax apathetically walks over to the rest of the cells, tearing them open as another ground-shaking boom shakes the stage. Even then, no one moves but rather they all stare at Ann and Jax.

"Let's go," Renn slowly says, hoping that someone will listen. "There's a tunnel just down there. It will lead to a secondary exit that comes up about fifty feet from the walls of City Hall and will lead us straight to the Mill," she explains, pointing to the far end of the foundation.

As Raiders begin to move and exit, making their way in the direction Renn pointed them, a woman runs up to both Jax and Renn.

"Where's my husband?" she asks, worry, anger, and hope on her face.

Renn waits for Jax to respond, as it seems that the question is directed more to him than it is to her. However, when he doesn't—when he just stares ahead, watching Ann leave—Renn looks to the worried woman.

"What's your name?" Renn asks, placing her hand on her shoulder.

"Céleste," she says. "Ma'am, where is—?"

But before the woman can repeat her question, the room shudders under another powerful blast.

———⟩⟩ ⋆★⋆ ⟨⟨———

"Hit it again," Kai orders, his blood filled with animosity, drowning out the surrounding chaos. They went in there, he knows it. If he must, he'll destroy this entire district to get to them, starting with City Hall.

With several Raiders rushing forward to answer Kai's order, they all line the entrance in their sights before firing a volley of rockets. Soaring forward and past the defending PPA troops and into City Hall, the explosions detonate just behind the soldiers, sending shrapnel and flames into their backs, but doing nothing to the transparent walls of the building.

"It's not working—!" one of the Raiders begins, his sentence going unfinished as a bullet cuts through the middle of his head.

"Damn it!" Kai yells out, taking cover and rallying another attempt. "Again!"

"We're surrounded, sir!" a panicked Raider rebuts, huddling next to Kai. "What do—?" but he too is stopped short as his life is taken from him, his body falling onto Kai's shoulder.

"You're bleeding men!" Caspian shouts out.

Gritting and shoving the dead coward off, Kai yells out to his team. "Sound off!" He waits for their call backs but gets nothing. "Sound off!"

"I told you," Caspian again yells. "Your options are limited."

Seeing a rocket launcher just off to his side, Kai's scrambling fingers reach for the pistol grip, gaining a firm grasp before yanking it to his chest. "Yeah, and what are my options?"

"Well, you have two really," Caspian responds, signaling to a number of his own men, repositioning them around both City Hall and the lone Raider.

"What's my first?" Kai asks, reloading his weapon.

"I can kill you with a bullet," Caspian states, firing off a round, striking the wooden cover next to Kai's head, the shattered splinters cutting Kai's cheek.

"And the second?" Kai asks before he fires a retaliating burst of his own that Caspian easily dodges.

"I can beat you to death."

"Hell of a choice!" Kai scoffs.

Just then, the ground begins to rumble from behind him, but as Kai turns to look at the alleyway from where it's coming, he sees nothing.

Motioning three of his men forward, Caspian fires three more shots, intentionally striking the same location as before. "So, what will it be?"

The subtle thundering does not lessen, but grows at an exponentially violent rate, the air from around City Hall cycling and picking up both dirt and debris. Kai can't help but smile as the Owl G6 soars up above. He doesn't know how Jax and Renn got out of City Hall, but he doesn't care. This is the ultimate opportunity.

Calmly slowing his breath, Kai shoulders the launcher, his grip tightening around the trigger well. Inhaling, the old metaphor of birds and a stone circle around in his mind as Kai whips out from behind his cover, watching the massive aircraft take its slow hover away from the capital. Taking careful aim, he watches the airship's ascent, and with Caspian falling just between Kai and the bird, the blood flees from Caspian's bony face as the trigger is pulled, sending the rocket his way.

Upon letting the missile loose, Kai drops the launcher and as if pursuing the projectile, he charges Caspian and his band of PPA. Firing shot after shot, Kai begins killing the astonished soldiers as they try to take cover from the explosive they think is meant for them. But, just before the projectile can hit Caspian square in the chest, it soars upwards towards the aircraft, striking the wing and igniting the dark night into a fiery glow. Veering left and then right, the aircraft makes a sudden dive for City Hall, and as Caspian watches, taken aback by the sudden turn of events, a slamming force tackles him to the icy ground.

Despite Kai's shocking strength, Caspian throws his body off him with utter ease—the frozen ground mercilessly catching Kai on the flat of his back. But, as if it didn't faze him, Kai reaches for his sidearm and pops out a shot that finds Caspian's shoulder. Rolling over, Kai dodges a crushing foot stomp that gives him an opening for his fist to slam into the inside of Caspian's thigh. Again, the power behind the man shocks Caspian. Deflecting another two strikes, Caspian wraps his fingers around Kai's collar as he pulls him to his feet.

"You're not strong," Caspian says, the curiosity within him surfacing. "But you aren't weak either. You have some of it, don't you?"

"I don't know what you're talking about," Kai says.

The fiery Owl crashes through the transparent walls of City Hall, sending glass in thousands of directions, the shattering sound drawing Caspian's widened eyes from Kai. With all his weight, the Raider shifts his body and drops his elbow down through Caspian's grasp, shoving the Stone towards the collapsing building before finding his own refuge as the airship craters the earth.

━━ ⋆ ★ ⋆ ━━

"Ann!" Jax coughs out, the black haze filling his lungs and clouding the surrounding atmosphere. Searching through the burning bent metal wreckage, Jax draws his sidearm as he continues to call out for any survivors. "Renn! Is anybody hurt?"

"I'm good!" Renn calls out, smacking her coat free from flames. Unbuckling herself from the seat, she falls near the emergency panel and hits the flashing button, sending white powder flying from the vents to asphyxiate the fires.

"Ann!" Jax calls out again. He too, undoes the straps, falling next to Renn.

"Jackie?" Ann's delicate voice calls out, sending a wave of relief through Jax. "Jackie, I need help!"

"Hold on," he calls back, getting to his feet and moving his way through the grey steam.

"Is there anyone else?" Renn calls out as she, too, moves through the vapor. Successive cries yell out, and all, save for one, have relieving news.

"Céleste is hurt!" Ann cries.

Rushing forward, Jax fervently inspects the little girl for any injuries.

"Not me!" she says, shoving him away. "Her! Céleste, she—" she stops, dreading that yet again she'll have to watch a life violently end.

"Hang on! Renn!"

As Renn pulls off her gloves, she delicately feels for any visible wound. "Internal bleeding."

"What does that mean?" Ann asks.

Before Renn can answer, a subtle metal twisting sounds from the back of the aircraft. The door resists, but eventually, it falls open to let in a gust of cold air that puts out the last remaining fire, and what little emergency power remains cuts out, leaving the passengers in darkness. Emerging from the outside, a faint silhouette steps in, and for what seems to be an eternity, not a muscle moves on the man's outline until slowly, his hand reaches for his pistol.

Noticing the veil of vapor that surrounds them, Renn realizes why the silhouette stands still. Motioning to Jax, she catches his attention from the corner of his eye.

"Move them out the side exit," she mouths, her hand signals communicating what Jax doesn't read.

"No, you. I'll stop him," Jax replies in the same silent manner. He knows he's the only one who can. Shuffling as many as possible from the ramp and towards Renn, Jax and everyone inside are startled as a shot abruptly rings out.

"Everyone outside!" the silhouette commands. But no one budges in hopes that they remain unseen. "Now!" he yells, firing another round into the dirt.

Standing, Jax moves forward to create the distraction everyone else needs.

"Leave them out of this, Kai," Jax shouts back.

Despite her injuries and pain, Céleste's eyes shoot open at the sound of his name. Noticing the woman's silent excitement, Ann puts two and two together.

"You've done enough," Jax declares. "They can still get out of the Area—"

"OUT!" Kai's echoing command rings. "Come out now, or I start shooting."

Renn keeps people moving but shakes her head as she knows exactly what Jax intends. Any good leader would.

"All right," Jax calls out, the dust and foggy residue beginning to settle. Turning back to see her, Jax's gaze locks with Renn's. "I'm coming out."

Kai shoots inside the aircraft this time, where it ricochets before finding a sudden stop. "I want everyone!"

"Kai, they can still get out," Renn is the one to yell this time, and as Jax continues his walk down the ramp, Céleste strives to get their attention. Before Renn or Jax notice the woman's plea, Ann jerks Céleste's hand back as she holds her finger to her lips.

"I know you still care about your people," Jax says, stepping out of the haze, feet from Kai. "Don't do this."

"There is no one I care about anymore!"

Jax shakes his head. "I don't believe that."

"Everyone I loved is dead! Dead, Jax! I figured you would have noticed that by now."

"You wanna bet?" Ann's strong little voice rings out from inside the haze.

"Who said that?" Kai yells, aiming and firing another shot inside the bird.

Everyone that didn't escape from the side of the aircraft quietly shuffles towards Kai and Jax, Renn being the last one.

"Is that everyone?" Kai asks, his aim directed at Renn's head, noticing that Ann is not among them.

Defiantly, Renn nods, a single tear streaming down her cheek.

Squinting, Kai sees right through the lie. "The little girl, where is she?"

With the utmost contempt, Renn shakes her head this time.

"Tell him the truth!" Ann cries out from inside. "Tell him what he just did!"

Storming out of the fog and down the ramp, Ann runs up to Kai, her boots kicking into his as she looks up with nothing but loathsome indignation.

"Tell him, Renn!"

With another tear streaming down the side of Renn's face, she looks to Kai before saying, "You shot her…"

"Who?" he seethes out.

"Your wife."

"She's dead," Kai scoffs. "For years now she's been—"

"The PPA got her. She was one of their successful experiments."

"You lie!"

"She's right," a cold, dark voice says from inside the downed aircraft before slowly, Caspian walks out, clutching a bleeding Céleste. "Her injuries were internal, but now…" He chuckles, letting the sight of the external blood on her stomach speak for itself.

Kai drops his gun as he reaches out to his dying wife. "Put her down!"

"Why," Caspian yells back in a laugh. "Last we heard, you don't care about anyone—last we heard *she* was dead."

"PUT HER DOWN!"

As commanded, Caspian opens his arms, letting Céleste's slumped body collapse to the frozen ground. Rushing forward, Kai slides next to her, immediately placing his hands over the gaping hole in her stomach where his cupped hands begin pooling with blood.

"I'm so sorry..." Kai tearfully pleas. "I didn't know..."

"That shouldn't have mattered, Kai," she says, gently holding his face and kissing his forehead.

"I've missed you so much," Kai cries.

"I have too..." she whispers back as she grabs at the charms on the bracelet. She gave him these when they committed themselves to each other, each one having a meaning—each one testifying of the potential she saw in Kai all those years ago. "Kai," Céleste says, struggling to say the words. "Kai, look at me."

Slowly, Kai lifts his eyes towards his cherished wife.

"Take care," she begins with a cough. "You need to take care of our people. Promise me..."

"I promise." Kai bows his head. "Can we be together again?"

Softly, she smiles. "We can, but not here. Not now." Céleste closes her eyes. "They need you, my love."

"Nobody trusts me anymore..."

"Then give them a reason to," she replies, her final breath leaving her body.

"Soon," Kai whispers. "We'll be together again soon."

"Shame," Caspian says, the tip of his gun pressing against Kai's temple. "Ironic, don't you think?"

Holding back the flood of tears and pain, Kai's hands tremble as he harnesses his ire, bitterness, and hopelessness. Committed to honoring her dying wish, he searches his mind for the one thing by which he can atone.

"Run," Kai says, the word barely a whisper.

"What was that?" Caspian asks, digging the barrel even further into the side of Kai's head.

"Jax," Kai says as he turns, looking to him as the brother he should have been. "Get our people and run."

"That's what I thought you said." Turning to the group of Raiders, Caspian moves his aim towards their direction. "Don't even think about it. We have a special Gathering planned for everyone here."

With a knowing nod, Jax sees the tool that Kai is now grasping in his hand. *There must be another way,* Jax thinks.

As if knowing his thoughts, Kai simply shakes his head. "I have to do this."

"Shut up!" Caspian yells out, firing three rounds into the air before swinging his fist at Kai's face.

To his demise though, Kai catches the blow.

"Run!"

In a last stand, Kai sweeps his enemy's legs out from underneath with immense force before shoving the grenade he's been grasping into Caspian's mouth. Teeth chip and crack as Kai wills the bomb deeper, and while a single resisting hit from Caspian breaks every single rib on Kai's right side, the Raider refuses to let up.

"Take cover!" Jax yells, taking Ann and jerking Renn to the nearest alleyway.

An additional blow breaks the other set of Kai's ribs, but he presses on. His knees dig in, pushing all his force downward and onto the last task beneath him. Pulling the pin, the spoon flips up, initiating the countdown. Kai's arm breaks, and while Caspian flails, his teeth continue to crack against the metalized force of the grenade between them.

Looking up to God, Kai prays, his final words being of gratitude.

"I thank you for this life."

Caspian slams his fist down, the impact landing on Kai's thigh, shattering his femur, but still, Kai kneels, steadfast and immovable.

"And please forgive me—for I was weak, and for that I am—"

But before his petition is complete, the explosive ignites, the flashing blast ending it all.

Epilogue

Area Thirty-Eight
December 25, 2037

"Mica?" Aila's voice finally comes into his earpiece. As exhausted as she sounds, his name spoken from her mouth puts Mica into a more composed state.

"How's it going, love?" he asks, studying every possible angle, but only finding one. One is all he needs.

"I wish you were here!" Aila cries out.

"I will be. Just keep breathing," Mica says, verifying the details of his sole option. "Lisa and Carter know what they're doing."

"Is that Aila? I can't believe the luck I'm having today!" Sullivan crows. "Tell her I say hi."

Briefly contemplating Sullivan's request, Mica decides to go with it—a few words can offer a lot of information and time. "Aila, Sullivan says hi."

"Where are you, Mica?" Aila asks, the panic in her voice rising.

"Everything's all right. I'm just talking with Sullivan."

Pulling out his sidearm and pointing it at Mica's head, Sullivan motions towards the ground. "Knees. Now…"

Defiantly, Mica stays on his feet.

"Are you okay with the name we talked about?" he asks his wife.

"Mica, I need you!" *How can I do this*, she thinks. *I can't do this alone.*

"Aila, are you okay with the name?"

"Yes," she breathes out, a heavy contraction on its way. "It's perfect, but I need you with me. I can't do this by myself."

"Down!" Sullivan repeats, his commanding yell echoing off the surrounding buildings and concrete structures.

Slowly, Mica kneels, formulating and perfecting his plan. "You're not alone, Aila," he says. "You have Carter and Lisa—your uncle and aunt."

"I'll keep this real simple, Mica," Sullivan begins, stepping closer, the barrel of his pistol touching Mica's head. "Join us or die."

"But I need you, Mica," Aila cries out. "I need *you* here…"

Mica stares his enemy in both his eyes, and Sullivan loves it. Seeing defeat and anger in the eyes of a formidable foe is a rare opportunity. Dan, he's nothing to shy away from, but Mica, he's the prize any hunter wants. The corners of Sullivan's lips turn up ever-so-slightly as he imagines the kind of pain he'll be causing Aila, taking away her boy's father before he's even entered the world.

"Is she pleading for you?" he asks, pulling back the hammer of his firearm, placing the cold metal tip of the barrel between Mica's brown and blue eyes. "Hope you said your goodbyes…"

"Aila, I love—"

As expected, Sullivan squeezes the trigger, and all Mica does is angle his head to the left, the bullet narrowly missing and cutting through the earpiece and his right ear instead, killing the connection. The obliterated device falls to the dirt as Mica shoots both his hands up, one on Sullivan's wrist and the other on his elbow. With all the force he can muster, Mica strains to break his arm, but Sullivan's muscles make it impossible.

"Clever!" Sullivan grunts, slamming his fist into Mica's sternum.

Mica stumbles backwards before regaining his footing, and as Sullivan throws a second punch, instead of dodging it, Mica aims a forceful fist, crushing Sullivan's hand on impact.

"Damn," Mica mumbles, not realizing how much that would hurt.

"I don't know why I thought you would die so easily," Sullivan says, shaking his hand, re-evaluating how to proceed. With all his PPA troops surrounding them, their guns raised in a shaky fashion, Sullivan commands them to hold fire. "I still don't want it to be that easy."

"You were part of the assassination, weren't you?" Mica asks, reflecting on President White's death.

"Very perceptive, Mica," Sullivan laughs. "Too bad it's only now that you're figuring this out."

"Why? After everything we've done—?"

"Because of Harris Crowe—he's promised us positions in the Nine."

"Harris Crowe?"

"Yes, Mica, the founder of the Ordean Reich. I'm rather disappointed, in fact, that no one in the Division managed to find him."

"So that's all it took to buy your loyalty? A single bullet and like that, you're in?" Mica says with a snap of his fingers.

"I wouldn't say it's entirely that simple." Sullivan reaches inside his coat, pulling out a small vial of brown liquid. "It's more because of this. It's already been put into place over in Europe—their laws being less stringent—hence, the Bale Act."

Mica examines it, figuring out exactly what it is that Sullivan is holding. "That's how Caspian got better, isn't it?"

"Not this particular formula, but to make a long story short, yes. Imagine it, Mica, a perfect human body with genetically pure blood. No more mental illnesses, down syndrome, or any sort of physical aberrations. No more homosexuals or transgenders and their lack of mental capacity to identify with their physical body. No more blacks or browns or people of color and their divisive cultures. This vial can accomplish that—it can unify our nation and the world into one kind of people. Think about it, the plague of human existence is individuality—choice, diversity, personality, an identity, all of this allows for *one person* to fight against progress. Our culture is focused on identity rather than merit and what someone can offer to society—sociologically, economically, and genetically. Mica… You know there is reason here."

Everything has just changed in Mica's eyes. His entire effort to redeem this country has been thrown to the wolves because of one simple vial.

"That vial, you think it can accomplish all of that?"

"I do. We'll start with our children, and if you join me, your son can be among them. Our children will be the future."

Taking a step forward, Mica sees the tantalizing opportunity despite its moral ambiguity. *This will be their demise*, he thinks.

"I'll take my chances."

Without giving another opportunity to the man he thought to be his friend, Mica extends his whip and lashes forward. Sullivan sees it too late as his wrist is seized and his shoulder ripped from its socket. The vial drops from his grip, and with his one good arm Sullivan tries to catch it. But Mica is too quick. He scoops it up, and in the same motion throws half a dozen pellets down to emit a cloud of smoke. Having been fooled once, Sullivan reaches out with his good arm, wrapping it around a fleeing Mica where, in a firm hold between his bicep and forearm, he squeezes Mica's throat closed as he pulls Mica into his body.

"You try so hard and look at where it has gotten you."

Mica scrambles for his whip, but it's useless underneath Sullivan's boot. He reaches for his knives, his clubs, for anything to free him from a certain death, but all Mica has are his hands, and as the blackness closes around him, Mica attempts one final defense. With his scrambling hands fumbling across Sullivan's face, Mica feels the chin and then the cheeks. His hands move to the center, finding the nose, and just above that is what will save Mica's life. Gripping his hands around Sullivan's massive skull, Mica quickly positions a hand perfectly, jamming his thumb into Sullivan's eye, gouging it out until the pressure is released from around his neck. Once breathing again, Mica simply digs deeper until he is finally able to scoop out his bloody thumb. Throwing down three more pellets, Mica picks up the vial before vanishing from Sullivan's presence for the last time.

―∴∗★∗∴―

Area One

Sullivan's feet echo down the desolate hallway. Never has he been more humiliated and crushed in his entire life. In a fleeting moment his wife, the co-author to the vision, was taken from him. Dead. Three shots and there was nothing he could have done to stop it.

"Sir," a PPA specialist says, holding his hand out. "You are going to have to wait. The One is not ready—"

Before the soldier can finish the order, Sullivan's grasp crushes his throat. As the limp body falls to the floor, Sullivan throws the doors open and storms into the room he knows all too well. Instead of the council being his judge, it is a single man whom no one has ever seen—the Chief Judge of the Nine.

Some say within the Oligarchy that the One is an idea, but Sullivan isn't naïve. Of course it's a person, but who? That's the question that needs answering. He's speculated with Bella countless times, and both always came to the same conclusion. It's Harris Crowe, the founder of everything they have here and now. The genius behind the Ordean Reich's World Union. Who is better equipped than him to lead the Nine?

"Did you kill my guard?" the One calls out, stopping Sullivan mid-step.

Having not seen a single person since entering, Sullivan looks around to see where the ominous voice is coming from.

"I'm in here," the voice casually states. "Just not where you can see. Now answer me, did you kill my guard?"

"I did." Sullivan doesn't stutter, but he's terrified beyond belief. "Area Thirty-Eight has been overrun."

"Say that again?" The shock in the One's voice isn't obvious, but it's there. "Caspian, your son, wasn't he the Area Leader of Thirty-Eight?"

Having not had the time to yet reflect on this, Sullivan grits his teeth before responding. "Yes. He was killed as he attempted to defend it."

Footsteps sound up ahead in the darkness as the Chief moves forward. Shadowed by a black cloak, he emerges into the light where for the first time, Sullivan lays eyes on him. "And what of Nine, Bella Stone? Where is she?"

"She too, is dead, my Judge."

A heavy sigh comes from under the hood. "We've lost much today."

Humbly, Sullivan falls to his knees. "I will retake the Area. Give me the resources and it will be done."

Gently, the One puts his hand on Eight's shoulder. "No, vengeance is not the key. It's not the answer to our growing problem."

"But my army is—"

"Your army is dead!" the One shouts out, his silencing statement echoing throughout the barren chamber. Grabbing his redwood cane and sliding off his hood, the Chief Judge looks to Sullivan, burrowing his bicolor eyes into his old friend. "We were never perfecting humanity. That was your vision, not Crowe's. Your serum was only a means to an end."